JOEL MANNERS

# THE
# THIEF'S
# TALE

*A Tale From*
## THE MARTYR'S WORLD

# THE THIEF'S TALE

By Joel Manners

This book is available in print and electronic format at most online retailers.

Cover art and map by Joel Manners

ISBN 978-0-9972594-8-3 (Paperback)
ISBN 978-0-9972594-9-0 (Hardback)

Colquhoun Books
Austin, TX.

www.JoelManners.com

# BOOKS BY JOEL MANNERS

THE CHRONICLES OF THE MARTYR

*THE MARTYR'S BLADE*
*THE MARTYR'S TEARS*

TALES FROM THE MARTYR'S WORLD

*THE THIEF'S TALE*
*THE ARTIFICER'S TALE*

For

Christie,

The girl who holds the key to all the locked doors in my life.

# THE THIEF'S TALE

Chapter 1.   Something Precious _____ 1

Chapter 2.   A Girl Could Get Used to This ___ 16

Chapter 3.   Promises Were Made _____ 25

Chapter 4.   The Honorable Nell Spicer _____ 37

Chapter 5.   Red Hair and Wide Smiles _____ 60

Chapter 6.   A Kinked Tail _____ 78

Chapter 7.   Easy as Wishing _____ 96

Chapter 8.   Butcher's_____ 125

Chapter 9.   A Real Device _____ 139

Chapter 10.  Everyone Smiling _____ 161

Chapter 11.  Baron Murtagh _____ 184

Chapter 12.  To Earn a Dragon_____ 202

Chapter 13.  Always an Angle _____ 220

Chapter 14.  Lady Blackberry's Ball_____ 244

Chapter 15.  A Bottle and a Tale _____ 265

Chapter 16.  Murderous Bastard _____ 278

Chapter 17.  Agony and Fear _____ 299

Chapter 18.  What They Deserved _____ 328

Chapter 19.  An End to Hiding_____ 354

Chapter 20.  Long Live the Queen _____ 367

Chapter 21.  Epilogue _____ 370

20.

21.

Carraig
Dhubh

Blackheath

7. Forge Hill

22.    8.

6. Cowgate

9.

Whitetemple

19.

Southgate

Chandlers Lane

2.

1.

3. Tinkers
Square

Newgate

18.    4.

Eastside

17.

16.

The King's Road

Mor

11.

24

10.

Littlemarket

23

Southwick
Common

Bankside

25.

Oldtower

5

Golden Fields

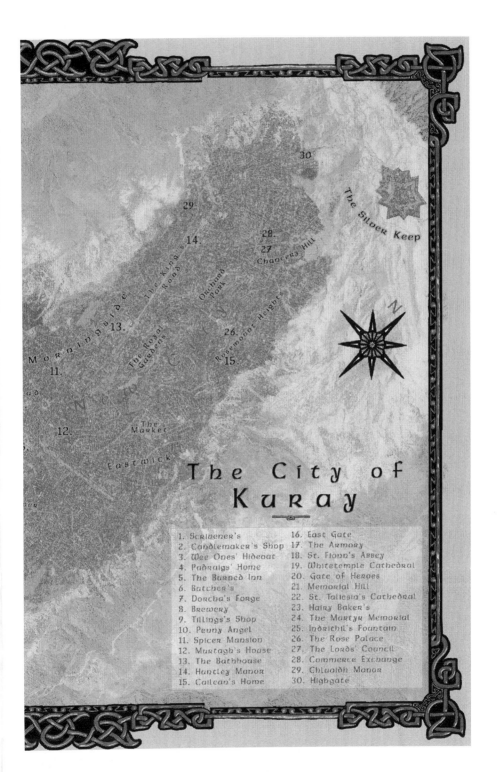

# The City of Kuray

1. Scribener's
2. Candlemaker's Shop
3. Wee Ones' Hideout
4. Padraigs' Home
5. The Burned Inn
6. Butcher's
7. Dorcha's Forge
8. Brewery
9. Tillings's Shop
10. Penny Angel
11. Spicer Mansion
12. Murtagh's House
13. The Bathhouse
14. Huntley Manor
15. Cailean's Home
16. East Gate
17. The Armory
18. St. Fionn's Abbey
19. Whitetemple Cathedral
20. Gate of Heroes
21. Memorial Hill
22. St. Taliesin's Cathedral
23. Hairy Baker's
24. The Martyr Memorial
25. Indrichil's Fountain
26. The Rose Palace
27. The Lords' Council
28. Commerce Exchange
29. Chluaidh Manor
30. Highgate

## CHAPTER ONE

# Something Precious

A shadow clung to the sheer face of the tower. Splayed against its weathered surface, she carefully tested her holds, her fingertips curled over slivers of frost-rimed stone no wider than a coin. Satisfied with her grip, she probed with one bare foot, and her toes found a crevice in one of the massive blocks that formed the tower.

She wedged her toes into the small fissure and pushed slowly higher, taking her weight on her pointed foot to grant her aching arms a moment's respite.

The summit of the Silver Keep was tantalizingly near, a sharp silhouette that seemed to sway against the slow seethe of coal-black clouds above it. Colossal statues ringed the top of Ruric's Tower, and the carved feet of one of the mighty figures jutted from the wall less than a body-length above her. Sculptors had shaped them into the likenesses of warriors, nobles, and sages with a delicate care that had endured centuries of wind and ice and rain.

Yet from the distant streets of Kuray in the valley beneath the Silver Keep, the statues were so small that even their gender was indistinct, and Wyn was surprised to discover that the figure above her was a robed man holding a staff bedecked with leaves and not, as she had always thought, an elderly woman waving a broom.

Wyn slid her hand higher, probing into the cracks between the ancient blocks. A small cranny allowed her to clutch a thin lip of stone and stretch cautiously upward.

The pedestal loomed over her, and her fingers found an ornate flourish to grasp. As she shifted her weight, lichen tore and slipped under her fingertips, mortar crumbled, and her hand came free in a rush. The violent motion twisted her against her remaining handhold, and her breath hissed sharply through her teeth as her toes slid on the smooth stone. For a heartbeat, she clung to her tenuous perch.

Then she jumped. Wyn uncoiled in a graceful whirl, following the pull of her body away from the wall. She twisted, back arched, feet pointed, eyes wide, as her limbs surged with the thrill, taunting the endless plunge beneath her.

One hand smacked hard against the edge of the statue's pedestal. Her fingers curled instinctively around a stone toe, holding her slender weight as she swung like a pendulum. For a moment, she closed her eyes and allowed herself to feel the rush of air past her legs and the strength of her fingers anchored against the drag of the abyss.

Then she strained savagely, tendons rigid in her arm, as she hauled herself close enough to the pedestal to grasp a second handhold amidst the statue's gnarled toes. She swung her legs and kicked, and with a final heave, she hooked her heel over the ancient plinth and squirmed into the space between the sage's ankle and the wall.

Wyn sagged against the statue's leg as she gasped for breath. The stone burned with frozen fire, but the icy surface felt good against her face, and its touch penetrated the fog of weariness that threatened to engulf her.

Her slim legs dangled on either side of the narrow base and her toes swung in a gentle circumnavigation of the outer walls of the Silver Keep. Wisps of long, blonde hair that had escaped their crude knot wafted around her face and affixed themselves to the pale, sweat-slick skin of her slender neck.

Wind slithered through the gap, stinging her back through the thin cloth of her tunic as it hissed across the drops of perspiration trickling down her spine, but its coils could not find a grip to pull her from her perch. Her tunic and leggings clung to her lithe shape, offering no loose cloth to flap and tug, and she wore no cloak or other garb that could catch the twists of air.

A satisfied grin spread across her lips, and her eyes were dark with joy.

"Knew I could make it," she whispered. She leaned against the wall at her back and sighed contentedly as she examined the castle spread beneath her.

The sheer wall of Ruric's Tower plunged toward the dark bulk of the Silver Keep's main halls. The distance reduced the high walls and soaring towers of the Keep to small lumps and thin spikes that nestled like a forest of spears beneath her, eager for her to fall.

Wyn snorted heavily and spat. The shining spittle spun crazily for a moment, then whipped sideways on the curling wind and splatted against the tower wall not far beneath her. Wyn sniffed in disappointment, then untied the small flask she carried on her belt and reveled in the icy water's touch as it rushed across her parched tongue. She desperately wanted to down the entire contents but forced herself to shove the cork back in after just a few swallows. The flask was tiny, all that she allowed herself to carry aside from a slim leather wallet containing a few choice tools.

A writhing blast of air from the mountains soaring above Kuray tore a gap in the sluggish, snow-heavy clouds, and suddenly the Silver Keep was bathed in bright moonlight. The stones of the fortress shone and glittered in the light, as if they were encased in ice or coated with a layer of polished metal.

Wyn gasped, instinctively curled her legs and arms into the shadow beneath the statue, and disappeared completely. For a heartbeat, she held as motionless as the statue itself. Then she laughed softly. *Who is going to see me up here?*

As if in answer to her unspoken question, a huge raven alighted with a flurry of wings on the foot of the statue less than an arm's-length in front of Wyn. The bird cawed loudly as it glared at her with its great, black eyes.

"Shhh," Wyn hissed at it.

The raven cocked its head and settled its wings into place. Its sharp beak opened slightly as it tasted the air, but it remained silent.

"Thank you," Wyn whispered. She grinned and winked at the massive bird. "Don't tell anyone."

The raven bobbed its head and launched into the air. Wyn could hear its mocking calls growing fainter as it soared away. *He's laughing at me,* she decided. *Well, it's not my fault I don't have wings. Let's see him climb up here with his little boney feet.*

She shivered and craned her neck upward. The dark underside of a balcony loomed over the top of the statue's head, adorned with stone flourishes and whorls to disguise the gutters and thick supports, a playground of handholds and ledges for her final ascent. She blew on her fingers, rubbed life into her toes, and puffed the hair out of her face, suddenly eager to be moving.

Wyn scrambled up the statue as effortlessly as if its folds of stone cloth were wide steps, slipped over the railing, and crouched in the pool of shadow against the balustrades, her head cocked to the side as she learned the sounds of the balcony.

Once satisfied that she was alone save for the dry brush of the wind through the railing, she crept to a window and peeked through its shutters. Embers pulsed gently in a wide fireplace set into the far wall, and their light warmed twists and curves of polished silver, crystal, and wood.

The window did not have a lock, but an iron hook sealed it against vagrant intrusions of wind. Wyn selected a thin, steel pick from her wallet, freed the catch with a gentle nudge, and soundlessly stepped over the sill.

She crept to the fireplace, ready to bolt at the slightest stir in the room's thick shadows, her arms clutched tight against her chest as she shivered and presented first one side of her body, then the other, to the lazy heat of the embers.

As she warmed, her gaze wandered over the enticing array of potential pillage that gleamed and twinkled around the room. A fortune lay within a few steps, even after the cut the Candlemaker

THE THIEF'S TALE

would take, but Wyn dismissed the room's contents with a wistful glance. She had not climbed Ruric's Tower just to nick a precious that could have come from any noble's mansion. She desired a very particular prize. Something small, something valuable. But, most of all, something that was, without a doubt, the Queen's.

Wyn padded silently across the luxurious carpets and eased the door's latch from its hook. The polished wood sighed smoothly open, and she silently thanked the generations of servants for their tireless work keeping the mighty, iron hinges oiled.

Outside the door, Wyn followed a hallway toward the center of the tower. She passed a drawing room and a library and slipped through a dining room with a table long enough for twenty chairs. The heavy silence was undisturbed save for a faint moan of distant wind against stone, but a band of light beneath a door signaled that at least one other occupant of the tower was awake.

Wyn crept carefully to the door, touched it lightly with her fingertips, and brushed her ear against the smooth wood. A shadow shifted beneath the door, and there was a creak of leather and a thump of metal on wood, so near that Wyn flinched, and she scurried quickly away, deeper into the tower.

A dozen steps brought Wyn to an antechamber with hallways exiting to the left and right, but her attention was caught by the wide door in the wall ahead of her. A warm glow bathed the edge of the door and spilled into the hallway, revealing that the door had been left ajar, just enough to provide a gap to peek through.

The room on the other side smelled of lavender and ancient, polished wood, a warm, comfortable scent that made Wyn think of thick blankets and a steaming cup of tea. A fireplace sighed with heat and lit the room with a soft glow, revealing a splendor Wyn had never imagined.

The chamber was ten strides across, at least, yet not a hand's-breadth felt ignored. A vast bed, covered in a duvet so deep and soft it looked like a cloud, dominated one side of the room, but space enough remained for a suite of plush chairs covered in luxurious fabrics and countless small tables with delicate, curved legs.

THE THIEF'S TALE

*The royal bedchamber, must be!* Wyn realized, and she held her breath to smother a gasp of excitement.

The bed could sleep five, comfortably, but it was currently unoccupied, its covers and mountain of pillows almost pristine. A small depression in a single pillow at the edge of the bed and a minor wrinkle in the sheets below it showed that Queen Gabrielle had recently used a small fraction of the bed's vast terrain, but there was no sign of her now.

*Where is she?* Wyn wondered. *A quick trip to the privy, or...* Wyn closed the door behind her. *Wherever she is, I'll not get a better chance.*

A dressing table revealed velvet-lined trays filled with gleaming jewelry, precious stones of every description surrounded by gold, silver, ivory, and wood. A pearl pendant encrusted with diamonds. A brooch in the shape of a fiery bird wrought from red and yellow gold. A string of polished onyx held in baskets of gold thread. Wyn let her fingertips rest on an armband of twisted white and yellow gold shaped like two snakes intertwined, feeling the cold weight of metal. Any of the pieces would make a spectacular catch, but none were what she was searching for.

Wyn checked under every flap of soft velvet in the drawer. *Where's her bloody crown?*

The glee she felt as she imagined the crown daringly perched on her brow as she enjoyed a mug or two surrounded by the adulation of the lads banished all thoughts of lesser baubles. Nothing could match the crown for its intimacy with the Queen. *Where is it?*

Much to her disgust, the writing table contained only beautiful, creamy vellum and quills. The nightstand held nothing more than an ancient, ponderous, leather-bound tome, carefully placed to conceal a ragged, well-thumbed, string-bound read. The end table bore only a small, silver magnifying glass, and, to her satisfaction, a pitcher of water that she used to refill her flask.

A soft, musical chime made Wyn jump and then crouch behind a divan, straining to hear past her pounding heart. Another gentle note drew her gaze to the mantle above the fire, where a small, golden egg nested in a series of slowly turning silver disks. At last, too curious to stay away, she crept to the mantle, poised to flee at any instant, and peered at the contraption.

THE THIEF'S TALE

She could make no sense of the rings, though markings of moons, stars, mountains, and rivers covered them. The egg itself was a wonder, its delicate surface crafted in sculpted gold petals of every color from white to red. As she watched, the shell slowly opened like a flower and revealed an inner surface etched with intricate runes and patterns in silvery metal.

*It must be a Device,* she decided. A tingling surge sizzled through her fingers at the thought. *Maker... it's just sitting here being magical, right in front of me! Wonder what it's doing?*

As if in response, the fine threads of silver metal shimmered like moonlight on water. Wyn gasped as the light rippled and flowed into the air above the shell, tiny stars that whirled and danced like motes caught in a shaft of light. One stream coalesced into a ball that shone like the moon, chased by two intertwined streams of light that twisted into the forms of two dragons, one silver, one black, striving against one another to catch the elusive sphere. The dragons clawed and bit and strained upward, but the moon evaded them and danced higher, until the dragons succumbed and fragmented, their light fading into embers that drifted into nothingness.

At last the moon hung placidly over the opened egg, pulsing with silver light. A bright tone sounded once, sweet and high, and the moon burst like a dandelion and rained light into the shell, which slowly closed, sealing away its magic.

When the shell clicked shut, Wyn let out her breath, blinked eyes wide with astonishment, and closed her mouth with a snap. After a moment's hesitation, she reached out a tentative hand and touched the shell with the barest brush of a fingertip, then smiled when she felt only the cool smoothness of the metal.

"Dragons chasing the moon," she whispered. *The Song of Pride...* she knew the story well, could hear Reverend Crawa's creaking voice telling the tale of Loriel's wager with the great dragons Ddraighnall and Tiernarnon.

Wyn waited expectantly for the Device to open again. But after a moment her smile faltered, her eyes slowly narrowed, and a small crease appeared between her faint brows. The single chime the Device had sung as the moon dissolved became a concern, then a conviction. *It's a timepiece,* she realized. *Maker, it's not first bell*

THE THIEF'S TALE

*already, is it?* She swallowed against sudden panic. *I'll never make it back down before sunrise.*

Wyn grimaced in frustration. *Then hurry,* she urged herself.

She glared at the room, her hands on her hips and her toes curled into the thick fur of a bearskin rug that lay beside the bed. *Crown, crown, crown. It can't be in a vault, she wears the damn thing, or, at least, she wears her little circlet, I've seen it.* Wyn frowned again. *In fact, where are all her clothes? Queens have loads of clothes, I reckon, but there's not so much as a wardrobe in here.*

She examined the ornate engraving of flowering ivy carved into the walls and soon discovered a small door lost in the shadows behind the bed. Wyn stepped through and gazed about in amazement. Tall wardrobes lined the inner wall, each an exquisite work of art in mahogany wood. In front of the wardrobes were plush settees arranged around a cluster of full-length mirrors and a row of stands bearing dozens of gowns, dresses, robes, and even, in one case, a long tunic of steel and silver chain so finely crafted that it appeared to be made of shimmering cloth.

Wyn wandered amongst the silk and lace and soft wool, rummaging in drawers, peering at shoes, gazing at gowns. At the far end she found a dressing table covered with more prosaic accoutrements. Hairpins with pearl grips, combs with ivory handles, a silver brush.

Wyn froze.

She stilled her breathing and let the sounds of the castle come to her. There had been a noise, so faint, so distant that it had not interrupted her thoughts. But she had heard it, every instinct told her, despite the empty silence of the dressing room. There was an absence of sound, an echo of what had been, that told her she was no longer alone.

Wyn replaced the brush with a faint click of metal on glass, never taking her gaze from the room. The bright bars of moonlight did not shift, the deep shadows beyond them did not stir.

Her head twitched to the side as sound brushed against her ear again. The distant thump of a door closing.

THE THIEF'S TALE

Wyn hurried across the dressing room on her toes and sank into the shadows against the door, her heartbeat throbbing in her ears as she eased the door carefully inward and peered through the gap.

A young woman in a billowing white nightdress slipped into the bedchamber through the outer door, and Wyn blinked in surprise. The woman's beautiful face, golden eyes, and her warm, copper skin were instantly recognizable. Wyn had seen her a dozen times as her carriage swept up the King's Road toward the Silver Keep, and even once so close that Wyn could have reached out and touched her boot as she rode past in a crowded square filled with joyous cheering and fluttering flower petals.

Queen Gabrielle slowly eased the door closed, grimacing as the bolt clicked. She collected the read from her nightstand, padded across the floor to the fireplace, and curled onto a thickly cushioned settee, her nightgown tucked securely around her legs.

Wyn watched impatiently as the young woman became engrossed in her book, each page greeted in turn with expressions of shock, wonder, or dismay.

She frowned as the Queen re-read a particular page several times, her eyes wide. *Martyr's tears, go to bed,* Wyn urged her, but there was little to indicate that her pleas would be granted.

Wyn jumped as a sharp rap boomed from the door to the bedchamber. The Queen gasped, almost dropped her book, and then quickly shoved the little volume beneath a convenient cushion.

"Yes?" she called out.

The door opened, revealing the form of a massive knight in steel armor so polished it gleamed like the night sky with a thousand stars shimmering across its surface.

"You have frightened my wits to death," the Queen chastised the knight. Her voice was rich and melodic, the graceful accents of her home as warm as that faraway land. Despite the Queen's awkwardness with the northern tongue, Wyn was struck by the feeling that the fault lay in the language, as if its sounds were too crude for such an elegant woman.

"I apologize, Your Majesty," the knight replied, although he did not seem apologetic. His craggy face looked as unperturbed as

THE THIEF'S TALE

granite. "Lord Karsha thought you would wish to know immediately. A messenger has just arrived from the King with a private correspondence for you."

The Queen's smile was a flash of white against her dusky skin. "Yes, absolutely. Please tell him to bring it right away."

"Perhaps in your study?" the knight suggested.

"Lord Karsha does not care to see me in my nightclothes," the Queen objected.

"Yes, Your Majesty. Does not care *if* he sees you, I believe."

"Thank you, Sir Ceredor," the Queen replied impatiently.

"I will send for him. Shall I wake Lady Bryn to assist you?"

"Let her sleep."

"Are you certain, Your Majesty? Lady Bryn will be extremely disappointed."

"I am able to read a letter by myself. I have done it before, I recall."

"Yes, Your Majesty." The knight frowned in disapproval.

Queen Gabrielle sighed. "Are you certain I am the Queen? No one acts as if this is true. Very well, please send for Lady Bryn."

"Yes, Your Majesty."

Wyn gently closed the dressing room door and waited until she heard the knight's footsteps clump through the doorway, followed by the tiny click of the latch, before she faced the dressing room, chewing determinedly on her lip. *Time to do the job and get out,* she told herself. *No crown for Wyn, more's the pity. The brush? Could be missed immediately, that would be a laugh on me, that's certain. What then?*

Wyn pushed her hair out of her face as she glared at the wardrobes and the headless gowns promenading in the shadows of the room. *Something that's hers, something small, something precious, something personal… what, what, what?*

Wyn's eyes went wide with delight as her gaze alighted on a chest of drawers. She shoved her fingertips into her mouth to stop a chortle of glee, scampered across the room, and fished a handful of lace-covered garments from a drawer, tucking them securely into the pouch on her belt.

THE THIEF'S TALE

Voices drifted to her from the bedroom, another woman's, laughing with the Queen. "... it will be there in the morning, I promise, Your Majesty. You need your rest."

"I cannot wait until morning to read his letter." The Queen sighed in exasperation. "In any case, I fear I must spend my morning being ill, again."

Light footsteps approached the dressing room door. "Just a housecoat, I am so frozen," the Queen called out.

Wyn darted to a window and yanked it open. Icy air pinched her face and ears. She thrust her body through to her waist, rocking and twisting to peer up and down the wall outside as her toes pointed and stretched to keep her balance.

This side of the tower faced west toward the mountains, nothing between Wyn and their ice rivers and sheer, granite faces except open air. Beneath her, the tower plummeted into a forest of lower towers and spires, then, impossibly distant, the rugged spine of rock that supported the Keep.

Between the windows stood more of the ring of stone heroes, their plinths anchored in the wall, their backs flush with the smooth stone, staring north and west with the same passion as their southern ring-mates with whom Wyn was already acquainted.

Wyn drew her legs onto the windowsill and crouched, judging the distance between her and the nearest statue, an armored knight whose face had weathered into vague pits and ridges barely recognizable as eyes and nose.

She pushed herself up, her fingers braced beneath the window's frame.

The wind gusted, snapping her hair across her cheek and mouth as she glared at the gap between her and the statue. It was not far... if one was strolling through the alleys of the Old City without a care for an impossible gulf of air beneath you. She tested her toes against the narrow, stone sill.

Voices drifted through the window. "Maker, no wonder! The window is open!"

Wyn sprang toward the statue, all her lithe strength exploding through her slender legs into the tips of her toes. She flew across the gap, wind rustling through her tunic, tugging at her hair,

THE THIEF'S TALE

singing in her ears, and wrapped her arms around the statue's leg as she smacked into it, driving the breath from her body.

Wyn gasped and hugged the smooth leg as her feet scrambled for purchase. She hooked a leg, drew herself up, and stepped around the knight's bulk as she heard the window clang shut.

"Ahhh…" Wyn sighed. "That was exciting." She wedged herself between the statue and the tower, pressed her back against the wall's freezing stone, and caught her breath.

*What now?* She peered down the tower, then frowned at the moon. *Not much night left… no chance I make it to the bottom before daylight.* She shivered as another gust of glacier-fed wind snaked around her. *Can't stay here, I'll freeze to death.*

A black silhouette blurred across the tower's shining stone and landed on the statue's shoulder with a thunder of flapping. The great raven carefully folded and refolded its wings into place as it examined Wyn with its gleaming, dark eye.

"What do you think, handsome?" Wyn asked the bird.

The raven croaked and preened his feathers with his wicked bill until his wings were perfectly arranged.

"My hair is a mess?" Wyn grinned at the bird and rubbed her hand vigorously through the tangles of sweat-streaked blonde hair that hung limply around her head. "Never!"

The raven croaked and bobbed its head in amusement.

Wyn smiled in return and began to gather her wayward hair into a knot, pulling it tight with a yank. "That's as pretty as I get, I'm afraid. Now what?"

The raven tilted its head, spread its wings, and launched into the air. Wyn watched it spiral slowly down the face of the tower until it swerved and seemingly disappeared into the solid stone wall. She blinked in surprise at the spot the raven had vanished.

"Now, then…" she muttered, frowning. "How about that?"

She rose from her perch and spread herself against the wall, her fingers and toes finding purchase on minute ridges of lichen-encrusted stone. Wyn's lips compressed into a thin line as the strain of her earlier climb made itself immediately known with a dull ache that started in her shoulders and rapidly spread to her thighs.

THE THIEF'S TALE

But the raven had not flown far before it had plunged into the wall, and Wyn reached the spot sooner than she had feared. Tall windows pierced the tower there, an elegant sweep of glass and iron save for a single pane that had broken and left a hole wide enough for an enormous raven to slip through.

She carefully snaked her arm through the opening and gently coaxed the latch free. The ancient hinges creaked in protest and refused to open further than a gap barely wide enough for her to squeeze through.

Wyn bent double over the windowsill, squirmed onto her hands, and gracefully curled her legs through the window after her. Then she rose, her eyes wide in astonishment as her gaze explored the room.

The tall windows framed a statue of a slender woman bathed in gentle, silver moonlight. She stood with her sword raised defiantly over her head, and at her feet lay a wounded knight wearing a seven-pointed crown. Wyn had seen statues of the Martyr in the same pose enough times to recognize her instantly, but this one caught her gaze and held it.

As always, the Martyr was young and beautiful, but Wyn had never seen her look so fierce, her lips parted in a snarl of resolve, her gaze narrowed as she challenged whatever unseen presence loomed over her. The Martyr was typically depicted with a peaceful and serene expression, as if she were dozing in front of a fire instead of battling for her life, and Wyn was suddenly overcome by a realization that the Martyr had been a young woman not much older than herself, who had laughed and frowned and sighed and wished, and who had somehow defied her fear to save her king. Wyn felt a pang of envy as she gazed at the Martyr's face. *How were you so brave? Can you show me?*

The statue's hair was carved into long, intricate braids that swept dramatically into the air behind her, and Wyn wondered who had sat behind the Martyr and created the flowing works of art, and had they laughed together, or shed tears at the thought of the upcoming battle? Had she known it was the last time she would hear the soft stroke of a brush through her hair?

Wyn pressed fingertips to her own lips as she swallowed against an ache in her throat and forced away a vision of bright

THE THIEF'S TALE

sun flashing on a polished wooden brush, a memory buried safely away for years. She drew long, steady breaths, and focused on the letters carved into the statue's plinth as she traced her fingers along their deep shapes.

*Bronwyn*… her own name, once. In a different life, lost long ago.

The shrine was as peaceful as the bottom of a pond, gentle and filled with soft shadows. Wyn smiled at the Martyr, glad to have seen her, despite the hated sniffles the encounter had brought with it.

Wyn pressed her nose against her sleeve and reluctantly turned her attention to the rest of the room. Huddled, shrouded shapes obscured the walls of the shrine, revealed by a nervous poke with a finger to be stacks of cushioned benches with dusty blankets thrown over them. A broad rug was rolled and wedged against the wall, and cobwebs festooned a small forest of candlesticks clustered in the corner.

The raven perched on the highest stack of benches. It had torn the covers of its tower into rags and made a comfortable nest at the top, leaving the shit-covered skeleton of wood exposed.

Wyn found the entrance to the shrine, a small door secured by an iron lock, and shoved a bench against it before allowing herself a breath of relief that she instantly regretted as her eyes watered from the acrid stench.

"Phew," she told the raven. "You might want to clean up a bit before inviting any lady ravens over. That's free advice, that is."

The raven ruffled its feathers but appeared content to watch her. Wyn deprived a stack of benches of their covers and made her own nest, as she gratefully wrapped one of the blankets around her and made a pallet of another near the windows.

*Not bad,* she decided as she leaned wearily against the wall. *No one's been in here for months, I'll wager, judging from the mess he's made. I'll wait here all tomorrow, nice and snug, and have a bit of a kip before heading down as soon as it gets dark.* She swished a mouthful of water around her mouth and wet her lips before tucking her flask away.

"Thanks for sharing," she yawned to the raven. "Don't worry… I don't snore…"

THE THIEF'S TALE

As the blankets warmed her, her eyelids became heavier, until she was barely able to raise them for more than a moment. Each time she forced them open, she could see the raven watching her with an unblinking gaze from its roost, and she relaxed under its unwavering guard.

Her head drooped forward, and she began to softly snore.

THE THIEF'S TALE

## CHAPTER TWO

# A Girl Could Get Used to This

Wyn clasped her cloak tightly around her shoulders and hurried along the edge of the alley as it wound its way through the dregs of the Old City. She slipped easily among the jostling figures eager to be somewhere dry and warm.

Rows of narrow, brick buildings crowded against the bustling alley, their windows glaring at one another over the street's cobblestone surface. Occasional lanterns swung from iron hooks on the walls, freshly lit by the City Watch as the grey light of a gloomy evening slowly leeched away. The lanterns' golden glow glistened on the cobbles and the iron gutters of the buildings, and made small spheres of gossamer haze from the drifting mist.

She squeezed past porters bearing vast packs across their shoulders, push-carts squeaking and rattling over the uneven cobbles, a fiercely bearded man violently scrubbing his doorstep with a stiff-bristled brush that matched his beard to a remarkable degree, and peddlers offering firewood, turnips, rags, a muddy sack of damp flour with a burst end, and an assortment of carved wooden animals.

A narrow opening between the buildings twisted into the darkness, and she darted into it. The cold stone and damp wood walls were close enough that Wyn could have touched both sides with extended fingers as she threaded her way along the alley, and the buildings frequently slouched against one another overhead, forming small tunnels.

A small sign with a simple image of a burning candle protruded from the bricks next to a narrow, black door. Wyn pushed through the door and closed it firmly behind her, and the faint chime of a bell sounded from somewhere deep inside the shop. A single, fat stub of mottled wax smoked on a small, rough-planked table, filling the room more with the stink of tallow than with light. Wyn pulled open a small door that lurked in the back of the room and descended the warped stairs beyond.

The cellar of the shop was almost as dark as the upper room but was as sweltering and cluttered as the entrance was frigid and bare. The sweet aroma of beeswax candles set in silver candelabras filled the room, and their light cast a warm glow on packed shelves that groaned under the weight of the boxes crammed onto them.

The man seated behind the scarred table in the center of the room appeared as if he were made from one of his waxy creations. His pale skin shone with sweat and hung in drooping bulges that rolled down his figure and swayed in thick curtains under his arms. Damp patches imprisoned by crusty, salt-rimmed borders stained the thick fabric of his tunic, and bulky rings strangled thick fingers. Tiny, pale eyes stared at Wyn from within thick folds of flesh, gleaming, sharp, and alive, as if all his liveliness had fled his sagging body and taken refuge in his gaze.

"Ah... Wyn," he greeted her, his lips pursing. He drew one hand from beneath the table and rested it next to the other, which was about as friendly a welcome from the Candlemaker as one could hope for. "I was wondering if you and Mellon were still amongst the living."

"Been a bit busy, is all." Wyn leaned nonchalantly on the empty chair that faced the Candlemaker across the table, resting her arms on its high back. She had known crossbows to release unexpectedly, and she felt a good deal safer with the chair's thick oak between her stomach and the barbed, steel bolt of the one beneath the table, whether the Candlemaker's hand gripped its trigger or not.

"And what have you brought me, today?" he asked, his gaze unwavering as his fingers twitched greedily on the tabletop. "Some baubles, perhaps? Some trinkets?" he giggled. The Candlemaker was as hard in his dealings as he was soft in his body, but Wyn and Mellon always brought their choicest finds to him. The Candlemaker paid coin, found buyers, and did not seem intimidated by even the most recognizable pieces of jewelry, which made him very valuable to Wyn and the lads. In return, they were able to provide the Candlemaker with a steady stream of choice gems and precious metals, high quality goods that few could deliver. Which made them valuable to him.

It was not trust, but it would do.

Wyn felt a grin spread across her face. "No, none of that shite. What do you say to these?" She slid a tiny slip of black silk and lace out of her pocket and spread it on the table.

"What...?" The Candlemaker leaned forward, his eyes almost lost in the deep wrinkles of confusion that were bunching his fat into fleshy, rolling hills. "What the fuck is that?"

"Have you never seen a lady's knickers?"

"What am I meant to do with those?" he asked. "I'm not a fucking clothier. Do you see a bunch of ladies in here buying knickers?"

"No, I don't," Wyn replied innocently, gazing around as if surprised she did not see a parade of noblewomen needing undergarments.

"Then get them dirty panties off my table." He sat back, his arms folded over his belly.

"Oh, you might want to reconsider that," Wyn said brightly, and she winked.

"Why's that?" he sneered.

Wyn casually placed a fingertip on the strip of embroidered lace at the top of the silk and tapped it significantly. The Candlemaker leaned slowly forward, his thick lips pursed as he squinted at the symbol stitched into the lace. His eyes widened, and he bent so low Wyn could feel his breath against her finger.

The Thief's Tale

"Never…" he whispered. "You never…"

"I did," Wyn giggled. "Her Majesty's panties are what you're sniffing."

He jerked away. "I wasn't… I was just… where did you…?"

"Where do you think?" Wyn laughed. She slowly raised her finger from the panties and pointed it upward.

"The fuck you did!" he spluttered.

"The fuck I did," Wyn assured him.

He stared at her for another moment, then licked his lips and glanced at the black silk, then back to Wyn's face.

"Maker's breath, you did, didn't you?"

"Yeah." Wyn could not stop grinning.

The Candlemaker shook his head, astonishment slowly oozing into the more familiar lines of greed and cunning across his face. "I suppose I might consider it, purely as a novelty. Not certain I could ever find a buyer…"

"As long as the novelty is the fair price you're about to give me," Wyn scoffed. She began to gather the black silk from the table. "Or I'll have a look to see if there's someone more willing…"

"No need," he allowed, his lower lip pushing out fiercely. "I'll pay, and you'll say yes." He placed a small purse on the table, but kept it covered by his thick fingers. "You can have this now, or take a share…"

Wyn's faint eyebrows arched in surprise. She had never been offered shares before, and it was tempting, she had to admit. But the soft clink of coins in the purse made her fingers itch. "Depends on how many coins are in that purse, and what they're made of."

"It's silver," he grumbled. "You're not getting gold, no matter whose arse this has touched."

"I'll take the purse," Wyn decided.

"Thought so," he giggled, and he snatched his hand away with a flourish.

"And three more," Wyn added. "Just like it."

He laughed, genuinely amused. "Why the fuck would I do that?"

THE THIEF'S TALE

"Because," Wyn informed him, pulling a spray of silk from her pocket, "Her Majesty also likes blue, green, and white."

———⚓———

Wyn tried to spend her silver, but the lads conspired to make sure one of them was always dipping into their own purse before she could dip into hers. Mellon made a grand show of paying, and Desmond would grin triumphantly when she finally realized he had already paid. Fergus had a quiet whisper in the publican's ear, and the sweating man would only stammer, "Your money's no good here, lass," in a shaking voice whenever she tried to give him coin after that.

"What are you lads up to?" she asked, fighting to keep her thick tongue from slurring her words. "Evens in, evens out."

"Maybe so." Mellon leaned back in his chair and drained his mug. "But you might be deserving of a bit of largesse on this one, a bit of above and beyond, as it were."

"Above is right," Desmond chuckled into his mug.

"Everyone did theirs," Wyn objected, smiling happily at a fresh mug that appeared next to her elbow even as she set down her empty. The thick suds sloshed over the lip and slid down the mottled side of the mug, and Wyn rescued the remainder by slurping noisily until the dancing surface was low enough to trust to a wobbling tabletop.

"There's doing a part, and then there's ringing the bloody bell." Mellon grinned wickedly, his smile sharp in his round face.

"Very true," Wyn agreed emphatically, and she waved her mug vaguely in the direction of the center of the table so that the foam plopped and sloshed.

Mellon raised his mug to her and took a long swallow, his throat bobbing up and down amidst the forest of black bristles coating his neck. Wyn joined him, smacked her lips in satisfaction, and thumped the mug awkwardly on the table. It tipped precariously before it was saved by a hand that shot from the far side of the table to steady it.

"Woah." Wyn blinked at Fergus. "My hero."

THE THIEF'S TALE

"As always," he replied, the low rasp of his voice so quiet that Wyn had to strain to hear it over the chaos of the tavern. Fergus released the mug, his scarred fingers retreating to their habitual place on the worn pommel of his sword. He leaned against the wall behind him, his long, lank hair framing a thin face with a hatchet of a nose and a chin as sharp as the gleam in his eyes.

"I may be a bit..." Wyn eyed her mug suspiciously, which was already leaning to the side as the table did its best to stand on its end. "... tipsy," Wyn confided to him.

A ghost of a smile crossed Fergus's thin lips. His mug was almost untouched, the foam barely below the rim, but Wyn knew that was about all the swordsman would drink, no matter the celebration.

"You might be," Fergus acknowledged.

Wyn abandoned trying to keep her mug stable and downed the rest of her ale, just to be safe. "Fucking Tallywags!" she cheered, and the lads joined her in a chorus of, "Tallywags!"

The room was spinning pleasantly, now, everything in it cheerful and bright and warm. Wyn beamed happily and began to slowly stretch her legs onto the bench opposite, nudging Desmond's lanky legs out of the way with the tips of her small boots.

*I did it!* She smiled and snuggled deeper into her cloak. *Everyone knows I did it.*

And there had been a never-ending stream of people approaching her. Small names anxious to congratulate the crew of the day, and, perhaps, offer their services. Mellon accepted their tribute and gave them nothing but an easy word in return, ushering them away when they tried to linger.

Mellon had dressed for the part, exchanging his usual shapeless wool jacket and hideous scarf for a long, high-collared coat, a red vest with silver buttons, soft leather boots, and cream-colored trousers. He had tamed his spray of hair but had retained his unshaven scruff, claiming it made him look tougher.

*Everything is going to be better, now, everyone will want our help, and be nice to us, like they are tonight. Who would have guessed that a pair of knickers would be the best thing I ever nicked?*

THE THIEF'S TALE

Wyn finally got her legs just right on the bench opposite, and she leaned back against a pillar with her new mug gripped firmly in both hands.

"A girl could get used to this," she sighed happily.

"You deserve it, Wyn." Desmond's smile slipped slightly and became fixed. "Listen, Wyn…" He leaned a bit closer, glancing at Mellon as he did. "I just wanted to… what you did was amazi—"

"You know what I deserve?" Wyn suddenly realized, her eyes going wide. She grinned at the other three in turn. "A bloody gold talen from Lord Sly."

"Deserves and gets are two very different things," Mellon observed.

"You don't think His Nibs will pay?" Wyn asked. "He's promised for years and years, though. First person to get in there gets gold."

"Not a chance," Mellon declared. "If he has a gold talen to give away, I'll shit a diamond."

"Shame," Wyn mumbled, wondering where the rest of her drink had gone. "I'd have liked to see you push out a diamond."

"Well, I'm willing to give it a try," Mellon said reasonably. "Hold my drink." He passed his mug to Desmond and stood, fumbling with his belt.

"Maker, no!" Desmond pleaded as Wyn giggled happily.

Waves of warmth washed over her as she slowly sank lower against the wall, chuckling contentedly at the increasingly dazzling wit bandied about the small table. She roused herself to take care of her share of another round of drinks that had appeared while she was not looking, then rested her eyes for just the tiniest moment…

"… she's gone, again," Mellon laughed.

Wyn jerked upright, her cheek numb from pressing against her arm. "Just a bit," she mumbled, checking her face suspiciously for drool. "Where's my mug?"

"Come on, before the puking starts," Mellon suggested reasonably, and benches scraped as the lads struggled to their feet. Wyn complained bitterly, but once on her own feet she had to laugh at the gleeful sway of the room and cling to Fergus's iron shoulders to steady herself.

As they approached the door, a group of men pushed their way into the tavern. Wyn recognized their leader, a thick-set brute with eyebrows like caterpillars and black stubble coating his jaw who collected debts for anyone who cared more about inflicting pain than recovering their coin. Wyn lowered her gaze quickly and tried to shrink behind Fergus, but as they passed the newcomers Wyn was astonished to see them step aside. The leader shocked her further by nodding respectfully to her and mumbling, "Good on ya."

The night air was bitterly cold and laced with stinging flakes of ice, and Wyn brushed absently at her cheeks as she chased their touch. "… snowing…" she observed thickly.

A single carriage drawn by two matched horses crowded the lane, its black paint glossy and gleaming, with a golden seal that depicted a stone tower beside a river prominently displayed on the door.

"Evening, Tallywags," the driver greeted them, tipping his tall, ribbon-bedecked hat. He hopped down from his bench and strode to the carriage door.

"Evening," Mellon returned the greeting. "You one of the Charioteers, then? Who are you, tonight?"

"That I am, that I am," the driver nodded his head eagerly. "Seems like the driver said it were the property of Lord Dampcloth, but I may have misheard him. He was not well pleased to donate his hat, so there was a bit of swearing all jumbled in." He swept open the door to the carriage. "Come on, then, in you go."

"Aren't you earning?" Wyn asked. "We don't mind walking."

"You're not walking, tonight, lass," he grinned. "Compliments of the Charioteers."

"Do you think everyone knows?" Wyn asked Mellon quietly, as a strange swirl of glee and dread churned in her stomach.

"Word will out, Whinny, you know it will," Mellon said sagely. "Might as well enjoy it."

"I suppose…" she replied. The churning was not dying away. "Hang on two shakes…" She retched against the side of the tavern, hands pressed firmly against the wooden planks of the wall for support against the swaying city. Mellon thoughtfully held her

THE THIEF'S TALE

hair as she finished and offered her his silver flask. Whatever he kept in it burned as she swirled the liquid around her mouth, but it cleansed the sour bile that lingered in her throat.

"Right," Wyn declared, wiping her lips with her sleeve. "Ready for my carriage."

The Tallywags bundled into the carriage and Wyn flopped onto the soft leather bench, her head thick with dense clouds of happy exhaustion despite the chill air. Mellon leaned against the cushions opposite her as the carriage creaked into motion amidst a flurry of shouts and whistles from the driver.

"Well, what do you think?" Mellon asked.

"About what?"

"Beauchamp's job. The commissary wagon? Any of this ring a bell?"

"Did Champs come by?" Wyn frowned. "I missed him. I think I might have had a little kip for a moment."

"I could never tell. Yes, Beauchamp has a job he thought we might be interested in. Two locks, a thousand crowns to vanish from a moving wagon, and it has to be done in daylight."

"Sounds amazing." Wyn smothered a yawn. "Who made the locks?"

"Gwylfai."

"Oh, yeah, no problem. Be nice to work with Champs again. He always finds the nicest locks to crack." Another yawn burst through her clenched jaw and squeezed her eyes closed with its ferocity.

"Poor luv," Mellon laughed. "You did yeoman's work here tonight, what with the scowling and the puking, so let's get you home before you add snoring."

"I wasn't scowling, I was trying not to yawn. And I don't snore," Wyn objected.

## CHAPTER THREE

# Promises Were Made

The ride to Scrivener's was quicker than Wyn had expected, no doubt hastened by the driver's fear of what she might do to the interior of his appropriated carriage. The cramped building was squeezed between a wainwright's shop and a small theater, which meant it was noisy all day with the banging of hammers and noisy all night with the drunken roaring of the crowd, but the eponymous clerk who owned the building kept to himself on the ground floor endlessly scratching copies of letters for his clients and let the top three floors of the building to the Tallywags for a very reasonable rent. The second and third stories featured empty rooms and dusty floors but the fourth, tucked under the peaked gables of the tall roof, they had made their home.

They staggered up the narrow stairs together, Wyn finding every creak and squeak of the worn boards hilarious. But as they stepped into the main room, it took only a small intake of breath from Mellon and a sudden stillness from Fergus to bring her completely alert.

A figure stood next to their stove, warming his hands, as unconcerned by their arrival as if they had stumbled into his home.

He was a young man, his skin a dull grey in the shadows, smooth-cheeked with a thin, trimmed line of beard along his jaw and across his lip, his short, black hair swept to one side rakishly. But what had once been a handsome face was now twisted into something far more dangerous, his nose thick from being broken far too often and his eyes dark within narrow slits, always watching. One corner of his mouth hooked around a puckered scar, and gold gleamed between his lips beneath the twisted flesh.

His gaze rested on Wyn for a moment, and she fought the urge to flee, suddenly a child caught on the wrong street, desperate to escape.

Fergus stepped slowly forward, his gaze never leaving the man's, the fingers of his sword hand slowly curling and straightening.

"What do you want, Ratter?" Mellon asked, his voice too loud in the small room.

The man's gaze left Wyn and returned to Fergus, but he made no answer to Mellon, and stepped to the front windows and closed their shutters.

Mellon balled his fists onto his hips and put a harsh edge on his rasp. "Ratter, what are you doing here?"

The man smiled crookedly and held a finger to his ear. A heartbeat later the heavy tread of boots on the stairs made Wyn's heart sink lower, and she felt sweat prickle down her spine.

Wyn scrambled out of the way as a second man entered the room. His gaze swept over Wyn without a pause, a slight sneer on the corner of his thick lips the only sign that he was not merely bored as he inspected the thick beams and warped floorboards before taking any interest in the room's occupants.

At first glance, the man might have been mistaken as a youth despite his size. His face was round, his mouth wide, and there was only the faintest shadow of a beard along his jaw. But there was nothing young about him, no trace of uncertainty, nor arrogance, nor petulance… none of the emotions that rested so comfortably on a young man's face. Only contempt.

THE THIEF'S TALE

A ragged, pink scar split his pale skin from forehead to lip, a knotted line that crossed his right eye but somehow had spared his sight.

He wore a grey tunic with black embroidery around the collar and a heavy, leather coat that trailed to his knees like a robe. A sword hung in a battered leather sheath at his hip, its grip worn, its pommel bare, unadorned steel.

He finished his inspection of the room and faced the Tallywags.

"Quinn," Mellon greeted the man. He adjusted his fancy brown coat and licked his lips. "Haven't seen you in a while."

"Mellon," Quinn replied. His voice was soft and cold as snow. "I hear you've been busy." Quinn stared around the bare room and sniffed. "Did I hear wrong?"

Mellon shrugged. "You know how it is. Easy in, easy out."

Quinn appeared not to have heard. He tugged his black gauntlet from his right hand and slowly rubbed his head, his fingers sliding over the short stubble that coated his skull like a cap.

"I heard you've been very busy." Quinn stepped closer to Mellon. "That you are to be congratulated."

"Oh, well…" Mellon licked his lips again as he stared up at Quinn. "We've had a bit of good fortune, that's a fact…"

"I have a job for you." Quinn yanked his gauntlet back onto his hand and hooked his thumb into his belt. "A simple matter for a crew that can break into the Silver Keep."

"We don't work for you," Wyn blurted, anger and fear sizzling out of her before she could stop herself.

Quinn's gaze met hers, his pale eyes cold and reptilian. Wyn quickly looked away and slunk into Fergus's shadow, her arms hugged across her chest, her jaw clenched as she fought the urge to flee.

"I think what Wyn means," Mellon said hastily, "is that we're not for hire. If there's a score you know about that you think we might be interested in…"

"This time," Quinn replied, "you will want to take the work."

"No…" Wyn begged her boots in a whisper. She risked a furtive glance at Quinn but was caught by his unwavering stare.

THE THIEF'S TALE

"Why is that?' Mellon asked.

"It would make me very grateful." Quinn inhaled slowly, then returned his gaze to Mellon. "And I would be very disappointed if you did not."

Mellon cleared his throat. "Well, perhaps if you told us a bit about what you might need…"

"My client wants two keys," Quinn informed them, "from two different owners, neither of whom can know that their key is gone."

"Keys to what?" Wyn asked.

"Why the fuck do you care?" Quinn asked sharply.

"Because, I thought, you know, why steal two keys when I could just pick the locks, instead," Wyn snapped back, horrified at herself.

"The keys are the job, not the locks."

*Why? That's bollocks…* Wyn thought angrily, but she desperately choked back the words. *Martyr's tears, please shut up, you stupid girl!*

"Two keys," Quinn repeated. "Talk amongst yourselves. Ratter will be back in the morning to hear your answer."

"That's all we get to know?" Mellon asked, his voice tight with strain. "Quinn, be reasonable. We have other work, at least tell us when this job is."

Quinn gazed at Mellon for a moment, then strode to the door. "Starts tomorrow, and you have two weeks," he threw over his shoulder as he left. "So, don't moan about it all night. Ratter will be back bright and early." Quinn's boots thumped unhurriedly down the stairs.

Ratter strolled from his place at the window to the door, his tongue probing the cleft in his lip.

"Maker's breath, Ratter, he can't expect us to drop everything when he won't even tell us what the job is," Mellon pleaded. "And two weeks? That's insane. A job like this takes longer than that just to prepare, and he wants us to do two of them. He can't ask us to do it in two weeks."

"Oh, I don't think I'd tell him what he can't do, if I were you," Ratter murmured as he followed his master through the door. "Goodnight, Tallywags. Bright and early."

THE THIEF'S TALE

Wyn listened to Ratter's footsteps descend the steps and the front door bang, then she sank onto the bench next to the table.

"I about peed myself," she groaned.

Mellon sat heavily beside her. "Well, it sounds like Quinn needs us, so he has to be civil."

"How civil do you think he'll be when we say no?"

"There's no harm in thinking about saying yes," Mellon said quietly.

"What?" Wyn's skin prickled with a rush of cold fire and her breath caught in her throat.

"I wouldn't mind him being grateful for us helping him out."

"No..." Wyn forced out. She glanced desperately at the other Tallywags. "Martyr's tears, we're not going to work for a bastard like Quinn. Do you not remember what Quinn is?"

"I know what he is, Wyn—"

"Then why are you talking about making him grateful? We can't work for him." Wyn cast about for a way to make Mellon understand more clearly, but her mind flailed uselessly, and she found her gaze riveted on her clenched fists, her knuckles white with strain.

"Wyn," Mellon tried again, his voice taut. "We should at least talk—"

"No!"

"Wyn, damn it, shut it."

"I'll not shut it, Mellon," Wyn hissed. "You know what he had that fucker Ratter do to Des and me when we were just bairns."

"I remember, Wyn, and I'm not anxious to find out what he might do to us now, if we disappoint him."

"There's others with names as hard as Quinn's," Desmond suggested quietly. His face was as pale as parchment, save for two bright red patches on his cheeks. "We tell them Quinn's throwing his weight around."

"Who would give a turd what Quinn does to us?"

"We could go to Patchwork or Scurrilous," Wyn said desperately, "or Lord Sly, he likes our work, I reckon. He wouldn't look kindly at Quinn for harming us."

THE THIEF'S TALE

"Black Morgan was hard as granite, and he got no closer than this." Mellon drew a finger down his face over his right eye. "What makes you think His Nibs wants any of that, just to help us out?"

"He wouldn't," Desmond agreed softly. He glanced from Wyn to Mellon, then down at his hands. "I dunno, Wyn… two keys? That sounds a lot easier than fighting with Quinn."

"Unbelievable," Wyn groaned. "What about you, Fergus? You've been silent as stone. Do you not have a thought on this?"

The lanky swordsman was slouched against the back wall, his limp hair hanging over his face, concealing his eyes. But his lips were drawn into a bloodless line. "If we say no, it'll be blades for certain," he said, his voice a quiet rasp. "Might as well draw first blood. That's our best chance of living through it."

"Martyr's tears, Fergus, I didn't say we turn to murder! We're not Quinn…" Wyn hugged her arms miserably around her chest. *Maker, why isn't Quinn murdered? He deserves it, he deserves a thousand murders for what he's done.*

Fergus shrugged. "You might not be."

"You're not like them, Fergus," Wyn told him angrily. "Not anymore."

"It's one job," Mellon replied. "We do it, nice and clean, and we're out. Fergus, you with Wyn on this, or me and Desmond? Your voice decides it."

Fergus climbed to his feet and shook his head. "We can't hide from him, Wyn."

"For fuck's sake, no…" Wyn whispered.

"Wyn, you're not a little girl anymore," Mellon snapped. "Can you stop thinking about what they did to you years ago and start thinking about what they're going to do to us all, right now, if we disappoint them?"

Wyn drew in a deep, shuddering breath as tears burned her eyes. Mellon's face slowly blanched and his eyes widened as he realized the hurt his words had caused, but Wyn could barely see him as the world swam and receded behind a fog of despair.

"I'm not saying we join his crew," Mellon tried to console her. "I'm just saying we do this one job for him."

"If we do one, he'll ask us to do another, as certain as fucking sunrise." Wyn whirled away and stumbled to the rear of the loft, where a small space crammed under the sloping roof served as her room.

She threw herself onto her cot and glared miserably at the raw wood beams spinning drunkenly above her head. She could hear the mutter of conversation continuing in the main room, though she tried desperately not to.

"... cruel... should know better than that..." drifted to her unwilling ears in Fergus's voice, cold and flat, and a weary "... fuck..." in Mellon's, until Wyn buried her head under her pillow and blocked them out.

*It's not fair,* she decided. *I've stayed clear of that bastard for years and then he just walks in and nothing's changed. Everyone too scared to say no. They're not scared enough, I say. You run from Quinn. You hide. You don't cozy up next to him where he can get you any time he wants.* Wyn's hands curled into fists around clumps of pillow. *How is Quinn not yet murdered? I'd do it if I had any kind of stones, and then I reckon they'd build statues of me all over the place, looking fierce and brave.*

She sighed and threw the pillow off, then fumbled awkwardly underneath her back until she found the pocket of her twisted cloak and pulled free a small bundle of soft, red silk.

*It's not fair,* she told the shining fabric. *This was a good night, and all.*

Wyn searched beneath the cot until her fingers found a small, wooden box. She pulled it out and rested the box on her chest. She traced the simple latch that secured it and brushed her fingers over the cracked paint on the lid.

Then she flipped the latch and opened it. A quick glance showed Wyn that the contents were in order.

"Her Majesty also likes red," she murmured as she tucked the red panties into the box and firmly closed the lid.

She managed to place the box securely on the floor before she passed out, her thoughts filled with the vision of a young woman, her lips parted in a snarl of fierce resolve, her gaze narrowed as she challenged a scar-faced presence that loomed over her.

THE THIEF'S TALE

The small gate opened with a creak and swung shut with a groan behind her as Wyn padded barefoot up the garden path. She shaded her eyes against a glare that seemed to come from every direction, making the small house in front of her swim and dance so that it appeared to grow and shrink as she approached it. Sunflowers with wilted and curled petals lunged at her face as she pushed toward the house.

The house's cracked yellow door groaned open as she shoved her way inside. A gaunt man with stained fingers sat hunched over a long table, the black of his clothes a blot against the faded white plaster of the room.

Wyn gazed frantically around the room. She knew she should recognize it, but wherever she looked, the room's contents turned hazy and indistinct.

"Mum?" she called. Wyn hurried to the back of the room and called again. "Mum?"

Only the scratch of the man's quill against the table's linen answered her. Wyn approached the table hesitantly. Long streams of black ink trickled over the edge and spattered onto the worn floorboards, leaving spreading stains on the tablecloth as it fell. Wyn tried to look at what the man was writing, but the table was too high for her to see.

"Do you know where Mum is?" Wyn asked.

"You're too late," the man answered, without looking away from his work.

Wyn backed away, then hurried deeper into the house.

"Mum?" she called out. A long passageway lined with doors stretched into the darkness ahead of her. She tried to open the doors, but none had handles. "Mum?"

A hand slipped into hers. Long, warm fingers intertwined with Wyn's, and something hard and smooth pressed into her other hand. Wyn glanced down to see what it was. Her fingers curled around the handle of an old, cracked hairbrush. Long strands of golden hair floated from its bristles.

"I'm here, sweetheart," a soft voice breathed in her ear

"I've been looking everywhere for you," Wyn told her mother. "For so long."

"I know," her mother replied. "I just wanted to see you, one more time."

Wyn nodded and led the way down the passage, gripping her mother's hand tightly. A priest stood outside a closed door, a dark frown narrowing his eyes to slits as he glared at Wyn.

"Where have you been?" he demanded. "You're too late."

Wyn pushed past the priest and through the door in a rush. Her mother's bedroom was dark and the air was stifling with incense. Shutters had been pulled closed against the sunlight, but Wyn could see a tall man standing next to her mother's bed, staring down at the small figure huddled beneath the thin blanket. He was holding her mother's hand, her frail fingers dwarfed in his grasp.

He turned to Wyn, and gold flashed from behind a twisted lip.

"You're too late," Ratter sneered. Blood began to drip between his fingers, pattering across the knotted rug beside the bed.

"No!" Wyn screamed. She lunged forward, but the hand holding hers yanked her back, pulling her off her feet so that she stumbled and sagged backward. She looked up.

Quinn gazed down at her. The long scar across his eye writhed as his mouth twisted in disgust.

"You shouldn't be here," he told her.

Wyn screamed again and tried to pull away, but Quinn's hand tightened, squeezing mercilessly. Wyn pulled desperately, but Quinn's grip was a vice, and Wyn could not free herself.

"Too late," Ratter said again.

Quinn finally released her and Wyn staggered back, staring at her hand in horror. Her fingers twisted in all directions, as long and thin as broom bristles. She tried to straighten one with trembling fingers, but it snapped with a dry crack.

"No!" Wyn cried. She tried to raise the hairbrush, but her brittle fingers could not grip the smooth wood. It spun out of her grasp, blonde hairs streaming in a long arc, and hit the floor with a sharp crack. Pieces scattered in all directions. Wyn fell to her

THE THIEF'S TALE

knees and tried to gather the fragments together, but her fingers would not work.

She crawled to the side of the bed and tried to rise to her feet, but she could not find her balance.

"Mum!" she called desperately.

Ratter laughed. "Too late."

Wyn woke as she wrenched herself upright in her cot, her hand reaching for her mother's. She gasped for breath, groaned, and curled miserably under her blankets, eyes aching as she fought against tears, an unstoppable flood of terror and loss and the heartbreaking joy of hearing her mother's voice.

As her ragged breathing slowly calmed, she peered blearily at the small slivers of daylight that speared through the cracks in the curtain and winced as pain seared across her forehead and ignited a brutal, pounding inferno behind her eyes.

But she had little time to suffer in peace. Footsteps stomped toward the thin curtain that covered the entrance to her cell.

"Get your boney arse out of bed." Mellon's voice was an unforgiving grind of nails on slate.

"Shhh," Wyn begged.

"None of that, luv, we've business to attend, and I've bought Jenny's entire cart-full today so the stove's nice and warm."

"Please fuck off," Wyn groaned. She buried her head in her pillow and tried to die as quickly as possible.

"I thought you might be a bit peaked, so I've done you a tea." Mellon held a steaming cup near the cot so that its warm scent wafted enticingly across Wyn's nose. "Put an extra lump in, and all."

"There's sugar?" Wyn mumbled.

"There is."

"Two?"

"Promises were made."

Wyn pushed herself slowly upright and swung her feet to the floor. Her head pounded miserably, and she groaned and pressed her face into her hands.

"What time…?"

"We're a lazy acolyte from morning bells."

"Just kill me," Wyn begged. She pried open one eye and squinted at Mellon. He had taken the small stool Wyn kept for reaching high things as a seat, but had managed to somehow recline regally on it, his back against the wall, his cup of tea held delicately to his pursed lips as he savored a long swallow. Coarse black bristles covered his ruddy cheeks and neck in a wiry pelt that was just on the scraggly side of the unshaven-beard divide, and Wyn's face itched just to look at it. His hair was just as shaggy and unkempt, although his hairline was beginning to lose the battle to remain on his head and had retreated almost half-way across his dome, leaving only a few wispy rearguards. He offered the second cup of tea to her again.

Wyn pushed her hair out of her face and accepted the chipped mug from Mellon. The tea was, as promised, sickeningly sweet and scalding hot, and she sipped greedily.

"Maker, that's good," she sighed. She slumped against the wall at her back and gazed blearily at Mellon. "Last night I dreamed..." she began, then suddenly realized what she was about to say and quickly changed her mind. "I mean, I had a stupid dream that you said we were going to work for Quinn."

"I know, lass, I don't want to work for him, either," Mellon said gravely. He blew softly on his tea and took another slurp. "But there's no good alternative. Tell me I'm wrong." Mellon held up a finger to forestall her response. "And don't bother with 'say no' because you should know better than most that making him angry will just bring a world of pain down on us. We do our job, we keep him happy, we live to do more jobs for better folks, right?"

"You don't know him, not like I do," Wyn insisted.

"True, but you're not the same wee girl, neither. You've got Fergus and me as well as Des, and we're the Tallywags, fresh from pilfering the Silver Keep."

"It won't matter," Wyn predicted sullenly. *It won't. The only sane thing to do is hide and hope Quinn gets what he deserves before he finds you, although Maker knows when that will be...*

"Well, aren't you the font of optimism this morning." Mellon sighed and rose from the stool amidst loud popping from his knees. "Come on, our new employer will be here soon."

THE THIEF'S TALE

"You mean his dog." Wyn downed another mouthful and sighed in bliss as the fiery heat blazed down her throat.

"That's right, but dog or master, you, as the brightest star in our firmament, must be present to impress them with our absolute dedication to their miserable job."

Wyn glared at Mellon over the lip of her cup. "Fine," she forced between her clenched teeth, and she raised a leg and pointed her toes at Mellon. "But only because you brought me tea."

"Every day, luv," Mellon reassured her. "Why are you sticking your foot in my face?"

"Boots," Wyn informed him. "The brightest star in our firmament requires her boots. I think they're under the bed."

"She requires a wash," Mellon disagreed. "You smell like a brewery. A homeless brewery." He strolled to the cell's entrance and paused. "You might find yourself a smile underneath that stench, you scrub hard enough."

"You might find yourself wearing the rest of this tea if you don't go away," Wyn promised.

Mellon eyed her archly for a moment, then strode from the room. "Get washed!" echoed back to her from the hallway, once he was safely away.

## CHAPTER FOUR

# The Honorable Nell Spicer

"There she is." Ratter sucked on his gold tooth and leaned against the freshly scrubbed brick façade of the building behind him.

Wyn peered across the busy street. A thick-set woman with iron-grey hair and skin the color of oatmeal had stepped into the sheltered portico of the Penny Angel. The woman grimaced at the low clouds and the few swirling flakes of snow that dared to approach her as she was joined by two tall men in matching long, black coats, and one short squidge of a man in a garish robe, none of whom she acknowledged.

The woman walked briskly across the street between two passing carriages, preceded by one of the tall men and followed by the other, the short man hurrying at her side. She wore a long dress with a thick, sculptured jacket and flourished a walking cane with a steel tip and an ivory handle. As she swept past, her cane tapping purposefully on the cobbles, Wyn spotted a thin gold chain that nestled around her neck, a wide ring with gemstones that sparkled on her gloved finger, and a brooch in the shape of a golden leaf that fastened her coat.

"The Honorable Nell Spicer," Ratter mused. "And friends, of course. Spends most of her day at the Angel or the Commerce Exchange. Mostly selling. She has several ships of her own, and she represents dozens of the smaller merchants."

Wyn watched Spicer stride away as the crowd parted for her entourage. "Who are her friends?"

"The tall lads used to be soldiers." Ratter sniffed, unconcerned. He adjusted his coat on his lean shoulders, and Wyn saw the hard shapes of leather and steel beneath, and a long, thin blade at his waist. "They're part of her household. Sleep in the house, and all. Always around, everywhere she goes."

"Splendid," Mellon snorted. "And the rather smug gentleman in the interesting robe?"

"He's an adept, name of Quany."

"She has an adept working for her?" Mellon asked, horrified.

"Them lads aren't your worry," Ratter scoffed. "I'll show you."

Madam Spicer's home would have qualified as a palace in any other city in Albyn. It sprawled alongside a vast park in the center of Morningside, a massive edifice with three wings of rooms and behind it, a cluster of stables, servant's quarters, and a carriage house surrounding a cobbled yard. The mansion itself was built from wide, carefully fitted blocks of stone faced with shining white marble cut so smoothly that it looked like pond ice. Tall, arched windows lorded over the front of the house, and a sweeping crescent of driveway passed under a soaring portico supported by a half-dozen pillars encrusted with carved leaves.

The peaked roof was capped with thick slate tiles and crowned with gargoyles, while two dozen chimneys lined the back, all belching long streamers of white smoke into the chill air.

"Her key is in there." Ratter pointed at the hulking mass of the mansion across the broad avenue.

"Well, that narrows it down," Mellon complained. "Which one was hers, again?"

THE THIEF'S TALE

"The sun."

"And the other key is the moon?"

"Don't worry about that one, yet." Ratter nodded at the mansion. "Go in while she's at the Exchange, you'll never see her or her goons."

Wyn shoved her frozen hands under her arms, stifled a sour burp, and glared at the mass of shiny marble gazing haughtily over the park. Her head was proper pounding, now, and the pain was starting to make her queasy. She needed someplace dark and flat, not bright and freezing.

She was not worried about the high wall that surrounded the mansion and its sculpted gardens, but she was not pleased about the pair of City Watch patrolmen who seemed to be permanently stationed outside the main gates.

"What about those two?" Wyn asked.

"Didn't think you'd be fussed at a couple of blackberries," Ratter said mockingly.

"I'm not fussed, but they're worth mentioning." *You prat,* Wyn added silently.

"Well then, she pays our local constabulary to keep a special eye on her gates. There, mentioned," Ratter sneered. "You happy, now?"

Wyn inhaled, a flurry of barbed retorts quivering on her tongue. But her ire was smothered by a choking swirl of fear when she met Ratter's narrowed gaze, and her lips stayed shut. He nodded knowingly at her, and her humiliation was complete.

"Spicer keeps her key safe and snug in a vault in her study," Ratter continued, apparently satisfied with Wyn's sullen submission. "Built special for her and hidden away."

"Built special?" Mellon asked. "By who?"

"Had it shipped from Criénne." Ratter's accent flopped heavily around the name. "Has some sort of new lock, can't be picked, we're told."

"Told?" Wyn asked sharply. "All this is second-hand?"

"Don't you worry about it, the information's good."

Mellon snorted. "I'm certain you won't mind if we do our own look-around."

THE THIEF'S TALE

"Knock yourself out," Ratter said magnanimously. "You still only got two weeks."

The Scrivener's loft featured a long, central room which boasted an iron stove, a dented iron pot hung near the stove on a hook, a table that Wyn reckoned was likely a relic of some age before the invention of carpentry, and a circle of battered chairs carefully selected for their absolute, perfect comfort for each of the Tallywags' posteriors.

Three grimy windows let in light from the front of the building and gave access to the steeply pitched roof. The back of the loft featured a narrow passageway with a single, tiny window at the end, overlooking the wainwright's yard.

On the one side were two smaller rooms, one with an old copper tub perched on clawed feet, the other with a heavy door, reinforced with steel locks and hinges and brick walls.

On the other side was a single, narrow room divided into four alcoves. Curtains hung over the entrances to the alcoves, creating small cells that contained a cot and just enough room to turn around in. Wyn's was alone on the back wall, as far from Mellon's snores as she could get.

The table in the main room was covered in a bizarre panorama of cutlery, twine, several chipped mugs, an old loaf of bread with its crust carved away in places, one of Desmond's shoes, and the pot that usually hung above the stove.

Fergus placed two blackberries on the edge of the mess. "These forks are the gates, right?" He frowned. "That's about it, then. Good enough to start with."

"Right, so what do we know about Madam Spicer?" Mellon asked.

"Her guards know their business," Fergus said quietly. "They followed her all day, always close at hand. Not much chance of overpowering those two without a ruckus." He shifted his leather vest slightly, and the heavy, steel rings clustered on his fingers gleamed dully as he widened the ties of his loose shirt. Wyn caught a glimpse of blue flames tattooed across the pale skin of his chest through the gap, the edge of a great swirl of fire spewed forth by a dragon that she knew curled over his ribs and across his back.

"Spicer's not supposed to know she's been robbed, so it's not like we can go around bonking her guards on the head, right?" Wyn asked.

Fergus shrugged. "If you end up wanting them out, it will be difficult."

"And they sleep in the mansion like Ratter claimed?" Mellon pointed at the loaf of bread.

"They went in with her."

Desmond set a small piece of carved wood beside the loaf. It looked remarkably like Nell Spicer, down to her stern visage, captured in the wood with a few gentle strokes of his tiny knife. He picked up a second chunk of wood and began to whittle it into shape, as well.

"I like her little frowny face," Wyn told him, her nose almost touching the miniature merchant on the table as she peered at it.

"Thanks," Desmond grinned. His thick, copper-colored hair stuck up in unconcerned waves that made Wyn's fingers want to dive in and ruffle madly. Desmond had apparently also given up shaving that week, along with Mellon, but his results were far less dramatic. There was a faint shine of ginger bristles on his cheeks and the length of his strong, straight jawline, but only when the lantern light fell on his fair skin at just the right angle. "I'll do those two guards next, shall I?"

"If you like. Might want to do the City Watch next, though, as I'm likely going to eat them, soon."

"Right you are," Desmond agreed.

"We'll need a damn interesting story to convince her to bring her key out of the house," Mellon mused to himself as he watched Desmond's guards take shape. "And if she does bring it out, we'll have to deal with those two. No, I don't like it... how about a bit of simple burglary, instead?"

"It's a bitch of a nut to crack," Wyn snorted.

"Those nasty spikes on the wall got your tummy in a twist?"

THE THIEF'S TALE

"Climbing over the wall is dead easy, and there's a hundred windows to choose from, even though the shutters are latched and locked—"

"Says the lass who broke into Ruric's Tower."

"Like I said, those are the easy parts. But we need to find out where Nellie's study is and get a peek at this unpickable vault while we're in there. I wouldn't mind knowing what I'm up against, and Maker only knows how she has it guarded. She has a bloody adept working for her, so there could be Devices all over the place, just waiting to kill me in all sorts of amazing ways. Give us a month to case it proper, maybe find someone on the inside to twist, give us access or find out who made the vault, and I'll bring you Madam Spicer's knickers with no one the wiser. Last I checked, we don't have a month."

"We don't need her knickers, we need her key. Without her knowing it's gone, mind you. Any ideas how we pull that off, assuming we figure out how to get in her study and open the unbreakable vault?"

"What if we don't steal it?" Desmond asked.

"I think you might be missing the point of all this," Mellon replied with exaggerated patience.

"I mean it. What if we don't steal it, but we do, at the same time."

"Did you slip on the ice and hit your head?"

"No. But we would still need to get into the vault."

"So that we can *not* steal the key?"

"Yeah."

"Fair enough." Mellon frowned at the table. "We'll get some help watching the place, find out as much about the comings and goings of the Spicer household as we can. Then, with any luck, we can figure out a way to get inside that place for a little look-around."

"Right, so, here he come, up the street, clop, clop, clop, past them gates, then up the lane, clop, clop, clop…" Old Padraig droned past the stub of gnawed pipe that stuck from the stained whiskers sprouting around his withered mouth. Wyn surreptitiously held her fingers under her nose to block the sour smell of the old man's breath as she watched the creaking progress of the wagon along the narrow lane that bordered Spicer's mansion. A second gate into the compound accessed the lane, this one wider and simpler than the soaring shafts of iron that barred the main drive. It was fashioned of iron-bound wood and swung into the yard behind the mansion to allow tradesmen and deliveries through the walls without disturbing the majestic gaze of the sweeping windows across the front of the house.

The driver of the wagon reined in his donkey at the gate, leaned out, and yanked on a small brass bell mounted on the wall.

"Clang, clang, clang," Old Padraig muttered. "Then this bastard come out…"

A moment later, a man in a black coat strode across the yard and peered through a slot window at the driver.

Wyn and Old Padraig were too distant to hear what was said, but the conversation was no mystery.

"Please may I get about my job?" Old Padraig whined. "Not until you lick my arse, I reckon." He spat a load of brown phlegm into the pristine snow under the shrubbery that concealed them from the mansion. "Then he open the gate, squeak, squeak, squeak, and in they go."

Wyn sighed. "He talks to everyone who comes?"

"No one goes in without his say-so, and he gives 'em all the fucking nuts, whether or no they're meant to be there."

"Lovely." Wyn turned away from the old man, pretending to muse on deep thoughts as she attempted to escape his breath.

Skinny Padraig gave her a bright smile, showing off his silver tooth. "Hello, Wyn."

"Hello, Skinny." Wyn frowned at the lad. He had already greeted her twice since she had joined him and Old in the park across the avenue from the mansion, but Skinny Padraig was always a bit on the odd side. He was not much older than she was, or perhaps a bit younger, difficult to know, given the fact that neither knew their real age, give or take a year. Or two. Skinny still had a boy's face, no trace of a beard save for a smudge on his lip

THE THIEF'S TALE

when the light caught it just so, and a boy's lanky awkwardness.
Still, he smelled better than his grandfather, and had attempted to
wipe his face clean, and press his mop of red hair into some
semblance of order under his knit cap.

"Hello," Skinny repeated.

"I see you, Skinny," Wyn laughed. "What?"

Skinny grinned wider and glanced at his feet. "Oh... sorry.
I've been watching the servants, is all."

"Good..." Wyn coaxed the lad.

"They all live in the mansion, in those buildings 'round the
back," Skinny told his boots. "They come and go for errands and
shopping, and such. Cooks off to the market. I made a list."
Skinny's hand dove into his worn coat and returned with a scrap
of folded parchment covered in charcoal scribbles.

"You can write?" Wyn asked. "Skinny! When did you learn to
do that?" Wyn accepted the parchment and squinted at the
blurred lines, trying to make sense of the scrawls and smears.

"I've been practicing," Skinny replied, and he dared to glance
up to meet her eyes for a moment. "Da says I need to write to get
better jobs."

"That's a fact, and no mistake," Wyn replied absently. The list
did make sense, in a way. A jumbled accounting of poorly
described people going to hideously abbreviated places. "Do the
servants use the back gate, too?"

"All of them, coming and going. They have to ring the bell,
too."

"Any chance of talking with them?"

"Oh, yeah, Red talked to a few." Wyn knew Red Padraig
would be the one to approach the servants. He had a quick smile
and an endless supply of words, enough to befuddle even the
most cautious of listeners, and Wyn avoided him fanatically,
ashamed of the mumbling incoherence she spouted whenever he
was around. She was not certain why he was singled out to be
named Red, since all Padraigs had red hair. All except Old, who
had no hair aside from his matted beard. *And Grey, of course.*

"He sold a little charm to a lass who works in the kitchen,"
Skinny continued, "but most are just getting things for the
mansion, not for themselves."

THE THIEF'S TALE

Wyn sighed in exasperation. "Well, we've no time for sweet-talking, in any case, not even for your brother."

"Red said he'd have a go if you'd like." Skinny scuffed a pinecone into a deeper patch of snow. "Has one picked out and all."

"Yap, yap, yap," added Old, helpfully. "Boy can talk a mule into moving."

"Tell him to leave off, for now," Wyn decided. *Not much chance we can twist someone proper in a couple of days. We'd likely just tip them that someone's sniffing around.* "That's it?"

"One last thing." Skinny grinned at the pinecone. "One time some thin old fellow come out, dressed like a proper gentleman with a black coat. He went to Donnager's."

"What's Donnager's?"

"You don't know Donnager's, Wyn?" Skinny glanced at her face for a moment, he was so shocked.

"No, Skinny, what's Donnager's?"

"Sorry, I thought you knew." He stared at her boots.

"The lass don't know, Skinny," Old muttered.

"What is it?" Wyn grinned. "Something horribly embarrassing?" Images of catching a pompous old fart doing something they could blackmail him with danced in her mind. *Gambling in one of the pits, maybe, or a mistress in a little cottage, or bribing some high-muckity, we might could do a quick twist with one of those...*

"No, nothing like that," Skinny shattered her daydream. "It's that place where they train all them servants to hire out to the nobs."

"Oh," Wyn said, disappointed. "Who cares about that?"

"I guess no one," Skinny mumbled, his smile wiped away. "I just thought, since the old gentleman was needing a bunch of servants for a party, two nights from now, it might be interesting, is all..."

THE THIEF'S TALE

"Skinny's right." Mellon frowned, puzzled at such a turn of events. "They're all aflutter about it at the Penny Angel. Quite the gala ball, it seems."

"I'm glad we finally got something from that place," Wyn groused. "It doesn't half cost us a fortune."

"I'm wounded," Mellon declared. "How many jobs have I found us simply by sitting in the Angel and listening to the other members?"

"Loads," Wyn admitted grudgingly.

"Exactly. Worth every penny. The marvelous wine and tea do not figure."

"A big party might be our chance, right?" Wyn beamed, suddenly cheerful again as she imagined the sea of jewelry draped around high-muckity necks and wrists such a gathering would produce. "Lots of fuss and bother, strange faces coming and going."

"Might be," Mellon agreed.

"What's the play, then?"

"Pondering this Donnager's angle. Might be something there. Spicer's servants think we're part of the Donnager's bunch, Donnager servants think we're part of Spicer's bunch. Not certain how to work it, though. But, however we play it, we know that Nellie will be busy and her mansion full of party guests and strange faces, so it sounds like the main chance, that's certain. So, Desmond, Wyn, prepare yourselves for a ball."

"Oh, no, no, no," Wyn stated firmly, crossing her arms and shaking her head for emphasis. "I'm not wearing a dress."

Mellon winked. "Let's hope it doesn't come to that, but dress or no dress, I'm certain we will need you in that house."

"You think there might be a lock or two involved in this caper?"

"There's a chance." Mellon grinned wickedly. "Might be nice to have a look inside before the party, hey?"

"Sounds like wisdom, that does. You finally get an idea on how to do that?"

"I did." Mellon shifted slightly, and his entire aspect changed. His voice lost its usual rasp and became unhurried and resonant, as if it would never occur to him that his audience did not hang

THE THIEF'S TALE

enraptured on his every utterance. Confidence became conviction, cool and aloof. "But a slight change in attire is required," he intoned. "Something drab and innocent, with perhaps a touch less ragamuffin. So, if you would kindly pillage the Wardrobe for something appropriate, my dear, as opposed to your typical slops, I am certain it would be appreciated."

"A sweet little mouse, is it? I think the Wardrobe can handle that," Wyn agreed. The secured and reinforced room next to the bath held far more treasure than merely their pooled coin. Various pieces of clothing and accoutrements they had collected for jobs over the years filled most of the room, ranging from a beggar's filthy shawl to a proper cloak and badge from the City Watch. "But, what's the plan for getting into Spicer's?"

"How do you fancy some flowers, my lady?" Mellon asked grandly.

"Flowers?"

"Flowers, it says," Mellon said firmly. "Twenty vases, assorted, twenty hanging, purple, and twenty table bouquets, also purple." Mellon turned the crisp piece of parchment to face the gate's slot window, then indicated the two wagons overflowing with blooms and Padraigs that crowded the lane behind him. "Flowers, it is."

Dark eyebrows frowned at him through the slot. "It might say golden crowns, but you are not on the list."

"Your list is bloody wrong," Mellon countered.

"Says you."

Mellon shook his head sadly. "It's your funeral, then. You think Master Parker will be pleased to pay for a bunch of flowers he never gets to see?"

"Parker?" The eyebrows lowered even further.

"That's right," Mellon sighed. It had taken little effort to discover the name of the old gentleman who had visited Donnager's, and only slightly more to find out that Master Parker

THE THIEF'S TALE

was the steward of Madam Spicer's household. "Listen, friend, these here flowers are cut, do you see?"

"Cut?"

"That's right. As in, they're dead a couple of days from now, no matter whether they are filling a grand mansion with beauty or sitting in a wagon. That means they're paid for, one way or another. And I reckon I know who's paying for them if they're left in these wagons, and it ain't Master Parker, and it sure ain't me, not with a bill of purchase, if you see what I mean."

"Let me see that parchment," Eyebrows grumbled. Mellon patiently held it in front of the slot, Master Parker's scrawled signature and the seal of the Spicer household prominent at the bottom of the bill, thanks to Desmond and a bit of quick work at Donnager's that morning.

Eyebrows tried one last stab at resistance. "Master Parker's not here right now."

Mellon shrugged. "Well, the flowers he ordered are." Wyn already knew that Parker was not present. Nor was Madame Spicer. They had waited patiently until Spicer's carriage had departed for the Exchange and Parker had left the mansion before trundling their wagons up the lane.

"Very well," Eyebrows sighed, and the gates rumbled open on their iron wheels. Mellon waved the wagons into the yard, where they stood patiently while one of the blackberries inspected them, and the Padraigs, for anything amiss. Wyn squeaked and shied away from his touch when it was her turn, and she received an apologetic smile in return.

"Sorry, lass," the blackberry said. "It's nothing personal, now."

"Sorry," Wyn apologized nervously. She made sure to flinch again when his hands reached her waist, and she glanced away from him in embarrassment when he finished.

"There, all done," he told her kindly, and she bit her lip and nodded as she stepped back in line.

"Why'd you make such a fuss?" Skinny whispered.

"Because, you ninny, that's what a wee innocent lass would do. Only a proper criminal would stand there as if being groped by a blackberry was nothing new."

THE THIEF'S TALE

"Oh." Skinny sighed. "That makes sense, that does."

" 'Course it does," Wyn snorted. "Everyone thinks girls are bloody useless, and it's not likely they'll let us forget that. We can't act like a bunch of hard lads showing their stones to each other. Not unless we fancy a busted lip." Wyn probed her lips with the tip of her tongue, instinctively searching for the tender swelling that had once seemed an unavoidable part of daily life. She grimaced and forced her tongue to stop.

"Bloody does," Skinny muttered as he glanced sideways at his cousin, a tall young woman with a shock of flaming red curls who was currently busy glaring at the blackberry.

"Well, we can't all be Bloody," Wyn muttered.

Once the blackberry had finished his inspection, the Padraigs swarmed over the wagons, hoisted armfuls of flowers, and paraded into the mansion through the kitchen entrance in a brightly colored mob following Eyebrows as he raced to stay ahead of the flood he had unleashed.

Bloody Padraig handed Wyn a tall vase stuffed with slender green shoots and a burst of yellow, red, and purple flowers. She clutched it carefully to her chest, the fronds tickling her nose, and hurried through the door after Eyebrows. He led them through a cloakroom, filled with simple, warm clothes that made Wyn's fingers tingle with the need to rifle through their pockets, and into the servant's wing, where a dignified woman with hair the color of storm clouds and a long, thin face confronted them.

"What on earth do we have, here?" she asked, more puzzled than angry.

"Master Parker ordered some more flowers, Mistress Callaghan," the gatekeeper grumbled.

"Did he? At least he remembered the colors, this time. Very well, you lot, follow me." She swept down the hall, dragging Wyn and the Padraigs in her wake, and up a narrow staircase to the palatial expanse of the mansion's main floor.

They were guided along wide passageways to a vast entrance hall with a circular gallery promenading around its second floor. In the center of the chamber, a wide staircase swept in two graceful arcs around a magnificent chandelier to join the balcony. Brilliant red carpets lined the stairs, the pillars were shining white stone,

THE THIEF'S TALE

and the railings burnished wood. Massive paintings, on a scale to match the room, gazed from the walls, and stern marble faces sat on pedestals around the balcony.

On the ground floor, a bank of doors led to a ballroom that was even larger than the entrance hall. Quiet commotion filled both rooms as servants hurried to prepare them for the upcoming ball.

"Now then," Mistress Callaghan said sternly. "We will have the bouquets on the tables in the ballroom, the hanging arrangements along the garden windows, I think. The vases we will have on the stairs, and along the hallways, if you please."

The Padraigs bustled to obey, a blaze of color and noise amongst the somber workings of the household. Wyn hesitated until the stern woman strode after them, finger raised, then hurried toward the servant's stairs, her vase wrapped securely in her arms.

The door to the stairs opened just as Wyn reached for the latch, and she snatched her hand back as a tall young man in rigid black jacket and trousers stopped just short of barreling into her.

"Careful, Flowers," he said with a grin.

"I'm so sorry, m'lord," Wyn replied quickly. His smile widened and he stood straighter, his confidence stroked. She widened her eyes and gasped breathlessly. "I didn't mean to be in the way."

"I think I shall survive," he declared magnanimously.

"I'm…" She hesitated and lowered her gaze. "I'm a bit lost…"

"I am certain it must be confusing, being in such a big house," he prattled. "Where are you meant to be?"

*Poncy git.* Wyn carefully bit her tongue until the urge to deflate the pompous twit had safely passed. She shifted the vase to her hip, stroked her hair behind her ear so that he could see her wide eyes, shining with gratitude, and gave him her brightest, most grovelly smile. "Oh, thank you, m'lord," she gushed. "Mistress Callaghan said take these flowers to the study, but I didn't dare ask her where…"

"The study?" He laughed, and he swept out his hand to give her passage to the stairs. "You are lost. Up one more floor, at the top of the main stairs. Next time, just ask. Callaghan won't mind questions, but she hates a poorly done job."

"I shall," she assured him gratefully, and hurried past him and up the stairs before he could think to ask any awkward questions.

The second-floor hall was empty when she peeked carefully through the doorway, and she quickly positioned her vase on a thin side table. Wyn was not going to count on the next servant she encountered being as gullible as the idiot who had given her directions, and the first person to question why a flower girl was searching for Madame Spicer's study would mean the end of Wyn's exploration. *Might become a bit interesting,* she decided. Far better to leave the rustling, awkward vase somewhere safe.

Wyn crept toward the wide opening at the end of the hallway. A sudden burst of conversation behind her sent her scurrying into the nearest doorway, pressing into its deep frame as two pairs of footsteps hurried to the servant's stairs with a rustle of starched cloth. She tilted her head cautiously forward when she heard the door click shut, grinned to herself, and continued to the study.

A pair of grand pillars framed the end of the hallway as it entered the sweeping balcony around the entrance hall. Wyn slipped into the shadow of the one against the outer wall and peered through the intricate filigree that adorned its base.

The landing ahead of her was a magnificent panorama of arched ceiling and stately columns almost ten strides across, open to the majestic rotunda of the entrance hall and bathed in light from the elegant chandelier hanging in the center of the circle. By craning her neck and peering around the pillar, Wyn could see two wide doors that lorded over the summit of the main stairs, emblazoned with the same golden leaf she had seen holding Nell Spicer's jacket together.

*Study,* Wyn thought smugly, but as she rose to step onto the landing, she froze. Two figures were ascending the last half-dozen steps of the main stairs, their heads clearly visible. Mistress Callaghan and a tall man in a spotless black coat which could not conceal the thick shapes of muscular arms and shoulders, barely contained by the fine tailoring, nor the barrel chest that strained the silver buttons on his silk vest.

THE THIEF'S TALE

He was clean-shaven, although it did him no favors. A twisted scar that ran to the corner of his mouth notched his chin, and his thick, muscular neck seemed ready to engulf his tiny, bald head.

Wyn sank onto her fingers and toes and pressed into the minute nook between the pillar and the wall. *One of Spicer's shadows… why isn't he with Nellie?* she wondered.

Callaghan and Pinhead reached the landing and stood in the center, staring into the entrance hall rotunda.

"No one is to be allowed up the stairs," Callaghan instructed her companion. "Stop them when they reach the top, so that you may use some discretion."

Wyn eased forward to get a better look. Pinhead's broad back was firmly turned toward her, but Callaghan had twisted slightly to speak to him, and her sharp profile was clear. A slight turn of her head and Wyn would be in full view.

"Two of the footmen will greet the guests at the door," Callaghan continued. She shifted to point into the rotunda. "And there will be additional footmen stationed at the base of the stairs…"

Wyn crept from concealment the instant the stern woman looked away. She stayed pressed against the inner wall, as far from the pair on the landing as she could get, and her gaze flickered between them and the wide doors ahead of her.

"… Master Parker has arranged for additional guards at the gates, but you and…"

Wyn's fingers brushed against the ornate frame of the doors, and her gaze traced the curls and twists of golden leaves and acorns across the dark, burnished wood to where a pair of gleaming, polished doorknobs beckoned to her.

"…evening bells, but many of the guests…"

Wyn slipped her fingers delicately around one of the doorknobs and gently twisted. The knob jerked slightly in her hand, and the door vibrated for the space of a single heartbeat. She heard a faint, muffled clunk.

Then, to her horror, the door pulled against her hand, dragging itself open.

THE THIEF'S TALE

*No, no, no!* she begged, but when she strained to stop the door, it simply yanked her into the room with it. She released her grip and whirled, ready to flee, but Callaghan continued her endless, boring instructions without pause, and Wyn felt a grin begin to creep across her lips as she realized that the door had made so little sound that Pinhead and Callaghan could never hear it above the racket being made by the Padraigs in the entry hall.

*All right... get it closed before they notice!* The doors had come to a gentle stop almost flush with the wall, revealing a wide room filled with brooding shadows, but Wyn had no time to take in the view. She hurried to one door and tugged the knob, but the door was as immovable as if it were hooked to the wall behind it.

*Maker's breath... what's wrong with a simple bloody door?* she snarled. She tugged uselessly, then twisted the knob. Immediately, the doors began to close, sweeping majestically across the thick carpet. Wyn stepped behind the door without thinking and glared at Callaghan and Pinhead, willing them to remain focused on the rotunda, until the doors closed with a soft thud.

Then she turned and properly examined her surroundings.

Spicer's study was imposing in a grand, austere manner. Heavy drapes blanketed the far wall. A massive desk dominated the back of the room, its deep mahogany surface shining in the thin light that managed to squeeze past the drapes. Colossal paintings in drab hues loomed on the walls.

Wyn walked slowly to the center of the room and stopped, her fists on her hips. *All right, then, Nellie, where's your special little vault?*

There were few hiding places in the sparse room, and Wyn found the small latch that allowed one of the wooden wall panels to swing open almost immediately. Behind it was a steel door, as wide as it was high, with a single handle and keyhole.

Wyn delicately stroked the keyhole with her fingertip, her faint eyebrows furrowed. *What's your secret?* she asked the lock. *Why are you unpickable?* The door's metal looked to be of good quality, but it did not live up to Wyn's expectations of what an exotic, thief-proof vault should look like. *If I had my tools, I could have a quick peek...*

THE THIEF'S TALE

She paused, her head tilted to the side. The drone of conversation outside the door had stopped, and Wyn had time to hope that Callaghan was finally ready to leave before she heard another voice call out, its commanding tone apparent despite the words being indistinct, and Wyn belatedly realized what Pinhead's presence in the mansion must mean.

*Nellie's come back...*

Wyn pressed the panel back into place and glanced quickly around the study, but there was nowhere to hide besides standing foolishly behind the drapes... *the windows!* She dashed across the thick carpet, straining over the throb of her heart for the sound of the doorknob turning, and yanked one of the drapes aside. Behind it was a tall window, dozens of panes of glass set in an iron frame, and a vista of the mansion's gardens stretching between the two long wings of the building.

Her hand had released the window's latch before she noticed the small mob of gardeners stringing lanterns across the courtyard directly beneath the study, and she quickly crouched, just peeking over the sill. There were far too many to count on all of them turning their backs to the mansion at once, and— *Maker's breath, they're all looking at me!* Freezing ice prickled up her spine, and her fingers and toes suddenly trembled with the need to flee before she realized the gardeners were concerned with their lanterns, and she had not been discovered. But unless they finished that instant...

A soft click sounded from the door.

Wyn twisted away from the window and launched herself toward the doors. She saw the crack of light down their center as they began to swing and swerved to the side, her slim legs a blur as she sprinted across the thick carpet. She skidded to a stop against the wall, crouched, poised on fingers and toes, and stifled her breathing.

The door eased into place against her shoulder, tapping it gently as it came to rest.

"It looks as if a First Day festival vomited over the entrance hall," Spicer declared as she strode into the study. Wyn caught a glimpse of her sweeping dress and a flash of her ivory-handled cane as she passed the small gap at the door's hinge. Callaghan

THE THIEF'S TALE

followed her, then a mountainous shape blocked the crack for a moment as Pinhead passed.

"Yes, ma'am," Callaghan agreed. "I will have the flowers removed, at once."

"Not all of them," Spicer decided. "Perhaps enough that they will no longer outnumber the guests."

"Yes, ma'am."

"Now then," Spicer's voice rose as she turned to the doorway. "Master Calixte, will you have enough time to prepare?"

Another figure stepped into the study, and Wyn peered through the crack as he passed, her eyes wide.

The man was of a height with Spicer's hulking guard, elegant in dark robes that hung in gleaming layers from his broad shoulders. His ink-black hair was cut close to the dark bronze skin of his scalp, but he boasted a thick wedge of a beard that was as grey as ash. His gaze swept over the study doors from beneath a forest of shaggy, black eyebrows, his brow creased, and Wyn shrank away.

"An amusing contraption," Calixte announced, his thin lips curled in disdain. His voice was deep and sonorous, well-suited to a temple or lord's hall, and rich with the resonant elegance of the south.

"The doors? Yes, I find them very convenient," Spicer said offhandedly, but Wyn could hear pride shining from every syllable. "It took rather a long time to get them just right, but I think it was worth the wait, don't you?"

"No, Madame. I am amused to see a Device mimicked with ropes and pulleys," Calixte scoffed. "That is all."

"I see," Spicer said coldly. "Then perhaps we should discuss the Device you have brought to me, since we are speaking of waiting."

"The Device will be installed before morning, but I doubt your man will master its Word in time," Calixte informed Spicer.

Wyn caught a glimpse of the merchant's hired adept trailing into the room behind the tall man, his pinched smile fixed painfully amongst the wrinkles of his cheeks, his tiny eyes narrowed to slits as he glared at Calixte's back.

THE THIEF'S TALE

"If you had delivered the Device on time, Calixte," Quany fussed, "that wouldn't be—"

"*Master* Calixte," the tall man intoned. "In fact, no amount of time may be sufficient."

The adept's smile became more rigid as the small bump of his chin rose even higher, but he remained silent.

"What do you suggest, Master Calixte?" Spicer asked. "I paid your Guild a fortune for that Device, but it does me no good sitting in a crate in my entrance hall."

"I will prepare the Device, as we agreed, and tomorrow night I will empower it for you, so that your guests may enjoy our work. After that, it will be up to your… man… to learn its Word. I make no guarantees."

"Very well," Spicer agreed quickly. "That is more than satisfactory. Please, sit while we retrieve the papers to finalize your payment."

Wyn listened to their footsteps pad across the room's carpet toward the desk. *Nellie will sit behind it, facing the doors… I have to go before she does. But… not too soon, or they'll hear.*

Pinhead's heavy footfalls were the easiest to follow, and the bodyguard moved relentlessly toward the desk. Wyn counted five steps and guessed that was half-way across the room for his long stride.

A muffled click sounded in the thick wood next to her, and the door trembled gently.

*Nooo… you must be having a laugh,* Wyn groaned as the door began to close, swinging inexorably away from her. She pressed against the door as it moved, stretching the last instants of concealment as long as possible.

*Now or never.*

Wyn eased around the end of the door, her gaze fixed on the retreating backs. Spicer was nearer her desk than Wyn had guessed, striding with a purposeful gait that whisked her across the distance. Master Calixte was much closer, having barely moved, his broad back a rigid wall that loomed over her. Wyn glanced between Spicer and the swinging door, judging which would reach their destination first. Her legs ached to hurl herself through the doors and flee as fast as possible, but she clenched

THE THIEF'S TALE

her teeth and forced herself to take cautious, quiet steps, hardly fast enough to keep ahead of the door.

*Too slow, too slow,* Wyn groaned. Spicer had reached the end of her desk, her gaze already on the high-backed chair awaiting her behind it, and Wyn was still three long steps from safety.

"What on earth are they doing?"

Wyn froze, convinced she was caught, before she realized that Spicer's attention was riveted on the gap in the drapes that Wyn had left behind.

"Lanterns, ma'am, hung above the gardens."

"Oh... that will look nice. An excellent idea, Callaghan."

Wyn slipped through the narrowing gap between the doors and felt a whoosh of air puff against her neck as they closed with a thud. A single golden hair drifted lazily against the emblazoned leaf, trapped by the almost seamless join between the doors. Wyn plucked it free and scampered to her refuge behind the pillar. She pressed her back against the wall and inhaled deeply, suddenly breathless.

"Martyr's tears..." she sighed in relief, and she let a small laugh bubble free. She blew hair out of her eyes, then took a steadying breath. There was not time to celebrate her escape from the study. The Padraigs knew to keep things slow and disorganized, but there was a limit to how long it could take to deliver the flowers without raising suspicion.

A quick glance over the balcony rail into the entrance hall convinced Wyn not to go that way. There was no sign of the Padraigs. Instead, a stack of wooden boxes bound in silver filled the center of the rotunda, their polished surfaces glowing with reflected light. Standing on either side were two soldiers, both as tall as Master Calixte, dressed in flowing crimson robes and breastplates of ornate metal. They each carried a spear with a broad, curved blade mounted on the tip, and their dark eyes glared suspiciously at every person who entered the hall.

Wyn gawked at the soldiers for a moment, then abandoned stealth and raced down the hallway, but she skidded to a stop with her hand on the latch to the servant's stair, her gaze caught by the vase of flowers she had left on the side table. *She said to get rid of the flowers...* Wyn hesitated. *There's no time...*

THE THIEF'S TALE

She darted to the table and scooped up the vase. *Somewhere Callaghan won't see it...*

Wyn hurried across the hall and peeked around the frame of the closest door, finding a music room, complete with raised stage and rows of velvet-backed chairs. She frowned at the chamber, picturing it filled with guests from the upcoming ball, come upstairs to enjoy a concert. *Do high-muckities do that at a ball?* she wondered. *Maybe the wrinklies do? Can't chance it.*

Wyn hurried to the next door, her flowers rustling and flapping around her face. *Now then,* she decided, *this will just about do.* Wyn had found a parlor, with flower-embroidered chairs and flower-embroidered curtains and a view overlooking the gardens. She peered through the window for a moment, marking a small pond with a statue in the shape of a rearing horse, directly beneath the window, and an apple tree with one limb raised like a warning hand between the fountain and the garden wall. *Yes, perfect.*

She positioned the vase carefully against the wall next to the door then swiveled it so that the brightest flowers were visible.

Sudden voices in the hallway sent her scuttling behind a long settee. Two housemaids hurried past, stifling laughter as they conspired in whispers. Wyn gave them only a count of six before dashing to the door and darting across the hall to the stairs, her strides lengthening into a jog as she passed through the cloakroom toward the safety of the wagons.

Wyn sped into the yard and froze, the grin sliding from her face like melting snow. Between her and the now-empty wagons were a dozen guards of the City Watch, their black cloaks, black coats, and the black leather of their belts a blot against the pale cobblestones.

She stared, wondering how the blackberries could have known they were robbing the place. *We've not even done any crime, yet, not unless decorating the place with flowers counts as vandalism.*

In fact, it was the strangest arrest she had ever seen. The guards were not looking at her, nor were they glancing toward the two wagons, filled with rigid Padraigs staring at her with wide eyes. The blackberries looked... bored. One was scratching under his leather cap, two were gawking around the yard and at the

THE THIEF'S TALE

mansion house, and only a few were paying any attention to the sergeant leading the patrol.

Wyn closed her mouth, lowered her gaze, and scurried across the yard. As she passed, she could hear the sergeant's monotone drone. "Three patrols in the gardens, then, starting tonight, and a patrol at each gate. They're paying double bonus, so look alive."

"Yes, Sergeant," the group agreed, their eyes becoming sharp at the mention of coin.

Wyn hopped into the lead wagon, Jolly Padraig snapped the reins and clucked at the donkey, and the wagon lurched into movement, wobbled across the cobblestone yard, and eased into the lane. Wyn huddled against the side of the bed, clutched her knees to her chest and glared at her boots.

"Nasty turn up," Mellon grumbled as he sat heavily beside her.

"That's a fact."

"Extra guards for the party?"

"Extra guards," Wyn agreed. "Patrols in the gardens, and so forth."

"Well…" Mellon grinned and leaned against the wagon wall. "It was all a bit easy, wasn't it? Nice to have a challenge."

THE THIEF'S TALE

## CHAPTER FIVE

# Red Hair and Wide Smiles

**W**yn knelt on the slate tiles and sat on her heels, clutching her hands together as she breathed warmth into them. Wisps of breath curled between her fingers as she watched the twinkle of yellow lanterns move between the trees in Nell Spicer's garden, then disappear around the corner of the sprawling mansion.

"Right, here we go," said Bloody Padraig. She leaned onto the brick parapet with her elbows, a frown of concentration on her face as she stared across the avenue. "One, two, three…" she whispered.

Wyn listened to Bloody and blew on her fingers as she waited. The front of the grand building was illuminated with dozens of lamps so that the edifice shone startling white, as if the sun had forgotten to set on one small patch of Kuray. More lanterns lit the gates and glowed softly along the sweeping drive. The blackberries patrolling the gardens were not satisfied with that, though. They carried their own lanterns and made a show of shining them into every nook and cranny of the mansion as they passed.

Wyn pressed her fingers over the tip of her nose and wrinkled it experimentally, probing the strange numbness that was produced in the ridges of frozen skin.

A new set of lanterns flashed as they appeared from the opposite corner of the mansion, following the same path as the first patrol.

"Thirty-five," Bloody announced. She sat back, adopting the same pose as Wyn, and the two young women sat in silence for a moment, watching the lanterns twinkle.

"There's three patrols?" Wyn asked.

"Three. Sometimes someone on the roof, not regular."

"Are all the sides of the house lit up like that?"

Bloody shrugged. "Near enough."

"What do you reckon?" Wyn asked. "You've done this more than me."

"What, break into a palace?" Bloody shook her head. "That's your kind of job, ain't it? You want a wagon to go missing, I'm your girl. What do you reckon?"

"I reckon thirty-five's not a lot of time to climb up and get those shutters unlocked. Not all lit up like it's the middle of the day."

Bloody cleared her throat and spat over the edge of the roof. "Yeah, that's what I reckon, too."

"Exactly." Wyn rubbed her nose, then moved her hands to her ears, pressing them against her hair inside her hood.

"Well, then," Bloody added.

"Why do they call you Bloody?" Wyn asked impulsively, curiosity bubbling out of her mouth before she realized it was on its way from her brain.

"Why do you want to know?"

"It's a bit of a hard name, isn't it? Nice and tough and scary, and all. Was just wondering, since the rest of your family all seem to favor more, uh, well…"

"They're all a bit of a mock, ain't they."

"That's it. Not yours, though."

THE THIEF'S TALE

"Ha… it's 'Bloody' for 'Bloody-minded,' " she chuckled. "But I don't mind people thinking it's because I'm a hard bitch. Makes life a bit easier, you know?"

"I can see that." Wyn snorted her appreciation. "I wish I had a hard name. Folks don't treat me very serious."

"Don't treat you serious?" Bloody asked incredulously. "That knickers caper was serious hard, and folks know it, don't you worry. Got nothing to do with a name when you've got pedigree like you have."

"Maybe," Wyn allowed, but Bloody's words had settled into her chest like a warm, contented cat, and she smiled happily.

"Anyways, you're a joyful sort," Bloody pointed out. "So, most likely we'd have named you Happy, or some such rubbish."

"Martyr's tears!" Wyn screwed up her face and stuck out her tongue at the thought. "Shit on that."

"Right? Or, now that I think on it, Golden, since you'd have stuck out amongst us Padraigs with your hair."

"Better than Happy, I suppose."

"Forty-two," Bloody announced as the third set of lanterns appeared.

"Close enough," Wyn sighed. She stood and stretched her back. "You ready to call it a night?"

"Too right. I'm starved."

"We can go past Hairy's."

"Now there's a thought," Bloody agreed eagerly.

They scrambled down and began the long trek back to the Old City. Bloody led the way with long, purposeful strides and a glare that sent the few toffs out for an evening stroll scurrying to the opposite side of the quiet avenues.

When at last they reached the narrow, twisted streets of Littlemarket and dove into the crowded throngs that filled them, Bloody slowed her pace and replaced her scowl with a fierce smile as she traded insults with anyone who dared meet her gaze. Wyn followed happily as she enjoyed a leisurely stroll along the street, instead of her usual habit of darting from side to side with her gaze fixed on the ground and her hood pulled low.

"Now then, ladies," a voice crooned to them as they passed a rabble of drunks loitering in front of a tavern. A wiry man with a pock-marked face and a long, drooping mustache sauntered into their path, his thumbs hooked over his belt.

"Now then, girls," Bloody replied smoothly, and Wyn snorted with laughter.

"No need for that, my lovelies," he assured her. Several of his companions joined him in the street, staring unabashedly at the two young women, so close that Wyn could smell the sour stink of their breath. "If you join us for a drink, you'll not regret it." He paused to give Bloody a sly smile. "I promise you that."

"Is that what your hand told you?" Bloody asked, much to the amusement of the man's friends.

His smile disappeared. "Fuck you," he said sullenly.

"Not a chance," Bloody assured him, "even if you had a cock."

His face flushed with embarrassment as his friends hooted with laughter. He forced his smile back into place and glanced at Wyn. "Maybe your lass would like a man for a—"

Bloody stepped close to the lout, their faces no more than a hand's-breadth apart as she glared fiercely at him. There was a flash of steel in her hand, and a small knife pressed into the man's groin.

"You touch her, you even think about her, I'll geld you right here and watch you choke to death on your balls," she hissed.

"Maker... Bloody..." Wyn gasped, shocked by the cold fury in Bloody's face. The man turned pale as ice, and his friends stumbled back, suddenly deathly quiet.

"You lads leave these girls alone," a deep voice intervened from the street. A stout man with a thick, iron-shot beard glared at the confrontation, his hands on his hips, the silver buttons of his coat straining to contain his belly.

"Fuck off, Grandad," Bloody told him. "I don't need your help with these bitches."

"Bloody, let's go," Wyn urged her. Bloody glanced at her, and Wyn gave her an imploring glare. "Let's go!"

Bloody gave the man a poke with her knife, enough to make him cringe, then pushed past him, leaving Wyn to hurry after her as the old man's indignant spluttering chased them along the street.

THE THIEF'S TALE

"Bloody, Martyr's tears, slow down," Wyn pleaded, and at last the red-haired girl shortened her stride.

"Did you see his face?" Bloody asked.

"He was terrified," Wyn said accusingly.

"Good. He'll think twice before he tries that shit again," Bloody smirked. "They were lucky my brothers weren't with us."

Wyn strode after Bloody in silence, her brow furrowed. She had enjoyed the sharp mocking that Bloody had given their accoster, but Bloody's quick threat of violence had left Wyn brooding. She was used to threats and blood and bruises, as common to her day as sunrise and sunset, and had endured far worse. But she hid from that brutal savagery. She feared those who worshipped pain and inflicted suffering. How could such a person be her friend?

*Those louts needed to be put in their place, that's certain, but how is threatening to cut their bits off any different from all the bastards threatening a beating to anyone who looks at them crosswise?* Wyn was not even certain whether Bloody would have carried through with her threat or not. *She never would have stabbed him, would she?*

By the time they reached Southwick Common, Wyn had convinced herself that Bloody had simply put a scare into the lout. Wyn nicked a handful of oatcakes from Hairy Baker's as they passed his bustling shop. The tall, massively bearded baker was renowned as much for the finely ground grain he used in his cakes as he was for the flowing red beard that gave his shop its name, and Wyn chewed her share of the loot in bliss as they walked.

"I'd lay coin that he's half a clansman, what with that beard," she confided.

"He probably grinds his grain with a hammer," Bloody agreed cheerfully.

Wyn's smile suddenly froze, and she quickly wrenched her eyes forward so as not to stare. Amidst the sea of faces she had glimpsed one gaze fixed directly on her. She waited a moment and then her glance darted past Bloody and back. Wyn caught a glimpse of the man as he turned away. Hair the color of ash streaming back from a high forehead, gaunt cheeks, and a ragged grey chin beard. Then he was gone, concealed by an eddy of the crowd swirling along the street.

THE THIEF'S TALE

"There's some bastard following us," she whispered.

"You certain?"

"Yeah." Wyn peered along the street, judging side alleys and walls. "I saw him all the way back in Littlemarket, and again just now." Wyn's gaze alighted on a narrow gap between two buildings with a low wall concealed just within its shadow. "Quick... here," she hissed, and she led Bloody across the street by the arm. "We'll be over the wall before he comes around the corner."

"What?" Bloody pulled away from Wyn's hand. "No... we can wait for him back here, ask him a few questions."

"I..." Wyn glanced longingly at the inviting shadows beyond the low wall. "Are you sure?"

"There's two of us," Bloody pointed out, her gaze hard, "and I don't like bastards following me."

"What if he has a knife?"

"What if he does?" Bloody snorted contemptuously as she reached behind her back and produced a long, wickedly curved blade from beneath her cloak.

Wyn glanced frantically back and forth between the wall and the knife. *Hide!* wailed a desperate voice in her mind, but she forced herself to stand next to Bloody and face the entrance to the alleyway. *Maker... what am I doing? You're not leaving Bloody, that's what you're doing.*

Moments passed with no sound except the rush of blood in her ears and the distant cackle from the street.

"Come on, come on..." Bloody whispered. Wyn risked a glance in her direction. The red-haired girl's eyes were wide and dark as she scowled furiously, and her lips formed a fierce, bloodless line, but Wyn's gaze was drawn to the quick, panting breaths that steamed from her nose into the chill air, and the tremble in the knife's blade. *Martyr's tears... she's as scared as I am.*

But as the moments passed and no grey-haired pursuer entered the alleyway, Wyn's heart began to calm and Bloody's breath began to still, until they exchanged glances and began to laugh.

"How many knives do you have?" Wyn wondered.

Bloody frowned as she considered the question. "Five," she decided. She glanced at Wyn's empty hands. "Where's yours?"

THE THIEF'S TALE

"I don't have one, and it's a good thing, too. I'd just as likely cut my own nose off as hurt anyone."

"You're braver than I thought."

"Me? I just run and hide."

Bloody laughed, then stopped suddenly when she realized Wyn had not spoken in jest. "You have to stand up for yourself, or they'll just take advantage of you. They think you're hard, they'll treat you hard."

"I dunno, Bloody. If they never know you're there, they'll leave you alone."

"Aye, but what about when you have to speak up? There's no hiding from that forever."

"I suppose."

"Don't worry," Bloody assured her. "People are no different from those monstrous high buildings you climb without blinking. They look proper terrifying to me, and to most everyone, but you just scamper up them, don't you?"

"They're not so hard," Wyn explained. "Up close, they're all covered in little cracks and nooks you can use, you just have to know how."

"Same as folks, then."

"Except I know I can climb anything, but I know I can't fight anyone. I mean, look at me, I'm useless. They'd just snap me in half."

"Oh, I doubt that. You've got a fire in you. When the time comes, just let it out. In any case, most of the time a sharp wit is all that's needed, and you've that aplenty, I'd say."

"I guess so," Wyn mumbled, absurdly pleased, and she took the opportunity to quickly smooth her hair back into place behind her ears and re-fasten her ponytail into something less ragged.

Bloody laughed. "Trust me. Anyone who would hang from their fingertips out the window has plenty of stones. You'd not catch me doing that."

"The fewer stones, the better, when you're hanging from your fingertips," Wyn pointed out.

"The fewer stones, the better, in most everything," Bloody agreed. "That's why boys are crap."

THE THIEF'S TALE

Wyn gleefully joined Bloody's laughter, and they returned to the streets with smiles for any passerby who chanced to meet their gaze.

They reached Scrivener's far sooner than Wyn expected, and she hesitated at the door, suddenly unwilling to curtail her evening.

"Well then," Bloody said with a smile. "I'll be seeing you."

"Yeah, see you," Wyn mumbled, and then continued in a rush, "Do you want to come up?"

"Do I want to come up?" Bloody asked. Her smile widened and her teeth flashed. "I was hoping you'd say that. Are you sure?"

"Of course," Wyn replied, relieved not to have to say goodbye. *Not just when we were starting to have fun.* "If Mellon is there, we can tell him what we saw at Spicer's."

"If Mellon..." Bloody closed her eyes, shook her head, and tried to suppress a wry grin. "Of course, you didn't mean..."

"It'll be dead dull... you don't have to..."

"No, it's fine," Bloody insisted, her smile growing. "Let's go talk with Mellon."

Wyn led the way upstairs, a small frown creasing her brow. She had missed something, she knew it, but she did not dare ask the older girl what had caused her so much amusement.

The door to the loft squeaked open to reveal a dark, cold room that smelled faintly of old smoke.

"Oh, they've let the fire go out," Wyn complained. She hurried to the stove and inspected the scattered lumps of ashen coal. A few prods with an iron revealed a faint glow, and Wyn rescued it with some careful poking and some energetic puffing.

"No one's here," Wyn apologized as she brushed off her hands.

"It's so quiet," Bloody said, amazed.

"Yeah, it's a bit lonely when everyone is out."

"No, I love it," Bloody said. She gazed appreciatively at the loft, her hands on her hips, as if she surveyed a sweeping panorama. "Do you get your own room?"

"No, well, sort of. It has walls, but just a curtain for a door."

"Bliss," Bloody assured her.

THE THIEF'S TALE

"Do you not?"

"Ha! Not a chance," Bloody snorted. She wandered to the front windows, then inspected the stove and the hallway before joining Wyn beside the table, where she examined the row of tiny, carved figures. "Oh! It's Nellie! Where am I?"

"In the wagon," Wyn told her as she leaned against the table next to Bloody.

"Oh, look at my hair," Bloody murmured as she held up her miniature self for inspection.

"I'll tell Des you like it."

"Des did it, eh?" Bloody turned the figure back and forth as she peered at it. "I look a bit miffed, don't I?"

"He likes to poke fun, is all," Wyn said defensively.

"Yeah, no worries. Your lad has talent," Bloody said approvingly.

Wyn felt a warm rush of gratitude. *I wish Des could hear that, himself. Why isn't he here, the git?* She glanced at the young woman beside her as Bloody carefully placed her figure on its perch, then bent over the table to examine more of Desmond's work. *What else can I show her that she'd like? Everything here is so boring. Oh! The Wardrobe! She'll love that!*

But, before Wyn could begin a tour of their prized possessions, she was interrupted by the sound of boots clumping up the stairs, instantly recognizable as Mellon's heavy tread followed by Desmond's long stride.

"Hello there," Mellon panted as he bustled into the room. He hurried to the stove and huddled over it. "About froze my fingers off walking home."

"Hello," Wyn replied. "Where have you lot been?"

"Down the pub," Mellon announced, patting his stomach. "They had a pig on the spit, loads of tasty crackling. It was superb."

"Oy, you could have waited for us," Wyn said indignantly.

"Too hungry," Mellon explained unapologetically as he unwound his scarf.

Wyn swallowed against an ache that a few oatcakes could not temper. "That's nice, that is. We near froze to death to take a look

THE THIEF'S TALE

at Spicer's, and you're snout deep in crackling. Oh! Des, Bloody liked your carving of her."

"You did?" Desmond asked Bloody.

"Yeah," the young woman assured him. "Can I have it when we're done?"

"Of course," Desmond beamed.

"Speaking of being done," Mellon interrupted, "what did you and Bloody discover at Spicer's?"

"It's a challenge, all right, so you got your wish, you daft bastard," Wyn accused Mellon. "Those blackberries aren't fooling around. Bloody counted forty heartbeats, give or take, between patrols, and the whole place lit up by lanterns."

"Forty?" Mellon scratched at the thick, black bristles that covered his cheeks, despite the fact he had shaved close that morning for his role as flower merchant.

"Give or take," Wyn agreed. "And we'd best hope on 'give' if we're going up the side of the house. Over the garden wall, across the garden, hoping all the way there isn't some high-muckity out for a stroll, then either hang about opening the latch on a window, lit up by a hundred hanging lanterns, or up to the roof and hope there's not someone up there. Which there is, sometimes."

"Sounds a bit tight."

"That it does. Not to mention Des following along behind. You think you can get up a rope to the roof that fast?"

"Probably," Desmond said uncertainly.

"Lots of 'probablys' and 'hopes' in that plan," Bloody muttered.

"I've a few more," Wyn announced. "Because once we're inside, it's hope Pinhead doesn't notice us wandering up to the study doors, which he probably won't, but they're at the top of the grand stairs, so anyone in the rotunda could see us, as well, and hope Ratter's source is right, and the key is hidden in that vault. Which it probably is, but… hope."

"Who's Pinhead?" Desmond asked.

"Nellie's bodyguard with the wee head. Callaghan told him to stand on the landing outside the study all through the ball, to make certain no one goes up there."

"He does have a tiny head," Desmond agreed.

THE THIEF'S TALE

"The good news is that Ratter doesn't know what he's talking about," Wyn continued. "Mysterious unpickable vault from Criénne." She snorted in contempt. "It's about as Venaissine as the Queen of Albyn's tits."

"She is Venaissine," Desmond said.

"Who is?"

"Queen Gabrielle. She's from Venaissin," Desmond reminded her.

"And so are her tits," Bloody added approvingly.

"Oh, yeah. Well, as Venaissine as my… err… bum…" Wyn cleared her throat and plunged ahead. "Hargraves's work, I'd guess, though there was no mark. His locks are solid, but I'll get it open, no worries."

"You hope," Bloody corrected her with a grin.

"Oh, yeah. Well, I probably can."

Desmond laughed. "Well done, you."

Wyn grinned, but it was a half-hearted attempt, and it soon faded from her lips.

"How about the invitations?" she asked. "Walking in through the front door is sounding better and better."

"I snagged one," Mellon replied, but he did not look especially pleased by the news. "Desmond says it's easy to forge."

Desmond shrugged. "Just a bit of nice vellum and some calligraphy. I've already made the seal."

"The issue is what names to use," Mellon continued. "The list of invitees I've managed to dig up is about as pompous a crowd as can be imagined, but it does limit our options. I could likely do old Sir Horace or Count Henri, but that doesn't help us since it's you two we want inside, not me."

"What about, oh, what was his name?" Wyn asked. "The banker Des pretended to be when we worked that old hoodlum at the Exchequer?"

"Oran," Desmond supplied.

"That's the one."

"Hmmm, I'm not certain Oran has the stones for a party like this," Mellon mused. "We need a bit more gravitas, I'd say."

"You always get to be the high-muckity," Desmond pointed out.

"A flaw of character I deeply regret at this moment," Mellon said unapologetically.

"Then what good does an invite do?" Wyn scowled. "At best, it gets Desmond being announced to a room full of high-muckities all glaring at him for not belonging there. And what about me? I've never done anyone who's half the nob your lot are, and we've not got time to create new ones."

"You're seeing my point," Mellon chuckled. "Still, an invite may be of some use in a pocket, in some circumstances other than trying to get in the main door."

"What circumstances are those?" Desmond asked.

"We'll have to work that out. In the meantime, I, too, have had a productive evening."

"Go on, then," Wyn urged him.

"Well, I confirmed that Spicer uses Sutton's and had a quiet word with one of their drivers, so we're set there. And I managed to procure…" Mellon paused dramatically, then swept a piece of parchment into the air. "… this!"

"Oooo, it's lovely," Wyn told him. She exchanged eye rolls with Desmond and reassured Bloody's baffled frown with a quick grin.

"This, my dears, is a bill of hire between one Master Parker and the esteemed establishment of Master Donnager and Associates. Every position to be filled, the names of the ladies in question, and the details of accoutrement."

"Well done," Wyn congratulated him. "And what do we do with all that?"

"Thoughts are stirring," Mellon assured them. "Where they might lead, now that is still a mystery."

"Speaking of stirring… can we stir up something to eat?"

"I couldn't eat another bite," Mellon replied.

"Right," Bloody declared. "Come on, then, Golden."

"Where are we going?"

"Our house. Gran will have something for us to eat, and she'll never forgive me if I don't bring you along to feed you up."

Wyn's stomach growled loudly at the thought of food. "I could eat a horse."

"Horse it is," Bloody promised grandly.

THE THIEF'S TALE

The Padraigs had settled on a winding street that nestled beneath the eastern wall of the valley. A long line of stone houses sat shoulder to shoulder on both sides of the lane, almost indistinguishable from each other save for the particulars of ancient disrepair, door color, or the angle of chimney. The frantic chaos of the Old City was a hushed murmur, quite overwhelmed by the screeches and laughter of a group of children playing skippenny in the street and the occasional yap of the dog dancing around them. The street surface was bowed and pitted but clean of refuse, and the only smell was that of wood smoke trailing from a dozen chimneys.

The house that Bloody led them to was as neat as any on the street, with its shutters in good repair, wooden shingles on the roof, and a door painted red with an enormous door knocker mounted in its center.

"Guess you don't have many callers," Wyn mused, eying the hideous troll face holding the ring between its tusks, disfigured beyond any troll's nightmare by leprous rust. "Or, if you do, this would scare most off, no doubt. Might be on to something, there."

Bloody snorted in disdain. "We could leave the door open. Nothing interesting ever happens here. Wish I could join a crew, get out of it."

"I don't know," Wyn said. "It seems all right, doesn't it? I grew up on a street like this... cottages, but still..."

Bloody scowled. "Maker, you must have been bored stupid."

"Yeah, likely, hey?" Wyn forced a chuckle. There were not too many memories of that life that were safe to dwell on. So many led to pain and were best left locked away. Bright sun on a yellow door. The smell of dried herbs and wood, the touch of an old, threadbare rug on bare feet. Safe and welcoming as the beautiful voice singing her name— Wyn scowled and swallowed the memories like a bitter draught. "I'd sooner slit my wrists and get it over with."

"It would be a kindness," Bloody agreed.

THE THIEF'S TALE

As Bloody opened the door, a wave of sound gushed forth, laughter, shouts, and singing, all buoyed on a surge of voices that sounded like a packed tavern was inside the house.

"Sorry about my family," Bloody said, and she pushed inside.

Wyn swallowed against a suddenly tight throat and followed Bloody through the door.

The house was not spacious, the hallway only a few paces long, with a narrow drawing room to the right and the kitchen at the end. Red hair and wide smiles were everywhere. Wyn counted ten Padraigs wedged into the front room, and more pushed and shoved their way through the doors at every moment. Heat blasted from a blazing fire in the hearth, and warm light filled the room from an array of mismatched lanterns hung on the walls.

No one seemed to notice their arrival, and Wyn stayed close to Bloody as she shouldered her way through the crowd.

The kitchen was, if anything, more crowded. A massive oven steamed against one wall and a long, sturdy table occupied most of the center of the room, leaving little space for the half-dozen Padraigs who were peeling potatoes, hacking apart cabbages, plucking chickens, and stealing unashamedly from a tray of buttery scones.

"Gran!" Bloody hollered into the din, and a tiny, stooped woman with bright eyes set deep in a nest of wrinkles appeared as if by magic.

"Yes, sweetheart?" the ancient woman asked. "You're just in time to help."

"Gran, I've brought my friend, Wyn. She's with the Tallywags, Mellon's crew."

"Good," Gran said happily. "Oh, such beautiful hair. We'll have food quick enough, if this lot will stop eating it faster than they make it." The old woman pulled Wyn's ear close and whispered, "I've made a clootie dumpling if you're quick enough to get a piece before the boys have had at it."

"Yes, please."

"Now, then, Bloody, help with the birds. Not you, sweetheart." She stopped Wyn with a quick wave of a hand. "You just enjoy."

THE THIEF'S TALE

"Yes, ma'am," Wyn agreed, delighted to be excluded. She found a small patch of wall and pressed against it as Bloody joined in the assault on the chickens. Wyn knew about half the Padraigs in the kitchen, she reckoned, from one caper or another, but the others she did not, and she realized that the family must be far more extensive than she had ever imagined. Every one of them seemed content to shout happily at one another, a steady stream of instructions, stories, and jest that was utterly bewildering, but which made Wyn smile with wonder from its sheer exuberance.

"Here you go," a low voice said in her ear, and a mug was pressed into her hand.

Wyn glanced up as she took the cup and felt her shoulders hunch forward.

"Hello, Red," she managed.

Red smiled broadly, his teeth a flash of white amidst the gleaming amber of his trim beard. "Hello, Wyn," he replied.

Wyn fought the urge to bury her face in her mug as her mind raced for a ploy that would allow her to slink away.

"It's a bit of a madhouse, isn't it?" Red asked, risking his own mug to gesture grandly at the kitchen chaos.

"Yeah," Wyn replied. "I don't mind," she added quickly.

Red laughed as if Wyn had made a particularly funny jest, his green eyes sparkling.

"I'm glad we're working together," Red confided. He glanced down and smiled again, and Wyn huddled a bit deeper into her cloak, suddenly keenly aware of how small she was and how shabby her clothes were. "I wanted to tell you, well done," Red continued, "for what you pulled at the Silver Keep."

"Oh... thanks," Wyn replied.

"Did you really nick her panties?" Red wondered.

"Yeah." Wyn risked a glance at Red, and a small smile curled the corner of her lips. "A whole handful."

"Wicked." Red raised his mug in toast and waited until Wyn had tapped her cup against it before drinking deep. "One day, I'll pull a proper job like that," he said wistfully. He smiled at Wyn again. "Perhaps we'll do it together. Something special, just the two of us."

THE THIEF'S TALE

"All right," Wyn replied, her gaze once again fixed on the foamy surface of her ale.

"Red," Bloody greeted her cousin as she joined them.

"Bloody," he replied easily. "How did you luck into an evening with Wyn, here?"

"She wanted someone good."

"Oh, aye? Did you show her how good you were?" Red asked.

"Twat," Bloody said fondly.

Red laughed and drank deep from his mug, and Wyn took the opportunity to pull her cloak more securely closed. The thick wool was starting to make her sweat, but that was preferable to revealing herself.

"Shame Skinny isn't here," Bloody told her. "He'll be right disappointed he missed you."

"Skinny?" Wyn asked, frowning in confusion. "I just saw him this morning."

"She just saw Skinny this morning." Red grinned at Bloody. "That's plenty enough for anyone."

"He's a bit strange, isn't he?" Wyn asked. "Always looking at the ground and mumbling so."

Red snorted with laughter. "Oh, dear," he chuckled. "Poor Skinny."

"Skinny just gets a bit shy, sometimes," Bloody said, glaring at her cousin.

"I dunno what he's got to be so shy about," Wyn said, her brow creased in puzzlement. "He even taught himself to write, that's not bad."

Bloody glanced between Wyn and Red, then she, too, snorted with laughter. "Poor Skinny," she agreed with him. "Not a chance."

"Right?" Red told her, then he smiled at Wyn. "Never you mind about Skinny, he's a good lad, that's true, but he still has some growing to do."

Wyn nodded warily, then returned to staring at her drink from behind her hair.

THE THIEF'S TALE

Red drained his mug and pushed himself away from the wall. He graced Wyn with a final roguish smile, told her, "I'll see you soon," and strolled from the kitchen.

"He's an idiot, you know that, right?"

"I never know what to say to him," Wyn admitted.

"Just don't say 'yes.'"

"About what?"

"About anything."

Wyn nodded agreement, although she was certain the warning was unnecessary. *Red's just having a laugh,* she decided glumly. *All them pretty lasses he's got, no chance he'd look serious at me. Just a mock.*

Gran bustled past with a raised eyebrow and a steel stare for Bloody. "Those birds won't pluck themselves."

"I did one, Gran," Bloody protested.

"One less to do, then," the tiny woman called as she disappeared into the kitchen larder.

"Sorry, it's always like this," Bloody told Wyn. "You see why I want to get out."

Wyn watched Bloody rejoin the small crew of bird pluckers, laughing and teasing each other as they ripped the feathers free, and Wyn smiled with them. Fergus insisted on doing all the cooking at Scrivener's as the veteran soldier could make almost anything taste thick and hearty, and the Tallywags had ample proof that Wyn could make almost anything taste like mud.

Although she enjoyed watching Fergus cook, there was never a hint of the exuberant chaos that filled the Padraigs' kitchen with heat and noise. And when Wyn helped her mother cook, she sat quietly on a stool and peeled or chopped whatever she was given, content to listen to her mother tell stories or sing or—

Wyn suddenly realized what she was thinking about and ripped her mind away. She wiped desperately at her eyes as they burned and the kitchen blurred, and she swallowed against a choking ache that swelled into her throat.

Wyn fled the kitchen, weaving desperately between barely seen figures as she sought the door. The night air slid across her skin, and she welcomed its freezing touch and the numbness it

THE THIEF'S TALE

promised. She began to run, anxious to be gone before anyone should notice and call after her to complete her humiliation.

Only when her lungs were ragged, red pain did she relent and stumble to a halt, her hands braced against her knees as she panted for breath.

*Maker... why won't it ever stop hurting?* Wyn slumped against a stone wall and sniffed miserably until, at last, her breathing slowed. Then she pushed away from the wall and strode deeper into the Old City, skirting the packed main streets along twisted alleys, stoking her anger to burn away her shame.

THE THIEF'S TALE

CHAPTER SIX

# A Kinked Tail

As Wyn skirted a particularly suspect pile of refuse in the center of a narrow lane, a low door swung open and a thick-set man staggered into the alley amidst a bellow of laughter. He knocked heavily into Wyn's shoulder and stumbled on, oblivious, as Wyn glared furiously at his back.

"Oy!" she called out. "Mind where you're going, you drunk bastard."

The man peered blearily at her, his face florid with drink, his eyes dull and glassy. "Whuh?" he muttered.

"I said, mind out, you old coot."

"Sorry, miss," he mumbled, and shuffled away.

Wyn frowned after him, dissatisfied by his quick capitulation. It had felt good to lash out instead of sneaking away, but she found herself craving a real victory. A proper lout to humiliate in front of his friends would be ideal. Wyn resumed her march down the alley, glaring fiercely at anyone who met her gaze, but most stared at the ground or glanced away. A woman wrapped in a thick shawl with a wrinkled walnut face shook her head in disapproval, and Wyn hurried sullenly on.

Laughter drifted into the alley through an ancient, crumbling archway. There was a cruel twist to the laughter that she recognized far too easily, a predatory glee that sent a surge of cold fire through her limbs.

Wyn stared into the short, dark passageway on the other side of the arch. She should keep walking, she knew that. The dank passageway led to pain, that was certain.

She heard the laughter again, and then a thin cry of fear, shrill and helpless, a child's voice.

Wyn hurried through the archway and to the end of the passageway, where she slid silently into a shadow and peered into the small courtyard beyond.

Two men stood in a pool of light cast by a lantern mounted on one of the high, brick walls surrounding the courtyard. The tall man had a long, angular face with drooping eyes and a strangely bulbous nose, while his companion was thick like raw dough, with a mat of greasy orange hair and a sheen of bristles across his jowls.

A young girl sprawled on the ground between them. Spindly legs wrapped in ragged strips of cloth stuck out of a threadbare dress, and thin arms pressed against the slick cobbles as she tried to push herself up. Her long, blonde hair was matted with filth and hung around her face like twisted ropes.

The tall man sneered at the girl at his feet. "What did I say?" he demanded.

"I didn't, I promise," she begged, her arms curled protectively over her head.

The other man giggled at the child's distress. He grabbed one of her arms and pulled her to her feet. Her dirt-streaked face twisted in pain, and she cried out.

"You dip around here, you pay your tithe," the tall man sneered.

"I didn't steal nothing," the girl protested.

"What's this, then?" the tall man demanded, shaking a small purse at her. "Where'd you get six bits, if you didn't lift them?"

"I begged them," she pleaded. "I promise."

"Well, there's a tithe on begging, tonight." He grinned at his companion. "Six bits, innit?"

"Six," the other man agreed, and he giggled again.

THE THIEF'S TALE

"And what for the dipping?" the tall man asked. "A finger?"

"Ratter would say two."

"Two it is," the tall man agreed.

The girl screamed and tried to pull away, but the heavy man only laughed harder, a strange, hiccupping chuckle that made his mouth purse like a gaping wound.

Wyn felt a fiery blade twist in her chest, and her fingers ached with remembered pain. She snatched a chunk of crumbled brick from the ground, strode two paces into the courtyard, and hurled it at the chuckling bastard's face.

Chuckles flinched at the last moment and the brick caromed off his skull instead of smashing his nose, but he yelped in pain and staggered away, clutching his head, as he released the girl.

"Leave her alone, you bastards," Wyn hissed at the two men.

The tall man stepped quickly away from Wyn as well, startled. "Who the fuck are you?" he asked, as the girl scurried behind Wyn.

Chuckles rubbed his head and then examined the blood on his fingers. "He knocked my brains out," he complained.

The tall man scowled and stepped toward Wyn. She could smell his sour stink as he loomed over her, a brew of filth and ale and rotten teeth. "You've made a mistake, you little shit."

Wyn herded the girl behind her. Wyn's heart was thundering in her chest, pulsing fiery certainty into her limbs until she could barely keep her hands from trembling. She scowled at Stench. "If you touch her, if you even look at her again, I'll cut your balls off and watch you choke on them."

For a moment, Wyn had visions of Stench blanching and turning tail, as frightened as the drunken lout Bloody had scolded. Then Stench's mouth twisted in a sneer.

"Shit, I think it's a girl." He turned to Chuckles and laughed. "A fucking girl brained you."

Wyn flushed with shame and fury. "That's right," she spat. "A girl, and a girl's going to rip your cock off in a moment if you don't fuck off."

"She wants to tug my cock." Stench leered at Wyn, showing the stumps of blackened teeth.

"Puss-puss," giggled Chuckles.

THE THIEF'S TALE

The two thugs began to circle to either side, Chuckles making wet smacking noises with his mouth, and Stench sucking on the remains of his teeth. Wyn pushed the girl toward the passageway behind her. "Go on, sweetheart, run," Wyn urged the child, and the girl scampered away without hesitation.

She heard the girl's bare feet slapping on the passageway's stones and away as her gaze flickered around the courtyard and back to the two men. The surrounding walls were nice and high, but there were few windows or ledges for a quick ascent, and Wyn worried that Stench would have the reach to yank her back down before she could get away. Nor could she turn tail, for fear of leading the two right back onto the girl who had just escaped.

More promising was a dark gap between two buildings on the far side of the courtyard. It twisted from sight, but it was narrow enough that Wyn thought she could dart along it far faster than the two bulky men if she could get past them to the entrance with any kind of head start.

Wyn circled toward Chuckles to stay away from the longer reach of Stench, but the taller man lunged at her with arms outstretched.

Wyn spun away from Stench's clutching fingers, and he staggered helplessly past her and tumbled into the wall. Chuckles swung wildly, his matted hair spraying drops of water in long arcs as Wyn darted right and then left under his meaty fists. He cursed as he twisted after her, then barked in pain as his boot slid on the smooth cobblestones and he crashed to a knee with a dull crack that echoed flatly from the stone walls.

Wyn did not wait to see if he would recover. The narrow gap at the rear of the small courtyard beckoned, and Wyn bolted into its deep shadows. Her shoulder smacked painfully into one wall as she twisted through the wriggling space, and she stumbled blindly forward for three agonizing strides before her boot struck a mass hidden on the ground and she sprawled into the trickle of grime-coated water that oozed down the center of the alley.

Long streaks of fire blazed across her palms as she tumbled. Her boots found the cobbles and slipped wildly as she scrambled to her feet, but as she braced to flee once more, she froze, her attention snatched by a heavy groan from the shadows.

THE THIEF'S TALE

A faint glimmer of light reflecting around the corner revealed two figures struggling together, and a third slumped across the narrow width of the alley at her feet, curled up like a grub. The larger of the two fighting men was on his knees, his fingers prying desperately at the arm hooked around his throat as his assailant inexorably squeezed tighter, driving his victim's head down from behind.

Wyn could not look away from the choking man's bulging eyes. He pulled helplessly on his attacker's arm, and his boots kicked uselessly on the wet cobbles, but it was over in less than a heartbeat as his eyes rolled up and he sagged to the ground.

At last Wyn was able to look away, and she slowly raised her gaze to the face of the last man standing. He was dressed in simple, dark wools and a long, hooded cloak, and was much slighter of build than the two men he had just felled. He met Wyn's gaze for an instant. Despite his hood, Wyn could clearly see a ragged, grey chin beard beneath a gaunt face, and slitted eyes beneath a harsh brow.

Wyn gasped in recognition and her eyes opened wide in shock, but in the next instant the man had whirled away and slipped over the high alley wall in a long, smooth leap.

Wyn blinked in surprise, and she took a hesitant step toward the two men slumped on the ground before the sound of running footsteps and shouts of rage from the small courtyard made her flinch away.

She dashed around a narrow bend and followed the alley up a half-dozen long, worn steps before a crumbling, low wall on her left drew her attention. A long leap from a windowsill took her up the side of the wall without slowing down. She rolled silently over the roof's lip and crept forward until she reached the edge of the roof overlooking the narrow path she had just left.

Chuckles and Stench had just reached the alleyway. Chuckles lagged behind as he hobbled painfully after Stench, but as Stench pressed forward at a run, he tripped and sprawled heavily over the two bodies, landing with a snort of pain that sounded remarkably like a goose honking.

The curled-up man groaned in agony as Stench cursed bitterly and crawled to his knees.

THE THIEF'S TALE

"What in the fuck?" Chuckles asked as he peered at the three men on the ground. He staggered forward another step, his hand against the alley wall for balance as he avoided putting weight on his knee.

"There's someone..." Stench snarled. "Fucking tripped me, the bastard. I'll kill the shite-faced fuck. Where's my fucking knife?" The long-faced man began scrabbling in the soaked filth for his blade.

"Wait..." Chuckles' face screwed into utter confusion, his top lip peeling away from his crooked teeth as he stared at the groaning man. "Wait... I think it's Huw."

"What?" Stench stopped searching and twisted back to his partner.

"It's Huw and Clach... I think Clach's dead."

Stench crawled to the motionless man and lowered his ear to the man's mouth. "Naw, he's breathing, just out cold." He glanced at the moaning man that Wyn guessed to be Huw. "Fuck me, what'd she do to them?"

*Me?* Wyn wondered.

Chuckles' giggle turned into a gasp of pain as he lurched towards Huw. "Huw... Huw! For fuck's sake, where's that bitch gone?"

"He dying or what?" Stench asked.

"How's I supposed to know?" Chuckles asked. He stooped over Huw and listened as the injured man groaned a few strangled, incoherent words. Chuckles glanced at Stench, his mouth pulled into a grimace of dismay. "I think he said his bollocks are smashed."

"Shit," Stench muttered. He glanced warily over his shoulder. "She didn't have but a moment..." Stench clambered to his feet and wiped his hands on his trousers, his gaze never leaving the dark depths of the alley. "Come on, grab one of these bastards and let's get out of here."

"Me?" Chuckles groused. "I can't walk. That bitch broke my knee, how's I'm supposed to carry one of these fat fuckers when I can't walk?"

"Maker, just grab Clach's arms and drag him..."

THE THIEF'S TALE

Wyn slid away from the edge and crept slowly across the roof until she could vault into the alley on the far side of the building. She trotted down the cluttered path, glancing behind her, her lips pursed in a puzzled twist. Her steps slowed until she came to a halt and she stood, fists clenched on her hips, and stared back the way she had come.

*What just happened?* Wyn glared at the darkened end of the alley as if its shadows concealed the answers to her question. *The grey-bearded bastard that's been following me just beat the bollocks off two other bastards not a stone's-throw from us, and I didn't hear a peep. And it's a good thing he did, because otherwise I would have smacked right into them, wouldn't that have been a laugh.* A smile crept onto the corner of her lips. *They think I did it…*

The smile faltered a bit as Wyn considered the possibility that Quinn might recognize her description from Stench and Chuckles. *They'll never tell him they were beat by a girl, not a chance.* Wyn shook her head emphatically. *Not a chance,* she reassured herself again.

*In any case, Nutless will soon tell them that it wasn't me who did them in…* Wyn glanced sharply behind her. There was a lonely sigh as the chill air stirred against the wet stone walls, but the silence was otherwise complete, not even a rustle of rats in the filth or a creak of a shuttered window.

*Because it wasn't me, was it.*

Wyn hurried along the alley, ducked around the first corner, and followed the twisted path down a series of steps. Wyn stopped abruptly at the bottom of the steps and stared back. A sliver of night sky thick with clouds churned between the black slabs of buildings. Her gaze darted from shadow to shadow, and her ears throbbed with the pulse of her heart as she strained to hear any telltale sound of pursuit.

Her breath poured out in a rush as she realized she had been holding it. A glance over her shoulder showed her the alley twisting between two buildings, and beyond that, the endless warren of the city.

But Wyn did not flee. Instead, she turned aside into a cobblestone yard that opened into the alley a few short strides away. It was not much wider than the alleyway itself, but it was a dozen steps deep and surrounded by tall buildings on three sides.

The rotted remains of a flight of stairs choked one side of the yard, and a dark pool of rank water filled the rest. Wyn surveyed the deep shadows behind the wrecked stairs and the sheer, smoke-blackened walls with satisfaction. If that grey-bearded bastard were following her, he would have seen her enter this yard. If he were following her, he would come this way, too. And then she would know.

He would be cautious when he saw the tall walls and no way out. But after he searched all the obvious hiding places he would have to conclude she had gotten away. She hoped.

Wyn's gaze roamed along the roof line above her. The ragged end of a rotted beam jutted from one of the buildings, and Wyn's eyes narrowed as she spotted a dark gap beneath the eave. It was a perfect hide, its entrance just one more shadow amongst the other shadows beneath the roof, with a sweeping view along the alleyway.

Two quick steps and she reached the wall. Her fingers found a web of cracks and chinks in the weathered stone and her toes a nub of wood, and she was up the wall with just the breath of cloth against the rough stone to announce her ascent. The gap was narrow enough that she had to squirm through it, but beyond she found more space beneath the sagging carcass of the roof, dark as a pit, and she eased onto her stomach in the deep shadow and pulled her hood low as she watched the alleyway below.

Wyn carefully merged with the thick beams beneath her. She matched their ancient, bowed silence, uncaring of cold or wet, uncaring of hunting or fleeing, until her breath barely stirred the air.

She waited. Every moment she was convinced she would see a figure step into the alley. A flicker of movement behind the dilapidated wreckage of an old wheelbarrow drew her gaze, but its source was revealed to be a ragged cat with a kinked tail that scurried furtively across the alley and disappeared through a crack in the wall.

Slowly the sounds of Kuray returned, absent while Wyn had stood exposed in the alleyway. A distant chorus of barking, a muffled cough from somewhere deep in the building, the faint rumble of wheels against cobbles, a distorted yelp of laughter.

THE THIEF'S TALE

*I'm crazy,* Wyn decided. *Two bastards get smacked by a man with a grey beard, why is that so strange? Nothing to do with me.*

A tickle of hair stroked her cheek, but Wyn ignored it, her gaze fastened on the alleyway as she counted the faint throbs of her heart. *Three hundred more, then I'm crazy, three hundred more, that's plenty,* she convinced herself.

At ninety-seven, the beam above her head groaned softly. Her heart thundered uncounted as she strained to hear. The beam creaked again, so softly it might have been felt, not heard. Cloth whispered against wood, and Wyn felt a brush of air stir against her cheek as something moved on the roof a hand's-breadth of timber and shingle behind her head.

Wyn's fingers throbbed with pinpricks, and she felt an uncontrollable shudder pass through her legs as she fought the need to wrench herself away from the presence above her. Sweat beaded across her back and left icy paths as it trickled down her ribs.

*No, no, no,* she pleaded. *Shite, shite, shite...*

The faint scent of wool and sweat wafted past her, and she felt another tremor of movement through the wood underneath her. Then nothing. Wyn fought her breathing into long, slow breaths as she sank even deeper into the shadows of her hide. She let the cold of the wood seep into her cheek and pushed that deep quiet into her arms and legs and chest, and slowly the trembling subsided.

An eternity passed, but Wyn did not stir. *Not until I starve to death or I hear you leave,* she grimly promised the unseen presence above her.

When the sound came, Wyn almost missed it. A soft brush of cloth no louder than a whisper. But as Wyn slowly tilted her head to hear, there was the unmistakable wet pop of a knee unbending, and a soft grunt of displeasure.

*Got you, you grey bastard.*

Wyn listened patiently to the soft groans and creaks of the building, carefully sorting which were ancient decrepitude and which were someone moving cautiously across the roof. As soon as she determined which way he was departing, she slid out of her hidey-hole and dropped lithely to the ground, then darted around the corner of the building and eased into the darkness of a deep doorway in time to watch a shadow climb silently down the far side of the building and hurry away.

Wyn slipped after him. She darted from barrel to doorway to collapsed wall, keeping her distance while he led her through the back alleys, then closing to within a stone's-throw when he joined the churning scrum of the main streets.

Grey Bastard did not want to be followed, either. He pushed through crowds then turned suddenly aside, reversed direction in the tightest of passageways, loitered in a tavern while he examined every patron's face, then ducked out the back and crossed Oldtower bridge, where Grey Bastard waited again, tucked out of sight as he watched those crossing after him.

Wyn enjoyed chasing him. As much as he twisted and turned, he stayed on the ground, likely, Wyn reasoned, on account of his grey hair and balky knee, and Wyn took advantage of his reticence. She watched him lay traps amongst the crowded streets from a comfortable perch, moved quickly across rooftops while he battled his way through the streets, and peered at him through a crack in the tavern roof.

The bridge was almost her undoing. But the moment Grey Bastard was across the bridge Wyn sprinted over a rooftop, leaped to a twisted balcony, and crossed the gap balanced on a laundry line hung over the tumbling stream below. She borrowed a brown cloak and shapeless dress from the same line and hurried back to the bridge on the far side, where it was she who lay in wait, hunched against the steps of a small temple, until she spotted him leaving his hiding spot at the end of the bridge.

A hundred paces later he ducked into a dark carriageway through the wall of an abandoned, half-burnt-down inn, and Wyn scrambled up the outer wall and crept through the charred shell until she found a nook overlooking the inn's courtyard.

A shining black carriage waited in the courtyard, devoid of any sigil or marking. Next to the carriage stood a tall man, thick in the way an old soldier grew stout, his stomach pressing slightly through the gap in his coat, but with a barrel chest and broad shoulders that made him look sturdy instead of soft, and he walked with a purposeful stride. A thin veneer of white hair was

THE THIEF'S TALE

cropped close to his skull, and a thick white beard, barely long enough to conceal his ruddy pink skin, covered his cheeks and jaw beneath rounded cheekbones more suitable for a kindly grandfather than a burly criminal.

As Grey Bastard approached, he nodded to the man and growled, "Cameron," in greeting.

Wyn nodded to herself... the man was exactly who she had expected to find as Grey Bastard's master. Old, posh, but tough as stone beneath the foppery. A broad-bladed sword with a black hilt was at his side, his coat swept behind it so that it hung free.

But the white-haired man merely nodded to Grey Bastard in return and opened the door to the carriage, standing aside and offering his hand to the person within.

The figure who emerged from the carriage was more of a surprise. A lady with a slender build and a pointed chin, her skin as pale as moonlight, her long, chestnut hair braided tightly around her head like a crown, leaving only a few loose threads to waft against her neck. Her long riding-coat was pinned at her throat by a silver amulet shaped like a ring, but she wore no other jewelry.

The lady walked gracefully across the cobbles to meet Grey Bastard, seemingly unconcerned that she was strolling within arm's-reach of a man who had just put down two of Quinn's brutes.

"I hope there is good news?" the lady asked, her voice soft and sweet with the refined tones of the nobility.

"Not as such, m'lady," Grey Bastard replied, his voice a dry scrape of steel on leather.

She tilted her head and her brow creased into a slight frown. "She lost you," she stated flatly.

"Aye," Grey Bastard admitted.

The lady laughed, a quick, bright sound accompanied by a flash of white teeth. "I told you."

"Yes, ma'am," Grey Bastard agreed. He shrugged. "It were a bit of a mess."

"Tell me."

"I followed her all night, just like you said, but she weren't alone 'til late." Grey Bastard pushed his hood back and gave one side of his head a vigorous scratch. "I thought to deliver your message then, but before I could she ran smack into a couple of lads intent on givin' a dipper they'd caught a proper thrashing. But she weren't having any of that. Went right at 'em."

"Did she, indeed?" the lady asked. "Then what?"

"I went to help. Thought the odds looked a bit long, and I weren't wrong, because there were two more of their crew waiting around the corner." Grey Bastard snorted and spat to the side. "I did for those two, quick as I could, but she comes running smack into me before I could finish. So I stepped away for a bit, thought to follow her when she moved along, but she vanished."

"Vanished?"

Grey Bastard nodded, unashamed. "She had me dead to rights thanks to them two bastards."

The lady sighed in exasperation. "I suppose that means you did not deliver my message?"

"No, ma'am. Sorry, ma'am."

"No, you did right," the lady mused. "I could wish it otherwise, but she needed help." She smiled, one side of her mouth curling slightly. "You will just have to find her and deliver my message tomorrow."

"Aye," Grey Bastard agreed.

The lady nodded, satisfied, and returned to the carriage. But as she mounted the steps she hesitated and turned back to Grey Bastard. "And, Dugan, make certain that you do," she instructed coldly. "We don't have time for another failure. Understood?"

Grey Bastard hesitated, then nodded low, almost a bow. "Yes, Hawk."

"Good," the lady said curtly. "I would hate to be disappointed." She ducked gracefully into the carriage and the tall man, Cameron, closed the polished door with a snap. He paused only to nod once more to Grey Bastard before he swung onto the driver's seat and cracked the reins. The horse stepped forward briskly and the black carriage rolled smoothly under the arch and left the yard.

Grey Bastard, or, Dugan, Wyn supposed, waited another moment, his hands on his hips, as he stared at the now-empty archway. He snorted and spat once more, then walked briskly in

THE THIEF'S TALE

the opposite direction, passing through a small passageway into the street beyond.

Wyn did not dare move until Dugan was gone, and by then it was far too late to pursue the carriage. Nor did she want to risk any more time in proximity to Dugan. *I think we've pushed our luck there far enough, tonight,* she decided.

She eased away from the small crack, crept from the inn, and trudged wearily home.

"Tell us about this lady, then," Mellon asked.

Wyn related everything she could remember about the woman who had appeared in the courtyard, along with her guard and the man who had tailed her across the city. "No one ever said her name, though her man was called Cameron, and Grey Bastard is actually named Dugan. He called her the Hawk," Wyn concluded.

"The... Hawk?" Mellon stammered. He gazed at Wyn expectantly, the corner of his mouth twitching.

"What?" Wyn covered her mouth. "Am I drooling or something?"

"No... just... really? You're not having a bit of fun?"

"How? You're not making sense. He's not, is he?"

"Sorry..." Mellon snorted with laughter. "Someone is having a bit of fun, that's certain."

"How's that?" Desmond asked, exchanging bewildered glances with Wyn.

"The Hawk... oh, come on..."

"Well, it's a bit of a poncy name, but..." Desmond said.

Mellon sighed in exasperation. "Maker, I'm surrounded by children. The Hawk is... well, a legend, the best thief, the hardest criminal, behind every great job you've ever heard of."

"I've never heard of the Hawk," Wyn complained.

"Nor I," Desmond scoffed.

"I have," Fergus said flatly.

"So... you think this lady is the Hawk?" Wyn asked.

"No!" Mellon laughed so hard he choked and had to splutter and catch his breath. "No, the Hawk isn't real, crews just say they're working for him, just to sound hard, or idiots say they heard the Hawk pulled a job, just to sound in the know. There's no Hawk."

"Grey Bastard called her the Hawk."

"She's having him on, that's all."

"He wasn't laughing. He was proper respectful, I'd say."

"Wyn, it's a story, that's all. I'm sorry I said anything."

"What if she was?"

"She isn't. Anyway, the Hawk is a man."

"Oh, yes? And why is that? I thought you said no one knew."

"They don't. Look, it doesn't matter."

"She should call herself Lady Hawk. That's a proper name."

"But everyone would know she was a lady, then," Desmond objected.

"Oh, yeah."

"Whether or not she is, in fact, the completely mythical Hawk, doesn't matter," Mellon reminded them. "Was the carriage clean?"

"Yeah, as far as I could tell from a quick glance. No badges or sigils. Just a big, black carriage in good nick."

"Hmmm," Mellon mused, his lower lip pouting out as he pondered Wyn's story. "Well, I can't say I like the idea of this Dugan lurking around while we try to pull this job, nor of some lady paying folks to watch us, but I'm not certain what we can do about it except take extra care we're not followed."

"We have to do something," Wyn insisted. "My skin crawls every time I think of that sneaky bastard, and he told her he was going to keep after me."

"No, we can't have that," Mellon agreed. "Fergus, she's never out of your sight tomorrow, right?"

The swordsman's gaze met Wyn's, calm and assured, and he nodded agreement. "I'll keep you safe."

Wyn smiled in gratitude as she felt the twisted knot of anxiety in her chest loosen, but she shook her head. "Fergus can't follow me around forever, Mel."

THE THIEF'S TALE

"I know, but just until we have a moment to sort this proper," Mellon allowed. "We can put out the word, see if anyone knows this Dugan, or if anyone has heard of a lady guarded by a man named Cameron. But that will take time, and we've a busy day tomorrow, so I think it will have to wait."

*W*yn waited until Mellon's snores reached their zenith before she eased out of her cot, using the horrendous, snorting din to mask any telltale brush of wool or creak of wood that would have given her away.

She did not need to dress, for she had lain fully clothed beneath her blankets as she waited for the lads to drift off to sleep, and she had only to clutch a bundle of cloak and boots to her chest before she was ready to creep across the bedroom floor.

She padded to the small window at the end of the hall. Wyn eased it open, crawled onto the sill, and carefully uncurled through it, balanced on her toes as she gripped the window frame and a weathered beam that supported the roof.

Wyn hooked one leg over the beam, hung for a moment to push the window closed, then pulled herself onto the beam and from there onto the roof.

She crouched for a moment, her heart racing. What had been anxiety while she sat at the table, warm and surrounded by friends, had slowly turned to fear as she lay alone in her cot, and had now grown into terror. *What am I doing?* she wondered. *Go back... there's still time.*

Wyn gritted her teeth and slowly stood tall, revealing herself to anyone who might be watching the building. *Anyone waiting for me.*

The steep pitch had kept the wooden shingles mostly clear of snow and ice, and Wyn walked sure-footed along the peak to the stone chimney that jutted from the center of the roof. Faint heat drifted from it, and Wyn perched on its top next to the vent and quickly transformed her bundle back into cloak and boots. Then she huddled against the frozen air with her arms wrapped around her knees. And waited.

She was certain that Dugan would not harm her. *He could have, easy, when I plopped in the muck in front of him,* she reminded herself. *A quick slice while I was busy gawping and no more Wyn.* And she was certain the lady who called herself the Hawk did not wish her any harm. *Just a message,* she said.

But Wyn had seen the bloody results of a 'message' being sent before, and there was no ignoring the fact that she was waiting, alone, for a man who had felled two of Quinn's thugs without breathing hard.

Wyn shivered and hugged her knees tighter against her chest. *What am I doing?* she asked again. *Just stay safe with Fergus while we sort it, like Mel said, that makes sense, doesn't it?* It did, Wyn knew it, but she knew she could not bear another day of looking over her shoulder, of expecting every moment to see Dugan emerge out of the shadows.

*Best to get it over with.* The thought had seeped slowly into Wyn's mind, an idle notion while surrounded by safety. But the idea had slowly mutated into a plan, and as it gained detail it also gained a dreadful certainty that she would do it.

*He'll not hurt me,* she reminded herself.

The building creaked as a gust of wind buffeted it, but Wyn heard the scuff of leather against wood as clear as a bell. She held her breath, then slowly looked over her shoulder.

"I thought you might be around," she told Dugan, hoping that he did not notice the tremor in her voice. "What took you so long?"

"I wanted to make sure you weren't about to vanish on me again." Dugan strolled toward her along the narrow peak of the roof, his step as easy as if he were on a broad avenue. "I'm too old to climb all the way up here for nothin'."

Wyn snorted her disbelief. "That's plenty close enough. You try anything, I've a friend with a crossbow who will put you down."

Dugan stopped, but he made no attempt to conceal the wry smile that twisted his lips. "Which friend is that? The one snoring like a pig?"

THE THIEF'S TALE

"No." Wyn frowned. "A different one. What do you want?"

"Just a word, I swear."

Wyn uncurled from her perch and dropped lightly to the wooden shingles. "Go on, then."

"I know someone who would like a chat. Asked me to pass along the message, as it were."

"Is that right? And what does this someone want to chat about?"

"They'd like to tell you that themselves." Dugan spread his hands. "I'm just here to set the meet."

"Tell them to come by in the morning, we'll chat. No need for chasing after me all over the damn city."

"Well, they'd not like to have it known, if you see what I mean. There's a need for discretion."

"What, then?"

"I'll take you there."

Wyn scowled. "Not a chance."

Dugan's smile spread. "You can bring your mate with the crossbow."

"If I said yes... *if*, right? If I said yes, when would this chat happen?"

"As quick as you like. Right now. Tomorrow night."

"I can't tomorrow," Wyn told him, her brows creased in a frown. "I have to go to a ball."

"Oh, aye?" Dugan snorted and, after a moment's careful consideration, swallowed whatever he had dislodged. "Now, then?"

"No, not now." Wyn sighed. "I'm bloody tired, and I'm bloody busy. I can't be running about playing silly buggers just because your someone wants to be mysterious."

"You tell me, then," Dugan said reasonably. "Long as it's quiet-like, my boss will say yes, long as it's quick."

"You wait for me down the pub, I'll come find you when I'm ready. But it won't be tomorrow, I'll tell you that for free."

"The day after, then."

"Maybe. Maybe never."

"My boss won't like that. Quite urgent, if you see."

"Then come by for a nice cup of tea in the morning. Otherwise, wait."

"Which pub?"

"The Silver Hart. And listen… if I see you lurking about, anywhere but there, the meet's off and your someone can go fuck themselves."

"I'll pass the message along." Dugan sucked on his teeth for a moment, his gaze fixed on Wyn's, until he finally turned away. "I'll see you at the Hart," he said over his shoulder, then he disappeared over the edge of the roof.

Wyn let out a long sigh of relief and sagged against the chimney, her eyes closed as she let the chill air slowly cool her skin.

THE THIEF'S TALE

## CHAPTER SEVEN

# Easy as Wishing

"You look flash," Wyn said with a grin. "You don't half clean up well."

"You think?" Desmond asked, attempting to lean casually against the doorframe. "I feel ridiculous."

"You look ridiculous," Mellon told him. "You're supposed to wear that jacket, not wrestle with it."

"It's... tight," Desmond objected, yanking at the jacket's collar. It certainly looked tight. Stiff, sage-colored fabric that glowed with a luxurious sheen in the lantern's light, black embroidery on the lapels, with a black waistcoat and silk necktie. But the rigid cut of the suit's jacket emphasized Desmond's long torso, thin waist, and broad shoulders. "Everything is... tight."

"Shows off your bum," Wyn told him with a laugh.

"What?" Desmond asked, panicked, as he twisted to try and look down his backside.

Mellon chuckled. "I thought you said you didn't know how to dance?"

"If I bend over I'll split my trousers," Desmond predicted glumly.

"Let's not do that," Mellon mused thoughtfully, and Wyn snorted with laughter.

"Did you get Wyn's?" Mellon asked.

"Ohhh, here we go," Wyn groaned miserably.

"I got it," Desmond replied, his thin lips twitching behind the ginger bristles that still refused to do more than form a faint sheen on his pale skin. He dropped a small sack on the table. "Fished it out of the laundry basket, so they'll not notice it's gone until tomorrow."

"Why are you grinning?" Wyn accused him.

"No reason." Desmond's smile grew until both cheeks were firmly dimpled.

Wyn opened the sack, pulled out a bundle of clothes, and stared, aghast.

"Martyr's tears! Lace! You picked this on purpose," she accused Desmond.

"No, honest, that's what they wear," Desmond objected defensively.

"Nooo…" Wyn groaned.

"And, you're having a bath." Mellon sniffed delicately. "No self-respecting young lady would leave her house smelling like that."

"I just had a bath." Wyn stuck out her tongue at him, but a surreptitious sniff under her arm made her decide not to argue.

"Get on with it," Mellon told her. He strode to the doorway and swept back the curtain with a flourish. "And it might behoove you to practice your diction while you bathed."

"Bother my diction."

"What a shameful fuss," Mellon tutted. "It will do you good to practice. We haven't had a chance for you to play high society in months, and it would be a shame to flub it." He pulled a dirty cloth cap over his thinning hair and yanked a worn pair of fingerless wool gloves on. "I'll be back with the carriage to take you to the ball."

THE THIEF'S TALE

Wyn crouched in the tiny copper tub and scrubbed until the water was grey and her skin was cream with blotches of pink from the bristles' vigorous attack. Then she rubbed soap into her hair and dunked it until her eyes stopped stinging, called herself clean enough, and huddled under a blanket until her shivers had calmed enough to get dressed.

All that was left, then, was her hair, a damp mop of dripping rat tails that lay like ice down her back. Wyn retrieved her small box from under her cot and carefully opened the lid. The red silk made her smile, but the grin faded as her fingers curled around the wooden handle of an old soft-bristled brush, the grip smooth from years of use.

She ran her fingertips over the familiar shape, gently inspecting the hollows where bristles were missing, the little crack at the tip, the chip in the edge.

Then she gathered a handful of her hair and began to brush. The bristles made a ripping noise as they tore through the tangles, and she was surprised at how long her hair was. *When was the last time I chopped it all off?* she wondered. She could not recall, exactly. *Years, I suppose. Too long, at any rate. It's all over the place.*

She pulled the brush through again, the sound tugging painfully in her chest as much as the bristles tugged at her scalp.

A soft knock sounded on the partition wall. "Are you dressed yet?" Desmond asked. "He'll be back soon."

"Yeah, just brushing my hair," Wyn replied. "Come in, if you want."

Desmond slid the curtain aside and stood in the gap, watching as Wyn ripped the brush through again, wincing as it tugged. "You know you're supposed to have some hair left when you finish."

"Ha, ha. I'm cutting it all off, tomorrow."

"Why?" Desmond wondered. "It looks pretty, all clean. Like sunshine."

*Like sunshine…* Wyn heard the words echo in another voice that made her throat tighten and her eyes burn. She yanked viciously at her hair, furious that she had let that memory sneak free.

The Thief's Tale

"I mean it," Wyn mumbled as she pulled another handful in front and struggled to tear the brush through it.

"Wyn, let me do it," Desmond said, reaching for her brush with a bright smile on his lips.

"No!" Wyn snapped, holding the brush as far away from him as she could. The sudden hurt in his eyes twisted in her chest, and she cursed herself again.

"Maker…" Desmond muttered. "I'll see you out there, I guess." He strode from her nook without another word and Wyn's shoulders slumped. She turned the brush back and forth, pressing the bristles into her hand, fighting not to remember. *Why don't I throw it in the fire?* she wondered. But the thought burned with a fresh ache, deep in her chest, and she swallowed it down as well, sucked in a shuddering breath, and raised her chin defiantly. *Done with that,* she promised herself. *Done, you hear me, you stupid girl? Done.*

She grabbed more hair and started brushing again, the steady rip alone in the silence.

**W**yn shoved a ragged cloth cap firmly onto her head and shrugged her shapeless wool coat into place. The coat was far too big for her, and the hem hung about her knees while the shoulders sagged to her elbows.

Baggy canvas trousers, frayed and ragged at the ankles, billowed around her legs on every step, and only a rough length of cord, wound three times around her waist and tied off firmly, prevented them from sliding straight to the ground.

A pair of stained boots, awkward as well as huge, completed her ensemble. Their toes snagged on every cobble, no matter how slowly Wyn shuffled down the alley.

A creaking wagon pulled by a melancholy donkey groaned its way across the entrance of the alley and halted to a chorus of angry shouts from the traffic trapped behind it. The wagon was piled high with coal covered by a torn, filthy tarp, and the driver looked as if he slept in the back with his load, so encrusted with coal dust was his skin.

Wyn clumped to the end of the alley and hopped onto the bench next to the driver.

"Nice wagon," she told him. "Will it make it to the New City before a wheel falls off?"

"Well, the price was right," Mellon answered with a grin. He clicked his tongue at the donkey, and the wheels creaked into life as they slowly nosed up the lane.

"Must have been the slowest getaway ever, I reckon," Wyn said thoughtfully, eying the plodding donkey.

"It weren't quick." Mellon guided the wagon slowly through the teeming streets of the Old City, avoiding sprawling stalls, darting children, scampering dogs, sauntering nobles, reeling drunks, and uncountable people merely going about their business, happy, dour, frenzied, or lackadaisical.

Wyn retrieved a lump of coal from the bed of the wagon and rubbed coal dust over her cheeks and forehead, caked her hands, and spread a liberal dose over her clothes. Finally satisfied that she was appropriately filthy, she tossed the coal into the bed and grinned at Mellon.

"Lovely," Mellon assured her, his smile flashing white amongst the spider web of black, filthy creases and dark smudges that covered his face.

The donkey slowly pulled them free from the maze of the Old City and entered the boulevards that swept gracefully between the walled gardens and tall, stone manors of the New City. Wide paths on either side of the road allowed the lords and ladies of the New City to stroll without fear of being trampled, and the streets were broad enough that even the creaking wagon was little obstacle to the trotting horses and shiny carriages that whipped around it.

The donkey moved no faster when, at last, they turned onto the King's Road and began the steep climb to Morningside. Mellon clucked, he begged, he wheedled, but the donkey appeared satisfied with its plodding pace, and Mellon soon gave up trying to urge more speed from the beast and stared contentedly at the slowly passing buildings.

THE THIEF'S TALE

The service gate into the Spicer mansion's yard stood open, and their wagon joined a queue waiting to pass through. The two blackberries who usually watched the gates had been supplemented by two more and a distinguished, wiry man who wore a black coat and hat. Black Hat consulted a long parchment each time a wagon reached the front of the line.

Ahead of their donkey, two carriages disgorged a dozen women wearing identical black dresses of a simple, functional cut, with no ornamentation save for a brush of white lace around the collar and cuffs. The women assembled in a line beside the carriage while Black Hat spoke with them, checking his parchment after each brief conversation.

Mellon nudged the donkey through the gates, and the wagon groaned as it turned reluctantly into the yard.

"Hold there, you old coot," one of the blackberries accosted Mellon.

"Coot, is it?" Mellon grumbled, glaring at the watchman.

"Where are you going with this lot?" the guard asked.

Mellon shrugged. "Coal chute, 'less you're wanting it in the hall."

"Master Parker, were we expecting coal, today?" the guard called to Black Hat.

The distinguished man glanced at the wagon, held up a preemptory finger to the young woman he was interviewing, and frowned. "Are they from Sutton's?"

"You from Sutton's, then?" the guard asked Mellon.

"I heard 'im," Mellon wheezed. He clambered down and ambled to the side of the wagon, seemingly unconcerned with the dark looks from the drivers of the wagons stuck behind him. He wiped his filthy sleeve along the warped, splintered boards that formed the wagon's stained side.

"Sutton's," Mellon announced, as faded white letters painted on a green background emerged from the soot.

"Sutton's!" the guard conveyed to Master Parker, who again interrupted the young woman to glare at Mellon.

"You were meant to be here this morning," Parker scolded.

"Yessir," Mellon agreed amiably.

THE THIEF'S TALE

"Very well, get on with it," Parker sniffed. "As quick as you can. As you can see, we are very busy this evening, and we cannot have you lot in the middle of everything."

"Nosir."

"Right," the blackberry said sternly to his squad. "Search the wagon, I'll check these two."

The other three blackberries groaned as they faced the filthy wagon, but for all their muttering they were thorough enough, checking beneath the bed and poking through the grimy load with their truncheons.

The first blackberry grimaced as he examined Mellon, clouds of black soot flying every time his gloves touched Mellon's clothes. Mellon helped by having a coughing fit half-way through, hacking and spluttering until he could spit out a blob of phlegm onto the cobbles.

"Come on, then!" the driver of the wagon behind them in the gateway hollered, his face beet red.

"Quiet, you." The blackberry scowled and showed the driver his truncheon. "Unless you want to be searched by this?"

Beets glared sullenly but did not open his mouth again, and the guard turned his gaze onto Wyn.

"Hop down, quickly now."

Wyn clambered off the wagon and submitted silently as the blackberry patted her down, stifling a grin as the coal dust kept him scowling and his hands from more than a cursory search. Enough to ensure she carried no weapons, but Wyn had not brought anything that might lead to a more thorough search, had it been discovered. *He likely didn't even notice he was searching a girl,* Wyn thought sulkily, her good humor vanishing. *Need a pretty fucking thorough search to discover that, I reckon. No one else has.*

The blackberry waved her back to the wagon, and she slouched onto the bench next to Mellon. He clucked at the donkey and shook the reins, and the cart creaked into the yard.

Wyn glanced at the line of women being interviewed by Master Parker. Some were as young as she, most a bit older, and two looked as if they had been carved from the Ironbacks when the mountains were young. As the wagon crept past, Wyn overheard Parker's voice.

THE THIEF'S TALE

"Let me see, Cara… Cara…" he muttered, his finger sliding down his parchment. "I find you have worked in Lady Alana's kitchens? Very well, you will assist Cook tonight."

"Yes, sir," the young woman agreed quickly, and gave the wiry man a quick bob of a curtsey that Wyn stored away for future use.

Mellon took his time maneuvering the wagon into place in front of the coal chute, or, rather, he did nothing to urge the donkey to move faster. But at last the wagon lurched its way near the wooden doors that covered the chute, and Mellon set the brake and climbed laboriously down, where he was confronted by a young steward holding a sheet of parchment that he unfolded with a dignity more befitting the reading of a royal decree in a throne room than a bill of lading in a noisy yard.

Wyn hopped off the bench and began to shovel coal into the chute. The roar drowned out whatever the steward had been telling Mellon, and Mellon shook his head helplessly and held a hand to his ear, and eventually the young man retreated, his parchment still clutched in his hand.

Mellon joined Wyn and took the shovel as Wyn sipped from her water flask and glanced around the yard. The blackberries at the gate had turned to Beets's wagon, Master Parker was interviewing the next servant, and no one was paying any attention to the filthy laborers in the corner.

Wyn slipped into the coal chute between shovelfuls and slid gently down. The mountain of coal in the bin at the chute's base shifted and spilled as she landed, but two quick steps had her out of the pile before the next load of coal came plummeting after her.

Dim light oozed through small, filthy windows set high in the wall, enough to guide Wyn to the steep stairs at the end of the cellar. A bright glow shone through the narrow crack beneath the door, blinding in the darkness.

Wyn crept into the shadow beneath the landing and sat behind a tarp-covered pile of crates.

And waited.

The light beyond the tiny windows faded, until only the glow from beneath the door kept the cellar from utter darkness.

THE THIEF'S TALE

Footsteps drifted down the stairs. Music began, thin and scratchy as it eked into the cellar. And then, finally, a growing cackle of distant voices announced that the ball was underway. Wyn sighed and tapped her fingers on the floor and muttered until the sounds of the ball slowly reached a crescendo, then she climbed to her feet and readied herself.

A clean rag, carefully hoarded in her inside pocket and endowed with a liberal application of fresh spit and the contents of her flask, wiped the black smears from her face and hands. The huge boots came off next, revealing a pair of small, stiff, shiny black shoes that had already pinched her toes numb. Then the vast coat and shapeless, baggy trousers, which fell away to expose a starched black dress with white lace around the collar and cuffs. Wyn pulled a pair of white stockings from the dress's pocket, carefully rolled them up her legs and tied them, and crammed her feet back into the shoes. She unhitched the skirt from around her hips and shook it out, and then, finally, her cloth cap was traded for a white lace bonnet which perched on top of her carefully pinned hair.

Wyn hated the dress. She hated the stupid frilly skirt that tangled around her ankles as she walked. She hated the stupid frilly collar that poked her under her jaw. She hated the stupid, frilly stockings that clung strangely to her thighs, making her want to pull and twist and pluck at them after every step. She hated the stupid, frilly bonnet she wore perched on her head, especially the stupid, frilly ribbon that dangled over her ear, tickling it mercilessly.

It was confining, tangling, irritating, uncomfortable, and worst of all, it made her look like a girl. A skinny, awkward little girl exposed for any bastard who came along who wanted to spit on her. And although she had to admit the chances of being beaten or shoved in the muck were probably low while she was in the Spicer mansion, she was certain there were plenty of humiliations available to high-muckities as well.

*Just be small, be quiet, be fast,* she told herself.

She smoothed the dress flat, breathed away every trace of knowing smiles and sharp retorts and replaced them with

THE THIEF'S TALE

downcast eyes and an anxious expression, then hurried up the steps.

The door opened into the ordered insanity of the servant's wing. Black-clad figures rushed busily in all directions, weaving around each other as if they followed the practiced steps of a dance. The kitchen was packed with cooks stirring, chopping, folding, and slicing, just keeping ahead of the relentless tide of silver trays bearing their creations away.

Wyn dodged nimbly through the chaos, hurried through a pantry with two young men frantically polishing a mountain of silver plates, and found the narrow staircase that led to the main floor of the mansion. Wyn joined a stream of dignified figures in black cloth and followed the flow into the entrance hall.

The vast chamber was alive with brilliant color and the hubbub of excited chatter and lively music from the ballroom. The scents of dozens of rich perfumes filled the air and blended into a sweetness that made Wyn gag. The ladies' dresses were more beautiful and extravagant than Wyn could have imagined. They put to shame the frilly gown that Mellon had purchased for Wyn to wear for a job a year ago, a sartorial decision that had ended poorly for all involved. Rich fabric clung to cinched waists and curved over sculpted bodices, elegant embroidery shone in the lantern light, lace ruffled softly at cuff and collar, and sweeping dresses trailed nobly across the red carpet.

The gentlemen did their best, with long coats fitted at the waist or dignified robes, vests of gold and red and green, and bright silk sashes, but they were no match for the ladies.

Wyn scooted through them until she could peer into the ballroom. A quick glance across the stately procession of dancers found Nell Spicer amidst an entourage of avid listeners. Satisfied that the mistress of the house was immersed in her ball and not lurking in her study, Wyn retreated across the entrance hall, clutching a soft fur stole she had borrowed from an inattentive guest as a flag of official servile business.

Up the steps she trotted, following the sweeping curve to the second floor.

Two men stood on the landing, eying the gaily colored crowd in the hall. Nell Spicer's shadows, the very same that Ratter had

THE THIEF'S TALE

promised they would not have to deal with. Wyn dropped her gaze and hurried between them, her eyes fixed firmly on the floor.

"Evening," the man on the left said casually. He was slightly taller than Pinhead, with a clean-shaven jaw that looked as if it were carved from granite, and thick, black hair covering the backs of his hands like a bear's pelt. "You with Donnager's lot?"

Wyn stopped, her hands clutched demurely around the stole in front of her. "Yes, sir," Wyn said hesitantly.

"What's your name, lass?"

"Elspeth, sir," Wyn whispered, her voice trembling. She widened her eyes fearfully at the man before glancing away.

"Do you know the rules, Elspeth?"

"Yes, sir, we were told, sir."

"All right then, lass," the guard said grandly. "Off you go, and ask if you need anything. I'll set you right."

"Thank you, sir," Wyn gushed with relief, and before she hurried past, she gave him the same quick bob of a curtsey that she had seen Cara give to Master Parker.

Wyn hastened down the hallway, her dress rustling loud enough to drown out a riot of geese. At the door to the garden parlor she darted to the side, closed the door firmly behind her, and fastened the iron latch.

The flower vase was precisely where she had placed it the day before, a burst of color next to a dour bust of pale marble, and she sighed in relief. She carefully lifted the spray of leaves and stems, revealing an oilskin-wrapped bundle in the bottom.

She collected the bundle, replaced the flowers in the vase, and unwrapped the oilskin on the floor.

A tiny knife with a blade as thin as parchment slipped neatly into the sleeve of her dress. A flat leather wallet tucked into the band of her stockings against the inside of her thigh. Last was a tightly wound length of rope, thin as a finger. Wyn uncoiled it as she crossed the room to the tall windows that overlooked the garden.

Wyn pulled both windows wide and hooked them open to prevent an inopportune gust slamming them closed. Footsteps scrunched on the gravel path outside the window, two sets of heavy boots with a measured pace.

THE THIEF'S TALE

Wyn tied one end of the rope around her waist as she waited for the sound of the patrolling guards to recede. A heavy latch secured the thick wooden shutters outside the window. Wyn twisted the lock and gently raised the bar as she counted ten heartbeats, pushed the shutters open, and dropped the free end of the rope out the window.

A dark figure rushed across the gap between the apple tree and the horse fountain, then swarmed up the rope. Wyn braced herself with her foot on the windowsill as his weight yanked on her. He reached the window quickly, Wyn grabbed his belt, hauled him over the sill, and pulled the rope back into the room. She gently closed the shutters, fastened them, and had the window sealed long before she heard the quiet crunch of the next patrol passing outside.

"Any problems?" Desmond panted, his face flushed despite the chill air.

"Easy as wishing," Wyn assured him. "Except my damn stockings keep twisting around. Any split seams?"

"I don't think so." Desmond craned and writhed as he examined his suit.

"Good." Wyn untied the rope and gathered it back into a tight coil. "We can't have you…"

Her voice trailed off as she glanced at Desmond. He was staring at her with a strange smile on his lips, his gaze flickering over her face.

"What?" she demanded. "Is something wrong?"

"You look pretty in that dress, is all," Desmond said quietly, grinning like a gormless idiot.

"Oh, har, har. Shut it," Wyn warned him. She felt heat throb up her neck, and she crossed her arms over her chest, suddenly aware of how clearly the dress's stupid, tight bodice revealed just how little she filled it out.

"No, I meant—"

"Shut. It." She tried to glare defiantly at him, but her hair got in the way and she had to brush it awkwardly behind her ear while still trying to keep her arms crossed.

Desmond closed his mouth.

THE THIEF'S TALE

"Here." Wyn thrust the rope roughly into his hands. "That goes in the oilskin, back in the vase. And be careful of the damn flowers."

Desmond quietly did as he was told, and Wyn positioned the vase correctly next to the door. She swallowed the last of her irritation at being mocked and turned to Desmond with a forced grin on her lips.

"Right, m'lord, are you ready?" Wyn asked.

Desmond patted his jacket pockets, yanked at his collar, and blew out his breath. "Ready."

They left the garden parlor and headed toward the study, Desmond striding confidently ahead, Wyn trailing dutifully behind, guiding him with subtle pokes of her finger in his back. The hallway was mercifully unpopulated as they approached the elegant, leaf-emblazoned doors. Music from the ballroom smothered any sound her stupid dress might have made, but the bright lights shining from the rotunda left no concealment on the spacious landing. Wyn approached the end of the hallway cautiously, peeked carefully around the pillar, then drew slowly back. Two fingers told Desmond that Hairy Hands and Pinhead were still stationed on the landing, an arm's-length away. Desmond pressed himself against the wall next to Wyn as she chewed on her lip, waiting, watching the guard furthest from her through a small gap in the filigree festooning the base of the pillar.

She could not see Hairy Hands, but Pinhead was in clear view across the opening. His attention was on the wide stairs that swooped in two great arcs to meet at his feet, but at the end of every pass of his gaze across the hall, he twisted and glanced over his shoulder, checking the study doors and the empty hallway behind him. Wyn counted thirty heartbeats between turns, then sixty, then forty-two. She could only guess that Hairy Hands was behaving similarly.

*Get to the door, two, twist handle, one, ten for the doors to open, Desmond comes, two more, ten for them to close. Leaves about ten to pick them if they're locked.* Wyn shook her head. *Going to be close.*

Wyn hiked up her skirt, removed the wallet from her stocking, and unfolded it. Inside the slim leather pocket were a dozen thin, steel picks, each twisted at a slightly different angle, or with a slightly different tip. Wyn selected a flat, bent one and one with a small hook at the tip and replaced the wallet in her stocking, only then realizing how much leg she had just exposed to Desmond. *Wonderful. More teasing when we get home,* she sighed.

She held the picks delicately in her fingers. If she was spotted, she would just have to palm them, as she could not risk the time it took to work them free from her hair or her other usual places of concealment.

Pinhead glanced over his shoulder, peered into the hallway, and turned back. Wyn rose onto her toes.

Then, much to Wyn's surprise, the lights in the rotunda dimmed dramatically, plunging the landing into deep shadow.

Wyn stepped confidently from concealment as if she were hurrying across the landing, but as soon as she made certain Hairy Hands was still staring into the entrance hall, she swerved and scampered to the door.

*Three,* she counted, already behind her rough schedule.

She grabbed the knob and twisted, but it was as immovable as if it were welded to the door. *Locked... bloody merchants never trust anyone.*

She knelt at the door and raised the picks to the knob, then froze. *Where's the lock?* Her eyes darted over the ornate steel, searching for a keyhole. In the back of her mind, she heard the music stop and registered the applause of the crowd.

*Eight...*

There was no keyhole. She tried the knob, but it would not turn, and a gentle shove proved that the door was not open.

*Fifteen... open it!* she screamed, but there was nothing to pick, no slot in the door, and the gap between the doors was covered by a thick piece of trim, preventing her from even seeing where the bolt was. The applause died away, and Wyn heard the drone of Spicer's voice from the floor of the entry hall, and the creak of a floorboard as Pinhead shifted his weight.

*Twenty!*

Wyn twisted away from the door and slowly crept toward the safety of the pillar. Her dress shifted and rubbed, and she froze.

THE THIEF'S TALE

*Twenty-five…* she thought desperately. She eased forward, willing her dress to hang quietly, but she was still five long paces from the concealment of the pillar.

*Thirty…* and Hairy Hands shifted his weight onto one foot.

A voice sounded like thunder from the entrance hall, a single Word that reverberated from the marble and sent a tremor through Wyn's feet and into her chest. Crystal chandeliers sang like wind chimes in a gale and flowers whipped their heads in a frenzy. Wyn gasped in shock as brilliant sparks, shining like diamonds, poured from the ceiling of the entrance hall and whirled through the air, a tremendous, curved river of light that swirled majestically around a central blaze of throbbing stars, bathing the landing in its glow.

Applause swelled from the unseen crowd, and Wyn scuttled back to the pillar under cover of its distant thunder. As she ducked out of sight she saw Hairy Hands's shoulder twitch as he began to turn his head, and she huddled against the wall, uncertain whether he had heard her, or, worse, seen her.

Wyn slid away from the opening, motioning Desmond to follow, and, mercifully, the music began anew, allowing them to tiptoe to the corner and out of sight.

"What happened?" Desmond asked.

"I think it was whatever Device the Guild brought Spicer."

"What was it?"

"I think… I think it was the stars," Wyn said softly. "The whole sky."

"Oh, amazing," Desmond whispered. He glanced longingly toward the entrance hall. "I wish I'd seen."

"It was beautiful," Wyn told him. She shook her head to clear the strange serenity that had enshrouded her. "You can have a look later. We've got a problem. The study door is locked, but there's no lock."

"What?"

"There's no lock." Wyn glared at Desmond, as if having no lock had been his idea. "There's nothing to pick."

"There must be," he said helplessly. "How else does Spicer get in?"

"Some other way to release the mechanism... I don't know." Wyn's lips pressed into a thin line. "Martyr's tears, how are we supposed to do this with no time to prepare?"

"I don't know." Desmond scowled. "What do we do?"

"I guess we improvise." Wyn laughed, then had to stifle a squeal of desperation. "We're not getting another chance better than this."

"We have a chance?" Desmond muttered, but Wyn ignored him.

"First, we get out of this hallway," she decided. Wyn crossed the hall and tried the first doorknob she could find. It was locked, but that was what she wanted. *A locked door means no one inside,* she hoped.

Wyn slid the bent pick into the keyhole and twisted it gently, then carefully nudged the second pick against the lock's delicate pins, feeling their weight. The lock was beautiful, well-oiled steel with tiny, spring-loaded pins hidden in an interlocking secondary barrel. It took her two rakes to convince it to open, and the lock yielded to the pressure of her picks with a soft click. Wyn added the picks to the pins already in her hair as she silently turned the knob.

The room on the other side was a library, with shelves of impeccably aligned leather volumes reaching to the high, vaulted ceiling and plenty of comfortable chairs to read them in. Thick drapes covered two tall windows, and with the door closed behind them, the room was as dark as a cave.

Wyn parted the drapes a hand's-breadth and eased the window open enough to peer through a crack in the shutters. The room overlooked the park, but Wyn could see no trace of the garden wall nor the street, so thick were the trees. The guards patrolling outside, however... them she could see. She ducked back as the golden beam of their lantern flickered over the shutters as they strode past, their breath steaming from the shadows beneath their hoods.

"All right," Wyn muttered. She opened the shutters wider and craned her head out. "All right."

"Do we have a plan?" Desmond whispered.

THE THIEF'S TALE

Wyn pulled back and closed the windows. "Yeah… I climb over the roof and down to the study and get in from the outside, then I open the door for you."

"Can you do that?" Desmond asked, and Wyn frowned at him. "I mean, I know you can, but didn't we say it was too risky?"

"Risky is what we have left," Wyn pointed out. "The only way into that room is from the outside, and dropping down is easier than climbing up. And, I don't have to haul you up after me. Easy."

"If you say so… how do I know when you're opening the door?"

"You don't… just be ready."

"What do I do if someone asks me what I'm doing standing around in the hallway?"

"I don't know… just… loiter. You're meant to be a muckity noble, tell them to fuck off, and sound pompous."

Desmond nodded. "See you there."

Wyn grinned at him, then returned to the window and listened to the quiet click of the door as it closed behind him. She removed her shoes and tucked them into her belt, then settled with her forehead pressed against the cold window pane, watching her breath pulse fog across the glass.

She did not have to wait long. Light gleamed through the trees, slowly sliding black shadows across the shutters as the lanterns moved steadily closer. The blackberries were following the well-trampled path in the snow without any deviation, and Wyn watched them walk past with a grin curling one side of her mouth.

As soon as they turned the corner, Wyn had the windows and shutters open. She stepped onto the sill and caught the top of the frame with her hands to steady herself. She pulled the window closed, pressed her fingertips into the gap between two square blocks of stone, lodged her toes into another crack, and began to ascend.

She had reached a lip of stone supporting a drainpipe when her stupid dress caught on the edge of a block and tugged her to a stop with a sharp, tearing sound. Wyn carefully transferred her weight until one hand was free and yanked the dress. She felt her

THE THIEF'S TALE

shoes come loose from her belt as she tugged, and she snatched at them, but she merely grazed a shoe's narrow tip before they were gone, landing in a bush beneath her with a sharp crunch and a gentle hiss of dislodged snow.

Wyn closed her eyes and softly beat her forehead on the cold stone, but there was nothing to be done about it. She had already lost too much time, and going down to find the hated shoes in the garden was out of the question.

She craned her neck upward. The gargoyles were only a body-length above her. Her stockinged toes found another crack between blocks, and she pushed herself up, feet straining as she reached for the gargoyle's clawed feet. Her fingers slipped into the stone curls, and she pulled herself over the low balustrade and onto the steeply pitched roof.

She scrambled across the roof on hands and feet, over the peak and down the far side without pause. At the roof's edge waited a narrow palisade no higher than the length of her hand, and a long gutter that ran beneath the bottom edge of the slate tiles and through the drainage spouts in the gargoyles' mouths. A thick layer of moss beneath a scum of ice filled the gutter, but Wyn hurried sure-footedly along the runnel, bent low in case she had the bad luck of sharing the roof with one of the blackberries that occasionally appeared above the front doors.

She reached the roof directly above the study windows before the lanterns of the patrol appeared below, barely, and Wyn dropped onto her stomach in the gutter, not even breathing as she sank into a gargoyle's shadow. Icy fingers of moisture slowly oozed through her dress and spread across her stomach and chest as she pressed into the gutter, but she was a frozen shadow as the lantern flickered its beam over the parapet and gleamed on the gargoyle's wet skin, then moved on.

Wyn rose to her fingers and toes and crouched on the lip of the roof. To her relief, the freezing air had kept the guests from enjoying Callaghan's lanterns, and the garden was deserted. Wyn gripped a flourish of scrollwork beneath the gargoyle's feet and slipped over the edge without hesitation.

She hung from her fingers, swaying gently as her stockinged feet probed for the snow-dusted ledge formed by a decorative

THE THIEF'S TALE

pattern in the stones. One toe brushed against it, then a second, and she anchored herself by the barest touch of her pointed feet.

Wyn checked the plunge beneath her, puffed a cloud of breath into the chill air, and began to work her way along the wall. A dozen crab-like steps and she reached the corner of the wall, where a well-placed ornamental flourish over the study window allowed Wyn to brace her feet, twist to grab the scrollwork, and gently lower herself onto the window ledge.

Wyn peered through the windows. Dark, thick fabric was drawn tight on the other side of the glass against the night air. The window ledge was wide enough for her to stand on the balls of her feet, and she only needed one hand to shake the knife out of her sleeve and into her grasp. She slipped the thin blade between the frame and the window. The short, iron handle of the window's latch was visible through the glass, and the small, shining point of her knife nestled against it. But it would not shift.

*Fucking shite!* Wyn peered at the latch. It looked the same as the one she had used to open the window in the garden parlor. *Shouldn't be locked...*

Wyn gave up being delicate and pressed against her knife with both hands. The blade bent, but she showed no mercy. It would break before she gave up.

She heard a scrape of metal and the latch twisted. Her knuckles barked cruelly on the iron frame with a rap that seemed to echo from the garden wall. Wyn tore the window open and slipped through.

Her breath fogged the glass in great patches as she panted, counting her racing heartbeats. She reached twelve when the lanterns darted through the garden outside. Their light passed over the study windows without a pause, and Wyn breathed out a sigh of relief.

"Knew I could make it," she whispered, grinning.

She eased from the drapes and crept across the floor to the study door, her stockinged feet soundless on the polished wood, and brushed her fingertips across the panels, searching for whatever mechanism secured them. There were no levers. No bolts. No latches or pedals. Nothing but smooth wood and the cold, metal doorknob.

THE THIEF'S TALE

Wyn glared at the knob. *Do you just open if I use you from this side? Can it be that simple?* she wondered. *Why not? If I were a high-muckity merchant, would I want to mess around with a fancy contraption every time I wanted out of my study? Or would I want a fancy contraption that was quick and easy to use?*

She slid her fingers around the knob, waited until the music from downstairs reached a crescendo, and turned it slowly.

Breath hissed through her teeth in satisfaction as she felt the knob start to move. *All right... careful, careful, we don't want them popping open before I'm bloody ready.* Wyn felt the slow grind of the mechanism through the knob as she twisted it, and she stopped the instant she felt the slight catch before the clunk that sent the doors swinging. *Now... how about giving us a bit of a peek?*

Wyn pulled gently, frowned, and pulled harder. A brief line of bright light appeared between the doors, but it vanished as soon as she relaxed. *Bastard is heavy.* She glared at the door, gripped the knob more firmly with both hands, and strained. The door shifted, the crack of light appeared again, and she felt a single throb of the mechanism through the knob. *Come... on!* Wyn planted a foot on the opposite door and heaved with her legs and back. There was another slow throb, and a third, and the door was open a hand's-breadth. She could feel her leg trembling under the strain, and she knew she could not hold the door's terrible weight a moment longer.

A shadow filled the crack, and Desmond's long fingers slipped around the edge. "Wyn, open it," he whispered urgently. "They're not looking."

Wyn felt the knob slip in her grasp. *His fingers!*

"Des... push!" she hissed. Her fingers clung desperately to the smooth metal as she heaved backward, the muscles of her arms and legs rigid with the strain.

The door eased open slightly, and Desmond stumbled through, knocking Wyn aside. Her fingers slipped, she staggered backward, and the door sank home with a soft thud.

"Maker's breath, I thought you were going to be squished!" Wyn groaned and flopped onto her back on the floor.

"Why wouldn't it open?"

THE THIEF'S TALE

"I don't know," Wyn said wearily. "It was really heavy without letting them open on their own."

"You were probably pulling up the counterweight," Desmond mused. He offered his hand, and Wyn gratefully allowed him to pull her to her feet.

He grinned at her as she caught herself against him, their fingers still intertwined. "You did it," Desmond whispered gleefully.

"It wasn't that hard."

"Perhaps not, for you. I reckoned we were done."

"Well, let's not pat ourselves on the back, yet, shall we?" Wyn was suddenly aware of how close they were standing, and she slipped her hand free and turned quickly away. "I'll get Spicer's vault open, you get your stuff ready."

Desmond dug through his coat pockets and laid two flat boxes on the desk, each made from identical polished wood with brass hinges and latch, while Wyn released the hidden catch and swung the false panel wide.

"Doesn't look too hard," Desmond muttered, peering over Wyn's shoulder at the steel door of the vault.

Wyn groped under her skirt to retrieve the leather wallet, browsed her picks, and selected several to hold between her lips as she explored the keyhole with the smallest shaft. The lock was beautifully made, with smooth springs to hold the pins in place, and a well-oiled barrel of such craftsmanship that there was almost no give to it at all. A second row of pins lurked opposite the first.

"Shouldn't take but two shakes," she mumbled around her picks. The double set of pins was a little tricky, but hardly the worst challenge she had ever faced. She inserted a flat, twisted pick and turned it gently, just enough to press the barrel against the pins, and began to scrape them with a slim, hooked pick, testing them one by one, teasing them into their shafts. Wyn pushed aside the muffled screech of the music, the damp cloth of her wet dress clinging to her stomach, the tuneless whistle of breath through Desmond's nose, the bitter tang of the steel picks in her mouth. In their place was the delicate push of the pins against her pick, the steel shaft alive against her fingertips.

THE THIEF'S TALE

The lock clicked sharply. Wyn smiled around her mouthful of picks and turned the handle. The heavy door swung outward with a sigh of air.

"Easy as wishing— Martyr's tears," Wyn groaned.

Inside the door was another sealed door, but comparing the two was like comparing a lapdog with a wolf. The inner door was like nothing Wyn had ever seen. Four handles were set at the points of a square around the center of its metal surface, each made from steel and wood so dark it appeared black. Between the handles were concentric bands surrounding a face that would have been at home on one of the gargoyles perched on the roof. In its mouth was a great steel ring. Four trees were engraved into the metal. They grew from the outermost band, their twisted trunks passing between the handles and splitting into a maze of smaller branches that reached to the sides of the door on each edge.

Wyn's breath whispered between her lips as she gazed at the door. Each of the concentric bands had numbers engraved on it, and she slowly turned the outermost band, feeling it slide with precise, oiled clicks.

"What is that?" Desmond asked.

"It's a lock," Wyn sighed. "A great bitch of a lock."

"Can you open it?"

Wyn scowled. "I've no idea how it works." She spun the outer ring of numbers and watched it slowly come to a stop. *But that's not entirely true, is it?* she thought. *It's still a lock, no matter how fancy. Means there's bolts being held in place, waiting for something to push the pins out of the way.* She spun the dial again, listening to the tiny, regular clicks. *Sooo... four handles... four rings... four locks?*

Wyn turned the band again, this time slow and careful, feeling every vibration of the clicks through her fingertips. She stopped, fingers resting on the metal. She shifted the band backward and forward. Two clicks heavier than the rest. *Probably.*

"Huh," Wyn grunted. She spun the band slowly onward, then reversed its direction until she heard another firm click. "Hmmm."

"What?"

THE THIEF'S TALE

"I think these dials are the key." Wyn sat on her heels and puffed hair out of her eyes. "They must have some kind of latch that goes into the lock when you hit the right number."

"That doesn't sound too hard."

Wyn snorted and flexed her fingers. The movement of the rings was so smooth, the variance in the tiny clicks so subtle, she was not convinced she could feel them with certainty every time. Wyn rose onto her knees and tilted her head next to the door so that the tip of her ear brushed the cold steel. *Just like feeling out a pin, but listening instead of touching,* she told herself.

The music did not make the task any easier, nor did the heavy footsteps that thumped outside of the study doors at irregular intervals, but Wyn carefully found the spot on all four rings that caused an extra scrape and click as it passed. Her knees were aching, the back of her dress now plastered to her skin with sweat instead of gutter water, but the bands were set. Wyn wiped hair out of her face with the back of her hand and reached for the handles.

They would not turn. Wyn tugged on them, but she might as well have been gripping an iron bar. "Shit!" she spat. She yanked harder on the handles, to no effect.

"Wyn, quiet!" Desmond hissed from the window, where he had taken up station, peering through a crack in the drapes.

Wyn glared at Desmond, though she doubted he could see her face in the gloom. *Why won't the handles turn?* she wondered. She spun the first band and frowned. *Wait… it's not clicking in the same place as before…* Wyn checked the other dials. Only the last still clicked in the place she had left it.

*Fuck,* she thought.

"Fuck," Desmond whispered. "The carriages are lining up in the driveway."

"How many?"

"Loads… all the way out to the street."

"Martyr's tears, it's not midnight already?"

"I don't know…" Desmond replied. "Can't hear the bells with all that music going on. People are leaving, though."

"Damn it," Wyn muttered. It would take time for the guests to truly begin departing, but the tide had started.

THE THIEF'S TALE

"Might be a good time to open that vault," Desmond suggested helpfully.

"Right," Wyn agreed. *All right... the right number moved. When did it move?* She positioned the outer band correctly, then the second. But when she returned to the first, it no longer clicked, and finding the new position made the second band lose its spot.

"Uhhh," Wyn groaned and sank back on her heels. "The order matters."

"So?"

"So, this will take all night," Wyn sighed.

"Why?"

"Because the order matters. There must be thousands of combinations."

"Ah, no..." Desmond disagreed warily. "There's four dials, right? That's, what, twenty-four different sequences?"

"What? No..." Wyn frowned. "Even if that's true, that's still going to take a long time, twenty-four."

"Only if it's the last one you try. You've already done one, anyway. It's not too hard."

"Maker, stop saying that," Wyn begged.

"You can do it, Wyn."

*I can do it,* she tried to persuade herself. She raised onto her throbbing knees again and started with the second ring. "Help me remember which orders I've done."

The bands blurred around, their soft clicking pulsing in her ear as her fingertips nudged them back and forth, searching for the subtle difference that gave away the correct position. Starting with the second was no good, nor starting with the third, nor fourth.

"Not many carriages left," Desmond warned from the window.

*Something easy to remember,* Wyn thought desperately. *She must do this all the time.* Backward from the fourth yielded nothing. *Too easy,* Wyn cursed. *Outside in?* The bands crept slowly around. *No, shit on it... inside out?*

"There's Fergus," Desmond whispered. "Waiting on a carriage in the drive. He looks cold."

THE THIEF'S TALE

"Got it!" Wyn hissed in triumph. "Two, three, one, four... they're all still in place!"

Desmond hurried to her side. "Open it..."

Wyn grasped the top handles and twisted. They turned smoothly, and Wyn heard a dull metallic clunk from two edges of the door. The second pair turned just as readily, and the door swung open silently, revealing a steel-lined closet filled with shelves.

Desmond stepped inside while Wyn investigated the back of the door, overwhelmed by the intricate gears and levers that were revealed.

"Parchment... coin... more parchment... Maker, look at the size of this emerald..." Desmond's voice muttered ceaselessly as he searched the shelves in the vault. "Ahhh..." He held up a small, wooden box with a seven-pointed star on its lid.

"Come on, then..." Wyn urged, her turn to pester and prod.

Desmond hurried to the desk and set the box next to the two smaller boxes he had carried in his coat. The lid to the star box popped open at a push of its latch, and Desmond stared into it, his eyes wide.

"Ohhh..." he groaned. "What...?"

Wyn peered over his arm. Inside the box, a key nestled in a bed of red velvet, but its shape was very different from any key she had encountered. Its shaft was as thick as her finger and covered in intricate ridges and symbols, from base to tip. The shaft was hollow, and many of the symbols were gaps that led into the dark interior. Desmond picked up the key and turned it back and forth. The end of the shaft was open, and when Wyn peeked down it, she could see a forest of small tines inside the cylinder, poking inward down its entire length.

"What am I meant to do with this?" Desmond muttered.

Wyn pushed one of the small boxes toward him. "Make an impression, and quick."

"An impression?" Desmond shook his head. "Wyn, an impression won't catch all of this... do you even see the insides? How can I make a copy?"

"It doesn't matter," Wyn said firmly. "Get as good a one as you can of the outside, that's all we need."

THE THIEF'S TALE

"What? What good is a copy of the outside?" Desmond complained. "It won't work without the inside."

"I know." Wyn opened one of Desmond's small boxes. It unfolded flat, revealing it contained flawless squares of soft, smooth wax in each half. "Just do it, Des… I promise I'll explain when we have time."

"All right," Desmond muttered. "But I'll need more than two molds…" He searched his pockets and drew out two additional slim, wax-filled boxes. "Always carry spares," he grinned.

Wyn paced the floor, peering anxiously through the drapes at the end of each leg. Only a few carriages remained in the driveway, and she quickly found Fergus, dressed in a beautiful green jacket and black cloak, huddled on the driver's bench of the one closest to the gates.

Wyn strode to the desk and stared at Desmond, her arms crossed. Desmond's fingers were fast and certain in their movements as he pressed the key into the wax, first one way, then the next, careful to capture each side of the key. The first box went back into his pocket, filled with impressions, then the second. The third he used to capture the end of the shaft and both sides of the head, pressing the blazing star into the soft wax.

"There, done," he whispered, tucking the third and fourth boxes into his coat, the key back into its own box.

Desmond replaced the box on its shelf and Wyn eased the door closed, set the dials back to their initial numbers, then closed and locked the outer door. The false panel clicked back into place, and they were ready to go.

Wyn let Desmond do the heavy heaving on the door this time, just enough to create the slightest of cracks for Wyn to peer through while she waited for Pinhead and Hairy Hands to turn their backs. Then she threw herself against the door as well, and together they wrestled it open wide enough to squeeze through and pad down the hallway to the small door that led to the servant's stair.

"Right, off you go," Wyn whispered to Desmond. "Left at the bottom, and then left again at the end of the hall, and you're back in the ballroom." Wyn passed him her knife and wallet, and he secreted them in his pockets.

THE THIEF'S TALE

"See you soon... Martyr, Wyn, look at your dress," Desmond gasped.

Wyn frowned and looked down. What had been uncomfortable, clinging damp in the dark study was now revealed to be a glistening stain of green sludge and black water from the gutter, smeared across her stomach and chest. Her stockings were as bad, or perhaps worse, as one foot had torn and Wyn's toe was poking through, its dirt-encrusted nail frowning at her.

Something freezing and wet squeezed onto the cringing skin of her stomach and slid downward as she yanked on the sodden cloth of her dress.

"Uhhh," Wyn moaned. "Disgusting... uhhh!"

"Wyn, shhh!"

"Marvelous." Wyn stuck her tongue out. "I've got slime in my knickers. Do you think someone might notice this?"

"Seems likely."

"There's cloaks by the back door..." Wyn chewed her lip as she thought it through. *Cloaks aren't much good if I can't get to them without being seen...* Wyn sighed. There were few choices outside of stealing some clothes, and she wanted to escape the mansion as quickly as possible, not rummage through wardrobes upstairs.

Wyn grabbed a small candelabra from a narrow table against the wall and held it clutched in front of her, its gleaming tines catching the light and, hopefully, the eye. "What do you think? Just another maid hurrying off to polish something?"

Desmond frowned as he eyed her critically. "I wouldn't hang about chatting."

"Not the plan," Wyn agreed.

"Look, I..." Desmond hesitated.

"I'll see you outside," Wyn told him.

"Yeah," Desmond said. "Good luck."

Wyn opened the door to the stairs and urged him through, then closed it on him with a sigh. *Martyr's tears,* she groaned. *Could I have looked more stupid in front of him? Stuck in a horrible dress, didn't notice there was no lock on the door, covered in muck... at least I managed to get the vault open, so I wasn't a total disaster.* She shook her head. *It'll be months before they stop teasing, I know it.*

THE THIEF'S TALE

Cold wetness trickled over her hip, and Wyn decided she had given Desmond enough of a head start. She slipped down the stairs and plunged into the chaos of the servants' quarters, twisting and dodging the hurrying figures as they raced to restore the house so they could snatch a few hours of sleep before rising to start the daily routine.

A row of scullery maids labored at steaming sinks, while a dozen footmen strode through the doors with an endless supply of dishes and crystal balanced in mountains on trays. The butler directed another stream of footmen returning bottles to the cellar and silver to the pantry, carefully counting each item into a heavy book. Housemaids hurried through the crowd carrying linens to the washing room, then raced back upstairs to attend to cleaning.

All under the stern eye of Mistress Callaghan. Wyn ducked through a doorway to avoid her glare, smiled hesitantly at the two young men polishing silver in the small room she had entered, then slipped out the other side before they could respond.

No one had time to notice her dress or her torn stockings yet, but she was terrified someone would chuck her into the kitchen to wash dishes for the rest of the night. She traded her candlestick for a large, empty bucket snatched from a cleaning cupboard, held it prominently in front of her, and sped down the hallway as fast as she could weave between the other servants.

The door to the cloakroom loomed open on her right, and she ducked inside. Without pausing, she snatched a hooded cloak and wrapped it around her shoulders as she plunged through the door.

The night air was shocking after the sweltering heat of the kitchens. Her feet burned against the cobbles, and a snowflake stung her cheek. Wyn shivered and muttered curses under her breath. They steamed into the frozen air in a cloud of vapor that swirled around her hood as she strode quickly across the yard. A chill breeze gusted beneath her cloak and found a thousand new paths into her clothes that had never been available when she wore trousers.

Two footmen in matching long black coats and white gloves trotted across the yard and into the mansion without glancing at Wyn. She took a final breath of air deep into her lungs, raised her

THE THIEF'S TALE

chin, pasted a cheerful smile on her lips, and hurried across the last stretch of snow-covered cobbles and out the gate. The blackberries watched her pass without a word, sullenly stamping their feet and beating their arms.

Wyn reached the end of the lane and skidded as she tried to step between the stone pillars that marked its exit, her stockinged feet numb in crusted slush. She steadied herself against the post, cursed, and walked cautiously down the street.

She shivered and pulled the cloak tighter, but that didn't help the ache that was rapidly creeping up her legs. It felt as if her bones were freezing, and her breathing became a steady flow of panted curses through trembling lips.

A high-muckity carriage rumbled past, drawn by two shining black horses clopping easily along the avenue. The carriage's wheels sprayed muck over Wyn's feet as it passed, stinging her skin so that she hopped slowly from one foot to the other, her teeth bared in pain.

Another carriage approached and she pressed against the high wall of a manor, anxious to avoid being splattered with more slush. But the carriage drew to a halt next to her and the door was flung open.

"Wyn, get in before you freeze," Fergus urged from the driver's seat, and Desmond leaped out and helped her stagger into the carriage.

"Here." He offered her a blanket as the carriage lurched forward. "You must be frozen."

"It's a bit nippy," Wyn stammered through chattering teeth. "Can you check if I still have both my feet?"

Desmond bent and tucked the blanket more securely around her legs, then suddenly froze. "Shit."

"What?" Wyn asked, her breath catching.

"I think my trousers just ripped."

THE THIEF'S TALE

## CHAPTER EIGHT

# Butcher's

**W**yn wrenched herself upright and sat gasping for breath in her cot, reaching for her mother's hand. She stared wild-eyed at her small cell, for a moment unable to recognize the shadowed shapes that surrounded her.

Then she groaned and curled forward, her elbows on her knees, her face in her hands.

She remained that way as the chill air began to bite at her skin. Her shoulders slumped and she dropped her hands into her lap. Burning sparks stabbed into her left hand with each heartbeat, and she shook her fingers gingerly to try and get the feeling back.

"Damn it..." she muttered, and with a groan, she sank back on the cot and pulled her blanket to her chin.

She listened intently to the darkened loft, straining to hear if her dream had woken anyone else. Mellon's rooting snores seemed undisturbed, but there was never any sound from Fergus's cell, and Desmond was a quiet sleeper as well. Wyn wondered if she had whimpered or muttered in her sleep, or, most humiliating of all, cried out.

*I'm certain they'll let me know in the morning,* she decided grimly.

She gave her hand one last shake as the needles faded away, then curled her knees to her chest beneath her blanket and stared at the wall behind her cot, her mind whirling endlessly despite the weary sting of her eyes. She was too cold to sleep, too warm to get up and steal a blanket from one of the lads, too sleepy to bring order to her musing, and too anxious to calm her thoughts.

She thrashed onto her other side and slammed her head into her pillow a few times before curling up, again.

*Martyr's tears, what is the matter with me?*

*Well, where do I begin? Loud, rude, and skinny as a twig.*

*Thanks, you're a real bitch.*

*Oh, I almost forgot that you're the idiot that didn't notice there was no lock on the door and rolled around in the filthy gutter until you looked like a pig.*

*Yeah, let's not forget those things, well done, you. Anything else?*

*Well, since you ask… pretty certain it was you flashing your leg at Des. How terrible do you think you looked? Groping in your stockings with your dress all hiked up?*

*Ohhh, Maker, yes, thanks, again.*

*By the way, you're a fucking idiot if you think he cares about getting a gawk at your scrawny leg.*

*I know,* Wyn sighed and clutched the blanket tightly. *I just wish someone did.*

*Martyr, could you be more pathetic, you stupid girl!* she shrieked soundlessly. She forced her thoughts to an image of a room full of locked boxes exploding open to reveal piles of gold talens, but even such a vision did not have its usual, calming effect on her.

Wyn watched Desmond very closely the next day, but he let slip no incriminating smile nor gave any sly glance, so she decided that he was not going to casually reveal her humiliations from the night before. More likely he was plotting the perfect time, when her shame would be greatest. *I'll be ready,* she promised his cheerful face.

THE THIEF'S TALE

Fortunately, she was given no time to reminisce on the previous night, as it seemed certain that Ratter would soon be searching them out if they did not come to him first. And Mellon was not about to face Ratter empty handed without understanding what, exactly, Quinn had dumped on them.

"I've seen symbols like that, before," Mellon sighed, staring at the open wax tablets on the table in the loft. "Those're Artificer's symbols."

"What, like, the Guild?" Wyn asked.

Mellon nodded. "Exactly like the Guild."

"Marvelous," Desmond groaned.

"The *Guild* Guild?" Wyn frowned, baffled.

"That's the one," Mellon agreed, glaring at the wax impression.

"That means it's a Device, I suppose?" Desmond asked.

"Do I look like a bloody grandmaster?" Mellon snarled. He pushed the wax tablet across the table, as far away as he could reach. "I'm just saying that's their symbols, sure as death."

"So…" Wyn chewed her lip thoughtfully. "The actual Guild?"

"Yes, Whinny, the real, actual, proper Guild of Artificers. The. Guild."

"Oh." She brushed a tickling strand of hair out of her face and tucked it behind her ear. "That Guild."

Fergus snorted, but the other two did not seem to find any humor in the situation.

"That's the plan ruined, then," Desmond grumbled. "I can't forge a Device, so we've got no key to give to Quinn."

"It was a good plan," Wyn offered. "And I didn't see anyone else jumping in with how to get a key to Quinn without Spicer noticing it was gone."

"It was a good plan," Mellon agreed. "Just we weren't told everything we needed to know."

"What if we explained to Ratter what happened…" Desmond tried.

"What, explain to him we were planning on giving him a copy instead of the original? I'm sure he'll be very understanding."

"No… perhaps not."

THE THIEF'S TALE

"No…" Wyn said slowly. "But… Des, you could make a key that looks like the real one, right? Using those?" She pointed vaguely at the wax tablets on the table.

"The insides will be different."

"But it will be the same, on the outside? As far as anyone looking at it."

"Yes. It will take a while, copying something as intricate as that, but I don't see why not."

"How long's a while?"

"A day or two. I'll need a blank key the right shape to start with."

"Perfect." Wyn beamed. "You get started on that, as soon as you can, and we explain to Ratter this is the real plan."

"What is?" Mellon asked, frowning in puzzlement.

"That the forgery's for Spicer, not Quinn. 'Course, we'll have to break back in and steal it for real, swap it for the forgery once Des is finished, but unless you have a better idea…?"

Mellon grinned crookedly. "Shit, that might work, luv. It's mad, of course, but at least this time we'll know where the key's kept, and how it's guarded. Not too hard."

"Everyone needs to stop saying that," Wyn muttered.

"Except, if it is a Device, the forgery won't function. Spicer might notice that." Mellon's grin vanished as quickly as it had appeared. "We'll need to find that out before we do anything else."

"Who can tell us if it's a Device?"

Mellon and Desmond glanced at each other, then said in unison, "Tillings."

The jeweler shuffled around his counter on small, careful steps, stooped as if he still sat hunched over his workbench. Thin white hair wafted from his skull in every direction and spiked from his eyebrows, and white bristles gleamed on the sagging skin of his round face.

"Mellon, is that you?"

THE THIEF'S TALE

"It is, indeed, Master Tillings, it is indeed."

"Well I never did… I thought you would be in prison by now."

"Not for lack of trying, Master Tillings."

"Well, come in, come in," Tillings murmured, waving one arm aimlessly in welcome.

The Tallywags carefully entered the shop, easing between workbenches covered in bits of metalwork surrounded by delicate instruments and tools. Fergus closed the door behind them and leaned on it while the other three approached the tiny jeweler.

"Good, good, oh, Desmond, wonderful to see you." The old man's blue eyes darted to Wyn, bright and twinkling, but almost lost amidst puffy eyelids. "And who is this?"

"This is our friend, Wyn," Desmond replied, and Wyn tried out Cara's curtsey on the old man.

"Good morning, Master Tillings, Des has told me ever so much about you from when he was your apprentice."

"Has he?" Tillings beamed, his sad eyes sparkling. "He was very gifted. A shame he gave it up."

"I still make jewelry, Master Tillings," Desmond objected.

"Well, I am glad to hear it. I must say, I was not entirely thrilled when Mellon suggested I take you on, but by the end of the year, I was very sorry to see you go."

"Thank you, Master Tillings. I was, too."

"Now then, as pleased as I am to see you, I assume this reunion has some business at its core?"

"Yes," Mellon agreed. "We've come across something that looks as if it might be your specialty, so to speak."

"An interesting alloy? Or intriguing craftsmanship?"

"Your… other specialty."

"Oh." Tillings' eyes darted between the three Tallywags. "I would rather not—"

"We didn't bring anything here," Mellon assured him. "Just an impression to look at."

"Well… Mellon, you know I am always anxious to help you, but I really would prefer to avoid any, ah, entanglements, that might gain me any attention from… them."

THE THIEF'S TALE

"We know, Master Tillings," Desmond assured him. "But you're the only one with the expertise. Could you not have just a quick look at the markings? See what you think?"

"Well, I suppose a quick peek," Tillings murmured. "Here, we will use this workbench." The bench held a tall stand with a dozen reading lenses hovering over it on jointed arms, and a sheet of black cloth which was quickly cleared of the silver rings he had been working on. Desmond produced one of his slim, wooden boxes from his coat and set it reverently in the center of the cloth.

Tillings opened the box and peered at the wax imprints through one of the lenses. "Oh, dear me," he muttered. "Dear, dear, dear."

"Good news, then?" Mellon asked.

"Well, this is certainly their work."

"The Guild, you mean?" Wyn asked.

Tillings raised his gaze to Wyn and examined her, and the friendly sparkle in his eyes had turned hard and cold.

"Yes, my dear, the work of the Guild of Artificers." Tillings swung several of the hinged arms over the workbench and aligned them above the wax. He squinted through first one and then another of the lenses, adjusting their height with a gentle twist of the tiny screws that held them in place.

"It's a Device, then?" Mellon asked.

"Yessss," Tillings replied absently as he examined the intricate patterns. "You can see the focus, right here, and a secondary declension along here, and this..." The tip of his tongue appeared between his lips, wagging back and forth as he frowned at the wax. "... I am not certain... some kind of reciprocal flow? I've not seen work like this before."

"But what does it do?" Wyn asked.

"I have no idea."

"You don't? But you can see all the little... parts... and the restful flow... and such."

"Yes, but the critical areas are not visible."

"Master Tillings, we've got left, right, top, bottom, right here. What more do you need?" Mellon asked.

THE THIEF'S TALE

"I would need to investigate the internal components," Tillings replied. "And even then, I very much doubt I can help you. This is sublime work, far beyond me."

"I thought you were the grandmaster of that place," Mellon said reassuringly.

"Hardly… a simple apprentice, and not one destined for greatness, despite my skills with metal. Even had I not made my, ah, mistake, I doubt I would have earned my master's robes. But that was of no concern. A lifetime of studying amongst the greatest metalsmiths of the world, working on the finest pieces… ah, that would have been a fine life."

"But you've figured out Devices before, I've seen you."

"Simple ones, yes. That I've been able to open and study. This is something different. No, I am afraid the only thing I can tell you is that it is some sort of Diviner, but beyond that…"

"So, it's useless. We can't make a copy."

"That is correct. I would need the original even to replicate the metalwork, and I'd never be able to imbue it. That must happen at the Forge, within the Guild itself, in Criénne."

"Don't you just say the Word, and it works?" Wyn asked.

Tillings shook his head sadly. "Oh, no. The Word of a Device frees the energy within, it does not create the energy. For that, you need the Forge. In any case, I doubt I could ascertain the Word of a Device this complex. You have truly stumbled upon something very rare. Or, at least, it has made an imprint upon you."

Desmond collected his tablet and tucked it securely in his coat. "Thank you, Master Tillings."

"Hmmm?" Tillings asked. "Oh, of course, Desmond." Tillings's brow creased as he glanced between Desmond and Mellon. "Listen, Mellon, I do not wish to know any details, but if you are in possession of this Device, you must take care."

"Oh, no, Master Tillings, we're safe as houses," Mellon assured him.

"Good, excellent," Tillings agreed, but his expression did not alter. "Because I would not doubt the owner of such a Device would be able to find it."

"How do you mean, Master Tillings?"

THE THIEF'S TALE

"There are Diviners that are crafted for just that purpose, to sense the particular resonance of a Device and draw the user to it. And for a Device like this one," he nodded toward Desmond, who had instinctively placed concealing hands over his coat pocket, "of such craftsmanship that it must belong to a puissant adept, I am certain its master would have such a Diviner, and the skill to use it."

"Good thing all we have is wax, then, isn't it," Mellon assured the jeweler.

"An excellent thing," Tillings agreed.

"What sort of, ah... care... would we need to take if we had more than wax?" Wyn asked.

"There is only one way to block a Diviner's gaze, and that is with a Veil."

"Is that a type of Device, too, then?"

"It is," Tillings assured her. "A most potent and subtle type, unlike Weapons or Wards, the ones you hear of most often. Of course, as with any Device, when a Diviner challenges a Veil, the craftsmanship of the Device and the skill of the adept who wields it determines victory."

"Well, it's a good thing it's just wax," Mellon repeated firmly. "We've taken up enough of your time, Master Tillings. Come on, Wyn."

Wyn nodded absently, but she took only one small step toward Mellon at the door. "Does the Guild use normal ways to find stuff?"

"Normal?" Tillings asked.

"Do they hire folks to track down, or, you know, follow people who might be, um... interested... in, uh... Devices?" Wyn finished lamely.

"They do have many agents, of course," Tillings replied nervously. "They are most determined to silence any outsider with knowledge of their secrets. In most cases that means those of us they have declared apostate, those who once studied in the Guild, but who have found themselves, ah... well... found themselves no longer there. But the Guild is also interested in anyone who might be involved in, shall we say, acquiring and redistributing Devices outside of the Guild's purview."

THE THIEF'S TALE

"Then they might have hired folks to follow—"

"Time to go, Wyn," Mellon said firmly.

Mellon was silent as he led the Tallywags through the throng, a heavy frown furrowing his brow. Wyn hurried to keep at his side, biting her tongue for as long as she could stand it.

"So that's it, right?" she blurted.

"What is it?" Mellon asked.

"We're done with this."

"Not at all." Mellon glanced at Wyn. "Why would we be?"

"Are you mad?" Wyn asked, her hands spread wide in helpless astonishment. "Let's see... because they can find the key as soon as we take it?"

"Nellie isn't going to know we took it, remember? She won't know to look."

"She'll have some Diviner, just like Tillings said. Her man, Quany, the adept, he'll have one."

"You said yourself he was a bit of a nonce."

"Well, the Guild master weren't too impressed, but..."

"Wyn, they won't know to look, that's the point. It must be why Quinn's client insisted the job goes down that way. In any case, we're just passing the keys along, so it's no worry to us."

"No worry... you are mad. What about Grey Bastard? He could be a Guild agent, just like Tillings said."

"First this lady is the Hawk, now she's a Guild grandmaster," Mellon laughed.

"You don't know."

"Wyn, I realize you didn't want to do this job, but we're in it now. If you want something to worry about, worry about Quinn."

"I am!"

"Well done," Mellon congratulated her.

Ratter was waiting for them at Scrivener's with a twisted smile.

"Quinn would like a word," Ratter informed Mellon with a sneer.

THE THIEF'S TALE

"We're a bit busy," Mellon replied with impossible aplomb.

"Now," Ratter insisted.

The morning had brought a reprieve from the snow and sleet of previous days, but the bright sun was far too low on the horizon to peek into the deep shadows of the Old City, and the city ached with a hard, spiteful cold under the pale blue sky. Clouds of white breath steamed around their heads as they strode after Ratter, dodging between the bustle of the crowded streets.

The thick stench of livestock announced their arrival in Cowgate, the convoluted expanse of stockyards and slaughterhouses clustered against the city wall at the very bottom of the valley. The cobbled streets rapidly gave way to trampled mud and dung and pools of water laced with scum-ice. The wide square that faced the squat towers of the Cow Gate itself was crowded with wagons laden with freshly butchered meat nudging their way through herds of livestock being driven toward the gaping mouths of the slaughterhouses.

A long building loomed across one side of the square. Four stories high and built with a steeply pitched roof, it towered over its neighbors on either side. The small, pale stones of the building's walls were streaked with black, as centuries of rain had smeared the thick smoke pouring from the building's chimneys against its sides. The building might have looked abandoned if not for the smoke and the flow of traffic through its gates.

A wrought iron brace was riveted into the wall next to the gates, supporting a sign with images of pigs, cows, and sheep, painted bronze to catch the glance of passers-by. The sign read "Southfield Slaughterhouse", but those in Kuray with a more notorious persuasion knew it as Butcher's.

The Tallywags were not ushered through the gates with the other beasts about to be slaughtered, but Wyn felt little relief as Ratter led them to a side door and inside.

A short hall gave access to the massive chamber that dominated the interior of the building. Pens of desperate animals lined the back wall, while the center of the room was dedicated to their slaughter. Long, iron gratings gashed the floor, and stone sluices crossed it, choked with blood and gristle. A cow was chained against the floor, lowing piteously, and as the Tallywags passed it, a lean man with a long axe hacked the cow's head free with three heavy, brutal swings that splattered blood against his smock.

A mangey horse was hitched to the carcass to drag it to the back of the chamber, and Ratter followed it. Here the butchers took over. Low beams slung across the room were laden with iron hooks and the swaying bodies of a dozen pigs and one cow. An army of smocked figures surrounded the carcasses, their long knives flashing as they slit and skinned and sliced. Blood and offal spilled into vats and slowly drained toward vast rendering tubs against the wall, and the stench of death was so overpowering that Wyn gagged behind her raised hand.

Ratter led them beyond the butchers, where a single pig hung from a hook, freshly slaughtered. Quinn stood beside it, his smock and gloves gleaming with fresh blood, a long, curved knife in his hand.

"Here they are," Ratter announced, and Quinn stepped away from his work and silently surveyed the Tallywags.

"Morning," Mellon rasped. He gazed around the slaughterhouse nonchalantly, his mouth pursed. "Business is good?"

"Where have you been, Mellon?" Quinn asked. "I expected a visit from you, gift in hand."

"Did you?" Mellon replied, apparently astonished by the news. "Why?"

Quinn stared at Mellon, his eyelids heavy, his gaze almost disinterested. "Where's the sun key?"

"Oh!" Mellon gasped. He smiled widely. "Oh, you thought... no, the other night wasn't to nick the key, it was to find it and get a look at it, that's all."

"Why?"

"Well, so we could make the copy for when we do nick it. Weren't we supposed to make it so little Nellie never realizes her precious key's been stolen?"

Quinn's thick lips twisted slightly as he absorbed Mellon's story, and Wyn forced herself to appear more concerned about the smell than the image of her own body swinging from the hooks at the back of the room.

THE THIEF'S TALE

"It'll take us a day or so to make, then we'll do the swap," Mellon continued smoothly.

Quinn glanced at the knife in his hand, as if deciding where he wanted to stick it. He turned to the pig and began to carefully slice into its shoulder. "You have used almost half your time, and you don't have the first key, yet."

"No, not yet," Mellon allowed, "but while we are discussing the schedule, let's talk about the fact that there's a bit more to these keys than we were told, which raises problems that we couldn't have accounted for. Not to mention we haven't been told anything about the second mark, so it's not as if we could have gotten started planning for the moon key, anyways."

"If you'd finished the first job, you wouldn't have to worry about having time for the second," Ratter sneered.

"That's all well and good to say now, isn't it, but I don't think you're listening, Ratter." Mellon's smile barely lifted his lips and got nowhere near his eyes. "These aren't simple keys, are they? Seems you might have mentioned they were Guild Devices."

"You're being paid to steal two keys. Why all the whining? Nothing's changed."

"Because," Mellon explained, "everything's changed. Do you not think they might notice when it stops bloody working?"

"They won't notice," Quinn assured him.

"Won't they?"

"No."

"How's that, then?"

"Because neither of them knows the Word for their key, that's why."

"Told you that, themselves, did they?" Wyn scoffed, then held her breath in terror, swearing to sew her lips closed to teach her mouth a lesson.

"Never you fucking mind. That's for others to worry about. You get on with your part of it."

"We are, no worries," Mellon said soothingly.

Quinn paused in his butchery to stare coldly at Mellon for a long, silent moment, and then he motioned briefly with his hand to someone at the far end of the chamber.

THE THIEF'S TALE

The sound of heavy boots assembling behind her made Wyn risk a glance over her shoulder and immediately wish she had not. A half-dozen brutes had gathered amongst the hanging carcasses, waiting wordlessly, and in their center were Chuckles and Stench.

Quinn's gaze flickered over his thugs for a moment, then he buried his knife in the pig and beckoned with his finger. Chuckles and Stench stepped around the Tallywags, glaring at Wyn the entire way.

"Is that her?" Quinn asked.

"That's the bitch," Stench assured him. "That's the one."

Wyn swallowed heavily against the pressure that threatened to close her throat. Her eyes darted to the grimy shadows in the corners of the abattoir, but they were a long way away.

"I hear you had a nice tumble with the lads, here," Ratter told her.

"I don't know what…" Mellon tried, glancing between Wyn and Ratter.

"They were going to beat on a little girl," Wyn told Ratter. "Just a wee bairn, the bastards."

"And?" Stench sneered.

"And you're a worthless piece of shit," Wyn told him.

"The mouth on her," Stench mocked, and Chuckles cackled in agreement. "You best watch out, little girl, because next time we see you, you're not leaving pretty."

Quinn stepped forward and his fist flashed out in a blur. The punch took Stench under the jaw with a flat crack that sounded like a stone shattering in a freeze. Stench was lifted off his feet by the impact and landed with a thud that sent ripples dancing across the pools of blood.

Wyn gasped in shock and stepped back as Chuckles let out a high-pitched giggle.

Stench curled slowly onto his stomach and tried to lift himself, but Wyn could see his arms trembling, and there was no strength in them.

Quinn glared coldly at the man struggling at his feet. Then he rolled Stench onto his back with his boot. Stench blinked at Quinn in confusion. Blood poured from his mouth in great rivulets, and his head lolled from side to side. Chuckles let out another half-swallowed chortle.

Quinn bent and smashed Stench in the face with another punch, cracking his head off the stone floor and shattering his nose. Stench began to claw at Quinn's thick arms, but Quinn brushed the injured man's hands aside and punched again. Heavy blows rained down on Stench, pulping his face, driving his head into the stone floor. Wyn quickly looked away, but she could still hear bones breaking under the assault.

At last it ended, and Quinn straightened to his full height. He cleaned his knuckles on his smock as he stared at the ring of watchers. Even Chuckles was silent. Then Quinn pointed at Wyn.

"She works for me." He glared around the circle until his gaze fell on Chuckles, who took a step away, his hands jerking up defensively like a puppet on a string. "I need her for a job. You fuck up the job…" His gaze moved from his terrified thugs to Wyn, and then Mellon. "You fuck up the job, you get fucked."

Quinn walked slowly to the pig carcass and pulled his knife free. "Get that shit out of here," he instructed, and his men hurried to gather Stench's corpse and drag it away. Ratter alone, remained, unconcernedly picking grime from under his nails with his knife.

Wyn finally drew breath again. Her hands had covered her mouth in horror, and she could not force them away. She hurt, deep beneath her ribs, as if she had been kicked, as if a snake was coiled inside her. She felt her breath catch again in her throat, and her eyes burned.

"Martyr's tears…" Mellon muttered.

"Don't disappoint me, Mellon," Quinn said flatly.

"We're doing the job," Mellon assured him. "We're doing it. But you still haven't told us anything about the second mark, so we're stuck, there."

"Then you should be happy," Quinn murmured. His knife freed the pig's leg, and he held it to inspect the cut. Satisfied, he turned his gaze on Mellon. "Because he's arriving today."

THE THIEF'S TALE

## CHAPTER NINE

# A Real Device

"That's him." Ratter wiped juice from his chin with the back of his scarred hand and pointed with his half-eaten apple. "Baron Murtagh."

The baron had entered Kuray through Newgate, as far from Cowgate as one could get in Kuray, both geographically and socially, but Wyn could still smell the blood and shit of the slaughterhouses. Its stench pervaded her clothes, her skin, her thoughts, and would not fade. She scowled at Ratter, hoping he choked on the next bite of his apple.

"His lordship rarely comes into town," Ratter continued, oblivious to the hard stares directed his way. "Prefers to stay at Glendon with his horses. But when he comes, he does it proper, don't he?" He sank his sharp, white teeth into the apple with a crisp crunch and chewed slowly as he watched the baron lead a phalanx of cavalry into the city.

Twenty riders accompanied Baron Murtagh. His cropped white hair shone in the weak sun, as bright as fresh snow, and deep lines cracked the wind-burned skin around his eyes and across his smooth shaven cheeks. But despite his age, he was as far from frail as the massive warhorse he rode. He sat tall in his saddle, and he wore his heavy breastplate of thick leather and steel as naturally as a tunic. His coat was padded wool, lined with fur around the collar, and he wore a broad-bladed sword at his hip. His powerful hands held the reins casually, and he joked easily with the rider next to him.

The other riders were as heavily armed as the baron, and behind them came two wagons, driven by more soldiers, their loads covered by canvas tied rigidly into place.

"His lordship don't trust locks and vaults and such." Ratter sneered at Wyn. "Too hard to keep the rats out, in his mind, so he keeps his key safe around his neck."

"You're joking," Desmond groaned.

"You laughing?" Ratter asked. "Then I'm not joking. Wears it on a little chain, he does, so he can feel it pitter pat against his heart."

"How are we supposed to nick a key from a noble, surrounded by knights and soldiers, without him noticing, in a week?" Desmond asked incredulously.

"I haven't heard you squeal like this since I caught you dipping in Cowgate," Ratter said thoughtfully. "I thought you'd grown a cock since then, but I suppose not."

"You were so brave, beating on children," Wyn said sweetly. "We aren't in Cowgate now, are we?" she asked Mellon.

"No, we're not," Mellon agreed.

"Then how about you fuck yourself?" Wyn suggested to Ratter with a bright smile.

Ratter glanced at her as he slowly chewed, and Wyn forced herself to return his stare defiantly, anger and fear churning in her stomach. Her arm twitched, ready to block a blow that came from five years in the past.

Ratter swallowed and chucked the core into the gutter. "At least one of you has a cock," he snorted. "Get those keys, Tallywags, or I'll be reducing that number."

They watched Ratter stride away southward, quickly disappearing into the twists and turns of the street, then Mellon hurried into an alley and was noisily sick between two barrels.

THE THIEF'S TALE

"Well done," Wyn comforted him, patting him awkwardly on the back. "You were amazing, the way you stood up to Quinn at Butcher's."

"Whooo," Mellon gasped. He held on to a barrel, breathing heavily. "Is anyone else preoccupied with the thought of swinging around on the end of an iron hook?"

"Yes," Desmond agreed sourly.

"Me, too," Wyn admitted.

"Well, you didn't sound like you were," Mellon told her. "Poking the rat in his eye as bold as brass."

"That was my mouth." Wyn shrugged helplessly. "It does what it likes while the rest of me shits myself."

"What do you think, Fergus?" Mellon asked as he wiped his mouth on the back of his hand. "Are we getting bloody the next time we go to Butcher's?"

The lanky swordsman shrugged. "They need those keys, but this ends bloody."

"Marvelous," Mellon spat. "Come on, let's scoot before the blackberries do us for vagrancy."

Mellon splurged for a carriage, and they bumped slowly down the valley to the Old City, Wyn's gaze drifting aimlessly out the window. Every surface of the city sparkled in the low, winter sun, dingy stone, warped shingle, and dark slate transformed by frost into a tableau to rival a jeweler's case.

Scrivener's was locked tight when they arrived, despite the late hour, and when they trudged up the stairs, they discovered why the old scribe had suddenly diverged from his utterly predictable schedule.

"Bloody, fucking, noxious hell, they've done our loft," Mellon cursed.

The main room was in shambles, the table turned over, the ancient chairs slashed, even the horrible hard-backed chairs and benches split and smashed. The old stove had been beaten until its pipe was bent and its door twisted loose, and the ashen remains of last night's fire spread across the floor.

Wyn hurried to the bedroom, her heart in her throat, barely noticing that the heavy door to the Wardrobe had been hacked from its frame. She raced to her cell and stared, aghast, at the torn bedding and shattered cot. She lunged forward and fell to her knees, searching desperately under the wreckage with her hands, hurling pieces out of the way.

She found her box cast against the back wall under the remains of her mattress, its contents strewn on the floor. Wyn picked through the torn canvas, splintered wood, and scattered rushes on her knees until she had found every piece that had been in the box. The brush had a new crack in it, but otherwise the contents had escaped harm. *They just chucked it in the corner when they saw it was crap,* she sighed in relief. Even the Queen's knickers were there.

The Wardrobe was not as lucky. Their visitors had not been gentle in their search, and the clothes and gear stored in the Wardrobe had suffered. The choicest pieces were taken. Jewelry, of course, and boots and cloaks, and the money box was ransacked, its lid split open, its contents gone to the last bit.

"Lovely," Mellon sighed, his fists clenched on his hips.

"There's a turd in the big pot," Wyn noticed.

"Well, that's supper sorted, then," Mellon snorted.

"Who shits in a pot?" Wyn wondered.

"Dogs," Mellon decided. "Did they find the stash?"

"No," Fergus answered from beside the stove. He retrieved one of the short, iron bars used to secure the windows and inserted it in a notch in the stove's curled foot. A heave on the bar and the stove twisted easily aside, revealing a small, steel-lined enclosure in the floor. "It's all here, looks like," Fergus reported.

"All right." Mellon picked through the hard-backed chairs until he found one with all its feet and sat on it. Wyn and Desmond righted one of the benches, and Fergus set the table back on its feet, its new wobbles and splinters entirely at home amidst the old ones.

"Let's just think about this a moment," Mellon began. "Quinn packs us off with Ratter and sends his lads here while we're gone to see if we're telling fibs about not having the key. And he doesn't give two shits that we know it's him, does he?"

"Just one," Wyn pointed out.

"That's a fact," Mellon agreed. "But he needs us, he needs us to get those keys, so... does he think we're too frightened by what happened at Butcher's to take offense? To shove back?"

"If he does, he's not far wrong, is he?" Desmond muttered. "How are we going to shove back on Quinn?"

"A fair point, my lad, but there's shoving, then there's shoving, ain't there?"

"What do you mean?"

"Fergus, you said this would end bloody, regardless. Seems like Quinn thinks he can push us around, forever, with no chance of a squeak from us. Do we push back hard?"

Fergus grunted. "We could hire some blades with what we have in the stash, but there's no telling if they would stick once they found it was Quinn we'd hired them to fight. Otherwise, we go for him ourselves, hope he gives us a chance at Butcher's like we had today, maybe I get him before his axe boys get to us."

"Maker, you paint a pretty picture," Mellon grumbled. "Perhaps not that hard? Find the lads that did this here and give them a message?"

"When you draw your blade, you need to be ready to finish it, all the way," Fergus said quietly. "No other way to fight. You ready for that?"

Mellon sighed wearily. "No. I wouldn't mind seeing Quinn's head a little looser on his neck, that's all. Something else, then. So's we're not sitting with our heads on the block waiting for the axe like those poddies at Butcher's."

"If we don't give Quinn the keys, we're for the axe." Wyn ticked off her points on her fingers one at a time. "If we take too long, we're for the axe, and if we do get him the keys and turn them over, I bet we're for the axe, too."

"It does seem likely," Mellon agreed.

"This is a bit, just a bit, mind you, just slightly like *exactly* what I—"

"Whinny, I hope you have something more helpful than 'I told you so.' "

"That's not what I was going to say..." Wyn muttered.

THE THIEF'S TALE

"Happy to hear it. Now, does anyone have any ideas on how we don't get the axe, either before or after we give Quinn his keys?"

The room was silent save for muffled hammering from the wainwright's shop next door.

"No one has an idea?" Mellon frowned. "I thought you were all proper thieves? It's just a job we've got to figure out."

"I do," Desmond said quietly. He glanced at the other Tallywags, with the same small, hesitant smile on the corner of his lips that he wore while he was working. "We need the Hawk."

Mellon scooped up the last trace of egg with a thick piece of bread and popped it in his mouth. He chewed in bliss for a moment, then took a long slurp from his tea and stifled a satisfied burp.

"Well, I approve of your meeting place," he told Wyn.

Mellon adored the Silver Hart, but Wyn was not as taken with it. The drinks were fine. More than fine, she had to admit. But the tavern was a bit too clean, a bit too polished, and a bit too refined for her to ever be completely comfortable.

The tables against the walls were surrounded by high-backed benches, turning each table into a private alcove, deep with shadow, which was Mellon's chief delight with the place. But being tucked away made Wyn feel trapped, and Fergus refused to sit with them, preferring a smaller table in the center of the room from where he could watch who was approaching.

"No sign of your man, though," Mellon groused. "I thought you said he'd be here."

"I said, starting yesterday. I thought he'd be here first thing, as anxious as he was to be quick."

"This was right after you told him to tell the Hawk to fuck off?"

"I was that tired, Mel," Wyn said defensively.

Mellon chuckled and slurped his tea again. "You certain you don't want an egg?"

"No, my tummy's not right," Wyn muttered.

"Ah, well." Mellon sighed contentedly and patted his stomach. "How long shall we wait? Much as I desire a day of leisure, I'm not certain we really have the time."

"I don't know…" Wyn's voice trailed away as Fergus loomed over their table.

"He's here," the swordsman said quietly.

Fergus reclaimed his seat as Dugan approached. The grey-haired shadow slid onto the bench opposite the Tallywags and gave Mellon's plate a hopeful glance.

"Wyn tells me you want to set a meet with your employer," Mellon said without preamble.

"Aye, that's right," Dugan replied easily.

"Who, exactly, would that be?"

"I believe they'd prefer to tell you in person."

"I see. And we can set the time and place?"

"My boss says that's fine. The exact words were, 'yes, whatever, just tell them to stop bleating on about it and be quick.' Although, as I say it, I'm not certain the thought was for me to tell you that flat out. Are you done with that?"

"Enjoy," Mellon told him, and pushed the plate bearing the remains of the thick slab of bread across the table.

"Ta very much," Dugan replied as he tore the bread into chunks and devoured them.

"Well, as Wyn explained to you, we're quite busy at the moment, so I'm not certain when we can meet with your employer."

"That's likely why you were down here waiting for me first thing this morning," Dugan mused. "Because you're that busy and all."

"We're always interested in meeting new people."

Dugan munched contentedly on the dense, brown bread for a moment. "Well, then."

"Tell your employer we'll meet tonight," Mellon replied magnanimously. "Whitetemple. First bell after midnight."

"Tonight it is," Dugan agreed. He shoved the last piece of bread into his mouth and slid free of the table. "I'll see you there."

THE THIEF'S TALE

Wyn watched Dugan depart, then stole Mellon's tea before he looked back.

"Whitetemple?" she asked. "Why there?"

"It'll be nice and empty by then, no one to see us, but lots of Temple priests and knights to come running if there's a fuss. Sounds perfect."

"I suppose. As long as we don't have to listen to a sermon."

"Oh, I hope we don't have to go anywhere near the place."

"But you said…"

"Come on, time to go," Mellon said firmly, and they collected Fergus and pushed toward the door, stopping only to shower a bushel of praise and a small sprig of silver on the publican.

"We'll go if we have to," Mellon continued once they were safely ensconced in the crowd. "But I'd much prefer to meet with her at a time when she wasn't completely ready for us. Just in case she wants to give us a surprise when we arrive."

"All right, but how do you figure we do that? She'll be a bit suspicious if we don't show up."

"No, it will have to be before."

"We don't know who she is or where to find her, and it's a bit late to decide you want me to try to tail Dugan, again."

"No, I didn't want to risk that, not when he's just met with us and likely to be on his guard against such shenanigans. No, I said I hoped, and it's a longshot, but we do have a day. Perhaps we can find her."

"Uh… Baron Murtagh's key isn't going to steal itself."

"Indeed not, but we need a day at least to shadow him and find out his particulars before we can start to plan, and the Padraigs can easily take care of that. While they do, we are free to pursue what leads we can. You never know."

"I might know how to find Cameron," Fergus told them, but he refused to give away any further details.

"I have an idea, too," Wyn informed him archly. "A better one, I'd wager."

"And what, exactly, are you wagering?" Mellon asked.

"Cleaning the dishes."

"We don't have any dishes anymore."

"Oh, yeah. Well, when we get dishes again, I'll clean 'em when it's Fergus's turn."

"I hate to take advantage," Fergus said. "But for dishes… you're on."

The sun shone as sharp as ice, dazzling as it blazed from a thousand crystal sparks on every surface, but somehow all the colder for its light. A cutting wind swirled between the walls of the buildings clustered along the narrow lanes of the Old City, bringing tears to the eyes of the folk caught in its blast, and turning their cheeks as red as apples with its bite.

But the frozen air did nothing to stop the people of Kuray from acting as if the sun's re-appearance meant it was high summer. Hoods were thrown off, cloaks left hanging by the door, and gloves shoved into pockets, all with a careless disregard for the snow lurking in the shadows of the buildings.

Wyn squinted against the sun's glare and a beaming smile lit up her face as she strode down Chandlers Lane. The wind whipped strands of her golden hair across her pink cheeks, but her joy could not be so quickly dampened, and she happily corralled the wayward wisps again and again as they refused to remain tucked behind her ears.

The bell above the Candlemaker's door jangled harshly as Wyn pushed into his shop, and she fairly raced down the narrow steps into the cellar.

"Ah, Wyn," the Candlemaker wheezed. "Always a pleasure to see your filthy boots on my stairs."

"Good to see you, too," Wyn muttered as she checked the soles of her boots, looking for filth. She did not see anything especially suspicious. Just cracked, faded leather.

"What do you have today? General Boone's codpiece? The Martyr's garter?"

"I might have a few bits and bobs." Wyn eased into her usual place behind the chair and leaned against its rigid back.

"Do they grow more appealing with age? Let's see them."

THE THIEF'S TALE

Wyn fished a small bag from her belt and spread the contents on the Candlemaker's table, a ragged jumble of unremarkable jewelry, all that remained of the Wardrobe's once-extensive selection.

"Hmmm," the Candlemaker murmured. His thick fingers pushed and prodded delicately at the small collection, briefly inspecting each piece before flicking it to the side. "What a pile of shit. A penny each, and you're lucky to have it."

"Slow week," Wyn muttered as the Candlemaker drew out a purse and began to stack a few silver coins on the desk.

"Was it?" The Candlemaker paused, a penny poised over the minuscule tower. His eyes narrowed, disappearing further into the shining folds of flesh surrounding them. "Now, that is a surprise."

"How so?"

"I must have been misinformed."

"You must have."

The Candlemaker nodded, placed the last penny on the stack, and carefully scooted it toward Wyn. "Don't bother me until you have something better to offer. Take shit like this to Precious, next time."

"Fair enough, fair enough," Wyn said placatingly. She tapped the little stack of silver with a finger. "Listen, I was wondering… speaking of being… busy…"

"Wyn, you know I love you dearly, but questions cost coin, no exceptions."

Wyn nodded and pushed the silver back across the table. "What do you know about someone called the Hawk?"

"The Hawk?" His lips curled into a sneer. "Fairytales."

"What if I knew what the Hawk looked like?" Wyn held his gaze. "What if I knew what *she* looked like? Would you know something then?"

The Candlemaker frowned and licked his lips, his hands suddenly still on the tabletop. "Much as I would love to regain the pittance I just gave you, I have no idea who that might be."

Wyn glared at him, dug in her pocket and drew out a purse. She stacked silver coins in a second tower one at a time until she had matched the first. "Saw her three nights ago. In Oldtower."

Sweat had broken out on the Candlemaker's pale skin, and he wiped his dome with the stained sleeve of his robes. "No idea," he insisted.

Wyn placed the purse next to the two stacks with an additional clink of metal. "What if I were to drop another pair of knickers on top of that silver. I bet you'd be snout-deep in it faster than—"

"I don't know her!" the Candlemaker bellowed, slapping his meaty hands on the table, upsetting the coin towers. "And if you are half as clever as you think you are, you don't know her either."

Wyn glared at him. *He does know, damn him. He knows the Hawk's a lady, so that means he really does know. And he won't tell me!* "Damn it, this is important! I have to know who she is, or else we could be in real trouble."

"Why on earth should I fuck myself along with you, then? It's hardly my concern."

"What? After all the deals we've brought you?"

"You were paid."

"It's all about the silver, then, is it?"

"Of course. What did you think?" The Candlemaker's lips writhed against each other as if more words were forming, but none came out. His fingers drummed frantically on the tabletop for a moment, then stopped.

Wyn desperately searched for the right words that would convince the Candlemaker to risk helping them. *What would Mellon say? Something cunning… gah, my bloody brain won't do cunning, it barely does words, right now. What would Lady Hawk say? Something hard… 'I'm disappointed,' but she'd make it stick. The Candlemaker doesn't care if I'm disappointed.*

"Speaking of knickers," the Candlemaker mused into the silence. "Had a visit from Faithless Todd."

"Why do you talk to the likes of him?" Wyn scowled.

"People walk in, they talk." He shrugged, massive waves shuddering through his flesh. "I listen."

"What did that bastard want, then?"

"He wanted to buy some information," the Candlemaker wheezed heavily through open lips. "Spread silver across this very

THE THIEF'S TALE

table, brand new crowns, every one, full weight. 'Just a taste,' he said, 'a promise of shares.' "

"A share of what?" Wyn asked, her hand tightening on the table's edge as her breath caught.

"He wanted to know about knickers," he giggled. "Said he's been contacted, been promised, been assured of just reward. Shares for an introduction, a lead. If it pays off with the one that took them, of course."

"What did you say?" Wyn's voice was a thin scratch across her nerves, and she swallowed heavily without effect.

"What did I say?" The fat man gurgled with laughter. "I told old Faithless the Candlemaker doesn't deal in promises and sent him on his way." He coughed wetly and pressed his fingers into his eyes to wipe his tears. When he pulled his hands away, his gaze was as sharp as a knife tip. "If he comes back with gold to match that silver, though…"

"Fuck you," Wyn whispered. "You'd give me up to Faithless?"

"Not Faithless, Wyn. I'd give you up for gold. But you know I love you, so I'm giving you this for free. Someone wants you for them knickers. Someone giving out fresh-minted pennies like they were pebbles to fools like Faithless Todd. So you may want to lay low for a spell, keep your head down, abstain from antics. And that's all you get for free."

Wyn nodded, her heart hammering, her hand clammy against her thigh, salt oozing through her teeth where she had chewed her lip raw. She turned, anxious to flee, but the Candlemaker's wet voice stopped her.

"You've forgot your little purse, dear."

"Keep it," Wyn grated between clenched teeth. "It's no mint of fresh pennies, but perhaps it's enough for a word of warning, should that gold ever arrive."

"That it is," he agreed. "Good luck."

THE THIEF'S TALE

𝕎yn stomped from the Candlemaker's shop in a foul mood, though the source of her disquiet swung like a pendulum between the thought of Faithless Todd's sinister patron and the thought of doing Fergus's dishes.

*I'll find her without you,* Wyn told the Candlemaker. *I did it once, I'll do it again.* She frowned at the crowded streets as she tied to will a shiny black carriage and a tall, white-haired swordsman to pop into existence for her convenient thief, but there was no sign of the Hawk or her guard, despite Wyn's increasingly sincere vows to the Maker concerning her future behavior. Wyn shook her head in disappointment. *I'll find her without you either, then.*

In the end, she decided she would pursue a different source of magic.

*If the Guild can use a Device to find a key, why can't I use one to find the Hawk?* she reasoned, giddy with the vision of herself stepping boldly in front of the Hawk, encircled by coiling dragons made of stars as she told the Hawk something hard, like, *I heard you wanted to speak with me.*

The fact that she did not actually have such a Device did not dismay her, for Wyn was convinced she had a pretty good idea where she might start looking for one.

"Hello, Master Tillings!" Wyn called out, and she gave the old jeweler her brightest smile.

He peered at her over his lens. "I'm afraid I am closed, young lady. You must leave immediately."

"It's me, Master Tillings," Wyn assured him. She took several paces closer. "Wyn, remember? I was here yesterday with…"

Wyn's voice trailed away as her gaze met Tillings's. His eyes were wide with fear, and he shook his head, the barest movement.

"No," he croaked. "Please go." He tried to adjust his lens, but his fingers were trembling so violently that he could not grip the screw.

"Master Tillings, are you all right?" Wyn asked hesitantly. "Do you need help?"

"I'm so sorry," he whispered.

The sound of the street swelled as the door opened behind Wyn, and heavy boots trod on the polished floor. Wyn took a deep breath, restored her smile, and turned.

THE THIEF'S TALE

Master Calixte appraised her, his eyes slits beneath his shaggy brows.

"Hello," Wyn tried. "I wager you're here to find something pretty for the wife. You've come to the right place." She began to stroll casually toward the entrance, careful to keep beyond the Guild master's grabbing range. "All right then, Master Tillings, thanks for everything."

Calixte's robes rustled softly as he raised one hand. A small metal disk attached to a golden chain rested on his outstretched palm. Its face was divided into a dozen rings, each one crafted of a different metal, each one covered in intricate markings fashioned from silver threads that flashed brighter than steel as they caught the sun.

The Guild master whispered softly to the metal disk. Wyn felt a deep thrum resonate in her chest, and the air around the tiny disk pulsed. Bright light leapt upward as if the burnished metal markings were spiraling off its face in long ribbons. Gold and silver and emerald entwined, wrapped around a deep violet hue.

Wyn gasped and stepped back, her hand raised against the glare. A bright ember floated free from the vortex, a tiny dandelion of light that wafted across the jeweler's shop and hovered before Wyn's face. It pulsed gold and yellow, as beautiful as a star, then swooped forward and brushed against her forehead.

Its kiss was warm and gentle, a touch of the sun through dappled shade on a summer day. Wyn blinked in surprise and glanced at Master Calixte, a smile of joy bursting across her lips.

Calixte slowly nodded and smiled as well, but there was no joy in his face, just cold satisfaction, and Wyn felt her smile wither in response.

"So," the Guild master said, his voice a low throb. "You will tell me about the key."

Wyn wrenched a stool from the floor and hurled it in one fluid movement, then raced for the door without waiting to see the result. Calixte swept the flying chair aside with his staff, and it tumbled into a shelf packed with clay jars that shattered in a cascade of colored powders. Wyn hurdled a workbench and darted forward as Calixte's staff struck the floor and the master bellowed a Word of power.

THE THIEF'S TALE

The impact of the Word was no gentle thrum this time. The engraved head of Calixte's staff pulsed as if it were seen through the fiery air of a furnace, and a wave passed through the shop and hammered on Wyn. Metal twisted and wood shattered as the power of the Word tore through them, filling the air with spinning shards as Wyn was hurled across the floor and into the wall with a crash that shook her teeth.

She struggled to rise as a rain of debris pelted her, but the world seemed to twist beneath her, and her boots could find no purchase. She watched, bewildered, as Calixte straightened to his full height, carefully tucked the shining disk into his robes, and strode purposefully toward her, his staff clunking methodically on each step as his boots ground splinters of glass and metal into the wood floor.

Wyn lurched to her feet and tried to run, but her legs seemed to be caught in thick mud. The Guild master's hand grabbed a thick wad of her cloak and yanked her back, and Wyn stumbled against him and clung to his robes to keep her balance.

"Who wants this key?" Calixte demanded, his accent thick with urgency. "Who do you give it to?"

Wyn sagged in his grasp as the ringing in her ears finally began to recede. Her fingers scrabbled across rigid shapes of metal beneath his robes as she struggled to regain her footing. Across the ruined shop, Tillings crawled to his knees behind his shattered workbench. Blood traced a shocking red path through the dust caked to his face.

"What key?" Wyn gasped as she beat uselessly on the master's arm.

Tillings' fingers rooted desperately amongst the debris, then hooked a small ring and pulled two narrow pieces of the wooden floor open on concealed hinges.

"Do not be foolish," Calixte growled. "If I must ask again, you will suffer."

Tillings reached into the hidden compartment and drew out a small, grey object. He set it on the floor, his gaze fixed on Wyn's, and slowly removed his hand. He paused to collect a second object and clutched it to his chest as he lurched to his feet.

THE THIEF'S TALE

"Speak," Calixte insisted. He held Wyn at arm's length and placed the tip of his staff against her chest. "Who wants this key?"

Tillings stretched his arm toward the Guild master, a gold pendant dangling from his clenched fist. His lips moved soundlessly, and then a Word rippled across the store. It was heat to Calixte's thunder, and a fat spark of lightning leapt from Tillings' pendant and arced toward the Guild master.

Calixte staggered as the spark struck his shoulder, and the smell of scorched metal filled the air. Wyn twisted like an eel and was free of his grasp. Calixte spat a curse and whirled to face Tillings, and his staff swung in a terrible arc toward the apostate.

Calixte's Word shook the building as destruction carved a trail that followed the staff. Wyn hurled herself beneath the devastation and tumbled through a shower of ruptured wood and metal. She slid through the debris on one hip and snagged the small, grey object that Tillings had left for her, then dove behind an overturned workbench.

Tillings had crumpled against the wall, his body twisted by the savagery of Calixte's assault. The apostate groaned and pushed himself to his knees but got no farther. Wyn could hear the crunch of Calixte's boots approaching, slow and dreadful, and as the Guild master loomed over Tillings, the apostate desperately snatched his pendant from the floor and raised it once more.

The older man shouted his Word and another bright spark leapt from the amulet. But this time the Guild master replied in kind, and his voice was stronger, a crack of thunder that overwhelmed Tillings' desperate croak. The sizzling mote veered aside and hung in the air beside Calixte, too bright to look at.

Tillings tried again, and again, his voice desperate and thin. Each time Calixte countered, his mouth twisted in a sneer of contempt as he swatted the sparks into an arc above his head.

Tillings sobbed out a final Word and collapsed as the Guild master waved that spark into submission as quickly as he had the first. He placed the tip of his staff against Tillings' chest and pinned the frail jeweler to the floor.

Wyn hurled herself onto his back, her fingers hooked deep into the flesh around his eyes. He staggered and went to a knee as Wyn strained to topple him. Iron fingers wrapped around her wrist and tore her grasp free as she screamed in helpless fury. Calixte shoved her away and her boot caught on an overturned box. Wyn tumbled backward and came to her feet in a rush, poised to fling herself at Calixte.

The Guild master did not give her the chance. Blood poured from long scratches that raked his face as his gaze met hers, and his lip curled in rage as he whispered a command that shook the ground.

The blazing motes of lightning suddenly snapped into motion, slicing through the air toward Wyn like stones from a sling. Wyn dove to the side as the first crackled past her cheek, then twisted and arced over the second, straining to find the third as she curled to meet the floor. Light blazed and scorched the wood beneath her hands as she tumbled and skidded to a stop next to Tillings's crumpled form.

"Come on," Wyn urged the old man desperately. She clutched at his tunic, shocked by how quickly the dark blood stains were spreading through the fabric.

"Run!" he urged her in a broken groan. She glanced at his twisted legs, shattered by the terrible force of Calixte's staff, and understood.

Wyn whirled to her feet, her gaze frantically searching the ruins of the shop for any hope as Calixte towered over her.

The Guild master raised his staff, his gaze fixed on Wyn. She dove over a ruined table in a long arc, snatched a small canvas bag from a strewn pile on the floor, and rolled to her feet in an instant, hurling the bag at Calixte's face as she rose.

Calixte swiped the bag out of the air with his staff, but the bag burst, spraying the Guild master with the fine sand the jeweler used for polishing his wares. Calixte cursed and wiped at his eyes, but Wyn did not give him the time to recover. She sprinted toward the front wall of the store, bounded off the end of a table, curled into a ball, and exploded through the store window into the street.

Wyn twisted, landed heavily, bounced off the side of a wagon, and darted into the crowd. She wove between a line of porters and scrambled into the beckoning entrance of a dark tavern. Voices cried out in surprise and anger as she shoved her way through the patrons and out the kitchen door into a cluttered yard. She hardly slowed as she threw herself at the stone wall of the tavern's neighbor and leapt from a barrel, caught the iron hinge of a shutter, then swung onto the tiled roof with a kick of her slender legs.

Wyn scurried over the crest of the roof and raced onward, hunched over to keep below the roofline, jumping from rooftop to rooftop until she finally slid back to the ground, her heart thundering, a good five buildings between her and any possible pursuit. She joined the crowded street once more, walking briskly with her gaze down. An inattentive cooper unloading his wares donated a new cloak, and Wyn pulled the hood low and tucked her hair securely underneath.

Another hundred paces and she turned again, then again, always heading downhill, until she reached a crowded square packed with wagons and stalls. The market was in full force as each vendor bellowed the quality of their wares at every passerby, dogs and children raced through every gap, and a small army of bards, tumblers, and jugglers plied their various trades.

In the center of the square sat a public well, a statue of seven chortling infants with jars over their shoulders from which streams of water flowed into a waiting trough. Wyn stopped to gulp a handful of the chill water and slowly brought her breathing and pounding heart under control.

Carefully, she withdrew from her pocket the ringed disk of metal she had stolen from Calixte. The brilliant light that had emanated from it was now gone, but its beauty was hardly diminished. The rings of metal were flawless and cunningly fitted together so that each ring could turn independently. The engravings and embossed metal thread were woven together so intricately that Wyn could hardly tell where one figure ended and another began.

Wyn ran her thumb over the face of the disk, feeling the cool brush of the polished surface and the subtle grain of the engravings. A smile curled unnoticed on the corner of her lips as she lost herself in the exotic beauty of the Device. *A real Device,* she breathed softly. Wyn could sense no magic in it now, but she could clearly remember the warm touch of its light against her forehead. *It kissed me,* she decided, her smile becoming a full grin. *I touched real magic.*

But that thought led quickly to the other Devices she had seen that day, and a grim disquiet soon chased away her contentment.

*I wonder if poor Master Tillings is alive?* It did not seem likely. Wyn chewed her lip as she thought back on the jeweler's terrified gaze and his attempted warning. *He knew Calixte was there, he said he was sorry... he knew it was a trap.*

Wyn shook her head and peered at the Device again. *Somehow this little knick-knack knew that I knew about the key. I'd wager coin that's why it kissed me, the little devil. It must be one of those Diviners that Tillings told us about.*

She traced the outer ring with her thumb, feeling the burnished gold slide under her skin. *This is worth more than everything I've ever touched in my whole life put together,* Wyn realized.

With a sigh, Wyn bent over the fountain and quickly shoved the Device into the pipe. It clanged twice as it plummeted into the well and was gone. *Find me now, Master Shithole.*

Only then did Wyn peek at the second item she had taken from Tillings's shop. The small, grey object looked like a plumb weight, a long teardrop of dull metal with a flat bottom. Wyn's fingertip found a row of engraving around its neck, tiny figures that closely resembled the markings on Spicer's key and on the metal disk she had just thrown down the well.

Wyn frowned and looked closer. A faint shimmer caught the engravings and passed, a subtle glow that could almost be believed to be a reflection if Wyn had not been watching closely. A dozen heartbeats later, the shimmer returned, and Wyn felt her breath catch. *It's a Device, too...*

"What does it do?" Desmond asked.

Wyn shrugged. "I dunno."

The grey Device rested in a place of honor on the table in the Tallywags' loft, its soft glow pulsing ice blue in a long, lazy

THE THIEF'S TALE

rhythm. Wyn leaned forward and rested her chin on the backs of her crossed hands as she gazed at the small object, occasionally puffing a strand of hair out of her eyes.

"It's likely about to explode," Mellon muttered darkly, glaring at the Device from the safety of the other side of the table.

"Not a chance," Wyn declared.

"You just said you don't know what it's doing," Desmond pointed out.

"The ones that explode go off in a terrible thunder," Wyn explained. "This one is just being sweet."

Mellon snorted. "You're quite the expert."

"Well, this is my fourth Device today," Wyn said modestly.

"My mistake, Grandmaster." Mellon bowed low. "And you're certain Tillings didn't say anything about it, or there was something you missed?"

"I told you, there wasn't time," Wyn replied, a note of exasperation creeping into her voice. *Fifth time he's asked,* she noted. *On ten I'm making him eat that thing, and we'll see if it makes his head go pop.* "All I know is he wanted me to take it. Gave me a proper stare when he left it for me."

Mellon shook his head. "It must be important. Martyr's tears, he must have said something. Are you certain?"

*Six.* "Yeah."

"I mean, proper certain."

*Seven.* "Proper certain."

"It doesn't seem fair," Desmond said quietly. "Master Tillings never did any harm, just made nice things for people. Now his shop's wrecked and he's probably dead. I wonder how they found him. I wonder how they knew we'd asked him about the keys."

"I think he told them," Wyn said simply.

"What?" Desmond sat back, astonished. "That's a shitty thing to say about someone, especially someone who just lost everything, maybe his life, to help you."

Wyn sighed sadly. "I know. But I don't see another way it fits. He's been hiding from the Guild for, what, thirty years? More? And they suddenly find him the day after we've been by to tell him about finding a key?"

"They could have followed us," Desmond suggested.

Wyn pointed at the entrance of the loft. "If they were onto us, Calixte would have walked through that door right there. No, Calixte knew about the keys, and that someone was looking for them, but he didn't know it was me until I went to Tillings's shop. And Tillings knew Calixte was there even before he came in. I'd wager coin Tillings twisted on us, maybe thought he'd found a way back in to study his lovely metals. But he must have known he'd made a mistake. That's why Tillings tried to warn me. That's why he said he was sorry. That's why he fought against Calixte." Wyn picked the grey Device off the table and held it up. "And that's why he gave us this."

"I agree," Fergus said quietly.

Mellon nodded as well. "That still doesn't explain what that thing does. Do you remember if he left a note or anything next to it?"

*Eight.* "No note."

"I know what it is," Desmond said slowly. "He told us what we would need to hide from the Guild once we had the keys. It's likely the same Device that kept him hidden all these years, but he knew it wasn't any use to him anymore."

"It's his Veil," Wyn agreed, her eyes wide.

Desmond nodded. "It must be."

"Then we're safe," Wyn announced triumphantly. "Master Calixte can't find us."

"If Desmond's right," Mellon pointed out, "and only as long as that thing works. Poor old Tillings wasn't any kind of adept, and he admitted himself he wasn't any kind of grandmaster, either. Remember, he said it came down to who was wielding the Veil and the, uh... the Diviner, and I'd give Calixte the nod, there."

"Well, it's a good thing I chucked Calixte's Diviner down the well."

"The Guild might have more than one Diviner, Wyn," Fergus said quietly.

"Oh, yeah," Wyn agreed glumly. "Well, some Veil is better than no Veil, and Kuray is a big place."

"If it's a Veil," Mellon reminded them. "Maker, Tillings, would it have killed you just to say something? Wyn, when you were getting out, maybe he shouted something after you?"

THE THIEF'S TALE

*Nine.* Wyn took a firmer grip on the tiny, grey Device. "No shouting."

"Mellon," Fergus said firmly. "She's answered. Leave it alone."

Wyn glared at Fergus.

"Fair enough," Mellon grumped. "All right, well, perhaps that's one problem solved, hiding the keys, but we have plenty more problems. For instance, getting the keys."

"And finding the Hawk," Wyn added.

"And finding the Hawk," Mellon agreed wearily. "If she's the Hawk—"

"She's the Hawk," Wyn stated firmly.

"Of course, lass, stubbornness makes it so. If she's the Hawk, there's still no reason to think she'll help us. She might just be looking for a pair of royal knickers to wear." Mellon scratched amongst the scruff coating his neck as he considered Tillings's Device for a moment. "Listen, not a word of any of this to anyone. Not even the Padraigs. If Quinn hears that the Guild of Artificers is on to us, he'll murder us quick as that." Mellon snapped his fingers, the sound harsh and dry. "Dump us in a vat to cover his tracks and find some other poor bastards to nick the keys. Is everyone clear on that?"

Wyn nodded glumly then slowly smiled, an unstoppable, fierce grin that soon had the others gazing at her in confusion.

"You look like you're ready to pounce on a mouse," Mellon observed.

"Not a mouse." Wyn chuckled to herself. "No, it's perfect. Too right we don't tell Quinn. We never tell Quinn. Turn over the keys, sweet as kittens, there you are, luv. Then we find a nice spot to watch Master Calixte pay that bastard a little visit."

Desmond's eyes went wide with sudden understanding, and Mellon grinned to match Wyn.

"Oh, I like that," Mellon crooned. "That's tidy, that is. All we need is to finish this impossible job, while also finding the legendary Hawk, so no worries."

"Oh," Fergus said quietly. "I found the Hawk."

## CHAPTER TEN

# Everyone Smiling

Forge Hill was not much of a hill. Its slight slope was hardly enough to roll an apple down, and only the most observant would notice that the buildings at the peak of the hill could see over the roofs of the buildings at the bottom. But it was an astounding forge.

The length of the main street was crowded, twisted, and filled with smoke and the pounding din of hammers against metal. Wyn and Fergus wound their way through the press of the packed street, squeezing between farmers, merchants, soldiers, tradesmen, nobles, shop keepers… everyone, for everyone needed the services of the blacksmiths who had made Forge Hill their home since long before there was an Old or New City.

The smaller establishments were sometimes little more than a canvas roof over the smith's workshop, while the larger had vast showrooms of cut stone and polished wood with space for a dozen smiths to work in the back, out of sight of the patrons. There were smithies packed with barrels of horseshoes and shovelheads, and forges displaying shining mail and flawless blades. All were throbbing with commerce.

"Maker, it's loud!" Wyn screamed at Fergus, and the thin swordsman nodded his head, his limp hair swaying beside his face.

"… very proud… some cattle," he replied.

"What?"

"Almost as loud as a battle!" he shouted.

"Oh." Wyn nodded and decided she did not want to hear one of those.

Carts and wagons snarled the center of the lane, barely moving despite the unending stream of bellowing and bickering from their drivers. A pack of children dashed back and forth between the patient oxen and mules, pausing only to gawp at the displays of bright steel weapons hung in the shop windows.

A terrible howl snatched Wyn's gaze toward a shop that featured a massive steel cage containing a shrieking troll. Wyn gaped at the creature as it shook the bars. Its hideously long forelimbs were as thick as her thigh and were covered in wiry brown hair matted with filth. The beast was not a very large troll, perhaps only as tall as Wyn when it stood on its short hind legs, but its barrel chest was as big as a donkey's, and its assault on the bars of its cage produced gasps of terror from the crowd gathered to watch.

"Have no fear!" the shopkeeper hollered above the noise. "My steel is more than a match for this brute!" He struck the cage with an iron rod, sending the troll into another paroxysm of rage. It leapt at the bars and began to gnaw on them, and Wyn suddenly noticed that the troll's fearsome tusks had been sawed off, and its long, powerful fingers ended in bloody stumps instead of wicked talons. Wyn scowled at the shop's proprietor and turned away, unable to watch any longer.

The next shop drew an even larger crowd than the troll.

"You'll like this," Fergus assured her, beckoning her to join him on the ridged base of a lamp post for a better view. From that elevation Wyn could see over the heads of the crowd into the small shop. It had a single anvil and workbench, and its only occupant was a tall man with long, iron-colored hair who was dressed in thick leathers. But Wyn's attention was riveted to a metal sculpture of a regal bird of prey perched on the end of the workbench, covered in hundreds of tiny metal feathers that gleamed in the light of the shop's lantern.

As Wyn watched, the smith seized a long blade in a massive pair of tongs and placed it on the bench before the bird. The blade was worn and had a jagged edge, its surface pitted by rust, but it must once have been a mighty weapon, broad and heavy.

The smith closed his eyes and paused dramatically. Then a Word rolled like thunder from his lips. Coats billowed, hoods blew off, and scarves whipped into the air as the crowd gasped in delight. Wyn felt the Word pass through her as if a great bell had struck within her chest, making her sway and clutch at the lamp post for support.

The metal bird slowly spread its wings and lowered its beaked head as if it sensed the blade at its feet. Then fire blazed across its wings in a sheet of light, and the air before it swam and rippled. The sword began to glow with heat, red then yellow then brilliant white, faster than Wyn could think, and its steel gave out a groan as if it were in pain as the glow spread from tang to tip.

Only when the entire length was blazing like a star did the smith begin to work the blade with his hammer, twisting and turning it to pound the impurities away and refresh the edge.

Wyn stared at the bird in awe, mesmerized by its shining feathers and the subtle movement of its neck, and when she finally tore her gaze away she found Fergus waiting patiently for her, an expectant eyebrow raised as he held out a hand to help her hop down from her perch.

"That was absolutely wicked," Wyn gushed. "I love the way his wings move. Did you see his eyes? I think he looked at me. Does that make the sword magic?"

"The smith claims it does, but I doubt that's true. What is true is that Device heats his steel like no other forge, hot and even, and the steel is flawless when he's done."

"It was amazing!" Wyn clutched her hands together and beamed at Fergus. "Did you feel the Word? What kind of Device is a fire bird, anyway?"

"I suppose it's a Weapon," Fergus decided. "If you put it on a wall and pointed it at your enemy, I would say they'd agree with that."

THE THIEF'S TALE

"Ewww," Wyn said, her nose wrinkled in disgust. "You always think of the worst things."

"Unfortunately, I am not the only one," Fergus reminded her, his hand sweeping to encompass the armaments on display around them. "In truth, it would make for an unwieldy Weapon. The Devices made for battle, the proper Weapons, kill faster than heating a man to death."

"Have you seen one? A proper Weapon? Are they all like Calixte's staff?"

"I have."

"And?"

"And?" Fergus sighed. "A moment ago, you wanted nothing to do with the terrible things that happen during war."

"I don't. Not really. Just tell me about the magic."

"It was beautiful, as if its wielder carried the sun in his hand, like an elvhen king from the stories." Fergus shook his head slowly and met Wyn's gaze. "It was the most terrible thing I've ever seen."

"Who was he?"

"A Temple knight, one of their templars."

They walked together without speaking for a while, with Wyn lost in her thoughts and Fergus ensuring she did not become lost in the throng.

"It's not really fair, is it?" Wyn finally asked.

"Weapons? No, they are far from fair."

"No, I mean all of it. Devices. They're so beautiful and special and wonderful, but the Guild keeps them all secret, and only lets just a few people have them, just those that can pay a mountain of gold, or whose grandfather did or whatever. And then, if you can use one, even if you're a complete prat like Quany, everyone kisses your arse and tells you your shit tastes like honey. It's not right. Think of how it would be if they made Devices to help folks who needed the most help?"

"I hear they are challenging to make."

"Pssht, I bet Des could make one. Anyway, difficult or not, they make them, so they could make them for anyone they wanted. They just don't."

"That's true."

THE THIEF'S TALE

"Well, that's my point. It's not fair."

"I agree."

"Well... well, piss on them, the bastards. I'm going to do something about it, steal them all and give them to proper folk."

"Steal all the Devices?"

"As many as I can, what's wrong with that?"

"Nothing, except you can't use a Device unless you know its Word. Do you think the previous owners will give you that while you're stealing their family heirloom?"

"Why aren't you helping, instead of...?" Wyn waved her hand dismissively.

"I am," Fergus stated. "For example, this is where we'll find Cameron." He pointed to a low, brick shop squeezed between its much grander neighbors like a string-bound read on a shelf of leather-bound tomes. Instead of a shingle above the door, the smith had hung a long sword with a brilliant, silver blade that seemed to ripple as the sunlight caught it.

The proprietor had torn away the walls at one side of the shop and replaced them with heavy doors of a cunning design that swung open to reveal the workshop. Two smiths labored at the forge, working a pair of bellows, while a third sat at a nearby bench, tapping gently to etch a finished pommel.

"When Dorcha is crafting a new blade, it is hard to see the smithy for the crowd," Fergus said, his thin lips twisting slightly in disappointment that such a sight was currently unavailable.

"Is she that good?"

"Her blades are simple but very strong." Fergus wrapped his hand around the hilt of his own blade as if longing to draw it.

"Her smithy doesn't look anything special."

"True," Fergus agreed. "Like her blades. She takes few commissions, but those who know her mark hope to be one of those few."

"Is your sword one of hers, then?"

Fergus shook his head slowly, his thumb stroking the pommel. "No. Perhaps when we finish this job I will have enough to commission one." Fergus glanced at Wyn. "To afford one of Dorcha's blades, you must be wealthy. Or work for a wealthy mistress."

THE THIEF'S TALE

"Especially one that might want her man to have a serious blade, eh?"

"That was my hope," Fergus agreed. "From your description of Cameron, I thought he sounded like a man who would frequent Forge Hill, and the smithies that make proper weapons, in particular. Once they had opened this morning, it didn't take long to find the shop doing some work for a man named Cameron."

"That's not bad thinking," Wyn granted. "You might be capable of more than just shitting on all my good ideas."

They settled in to wait, lounging against the wall of the shop opposite. As the shadows of the western buildings touched the eastern side of the lane, Wyn spotted the tall figure of the Hawk's bodyguard striding through the chaos of the street, dressed in a long jacket of brown and gold that reached his calves, a burgundy vest buttoned with shining silver studs, and black trousers.

"There he is," she grunted to Fergus. "That's Cameron."

Fergus watched the man step purposefully through the narrow door to Dorcha's workshop, then he sniffed and glanced at Wyn.

"Ready?"

"Yeah."

They threaded their way between a wagon filled with charcoal and a noble begging a smith to take his commission. A towering clansman with fierce tattoos swirling across his face guarded Dorcha's door, half his head shaved clean and half his head a mess of iron rings and spikes of hair.

Fergus showed him an iron coin with an imprint of tongs crossed with a hammer engraved on it and received a nod granting them leave to enter.

Wyn scurried past the giant and into the shop. The interior was dark and cramped, with a minimum of space set aside for a writing desk and a single stool. Racks displayed Dorcha's work for the handful of customers invited into the crammed room.

A tall woman with steel posture admired a slender blade displayed prominently in the center of the room, and a squat man examined a rack of heavy, bearded axes while tapping at his protruding lip. Fergus led Wyn to an open chest that had a dozen

THE THIEF'S TALE

knives laid out on black velvet, and she bent low to peer at their shining blades.

Cameron stood next to a small woman with pitch-black hair cropped as short as a boy's, who had a pointed chin and a button nose entirely at odds with the stone-hard muscles bulging on her scarred arms and bare shoulders. Cameron held a short blade in his hand, holding it to the light as he turned it back and forth.

"Sterling work, Mistress Dorcha," Cameron announced, his deep voice curling with country vowels.

"Are you certain you won't let me make you a new hilt?" the short woman asked. Wyn was surprised that her voice was lilting and sweet and honeyed with the rich burr of the hinterlands. She had expected to hear a rasping, heavy growl, thick with smoke and steel splinters. "Yours has cracked so many times, I'm surprised the wire still holds it together."

"True, but it fits these mitts of mine," he replied. "Most are too dainty. I'll hang on to it until it's naught but dust."

Cameron passed Dorcha a small purse which the smith tossed unconcernedly into the writing desk, examined the leather and steel sheath the smith had crafted for his new sword, then left the smithy, his deep-set eyes gleaming happily.

Fergus and Wyn followed a dozen steps behind him.

Cameron was an easy man to tail. He stood a head taller than most of the people on the street, and his white beard and fine clothes stood out amongst the drab hues of homespun wool that made up the bulk of the ordinary dress. Cameron strode through the crowded streets and the throng parted naturally around him, and he rarely glanced aside. Wyn was convinced that he was faking his nonchalance to lure any follower into revealing themselves, but she could not find any cohorts lurking around him to spot a tail, nor did he bother with any of the dozens of simple, innocuous ways of forcing a tail into the open.

His long stride quickly took them out of the Old City and into the broad avenues of the New. Wyn half expected him to head toward the grand mansions of Morningside, but instead he turned east into a neighborhood of more modest manors built on quiet, twisting, tree-lined lanes and cul-de-sacs.

THE THIEF'S TALE

The streets were deserted, and Wyn was forced to hang back at a corner while Cameron strode to the fourth house along, stomped up the steps, and let himself through a freshly painted blue door.

Wyn absently brushed strands of hair from her face as she examined the empty street.

"All right, wait here," she told Fergus.

She hurried along the side of the street, her head low, cloak pulled around her shoulders.

The manor with the blue door was tall and narrow, constructed of white stone, with a row of arched windows on the second floor above a balcony, two massive sets of curved windows on either side of the door, and a row of chimneys above its slate tile roof. Two pillars supported a portico over the door, and Wyn glanced at the stone carvings on its face. A small sigil graced the keystone, a simple design of a bird of prey with a fish held firmly in its talons.

Wyn kept walking until she reached the next lane, then circled back to Fergus.

"We need Mellon," she decided. "He knows all this stupid high-muckity bullshit."

"Her name is Lady Cailean," Mellon announced.

"Never heard of her."

"You're not the only one. No one at the Hall of Records recognized her fishy bird, so I spent forever gawping at pages of bloody sigils in this great bastard of a book."

"You've already said you know who she is, so skip ahead past all the moaning," Wyn suggested.

"No sense of drama, this one. Yes, I tracked her down. She's the lady of a little village named Dalby Combe, a few days ride down the river."

"Dalby… never heard of it, neither."

"Book says it's tiny. Lots of sheep."

"Amazing. So, do we go talk with Lady Cailean at her house?"

"She won't be eager to have herself revealed as the Hawk," Fergus cautioned. "Her first thought could easily be to kill us all so that her secret doesn't get out."

"She was the one wanting to talk with me, remember?"

"As the Hawk… not as Lady Cailean," Fergus pointed out.

"Well, I suppose that means we should make sure the discussion happens in a way that killing's not an option," Mellon replied. "Now that we know where her bed's at, I'm certain someone with proper training could devise a way to surprise her with a bit of talking before anyone thinks to draw a blade."

"You want to ambush her… to talk to her?" Fergus asked.

"Seems like the best chance to actually get to the talking, rather than swords and threats. Soon, as it's just gone evening bells and we don't have much time before we're due at Whitetemple. Somewhere she's on her own, or near enough, when she's Lady Cailean, not the Hawk."

In the end, trapping the Hawk was far easier than Wyn would ever have guessed.

Early in the evening, Lady Cailean departed her manor in her carriage, and Desmond parked their own freshly borrowed carriage in a small lane near the King's Road to await her return.

Wyn sank deeper and deeper into the bundle of blankets she had wrapped herself in as their heavy warmth slowly, inexorably pulled her eyelids closed.

She awoke with a start when Mellon kicked her foot.

"Quit snoring, snoozy. Fergus says we're up."

"I don't snore," she mumbled through a yawn.

The carriage creaked as Desmond eased it down the narrow lane, freshly piled snow squeaking under its steel-rimmed wheels. Wyn unwound her blankets as she swayed with the carriage's movement and rubbed at her eyes as the chill air shocked her awake.

THE THIEF'S TALE

She could hear the muffled hoof beats and the creak of springs as another carriage turned toward them from the King's Road.

"Here we go," Desmond called softly from the driver's bench, and the carriage rocked as he snapped the reins and the horses lurched forward. The carriage trundled out of the lane and into the avenue at its base and Desmond immediately hauled in the horses and set the brake, blocking the road completely.

Mellon opened the door and stepped down into the lane, and Wyn followed.

Lady Cailean's carriage had come abruptly to a stop a dozen paces from their own. The horses stamped and snorted steam in the light of the twin lanterns mounted on either side of the driver's seat. The driver tried to coax the team backward, but the Tallywags had chosen their spot well, where a tight turn and an incline worked to make a difficult maneuver almost impossible.

Cameron jumped down from the seat and took a step toward Mellon, his hand sweeping his long coat away from the pommel of his blade.

"Oh, I'd think twice about that," Mellon advised the tall man, and Cameron's eyes flickered to the side, where Fergus materialized out of the shadows, his crossbow held steady on Cameron's chest. "Unless you're intent on having a discussion with the sharp end of that."

For a man on the wrong end of a crossbow held by Fergus, Cameron seemed unconcerned. He slowly moved his hands away from his sides and frowned at Mellon as if irked by an unpleasant smell.

"That's it," Mellon grinned. "Now, we'd like a word with Lady Cailean, if you don't mind."

Cameron stepped to the carriage door, placed himself between Fergus and the opening, and knocked on the polished wood. "It's the Tallywags, my lady," he called in his grave, rumbling voice. "They appear to be... serious."

The window's shutter slid down, and the Hawk leaned forward. Her gaze flickered over Fergus with his crossbow, lingered on Wyn, then came to rest on Mellon. "So they do," she

THE THIEF'S TALE

agreed. "Well then, please join me." The door clicked open and she sat back.

Mellon strolled to the carriage and sprang up the step and in. Wyn followed more slowly, and as she passed Cameron, she glanced up and found his cold, unblinking stare appraising her, so like Fergus's eyes, yet in such a different face, that Wyn found it profoundly disturbing.

The interior of Lady Cailean's carriage was a good deal more comfortable than the Tallywags'. Deep cushions lined the benches, with padded rests to lean against, and there was even a small, covered brazier mounted between the seats that glowed with welcome heat.

The Hawk watched them settle themselves, her gaze so open and direct that Wyn had to stop her hand from tugging on her hood to lower it. *We're the ones in charge, here,* she reminded herself, but it did not feel like that to her, and nor did it feel like that to Lady Cailean, apparently, because the noblewoman looked as calm and at ease as if she were sitting in her drawing room, instead of held up by impromptu highwaymen.

She was dressed for high-muckity society, in an elegant gown with a low-cut bodice and tight corset that made Wyn cringe to think of wearing, tailored from a dark green fabric that shimmered when she moved. Her hair was sculpted into a tower of graceful curls, and long earrings dangled alongside her slender, bare neck, where a slow pulse beat languidly beneath her smooth, fair skin. Wyn was suddenly aware of how shabby her own clothing must seem, with its patches and split seams and frayed hems. She pulled her cloak more firmly around her shoulders and tried to cover the worst of the holes where her wool stockings were bursting through her leather trousers.

"I thought our appointment was for the first bell after midnight?" the noblewoman asked.

"To be honest, I never was much for going to temple," Mellon admitted.

"They told me they saw a young blonde woman walk by the house, this afternoon, and I wondered if it might be you, Wyn. I decided it was impossible you could have found me, and I put it

THE THIEF'S TALE

from my mind. I should have known better, I suppose, than to underestimate the woman who broke into the Royal Apartments."

"Yeah, finding you wasn't near as hard," Wyn replied. "Only took a few days."

"A few days..." Cailean repeated slowly. "Ah, the evening you lost poor Dugan. You followed him, and he led you to me."

"He might not be as good as he thinks he is," Wyn said smugly, but she was taken aback at how quickly Cailean had pieced together the truth. *Careful what you say, you twit.*

"Oh, Dugan is just as good as he thinks he is," she corrected Wyn. "Yet you twisted him around, regardless."

"Speaking of poor Dugan, I believe this is the moment you tell us why you've set your dog to tail our Wyn," Mellon said coldly.

"I have a job for you."

"Why us?"

"After what you accomplished at the Silver Keep, I knew we could help one another. I asked some trusted sources, and they vouched for your skills. More importantly, they vouched for your quality. A discreet, careful crew for a discreet, careful job."

"The Tallywags aren't for hire," Mellon explained patiently. "Why does no one listen?"

"I've heard differently," Cailean replied. The corner of her mouth twisted into a strange half-smile, ferocious and sly at the same time. "I've heard you're working a job for someone right now."

"Have you," Mellon growled. "Well, if that were true, then we'd be a bit too busy to take on another job now, wouldn't we?"

"Not this job."

"And why is that?" Wyn asked.

"Because the job I would like to hire you to do is to obtain two keys for me, without their owners realizing that they are gone, before the end of the week."

Mellon stared at the noblewoman in shocked silence, but Wyn slumped savagely against the cushioned bench and cursed. *I knew she was trouble, just sitting there all pretty pretending to be some useless nob.* Wyn glared at Mellon. *I told you she was the Hawk.*

"You see?" Cailean said matter-of-factly. "No extra work."

THE THIEF'S TALE

"Now, how would you know all about this?" Mellon asked in a low rasp. "Who did you twist?"

"Did you really think a prize this valuable would go unnoticed? That Quinn, of all people, would be the only one who realizes it's there for the taking?"

"I don't know, do I?" Mellon grumbled. "No one tells me anything."

"How do you know we're working for Quinn?" Wyn asked.

"Dugan, of course."

Wyn scowled. "It's a wonder we don't trust you."

"You shouldn't." Cailean reclined against the cushioned bench. "Not yet."

"Listen, if you know Quinn, then you'll know he's not too keen on his partners backing out of deals," Mellon said quietly. "It makes him a bit twitchy, to be honest, and when he twitches, people tend to end up with their brains smashed all over the floor. So if it's all the same to you, thanks very much for the offer, and we'll just say next time, shall we?"

"You don't know my offer," Cailean said reasonably.

"Unless it includes not getting hung on a hook down at Butcher's, it don't compete," Mellon said. He lurched to his feet and reached for the door handle.

The Hawk's eyes narrowed dangerously. "It would certainly include that," she said, her voice suddenly cold.

"How's that?"

"As part of your payment, I would be willing to extricate you from your dealings with Quinn," Cailean replied. "Permanently."

"And what exactly does that mean?" Mellon asked. He turned clumsily and found his seat again.

"Quinn is nothing more than a savage dog, one that may even try to bite me, given time. He has certainly pissed where he should not have, and that encourages other dogs to behave similarly."

"You're saying you'll shed no tears if Quinn gets put down? We'll not argue with you there."

"I am saying I will put him down," Cailean stated calmly.

"And how, exactly, will you do that? Last I checked, he's got dozens of big fuckers surrounding him just waiting to prove how hard they are," Mellon pointed out.

THE THIEF'S TALE

"Quickly and quietly," Cailean replied.

"You're a fool if you think you can off Quinn just like that." Mellon snapped his fingers.

"Yes, just like that."

*I believe her,* Wyn realized. There was steel in Cailean's quiet certainty, and a fierceness to wield it, that reminded Wyn of Fergus when the swordsman spoke of blades. Wyn discovered that she was not afraid of whatever knife hid beneath Cailean's ruffles. She was frightened by how clearly the Hawk's dark eyes seemed to see her, and by the conviction that the noblewoman had already planned for whatever Wyn might say or do or think, a dozen times over.

*She's like Calixte, but she doesn't need a Device to cut you apart.* Wyn suppressed a shiver, but it was not fear that made her skin prickle with cold fire and her heartbeat surge in her throat. It was exhilaration.

*How does she do it?* Wyn wondered. Cailean was dressed in the most useless of gowns, which emphasized her delicate features, her slender form, and the noblewoman should have, to Wyn's mind, looked helpless and weak. Yet she seemed as fierce and mysterious and strong as she had the night Wyn had spied on her meeting with Grey Bastard. *She may not be brutal strong like Quinn, but I'd wager she's just as deadly.*

Wyn realized that she was gazing, enraptured, at Cailean's face, and quickly looked away before she was caught.

"Are you really the Hawk?" Wyn suddenly blurted before she could stop herself.

Cailean's gaze met Wyn's for a long moment. "Heard that the other night, did you? You do have good ears."

"It takes more than calling yourself the Hawk to deal with Quinn," Mellon grumbled.

"I am certain it will," Cailean replied. "Quite a lot more, but I am willing to pay that price, as well as compensate you for the keys. I think you'll agree that's a better offer than you have from Quinn."

"I don't think you understand," Mellon snarled in exasperation. "If Quinn finds out we even talked to you, we're dead. If we were smart, what happens next is you don't get out of this carriage ever again, and we deliver it to Quinn to show him what good little soldiers we are."

"Is that why you brought your crossbow along? Perhaps I do not survive our chat, but that would not help you with Quinn, would it?" Cailean did not flinch away, Wyn had to give her that. She still sat straight and proper on her seat, hands folded in her lap, her chin raised high. But Wyn swore her skin had paled.

"Wouldn't hurt," Mellon smiled fiercely.

"Now *you* are being foolish." Cailean looked disappointed. "You would not walk away smiling from something like that, and you need help to survive what Quinn is going to do to you. We both want the same thing, Mellon. Why don't we help each other?"

"Help each other? Lady, you're the one that's got to make things solid, not us. We're the bloody victims in all this."

"Please," Cailean scoffed. "If you were just victims, we would not be talking."

"I feel very victimized," Mellon assured her.

"You are frightened, and you do not care to have worse visited upon you," Cailean corrected him. "But worse is what is coming for you, and there is nothing you can do to stop Quinn."

"We'll see about that," Mellon promised.

Cailean raised an eyebrow but otherwise did not acknowledge the boast.

"All right then, you kill Quinn off, we don't have him to worry about, you don't have him piddling on your rug." Mellon ran his tongue over his teeth as if tasting the possibilities. "On our side, we leave you with no extra holes. Sounds fair to me."

"Mmmm, not quite." Cailean laughed softly, and Wyn noticed that she had the first traces of lines around the corners of her eyes when she smiled. "There is still something I want. Two somethings. You bring me the keys, I pay, and we end with everyone smiling. The best kind of deal."

*Wonder if Quinn will think so,* Wyn wanted to ask, but she managed to keep her mouth closed, this time.

"And if we say no?" Mellon asked.

"I need those keys." The Hawk was still smiling, but there was nothing pleasant about the curl of her lips, nor the hard gleam

THE THIEF'S TALE

of her eyes. "If you are not going to give them to me, I will need to retrieve them from you."

"Very noble," Wyn said without thinking. "You're no different than Quinn."

"Not at all," Cailean snapped. She glared angrily at Wyn for a moment, a bright flush glowing on her high cheekbones. Wyn fought the urge to flinch away and apologize immediately, but she swallowed the words and held rigid, furious that she had insulted the noblewoman, and furious that she would so instantly cave when confronted. *I shouldn't have said she was like Quinn, but I'm not bloody wrong, either, and she should know that.*

Cailean exhaled slowly, and an icy calm replaced her rage so completely that Wyn wondered if some magic were involved. "You have nothing to fear from me. But if we are not working together, we are competitors, and you may count on those keys being in my hand when the race has run." Cailean glanced down and rearranged her skirts over her lap. "Now, you must decide whether you trust me more than Quinn to have your best interests at heart."

"We'll have a word with our associates, then." Mellon straightened his coat on his narrow shoulders. "While we are pondering your offer, it might be helpful to know what your offer is. The amount for the keys, exactly."

"A gold talen," Cailean replied. "Each."

To his credit, Mellon was able to close his mouth after only a moment, and when he continued, his voice was calm and even. "We'll consider that. See if it stacks up. If we agree, how do we let you know?"

"You know where I live."

"Right you are." Mellon reached for the door handle.

"Mellon," Cailean halted him. "Decide quickly. If I don't hear from you tomorrow, I'll assume the deal is off, and I will make my own arrangements."

"I hear you, Hawk," Mellon acknowledged.

"Good," Cailean said firmly. "Now then, if you will excuse us, Mellon, we ladies want to chat."

"We do?" Wyn asked.

"We do."

THE THIEF'S TALE

Mellon glanced from Wyn to Cailean and back. Wyn raised her eyebrows and shrugged, as confused as he.

"Just you ladies, eh?"

"Just we ladies," Cailean agreed.

Mellon ducked his head and doffed an imaginary hat, then clambered free of the carriage, leaving Wyn sitting awkwardly on the bench with her hands clasped between her thighs.

"Alone at last," Cailean murmured. Her gaze moved slowly over Wyn's face, examining every detail with an unhurried openness that made Wyn squirm and stare at her knees.

"You are younger than I expected," Cailean announced.

"Sorry to disappoint," Wyn muttered.

"On the contrary, I am even more impressed," Cailean assured her. "From everything I have heard about you, I assumed you would be much older. That you have already accomplished so much is astounding."

"Oh," Wyn replied, at a loss. She forced her hands apart, found she had nothing to do with them, and crammed them back into her lap. *Say something,* she begged, but her mouth refused to utter a peep.

"I have been looking for you," Cailean continued, apparently unaware of Wyn's embarrassed silence. "Ever since I heard that someone had broken into Ruric's Tower. Did you really climb it?"

"Yeah." *Say... something... more!* she demanded. "It was... fun." *Brilliant, well done,* Wyn groaned inwardly.

Cailean's eyes narrowed, and she smiled. "I think you mean that."

Wyn felt herself smile in response. "It was, actually."

"I have stood on that balcony." Cailean shook her head in wonder. "All I could think of was how ancient the railing was."

"It was a bit crumbly," Wyn agreed with a grin. "Made the climb a touch exciting, here and there. But you can see forever once you're up there, can't you, like you're a raven." Wyn risked a glance to meet Cailean's gaze. "Or a hawk."

"Like a hawk, just so," Cailean laughed, a bright giggle that took years away from her, and Wyn suddenly realized that the Hawk was nowhere near as old as she pretended to be. She absent-mindedly adjusted one of the sparkling earrings that

THE THIEF'S TALE

dangled against her neck as she gazed at Wyn. "Did you really steal the Queen's undergarments?"

"I did," Wyn admitted, and her smile turned sly. "As it turns out, Her Majesty has quite naughty taste."

"I am sure she does," Cailean murmured, but her attention had suddenly turned away from Wyn, and her smile had disappeared, replaced by cold distance.

*What did I say?* Wyn wondered. "Sorry if that was too much."

"What? No." Cailean shook her head, sending sparks dancing from her earrings, and her gaze returned to the carriage. "Why not a jewel or two instead?"

"Everyone has jewels to nick." Wyn shrugged. "I wanted something of hers."

"Perfect."

"Is that what you wanted to talk about?" Wyn asked, a faint line creasing her forehead. "Knickers?"

"Mmmm, somewhat," Cailean replied. "I said that I wanted to hire the Tallywags, but I really wanted to know more about you, Wyn. Your skills speak for themselves, but they don't tell the entire tale."

"It's not much of a story," Wyn mumbled as she sank as deep into the cushion behind her as she could. "I do all right, I suppose, but I don't have a clue what I'm doing most of the time." Wyn groaned inwardly. *Why did you tell her that?*

"That simply means your instincts are good."

"If you say so."

Cailean gazed at Wyn for a long moment before continuing. "My instincts are good, as well. If you are everything I think you are, I could use your help."

"Mellon said we'd think about it."

"I hope you do. But I meant beyond a single job."

"The Tallywags don't work for others."

"Not the Tallywags, Wyn. Just you."

"What?" Wyn swallowed heavily as her throat tried to strangle her. *Leave them?* "Oh... I couldn't... I mean, we're, you know, a crew."

Cailean laughed brightly. "Crews change all the time!"

"Not us," Wyn insisted.

THE THIEF'S TALE

"If you say so," Cailean agreed easily. "But if you manage to pull this job for me, I'll be asking you again. And you'll say yes, I promise you."

"Why would I say yes?"

"Because you're going to think about it, and you'll realize how much is waiting for you if you do."

"Coin and such?"

"I thought you just said jewels don't matter to you? No, not coin. Everything you deserve."

"And what do I deserve?"

"When the time comes, you'll tell me, and I'll make sure you get it," Cailean promised. She reclined against her cushions and folded her hands elegantly in her lap. "I look forward to hearing what you decide."

"Um, me too." Wyn suddenly realized the conversation was over. She escaped the carriage as quickly as she could, hurried past Cameron without meeting his gaze, and took shelter behind Fergus.

They watched the Hawk's carriage leave, then clambered into their own to return to Scrivener's.

"What did her nibs want?" Mellon asked, once they were safely gliding along the broad avenues of the New City.

"She wanted to know if I really stole the Queen's knickers," Wyn answered. She was not certain why she concealed the rest of her conversation with the Hawk, but she ignored the twinge of guilt that the omission sowed in her stomach. *Mellon has enough to worry about,* she soothed her conscience.

"She want to buy a pair?" Mellon wondered, his eyes suddenly feral. "She's willing to pay a gold talen for a key, I wager she's willing to pay more than the Candlemaker did for some royal undergarments."

"No, she just wanted to know if it were true," Wyn told him.

"Oh," Mellon sighed, disappointment flooding his face. "Just two ladies gossiping, eh?"

"Oy, look who's calling the kettle black," Wyn complained. "You're like a pig in shit every time you go to the Angel."

"Indeed I am," Mellon granted. "I'm just pleased to welcome another pig to the puddle."

THE THIEF'S TALE

"No, thanks," Wyn muttered. "I've had enough talking to high-muckities."

They rode their carriage down the long valley to the Old City in silence, listening to the creak and clunk of the springs as high walls and gardens gave way to crowded streets.

Mellon donated the carriage to the Charioteers for their evening's work and led the Tallywags to the Silver Hart, much to Fergus's disgust.

"The Hart, Mellon?" he asked, frowning, the highest mark of his distemper. "We were just there."

"For breakfast," Mellon pointed out. "Supper is different. And I need a bit of the Hart, tonight, to do some proper thinking. We all do."

They ransacked their pockets and found enough pennies and bits for a pie filled with venison and rabbit and roasted potatoes swimming in gravy, accompanied by a rich wine, heated and simmering with the aroma of spices.

Mellon explained the deal they had been offered to Desmond and Fergus as they ate. Fergus's frown never wavered, but Desmond's eyes lit up hopefully.

"That's perfect, that is," he said when Mellon had finished. "We get rid of the damn things, and she gets rid of Quinn. And we get paid for the job. That's even better than we were hoping for."

"It is," Mellon allowed. "There's just two things to consider, I'd say. First, how to take the deal without leaving ourselves open to getting taken for a ride, and, second, to have a good, hard think about walking away. Because, when a deal is better than expected, and you really have no other option…"

"It's probably too good to be true," Desmond finished sadly. "Do you really think so?"

"I don't know, which is what gnaws at me. I fear we are in deep water with this Lady Cailean. She seemed sincere. Wyn, you were there, too, lass, speak up."

THE THIEF'S TALE

"I believe her, but I don't know why," Wyn replied wearily. "Don't listen to me, I'm that twisted around about her. Every word out of her pretty little mouth could be a lie, but I'd never know."

Mellon nodded. "That's the place to start. Plan as if Cailean is a liar, and that she will bite us as fast as thinking about it. So, the first option... we walk."

"Before we give the keys to Quinn?" Desmond asked. "Then... we hide?"

"No. We can't hide forever. If we're here, Quinn will eventually come for us. We'll need to leave. Hop a carriage tonight, get as far as possible," Mellon said.

"Where would we go?"

"Greymouth?" Mellon replied. "I used to work there. Not a bad place."

"Ugh," Desmond groaned. "Start over."

"What about the Wee Ones?" Wyn asked softly. "The Padraigs? Them and anyone else we're friendly with. We just leave them?"

"We can warn them, but, yes."

"Lord Sly won't protect them once we're gone, you know that."

"Probably not," Mellon agreed.

"Then I'm not leaving," Wyn said firmly. "I'll not run away and abandon them."

"All right, then, Wyn, but we're just figuring options here, not deciding," Mellon soothed her. "Option two..."

"Steel," Fergus said quietly.

"I... very well, let's talk about steel. You said last time that we couldn't trust any brutes we hired to stay the course."

Fergus shook his head slowly. "No brutes. We cut the head off the snake. Tonight."

"How is that?"

"We tell Quinn we want a meet to give him the keys. If he agrees, I take him at the meeting. If he doesn't, I go find him in Butcher's while his lads are coming for us."

"He won't come alone, there'll be a bunch of brutes just waiting to lay into you."

THE THIEF'S TALE

"One thrust is all it takes. I'll figure out how to deal with the rest of them when the time comes."

"That's absolutely daft," Wyn objected. "The whole thing. You'll just go after Quinn in the middle of a dozen bastards who will kill you whether or not you get Quinn?"

"I thought we were discussing options," Fergus replied calmly.

"Proper ones, which means ones that aren't bloody suicide."

"Wyn, there's not going to be an option where there isn't a risk of someone getting bloody," Mellon said softly.

"I'm not helping him kill himself," Wyn snarled. She sank back against the bench and crossed her arms, glaring at Fergus.

"All right, another vote of confidence from the lady," Mellon sighed. "Option three is Wyn's lovely little plan, in which we drop the keys on Quinn, make ourselves scarce, and hope Master Calixte does him in before Quinn decides to tidy us up."

"I like that better than one or two," Desmond said.

"Me, too," Wyn agreed. *Although that would mean no getting everything I deserve from the Hawk. Not that that matters,* she reminded herself.

"But not better than getting two gold talens," Desmond added. "And who's to say the Guild actually goes after Quinn? Maybe Quinn's client has a Veil, maybe Calixte doesn't have another Diviner."

Mellon shrugged. "Maybe Calixte is taking a squat when his knick-knack goes off. It don't seem likely, but there it is. Any other options besides, four, trust Lady Cailean and hope we don't get fucked? No? Then, it's time to decide and start on the details, and we've not much time."

"You know I'm not doing one or two," Wyn insisted. "I say four is worth the risk, though I've already said you shouldn't listen to me."

"I say four, as well," Desmond agreed.

"Fergus?" Mellon asked.

"It doesn't matter, to me."

"Shit on that," Wyn scoffed. "You don't care if we leave our friends, or if you die?"

"I care," Fergus said quietly. "But I care more about keeping you all safe. That's my job. And all four options are going to get bloody, one way or another. It's just about when."

"Then pick the one that is the best, otherwise," Wyn insisted. "And don't say steel. We're not safest with you killing yourself."

Fergus held Wyn's gaze for a moment, and she was certain he was going to say steel. "I'm with them," he answered eventually, to her relief.

"And I'll make it unanimous," Mellon chimed in. "Now... the details."

THE THIEF'S TALE

## CHAPTER ELEVEN

# Baron Murtagh

"It's the one with the black door," Skinny told her, pointing to the row of tall brick townhouses that lined the quiet street.

"The one with the balcony?"

"That's it," Skinny agreed. "Lucky followed him here from the King's Road, and Birdie and Bump played conkers in the garden until they were shooed away, and saw the baron have a peek at them from the back windows."

They pushed their creaky cart a bit closer to the house in question while Wyn trotted up to each door along the path, knocked, and offered their services polishing silver. She made sure to sniff and wipe her nose frequently, and there were no takers.

The house the baron had rented was five floors high, with sweeping windows on the first three floors and a balcony on the third, as well. Its bricks were a sandy color, and the wooden frames of its windows and doors were painted black. Narrow paths ran past it on both sides, deep in shadow from the neighboring buildings even in the middle of the day, leading to a thin, walled garden in the back. The roof was a range of pointed gables and dormer windows, and a forest of iron pipes zig-zagged down the sides from the gutters.

"How many servants?"

"Lucky thinks three. A housekeeper, a cook, and a parlor maid."

"They sleep in?"

"Yeah… the little windows at the top are their rooms. Plus, there's the four soldiers."

"Where's he keep his bloody great horse in that house?"

"There's an alley at the back that leads to a stable at the end. Their horses are there. Two lads mind the horses and gear, and sleep in the stable loft."

"And the baron?"

"Fourth floor. Lucky thinks his bedroom is at the back and his study at the front. Anyway, he's hardly here except to sleep. Left at the dawn bell, or just about, straight to the Keep, then came back around midnight. Lantern on in his study until about two bells, then all dark and quiet."

"He didn't stop anywhere?"

"Don't think so. Not that we saw."

*Well, gives us a little while to nick the key from the house while he's sleeping, but not long.*

"There's a strange tower on the roof," Skinny said, frowning. "A lot of these houses have them… not sure what they are."

"Show me."

They wrestled the cart through the narrow gap between two of the houses and into the alley behind the garden walls. The townhouses seemed even more similar from behind without their different colored doors to tell them apart.

"There, that little, squat tower that looks like a barrel, perched on the roof. They all have them."

"Oh." Wyn scowled, disappointed. "It's a water tank."

"What?"

"It's full of water. Then, when they want some inside, there are these little pipes that let the water out, right into the basin or bath or whatever."

"Oh," Skinny murmured. "That's nice, ain't it? No hauling buckets up the stairs from the kitchen."

THE THIEF'S TALE

Wyn laughed. "Oh, there's still hauling. Servants have to fill the tank, then the high-muckities can have it pour out their little spigots like gold whenever they want it."

"Oh, 'course." Skinny shook his head. "There's no privy in the garden, neither, and I didn't see a night soil cart this morning. Do they really crap gold, do you think?"

"Probably," Wyn decided. "They just squat over their little purses and push out a talen whenever they need it."

Skinny stared quietly at the weeds against the garden wall for a moment. "Bloody said to tell you hello," he informed the thistles. "Red, too."

"Oh," Wyn said, suddenly as interested in the plants as Skinny was.

"Yeah," Skinny added.

"Well, say hello back."

"You can tell Bloody yourself, if you like. She said she'd come to watch the house tonight. Said maybe you'd like to have a drink, afterward?"

"Oh," Wyn repeated. She desperately wanted to see Bloody again, to explain why she had disappeared that night, but she had no idea how to do so. Her mind seemed to be paralyzed with humiliation. "No, I can't wait about tonight," she offered lamely.

"We could go now if you'd like."

"Go where?"

"You know, a tavern. If you're wanting a drink."

"No thanks, I'm fine." Wyn sighed wearily. "Keep watching the baron. We've only got a couple of days, but maybe he'll do something different tomorrow that's better for us."

"I know where Baron Murtagh goes," Mellon announced. He stomped into the room and hurried to the stove, scowled at its twisted, cold pipe, and huddled deeper into his coat. "His lordship spends all day in the Silver Keep closeted with Duke Thornton and a few dozen other lords, going over maps of the Ironbacks and talking about strategy and such forth. I have it from one of the clerks in the Royal scribes that they do this every winter, discussing how to slaughter as many of the Ironback clans as they can, come spring. Apparently, they'll be at it for another two weeks or so, get the King's blessing, then it's off home to sharpen their swords."

"Is that the same clerk who got me into the Silver Keep?" Wyn asked. "Can he do that again? If Baron Murtagh is in there all day, we could pull the job there."

"Yes, it's the same chap, but I'm not certain he can help us this time."

"But it was his lovely Wit of Audience that got me into the Keep."

"Writ," Mellon corrected.

"Is what?"

"It was a Writ of Audience."

"That's what I said." Wyn frowned, puzzled, and slowly wiped tickling strands of her hair out of her face. "What did I say?"

"You said, 'wit', luv."

"Did I?" Wyn snorted. "That was witty."

"Nice one," Mellon agreed. "If the writ hadn't worked, I'd have been bloody annoyed. We paid enough for it."

"I thought your little scribe gave it to you?"

"He did… after I pointed out that I'd bought all of his debt from Scurrilous."

"Oh… that's right." Wyn nodded sagely and pushed her hair out of her face again.

"But he can't just hand over four more. They only give out a few each day, and if you remember last time we had to wait weeks while he finagled a space on the list. How would it look when we four pop up all of a sudden? We'd have to wait, and the baron's only there for two more weeks."

"Well, we don't have two weeks, in any case," Desmond muttered.

"Nor we don't," Mellon agreed. "So, unless any of you have another idea of how to infiltrate His Majesty's War Council, we'll need a plan to take the key outside of the Silver Keep."

THE THIEF'S TALE

"His soldiers look like hard fighters," Fergus said quietly. "Ten-year veterans, all of them. Ten years of fighting the Ironback clans, no less. Two of them with the baron, two at the house, the rest billeted at the Keep."

Mellon shook his head. "Doesn't sound like a robbery I want to be a part of."

Fergus shrugged. "It would be bloody."

"What about the house, then?"

"Not too bad." Wyn rocked back and forth on her seat, her arms crossed tightly across her chest, her knees drawn up to her nose as she tried to ward off the shivers. "Could get in through the roof, easy, but then it's the same nightmare as Spicer's. We've no idea where he keeps the key, except around his neck, which if that's the case even at night, we've got to get into his bedroom. And that house isn't that big, not with one of them soldiers on guard."

"All right, what about on his way to the Keep? Any chance of a simple lift?"

"None." Wyn pouted. "Not unless we can figure out how to get up on his horse with him, and even then… a key on a necklace? That's no laugh."

"Well, that rules out everything," Mellon grumped. "Shall we go and tell Quinn we're through?"

"Can we get the stove fixed?" Wyn asked.

"What's the stove got to do with any of this?"

"It's cold," Wyn pointed out.

"Do you not think we've got a few more important things to try to work out first?"

"No. I'm freezing."

"Me, too," Desmond said, blowing on his fingertips. "I can't really do the fine etching with numb fingers." He nodded forlornly at the half-finished key on the table in front of him.

"Now, that's a proper reason," Mellon declared.

"I can't really pick a lock with all my fingers snapped off from turning to ice," Wyn grumbled.

"I don't think it can be fixed," Fergus said glumly, swinging the stove's creaking door back and forth on its twisted hinges.

THE THIEF'S TALE

"Can we all please stop talking about the stove for just a moment?" Mellon begged.

"What if we banged the pipe back into place and just used it as a fireplace?" Desmond suggested.

"Not worry about the top?" Fergus asked thoughtfully. "What would we cook on?"

"There was a turd in our pot," Wyn reminded them.

"Oh, right…"

"Yeah, no cooking, but we'd be warm."

"Please?" Mellon tried again.

"There's a fireplace on the second floor," Fergus said.

"Oh, yeah!" Desmond perked up. "I forgot about that. It'd be blocked up, though, wouldn't it?"

"Set fire to my bed," Wyn decided. "I don't care, I just want to be warm."

"Please…?"

"Mel, this place is a shambles," Desmond retorted. "They broke everything, and it's freezing. We need to fix it or go someplace else."

"Leave?"

"There was a turd in our pot," Wyn pointed out.

"It's not a bad idea, Mellon," Fergus said softly. "Someplace they can't find us on a whim."

"All right, I can sort something, but, right now, what say we figure out how to take the nice baron's key and not get hung on hooks?"

"Did you know?" Wyn asked. "The house the baron is staying in… it doesn't have a privy."

"What do you mean?" Desmond asked.

"There's no crapper in the garden."

"Oh, it'll be inside."

"No, I thought of that, but there were no chutes in the walls, I checked, and, in any case, the whole street smelled sweet as silver."

"Maker, you're fixated on crap, tonight," Mellon complained.

"A turd, Mel. In our pot."

"He probably just gets the servants to chuck the chamber pots into the night soil cart," Fergus mused.

THE THIEF'S TALE

"No," Desmond said brightly. "No, the sewer is under the house. The privy goes straight into it."

"What?" Wyn frowned.

"They have little holes that go all the way down to a big pipe under the street, and they bung water down the holes to wash it all down. I saw it in a house Tillings took me to when he was hired to do filigree on its mantle."

"Why would you want to keep all your shit under your house?" Wyn asked.

"It all washes away, honest."

"Well I never…" Wyn shook her head, her thoughts racing.

"Hooks? Axes?" Mellon tried hopelessly.

"Oh!" Wyn was so startled she stared at the other Tallywags with her mouth open for a long moment before she could continue. "Oh! That's it!"

"What is?" Mellon asked. "You gave me such a scare. I thought Quinn was behind me with a hook."

"No, no… wait two shakes… I've almost got it… it's coming…"

"Do you need the pot?"

"No, ewww… I think… yeah… so, the baron can't wear the key all the time, can he? What if people knew he was wearing a Device around his neck?"

"That's likely why he keeps his shirt buttoned."

"Yes, but what about when his shirt gets unbuttoned?"

"What's your suggestion?" Mellon grinned. "You volunteering to seduce his lordship with your tender ways? Wear a dress again?"

"I'm not wearing a dress."

"No? Shame."

"Anyway, it's Des's turn."

"I'm not wearing a dress, neither," Desmond said firmly.

"So much for sweeping his lordship off his feet." Mellon sighed. "It was our only hope."

"Not our only hope," Wyn said, her eyes wide.

"I like that look." Mellon grinned back at her and rubbed his hands together. "Whinny has an idea!"

THE THIEF'S TALE

"He'll also take it off when he has a bath, sure as there was shit in our pot."

"But, Wyn, he'll have a bath in that house of his, no doubt. Even we have a tub. We can't just wait for him to decide to have a nice trip to the Bathhouse."

"No, I know. But… we'll need some pig's blood, a cart, a rat, oh, and Fergus, you'll need to have a bath." Wyn laughed and clapped her hands. "Oh, you'll like this!"

"I don't like this," Mellon muttered.

"Why?" Wyn asked, frowning.

"Because it's a disgusting shithole?"

"Oh." Wyn wrinkled her nose at the smell that oozed from the pipe along with the drip of dark water and a ragged beard of thick moss. "It's not that bad."

"No, I take it back, it's lovely," Mellon scoffed, then he gagged and spat into the brick-lined channel beside him. "Looks like it's not true about the high-muckities shitting gold."

"More's the pity," Wyn agreed. She eyed the water trickling down the center of the sewer tunnel with suspicion. "Do you think trolls really live down here?"

"What?" Mellon froze, his eyes wider than Wyn thought possible. "What trolls?"

"Oh, nothing," Wyn said quickly. "Just something I heard."

"About trolls?" Mellon's skin had gone pale under his black bristles. He shone the light from his small lantern into the choking darkness of the tunnel in each direction, the weak beam shaking and fluttering.

"Yeah, shit trolls. Terrible nasty creatures, I heard," Wyn whispered anxiously.

The lantern's light slowly steadied, and Mellon's lips curled into a smile. He glanced at Wyn. "Shit trolls, eh?"

"Terrible nasty." Wyn blinked wide eyes at him.

"You cruel bitch," Mellon chuckled.

Wyn giggled. "Your face."

THE THIEF'S TALE

"My face? Martyr's tears, you'd smell what just happened in my pants, except..." Mellon indicated the foul tunnel with a sweep of his lantern.

"Very convenient."

"True," Mellon conceded. "The soul of consideration, you are."

"It's been said."

Mellon hefted the wriggling, bulging sack he carried, twin to the one Wyn was holding as far away from herself as possible. "Shall we give Baron Murtagh his own little shit trolls?"

"Yes, let's," Wyn agreed in her most poncy voice.

"Let's get on with it, then." Mellon cleared his throat and spat. "This is the one." He shone his lantern on a drain festooned with filth.

"Come on then, my lovelies," Wyn crooned at the squirming sack she held. She wore one of Fergus's thick leather gauntlets on one hand, but she opened the bag gingerly, nonetheless. Inside, the sack seethed with black fur, sinuous pink skin, and staring eyes that glowed red in the lantern light. She snatched a rat out and held it, wriggling, to the light. "Are you ready to do your duty, you disgusting creature?"

The rat coiled and lashed at her with its claws but could find no weakness in Fergus's gauntlet. "Too late for that," Wyn told it. "I banish you to the land of Shithole." Wyn shoved the rat into the dripping pipe and it slithered away with a final whip of its tail.

"Who's next?" Wyn asked the bag, peering inside.

"Lord Bumnipper, here." Mellon produced a rat with one long, jagged tooth from his bag. "In you go, my lord."

Wyn and Mellon continued shoving rats into the drain until more than a score had scampered and slithered their way up the pipe and they were left with a half-dozen dead rats in the bottom of their sacks.

"Perfect," Wyn declared. She jammed the carcasses into the pipe until their bodies had sealed it completely. Her sack was empty save for one last corpse and the rags soaked in pig's blood that had lured the rats onto the canvass in the first place. Wyn retched for the umpteenth time, spat, began to wipe her mouth, and then thought better of it.

THE THIEF'S TALE

"A bit disturbing, this," Mellon muttered, examining their work with his lantern held close to the tangle of pink tails bursting from the end of the drain.

"Imagine how disturbing it will be on the other end," Wyn chuckled evilly. "I wish I could see Murtagh's face when he spots old Bumnipper staring back at him from the privy."

"Let's hope it convinces him to avoid his privy."

Wyn shuddered. "I'd be convinced."

"In case his lordship is made from sterner stuff than we, are you ready for part two?"

"Ready," Wyn said brightly, hefting her almost-empty sack. "Rat-infested shithole, part two, coming up."

$\mathcal{W}$yn scampered along the edge of the roof, sure-footed on the frost-slick slate tiles and iron gutters, patches of rotten ice and scum-rimed mounds of snow lurking in the shadows. Smoke gusted at her from a black-stained chimney and tried to choke her, but Wyn dodged the eddy without breaking stride, leapt from the eave, and rolled gracefully to her feet on the steeply pitched roof adjacent.

She crouched low as she neared the peak, scrambling the final arm's-length on hands and feet until she could peer over the crest.

The far slope of the roof slid away from her fingers where they curled over the tip of the tiles, a precipitous incline that ended in a dark chasm of an alleyway and a cliff of sandy brown bricks on the far side, pierced by narrow, shuttered windows.

She crept down the steep slope, cautious on the slick tiles. The jump was not far, but the footing would be treacherous on the edge, so she braced herself on a small stone flourish holding the gutter and carefully leapt across, neatly snagging the opposite drain at the apex of her flight.

Wyn dangled easily from her fingertips, her legs swinging gently back and forth. Far beneath her small boots, in the depths of the alley, she could see the thick mush of snow and ash that

THE THIEF'S TALE

piled between the tall houses, disturbed by hundreds of servile shoeprints.

She adjusted her hold, carefully exploring the uneasy shift of tiles. A shoosh of snow nudged free and plopped onto her head, sending icy chunks sliding down her neck, jamming in her ear, and stinging her eye. She blinked balefully at the eave, squirmed uncomfortably as some snow slid deeper inside her tunic, and decided that was plenty enough caution.

A quick pull and twist levered her arm over the edge, an impatient swing of her legs threw her knee over as well, and Wyn rolled into a crouch an instant later, still as ice as she gazed at the row of dormer windows staring at her. None showed any sign of being thrown open in alarm, however, so Wyn scurried up the slope between them and reached the small, flat balcony that supported the water tank.

The balcony was an archipelago of icy patches between the small door leading into the house and the raised platform that held the giant water barrel. The shadowed corners of the balcony were thick with piles of crusty snow, the work of a wide-bladed shovel that leaned against the wall next to the door.

Wyn hurried to the tank and hopped onto the platform. The top was fashioned from sloped metal with a heavy latch. Wyn slid the iron bar aside and pushed the creaking lid open, straining against its weight. Moist air brushed against her face, and she grinned at the black, glossy reflection of her head silhouetted against the dim square of sky.

She lowered the lid as she struggled with the small bag tied to her belt, trying to detach it without touching the lumpy mass within. The bag had acquired a greasy stain since she had tied it on, and for a moment Wyn twisted and craned her neck, anxious that there was a matching blot on her trousers.

Finally convinced that her bum was free of disgusting stains, Wyn tugged the bag slightly open and peered inside, wrinkled her nose in disgust, and shoved the lid of the water tank open. The bag upended over the water with a deep splosh, and Wyn stared at the soggy mass bobbing in it.

THE THIEF'S TALE

"Sorry, Floater." Wyn could not stop a wry grin from twisting the corner of her lips. She blew the carcass a kiss, lowered the lid, and tapped the latch closed with a fingertip as she turned away.

Wyn hopped to the roof and paused as a whiff of smoke caught her nose. A small wrinkle appeared between her faint brows as she bent and peered upside down under the barrel's platform. A squat stove lurked there, steaming slightly in the chill air, and another waft of coal smoke made her nose twitch.

*Bloody high-muckities.* Wyn shook her head. *Burning coal just to keep their water warm. Pity the poor bastard who slogs up here every day to feed the fire and fill the tank.*

Wyn glanced at the door to the house, biting her lip. The rat's rotten carcass would foul the water by morning, but it was not certain that the odor would be noticed immediately. *Better make sure his lordship's bath is ruined,* she decided.

The stove's door swung open easily, and Wyn carefully dumped snow into it, watching the steam boil from the coals to make sure no puddle formed to give away her sabotage. With each handful the coals glowed less cheerfully, until the snow barely sizzled when she tossed it in. She closed the door and latched it, then skipped across the balcony, gleefully hopping between the patches of ice as she imagined the glory of icy, rat-rotten water pouring into Baron Murtagh's bath in the morning.

The clear skies lasted into the next morning, too, plunging the depths of the valley below the Silver Keep into a chill so cold it burned the skin and made bones ache. White smoke billowed from every chimney, smothering the Old City in a shroud that choked the inhabitants and gave the sun a grey halo.

There were no more smiles or bare heads in the crowds. Faces were muffled in scarfs or hidden under hoods, caps were pulled low and collars turned up as people hurried to their business, slipping on the patches of slick ice that had coated the cobbles. Worried gazes turned to the jagged ridge of mountain peaks that loomed over Kuray to the north and west. The

THE THIEF'S TALE

Ironbacks trailed long streamers of white to the south like pennants, and you did not live in Kuray without knowing that meant foul weather was lurking somewhere behind the barrier peaks.

Wyn rubbed furiously on her nose, then blew furiously on her fingertips, then stamped furiously on the cobbles, trying to find some sensation to prove that her extremities were still alive. She had dressed in the warmest clothing she had left, but she had few garments that were not worn through, and with the loss of most of the Wardrobe, her choices were slimmer still.

She had done her best, however. Thick wool stockings hugged her legs beneath her least holey pair of leather trousers, the soft white showing through the cracked brown at every crease and rip. She had stolen a pair of Fergus's boots, large enough so that she could wrap extra strips of blanket around her feet over the stockings. The boots were a tad heavy, but they buckled snugly to her legs and had thick soles that gripped in slush and snow and gave her a bit of relished extra height. She wore both of her two remaining tunics, a thick, grey, woolen coat of Desmond's that reached her knees, a black wool cap to tuck her ears under, and one of Mellon's least smelly scarves.

She was also wearing her habitual wool gloves, but she had cut the fingers off the gloves long ago to free her fingers for delicate work, and now she could not move her hands from under her arms for more than a moment or two without her fingertips turning numb.

As she turned onto Tinkers Square, the din of a hundred small hammers filled the air so that Wyn could hardly hear the young boy who rushed to confront her.

"Flower for the lady?" he piped, holding a suspect clump of purple thistles toward her as if they were made of gold. "Just a penny."

"A penny for a flower?" Wyn asked incredulously. "They've got bunches of them growing all over the place."

"Five bits, then," the boy chirped happily, trotting backward ahead of her. "They'll look right beautiful in your hair, m'lady, you'll see."

THE THIEF'S TALE

"Go on with you," Wyn scoffed. She felt a subtle tug on her purse and snatched a thin wrist that had slipped beneath her cloak. "Got you!" she laughed as the small girl who had darted behind her gave a shriek.

Wyn scooped up the girl and twirled her in a circle. "Got you, you little pixie!" The girl giggled helplessly and Wyn settled the beaming urchin onto her hip and smiled. "That was very good," Wyn told her, brushing curly hair off the girl's filthy forehead.

"How did you know?" the girl asked, grinning back at her.

"Just a tiny tug," Wyn assured her. "And you!" She held out her hand for the boy with the thistles, who took it in his grubby mitt and clung on tightly. "A penny for a flower! Does anyone actually give you a penny?"

"No, Miss Wyn, but if they give us the five bits, we leave them their purse."

"Very fair," Wyn agreed. "Now, listen you two, I've a wee bit of a job for you if you'd like, and it pays silver..."

"Yes, please, Miss Wyn!"

"All right, then, let's go and talk to the boss."

The children led Wyn through a maze of small alleys that followed the path of ever-increasing decrepitude of the buildings that bordered it. Smoke swirled into the narrow lanes along with a stink heavy with boiled fat and open sewer. Dogs and pigs wandered freely through doorways with no doors in their yawning frames, and hollow coughs echoed from the darkened rooms within.

The children skipped through it all without concern and soon came to a junction of five streets intersecting in a small, open plaza where the surrounding buildings regained a semblance of sturdiness and occupation.

A narrow doorway between a carpentry and a cobbler's shop led to a warren of small, low-ceilinged rooms that spread beneath both buildings. The two children raced eagerly ahead of Wyn, calling out, "Miss Wyn's home!" and "Whinny's back!"

She strolled along the small hallway at the base of the stairs, absorbed in the familiar rough brick arches and creaking wooden floorboards, the smell of boiled cabbage and young, unwashed bodies, as she approached the single door at the end of the hall.

THE THIEF'S TALE

The floor had been recently swept, and the doorframe scrubbed of any fingerprints that might have dared to smudge it, and as Wyn stepped through the door into the long room beyond, she felt thick, warm air envelop her.

"Hello, Wee Ones!" Wyn called out, and a dozen small figures rushed to greet her from the depths of the room. Many bounced up and down on their toes, too excited to contain themselves, while others simply beamed and stared. Wyn knelt and hugged and smiled and greeted them all by name, and wondered at how tall and how strong and how pretty they had all become.

"Hello, Miss Wyn," a voice quivering on the edge of manhood greeted her, and Wyn beamed from the tangle of small arms encircling her neck at a tall lad with a proud smile who watched from beyond the horde of smaller children.

Wyn rose and hugged the boy, marveling at how much he had changed since last she had seen him. "Maker, Brodie, where did you steal these from?" she asked, holding him at arm's-length and gripping his shoulders. She realized with a shock that she now had to look up to meet his serious, dark gaze.

"I don't know," Brodie replied, an awkward grin breaking through. "I just keep growing."

"I'll say. You'll be as tall as Des if you keep this up."

"Miss Wyn, where've you been?" a high voice near her hip demanded, followed by a chorus of indignant questions from the children.

"Sorry, luvs, I've been right busy."

"Did you really steal the Queen's dirty knickers?" a voice piped.

"I did!" Wyn announced to the delight and awe of her congregation. "Though they weren't dirty, who'd want dirty knickers?"

"Ewww!" agreed the crowd.

A handful of older children came forward, and Wyn greeted them each with a fond embrace. Slender Elise with her hair cut short and hidden under her cap. Jester with his pale eyes and crooked nose, now with a smudge of hair on his lip. Keeva, with more freckles than ever.

In the back of the room three pairs of eyes stared at her, wide and frightened, from the faces of three of the smallest children.

"Hello, sweethearts." Wyn knelt in front of them and smiled. "I'm Wyn. I used to live here, too, when I was little, so I know it's a bit scary, at first, but don't worry. They'll take care of you here."

One of the children nodded her head warily, but the other two were too shocked to respond. Wyn smiled again and let them be.

"How long have those three been down here?" she asked Brodie.

"We rescued them from the home on Whitetemple street, four, five days ago."

"They doing all right?"

"Two of them are doing chores, keeping things tidy. One still has the blubs. They all eat their share and no mistake."

"Seems I remember you were a bit ravenous your first week," Wyn pointed out.

"Suppose we all were."

"Where are the others?"

"Vail and Thorn took the rest of the bairns down to Goldenfields to teach them up a bit, so no telling when they'll be back. Red Peter and Nuts got asked to join Kane's crew, and Little Peter was picked up by the blackberries for dipping a couple weeks ago, so we're down to six earners."

"Maker... for how many bairns?"

"Twenty-one, with these three new ones."

"Brodie, why didn't you say? I've got a bit of silver, and I could help you for a day or two, as soon as I can—"

"It's all right, Miss Wyn," Brodie assured her. "I put a few bits aside over the summer, when we had more earners, and some of these bairns are about ready to work."

"Who?"

"Pixie, Two-Bits, maybe Alfred Ears."

"Oh, no..." Wyn felt her throat constrict as her heart raced. "Brodie, they're too little, you can't put them out to earn."

"They're doing really well, better than—"

"Look at them," Wyn whispered urgently. "They're babies, Brodie." *Keep them safe, Brodie...*

THE THIEF'S TALE

"Miss Wyn," Brodie said carefully. "Pixie's older than I was, and much better at dipping, than when I started earning. And, if they're not ready, we need to know, because if they're not going to earn for us, we need to find them normal work… buy them a chance at a seamstress or a tavern or something."

Wyn chewed on her lip, her stomach churning as she glanced at the bairns chatting and laughing at the other end of the room. *Brodie was so much older when he started going out with Des and me, it weren't just that I was littler…*

"Wyn," Brodie said softly, and the gentle touch of his hand on her shoulder made her flinch. It was the first time he had ever said her name simply, as an equal, and it sounded strange and awkward to her. "We can't shelter them forever. We first need to help those that can help us. Then help those others to do something else, if we can."

*He's hardly a lad, anymore… I never thought like that, when I was boss. I just fought every day, trying to find a few more bits for some food. Maker, he's got coin set aside, folks moving on to proper crews, and even a thought on what to do with the hopeless ones.*

Wyn swallowed against an ache in her throat. *Shows you what a proper boss can do, instead of a scared girl with no idea what she is doing. Best thing I ever did for the Wee Ones was leave.*

"They're lucky to have you as their boss," she forced out against her rigid throat.

"I'll take care of them, Wyn, don't worry. I'm not fierce, like you, but I'll take care of them, no matter."

"Thank you."

"Anyway, being boss is dead easy when you don't have to worry none about tithes."

"Is Lord Sly still holding up his end of the deal, then?"

"Kane comes by every few days with blankets or what's needed, and we've not been asked for a tithe from anyone. One of Kane's lads told Nuts that Little Peter is being taken care of while he's His Majesty's guest. But, if his Nibs ever changes his mind, we're in trouble."

"He won't," Wyn promised. "If Lord Sly ever says anything you let me know, and I'll work it out with him. Nick him another diamond, that should make him friendly for another year or two, just like last time, I reckon."

"Maker, if I got ahold of a diamond, I'd not give it up for bread and blankets, I'll tell you that for free."

"Yes, you would, Brodie, in a flash, if it would keep Lord Sly protecting the Wee Ones."

"I guess," Brodie muttered as his cheeks blushed pink. "I'm glad you've come by, Miss Wyn. The bairns have missed you."

"I've missed them, too, but I also have a job for you if you want it."

"You don't need to ask, you know that. What's the job?"

"I need some hard criminals, Brodie, some right bastards with no remorse."

"To do what?" Brodie asked, completely befuddled.

"To head down to the park across from the Bathhouse, right away, grab up as many snowballs as you can, and whack every high-muckity you can find in the face."

A sly grin spread across Bodie's face. "I think I know just the crew."

"Thank you, luv." Wyn gazed around the dark room. There had been years when she could not have imagined ever leaving the warren's low, claustrophobic safety, but now she could not believe how small and fragile the few rooms under the ground seemed, an egg whose shell could crack at any moment. Her lips set in a fierce grin. "Wee Ones, what's the word?"

"Don't get caught!" a dozen tiny voices sang back.

"Damn right," Wyn agreed.

THE THIEF'S TALE

## CHAPTER TWELVE

# To Earn a Dragon

The carriage jerked to a stop as the driver hauled on the reins, halting the wheels just short of the sluice of filth that had poured across the narrow lane from the tipped-over night soil cart. The horses snorted and stamped, and the carriage rolled dangerously backward before the driver could grab the brake. The rear wheels cracked into the stone wall of the building behind it and shuddered to a stop.

Baron Murtagh wheeled his horse to the side of the narrow street, a scowl blackening his face, but there was no room to pass the wedged carriage unless he cared to plunge into the mound of excrement.

The shutters on the carriage window snapped open and Mellon's head lunged out, his face red with righteous fury beneath his thickest beard.

"What are you playing at!" he bellowed at the driver, a tall lad with a worn uniform that waved forlornly around his wrists and ankles.

"I'm sorry, m'lord," Desmond stammered. "They've tipped the night cart into the street."

"So you crashed us into the wall?" Mellon screamed, his face turning crimson.

"Will you move?" demanded Baron Murtagh impatiently.

"Do you mind?" Mellon snarled. "I am having a word with my man here."

"Move your damn carriage," Murtagh said archly. "I have business at the Keep."

"What a novel idea," Mellon sneered. "Did you hear High King Ruric, here? Simply move the carriage!"

Desmond struggled helplessly with the reins, attempting to straighten the carriage without driving the horses into the oozing pile, as workers garbed head to toe in thick cloaks and gloves began to shovel the night soil aggressively out of the street, spraying clods in the air in their haste.

Murtagh's horse shied as the carriage creaked free of the wall, but the baron rose deftly in his stirrups and glared at the confusion as if about to issue a blistering stream of court martials to everyone involved.

Wyn pulled her hood low and scuttled into the street until she was almost touching the baron's shiny boot.

"Apple, m'lord?"

Murtagh glanced down, frowning thunderously.

"What?"

"Apple?" Wyn asked tremulously. She scooped one of the brown, withered fruits from the tray she wore around her stooped shoulders and offered it to the noble, her hand shaking nervously. "Three bits, m'lord."

"Get away."

"Two bits, m'lord!" Wyn whimpered. "For your pretty horse, m'lord."

Murtagh inhaled sharply, less than pleased to have his magnificent black warhorse described as "pretty."

"That's enough, you," a gruff voice challenged Wyn. She spun as hooves struck the cobbles behind her. One of Murtagh's soldiers loomed over her, his horse snorting as it scented the apples.

Wyn shrieked piteously and staggered against Murtagh's boot, her tray tipping over and scattering apples across the lane. She

THE THIEF'S TALE

clutched his stirrup as she teetered, gazing with wide, terrified eyes at the soldier. As Murtagh spluttered and the soldier tried to soothe her with raised palms, Wyn's hand darted underneath the horse and yanked the buckle on the saddle's girth free.

"Here, now!" A heavy, armored gauntlet descended on the back of Wyn's cloak and dragged her away from the baron. Wyn sagged uselessly, kicked a flapping, worn shoe into the air, and shrieked again.

"Will you deal with her!" Murtagh thundered to his soldier, then he turned his wrath on Mellon. "And get your fucking carriage out of the way, sir, or I shall drag you into the street as well!"

"Go, you useless bastard!" Mellon screeched at Desmond.

"Ya!" Desmond screamed at the horses and cracked the reins.

The team strained forward, the brake seized, tore free, and snapped a chunk of the axle loose with it.

Wyn slipped free in the chaos and shouting, darted behind a stall, and crouched low, peering gleefully through the boards.

Baron Murtagh gazed at the carriage in disbelief, and Wyn held her breath to stifle her laughter, anticipating the moment when his rage caused him to act.

But the moments passed, and the noble did not pompously push past, nor did he haughtily lean over to sneer at Mellon, nor arrogantly put his spurs to his charger to leap the pile. None of the things, in fact, that Wyn had giddily imagined. Instead, Murtagh began to laugh.

"As bad as that wagon on the road to Ráthmór," the baron chuckled to one of his soldiers. "Martyr's tears, what a mess that was."

"No blizzard, this time," the soldier replied, a smile cracking her stern visage.

The baron nodded. "No, thank the Maker. All right, down you get, you two, and help clear this lane."

Wyn watched in horror as the soldiers dismounted and hurried to the carriage, one expertly corralling the horses by their bridles, the other examining the broken axle. Wyn caught Mellon's despairing glance. Murtagh was not going to do anything but sit patiently on his horse, that was clear.

THE THIEF'S TALE

So Wyn helped him. She scooped up a jagged piece of stone, stepped into the street, and plunked the baron's horse on its rump with as vicious a throw as she could manage.

The horse startled as if it had been stung by a bee, reared, and leapt forward. The baron rocked backward, expertly kept his seat, then squawked in dismay as the saddle came free. Murtagh clung to the horse's neck for an agonizing moment, somehow resisting all the natural laws that were urging him downward. Then the horse ducked its head, snorting against the weight of its master, and Murtagh plunged into the pile of shit.

"It was beautiful," Wyn chortled. "Shit in his hair, shit in his shirt, shit on his face."

Fergus nodded, his long face as impassive as stone. "It sounds as if it worked as you hoped."

"You take the fun out of dumping a high-muckity in a pile of shit, you know that?"

Fergus shrugged, his long, lanky hair swaying around his shoulders. "I'm not a child."

Wyn squinted as she examined the swordsman's face. His gaunt cheeks and long, drooping nose made it hard to tell, but she was certain there was a trace of a curl to the corner of his thin lips. She beamed at him. "Knew it was funny."

Fergus nodded slightly. "Now for the hard part."

"Pfft, what's hard about having a bath?"

"I still don't see why I have to—"

"Because we need him to have a lovely, long bath, not just a quick plunge to get clean, and that means someone has to be in there with him to make sure."

"No, I don't see why me. I can't fool people the way you and Mellon can."

"So don't. Be a soldier, he'll lap it up, I promise. And if things go wrong, I need you in there, Fergus."

THE THIEF'S TALE

Fergus considered her words for a moment in silence, then nodded his head once and passed her the tightly wrapped bundle of clothing he had carried.

"I will see you in there," he said.

"Hopefully not," Wyn replied. She fairly skipped up the broad avenue that curved grandly past the great Bathhouse, she was so full of bubbling excitement. The tall pillars and marble sweep of the majestic building, the stacks of lordly balconies, the long clerestories, the endless tiers of roofs, all towering over her with cold grandeur, could not dampen her spirit. She slipped through a gap in the perfectly trimmed hedge, and her boots scuffed the manicured gravel path as she darted past a steaming fountain, hopped a balustrade, and vanished into the shadows between the sprawling buildings.

Desmond was waiting for her there. He had stripped off his faded uniform coat, revealing a ragged, threadbare tunic and ripped leggings, held around his waist by a strip of knotted rope, and he had traded his cracked leather boots for a pair of worn shoes. He pulled his cloak around his shoulders and gave Wyn a smile of welcome. "Am I disreputable enough?"

"Rub some dirt on your face," Wyn decided.

Desmond set to with a will as Wyn examined the wall behind them. The sheer, polished stone ascended three stories before giving way to a series of balconies. She looped the bundle of clothes over her shoulder and scrambled up a tree, leapt to a small ridge in the wall's facing, then wedged herself into the corner of two adjoining walls to reach the first balcony.

The balcony gave access to a series of doors into small, private rooms used by the Bath's patrons for massage and treatment, and Wyn quickly found an empty one and slipped inside. She bolted the door and tore off her own beggar's garb, replacing it with the first set of clothes in her bundle, a long, flowing robe made from soft, white wool with a deep hood, embroidered hem, and a sash made from black silk. She slipped on a pair of sandals and arranged the hood to shadow her eyes. A quick trip to the balcony allowed her to dump her ratty old costume over the rail for Desmond to conceal.

THE THIEF'S TALE

She gathered the remaining clothing bundle, set a pile of soft towels on top of it, and carried it into the hallway, remembering to walk slowly and gracefully, an ethereal presence, just as all the Bath's attendants were instructed.

Wyn glided down the hallway and into the tiled chambers that housed the baths. The air was warm and thick with moisture, the walls echoed with the soft trickle of water and the hushed murmur of conversation, and Wyn felt her toes thaw for the first time that day.

"Maker, what a nightmare." Baron Murtagh's voice rolled through the baths like thunder.

Wyn slipped through the steaming rooms in the direction of his voice.

"I'm not sure I will ever be clean, but sitting in another bath won't change that. I'm well-scrubbed, and very late."

Whoever the baron was arguing with murmured something that Wyn did not catch. She sidled up to a corner and pressed against the tiles. The baron sounded as if he was in the next room.

"Very well, but just for a moment, and as hot as you can," the baron said shortly. She heard bare feet splatting against wet tile and followed at a discreet distance. The baron's footsteps led her through a doorway and into a low-ceilinged room so steamy that the lanterns created golden halos of light around them. Wyn could make out a wide pool with gleaming water, surrounded by stone benches. Three figures appeared vaguely through the steam on the far side.

"Good morning," she heard the baron say.

"Good morning, m'lord," Fergus replied from the depths of the room.

Wyn hurried to the far end as quietly as she could, where the men's private changing rooms were located.

"Did you earn that, sir?" the baron's voice barked, and Wyn hesitated, unnerved by the accusatory tone. *What's happened?*

"I did, m'lord. Served twenty years out of Irongate."

"Did you, indeed?" the baron replied, suddenly friendly. I've known many good soldiers who never earned an entire dragon."

*Maker, his tattoo,* Wyn realized.

"I was fortunate, m'lord."

THE THIEF'S TALE

"Takes more than fortune to earn a dragon," the baron scoffed. "I know, sir. I have fought in the Ironbacks, as well."

"Yes, m'lord. I saw your attack at Dún Carrick," Fergus told the baron. "Black Manannan never had a chance, m'lord."

"Do I know you, soldier?"

"No, m'lord, I served with Sir Cullen."

"Maker's breath, one of Cullen's, eh?" Wyn heard the baron leap to his feet and the smack of hand clasping hand. "If you lads had not held the Dún, Manannan would have been safe behind its walls when I arrived, not nicely spread out trying to climb them."

"Yes, m'lord. It was a near thing."

"It was indeed. Please, join us."

"Thank you, m'lord." The water surged as the men settled back. "Never thought I'd be warm again after that winter."

"It was bitter cold," Murtagh laughed. "You chose the black dragon, I see. Did she help you find justice?"

"She did, m'lord, but I sometimes wonder if it was worth it."

"Aye, justice does not come cheap."

Wyn slunk out of the room, a satisfied smile on her lips. *Nicely done, and they're off to endless stories, I reckon,* Wyn thought gleefully. *And he had one of his soldiers with him, so that leaves one watching his changing room. I'll guess the lady, since it would be a bit awkward having her in the men's baths.*

Wyn left the baths and entered the broad, well-lit hallways of the changing rooms. She checked each hall until she found what she had been searching for. The soldier stood guard outside one of the countless dressing room doors, her eyes never wavering as her gaze swept the passage, her hand resting comfortably on the pommel of her thick-bladed sword, marking Wyn's target as surely as a circle of red paint.

Wyn ignored her. Soldiers always guarded doors, as if that were the only way into a room. She turned down the next hall, found the room that backed onto the one Murtagh had been given, and ducked inside. Each room had a small window that looked over the manicured lawns, and Wyn immediately opened it and leaned out, waving frantically until Desmond glanced up from his hiding place amongst the shrubberies and hurried to stand at the base of the wall far beneath her.

THE THIEF'S TALE

Wyn slipped off her sandals, scooted onto the window ledge, and got her feet under her. A long stretch brought the row of bricks above the window into reach, and she swung nimbly across the gap between her window and the window to the baron's room. She dangled there from one hand while she worked the window's latch with the slim blade of her tiny knife until it popped open. A single shove and the window gaped wide to allow her to step inside.

The attendants had laid out the baron's fresh clothes in perfect order, with no wrinkle or crease to be seen. His sword rested casually against the wall where he had left it, the attendants not daring to touch it.

Wyn padded across the tiled floor to the dressing table. She rolled her eyes as she tugged on the first drawer and found it locked. Inside, she discovered a sheaf of parchments covered in columns of tiny script, three gem-encrusted rings, a golden necklace with a pendant...

... and a steel chain with a key secured to it, its hollow, engraved shaft and wide head with its crescent moon a familiar relief. The steel clasp was sturdy and straightforward and held the key through one of the flourishes in the key's grip. Wyn removed the key, tied one end of a long piece of cord through it, and lowered it out the window to Desmond.

She peered down impatiently while he examined it, pressed its head into one of his wax tablets, then re-secured the key to the cord. He gave Wyn a thumbs-up and disappeared into the shrubberies, the sign that the keys were identical, save for their ornamental grips.

Wyn pulled the key safely back through the window and returned to the dresser. She slipped it back on the steel chain, then paused to examine the latch, running her fingers over it again and again to get the feel of its release, finding precisely the pressure she would need to open it, when the time came. It was well made, with just a tiny hitch in its motion, and she soon could open it with the slightest movement of a finger. Then she carefully positioned the latch next to the key and gently scored the steel so that the key snagged on the chain there, catching the latch snugly

THE THIEF'S TALE

against its weight. When the baron next put it on, the latch should stay at the bottom, right next to the key. *Hopefully.*

Wyn heard the guard outside the door clear her throat and decided there was nothing more she could do. She tidied the drawer away and slipped back to the first room through the windows. There was no sign of Desmond on the ground below, but that was according to plan. He would be hidden away, somewhere nearby, frantically etching the moon pattern onto the grip of the forged key he had made the day before.

Wyn unwrapped the rest of the bundle of clothes and sighed.

Mellon had borrowed the dress from a washerwoman who did laundry for several families who lived on the upper slopes of the Old City, and while it was not the gown the Hawk had worn so elegantly, it was a far cry from the simple maid's dress Wyn had worn to Spicer's ball.

Wyn climbed glumly into it. It had a corset covered in bronze and black flowers that gripped her waist and chest snugly and flared over her hips, a wide collar that opened across her shoulders, and a long, black skirt that swept the ground. Under the corset was a shirt of beautiful, soft silk, blindingly white, with billowing arms that buttoned around her wrists.

Layers of petticoats swirled around her legs and rustled as she moved, and Wyn snorted in annoyance as she struggled to lace the front of the corset's stiff fabric closed.

*Maker, I can't breathe in this bloody thing.* She angrily sucked in her stomach and tried again. *I'm skinny as a twig and it's squishing my ditties... how do real girls manage?*

But at last the dress was fastened, and Wyn wrapped a thick, soft, fur-lined shawl around her bare shoulders and was ready.

The bath attendant's robes were quickly wadded up and chucked in a basket filled with towels, and Wyn hurried out of the changing rooms, slipping inelegantly on the tile floor in the shiny, hard boots that were pinching her toes.

The park across the King's Road from the baths was home to wide footpaths for strolling alongside flower banks beneath soaring trees. Despite the cold, Wyn did not have the gardens to herself. Gentlemen and ladies taking the air dotted the paths, muffled in thick furs and soft wools as they admired the snow-laden trees or the icy tumble of a stream.

There were no blackberries to be seen, as the Wee Ones had successfully cleared them out by chucking snowballs at the high-muckities until the City Watch had chased after them.

Wyn loitered innocently at the base of a small statue set directly across from the Bathhouse entrance. She perched on a stone bench pretending to read a book, then strolled slowly around the statue, as if interested in its dramatic pose. Mostly, however, she gradually lost sensation in her fingers and toes. Then her ears. Then her nose.

*I should have dressed as a bloody bear,* she decided as she puffed surreptitiously on her fingertips and stomped her dainty boots.

Wyn kept a wary eye on the other denizens of the park, silently entreating them to keep their distance when they threatened to encroach on her domain.

But one pair of wanderers persisted in meandering steadily closer, a young couple who spent more time gazing at one another than at the winter splendor around them. The lady's hand rested gently on her lord's arm, and her hip brushed against him on every step. Wyn tried to conjure an image of herself doing the same, touching someone so intimately, but all she could imagine was the look of distaste or worse, the laughter, that such an act would produce.

Wyn could not look away, although the longer she stared, the more her chest ached.

The lady glanced at Wyn at that moment and met her gaze. Wyn flushed in embarrassment at being caught staring so brazenly, but the young woman simply smiled and nodded and murmured, "Good morning."

*Well, she didn't laugh,* Wyn sighed in relief. She watched the lady for a moment longer, glanced surreptitiously around to ensure she was not observed, then tried to match the young woman's long, graceful stride, the elegant sway of her hips, the tilt of her head.

For a moment Wyn felt as if she were walking on fresh ice, with every movement careful and deliberate and on the verge of

The Thief's Tale

disaster. And then her body slipped into a new rhythm, as natural as scaling a wall, as easy as balancing on a narrow ledge.

Even her dress stopped fighting her. It swept effortlessly with each step, matching her sway. Wyn glanced down in surprise and had to force herself not to immediately investigate beneath the dress to see if somehow the petticoats had come loose.

*It's not… terrible,* she admitted as she watched the black dress swirl around her legs. The hated corset and skirts emphasized her narrow waist and gave her the hint of a curve over her hips as she strolled. *I sort of look like a proper girl.*

Wyn took another turn around the statue, every step more comfortable than the one before as she settled into her new-found gait. *I wish I'd worn this when we went to talk to the Hawk,* she suddenly thought, *instead of looking like a dirty little sprat.* Wyn tried to recall every detail of their encounter in the carriage, as well as the meeting of the Hawk with Grey Bastard in the courtyard. *She looked the same, both times, whether she was wearing a frilly gown or real clothes. And she weren't just pretty, she looked proper fierce.*

Wyn raised her chin and forced her shoulders back, mimicking the Hawk, although she felt as exposed as if she had just stepped from thick, comforting shadows into brilliant light. Then a smile began to curl the corners of her lips as a fierce joy thrummed through her, as if she were climbing free of fear and anxiety, alone on a high tower where every moment was a victory of strength and boldness over death. Wyn had never felt as alive as she did in those perilous moments high above the earth, but now that joy began to stir inside her. *There I am,* she breathed in deep satisfaction.

Mellon appeared along the path, resplendent in the long coat and cape he had worn for his part as a merchant in the carriage but with his beard now shaved off as a disguise. His step faltered as he approached Wyn, and she almost laughed as his eyes blinked wide in surprise as he stared at her. Then he grinned and nodded and gave Wyn a wink.

But as he sauntered past to his station along the street, he gently raised one hand in caution, with an arched eyebrow for emphasis.

THE THIEF'S TALE

*We don't want the baron meeting the Hawk,* Wyn agreed. *I'm a little bird, fresh from the nest, no notion of cats on the prowl.* Wyn carefully dampened the fiery elation that had so recently kindled, concealing it beneath an innocent smile, although its blaze continued to smolder beneath the surface.

*Come on, then,* she told the closed doors of the Baths across the avenue. She was eager for them to open and disgorge her prey. *I'm ready for you, Baron.*

But as more time passed, Wyn's impatience became anxiety. There was no sign of Desmond and, therefore, no freshly forged key for Wyn to exchange. Wyn's strolling took on more of an appearance of pacing, and she cast frequent dark scowls at the far end of the bath buildings.

At last, she spotted him hurrying across the street to the park, half-jogging in his haste. But, before she could draw a breath of relief, the doors to the Bathhouse opened and Baron Murtagh stepped through, accompanied by his two soldiers and Fergus. The baron was declaiming grandly as he clattered down the steps, his arms sweeping out to indicate some acutely military situation that was utterly lost on Wyn.

Wyn caught Mellon's glance. He slowly rolled his eyes toward the rapidly approaching Desmond. There was no chance he could reach Wyn to pass her the forged key without Murtagh noticing him. Mellon raised an eyebrow questioningly.

*We're going,* Wyn decided in a rush. She turned from the statue and began a leisurely stroll toward the baron. Mellon hesitated for a moment, then began a brisk walk toward the Bathhouse steps.

*Come on Des,* Wyn urged him on. She buried her gaze in her book, unable to stop herself from staring at Desmond in any other way. *Come on...*

From the corner of her eye she saw Mellon start across the avenue, passing close to the baron and his entourage. One of the soldiers took a step toward him, but just watched warily as Mellon casually doffed his hat and kept going. The soldier turned slightly to watch him depart.

The second soldier had seen Wyn, absently wandering into the baron's path, and stepped forward. Neither saw Desmond until he broke into a run and collided with Wyn.

THE THIEF'S TALE

Wyn screamed helplessly and threw her book in the air. Pages came free in a rush and spiraled madly around her and Desmond. She felt the hard shape of the key pressed against her hand, and she palmed it even as she collapsed to the ground.

"Thief!" Mellon bellowed, outraged, as he thrust his walking stick violently in Desmond's direction. "Thief!"

The baron started forward without hesitation, but his soldiers reacted just as quickly. They shouldered between the baron and the commotion, holding him back as they drew their steel.

Fergus charged ahead as the baron struggled with his guards. "Come here, you bastard!" Fergus shouted, and Desmond sprang to his feet and sprinted into the park with Fergus pounding down the path directly behind him.

Murtagh looked to be on the verge of giving pursuit, despite his guards' best efforts to keep him safe. Wyn turned a shocked, helpless, desperate gaze on him, her hands clutched uselessly to her chest.

"Oh, my dear!" Mellon fussed as he hurried toward Wyn. "Oh, my dear girl, are you injured?"

The baron strode to her side as well, frowning in concern, the now-distant pursuit of Desmond forgotten. "Here, do not try to rise, let me ensure you are well," he said kindly.

"He knocked me down," Wyn said hesitantly, her eyes big and bewildered. She raised her hand and Murtagh took it unthinkingly. She clambered to her feet, staring at her ruined book, its pages scattered around her. "My poor book."

Murtagh glanced at the pages and Wyn staggered, clutching his arm for support as her free hand fluttered across his chest. "Oh, my," she said woozily. The hard lump under his shirt was slightly lower than Wyn had expected, but still above his vest. *Not too bad,* she told herself.

"My dear, you must sit before you do yourself further harm," Mellon insisted loudly, distracting the baron and his soldiers further.

"Thank you, sir." Wyn glanced shyly at Murtagh, then slipped into the crook of his arm, pressing against him as she waited for him to escort her to the nearby bench. The baron moved forward instinctively, well-trained in what to do with a lady on his arm.

THE THIEF'S TALE

"Oh!" Wyn cried out in sudden realization. "My book..." She twisted across Murtagh, leaning to see around him at the remains of her read. Murtagh turned to look, as well, as did the soldiers.

*Here we go...* Wyn held her breath. She had dipped purses, rings, envelopes, earrings, bracelets... almost anything that could be worn or stuffed into a pocket. But she had never tried a dip in front of two guards, blades drawn, let alone a heavy key on a chain around the mark's neck. Under his shirt.

Wyn slipped the fingers of one hand beneath the button of his shirt and twisted it neatly free as she leaned into him and gripped his far shoulder with the other. Her fingertip slipped through the gap and brushed the heavy metal of the key. *Now...*

"Oh, you're stepping on the pages!" she gasped and pointed at Mellon with an accusatory finger. At the same moment, she pressed the key firmly against Murtagh's skin, then slipped the latch with one finger, allowing the key to fall neatly into her hand. A quick twist and it was trapped between her chest and his ribs as Desmond's replacement appeared in her fingers. A heartbeat more and her fingertip had swiped the latch closed, and Murtagh's key fell neatly into her hand as she stepped away. "Please, sir, your boot!"

"Oh, my goodness," Mellon cried out, trampling more pages as he tried to stumble back. "I am very sorry."

They bent and reached together and bumped shoulders. Wyn said, "Oh!" and sat down hard as the key passed to Mellon's awaiting hand. "Oh, I feel faint..."

"Here, my dear, take my arm," the baron said soothingly. "Let us get you seated more comfortably."

Wyn allowed herself to be escorted to the stone bench, but her contentment vanished as she noticed the silver button on the front of the baron's shirt was only half-hooked. She almost lunged for it, but Murtagh's attention was firmly on her, now, and she did not dare.

She perched daintily on the edge of the bench and gave flustered answers to the baron's questions. "No, my lord, I shall have a bruise or two, no more, but I grieve the loss of my book."

"Let me see it." The baron gestured impatiently to Mellon, who passed the collected pages to him in a wad. Murtagh shuffled

THE THIEF'S TALE

the parchment vainly, barely glancing at the flowing script that covered them. Wyn stifled a frown of annoyance. She had spent forever in a very dull shop selecting the perfect folio of ridiculous poems for a scatter-brained young lady, and it was as wasted on the baron as if the pages had been blank.

"I am afraid it is beyond my skills," the baron admitted. "But, surely, a small price to pay. You were fortunate to survive with only a bruise, and nothing else lost."

"Lost... oh!" Wyn cried out, and she slapped her hand to her belt. "My purse! Oh, he took it!"

Murtagh instinctively pressed his hand to his chest and, finding the familiar shape of his key safely there, became overwhelmed with concern for her. He urged her to take his purse, for surely he should have acted faster to aid her. Wyn demurred, praising him for his bravery. He begged her to allow him to hire her a carriage to get her home, but Wyn demurred, claiming a quick walk across the park was all she needed to clear her head. He suggested an escort, but Wyn demurred, begging his lordship not to concern himself over such a trifle.

Mellon congratulated the baron on his quick action, then resumed his walk to the Baths as Fergus returned with a tale of chasing the thief the length of the park, only to lose him in the crowded streets around the Grand Market.

"Never mind," the baron consoled him. "You were much faster than I was, more's the shame of it. Still, had I a few less years on my legs, I should have given you a run for the glory."

"Yes, m'lord, I am certain of it," Fergus agreed.

With a few final instructions on keeping safe and treating bruises, Murtagh took his leave. Wyn gave him Cara's curtsey and a grateful smile. She could hear his resonant voice contentedly recounting a hound he had once owned for chasing hares as he and Fergus strode away, his soldiers trailing respectfully behind.

Wyn sighed and rubbed her elbow where it had whacked against the hard cobbles of the street. She carefully sorted the loose pages back into order, as a young lady so concerned with her book would undoubtedly do, then completed her stroll across the park, ambling aimlessly until she reached the Market.

THE THIEF'S TALE

Desmond was waiting for her near the entrance of the Market, and they sipped tea at a nearby café until Mellon arrived, followed soon after by Fergus.

"Whinny, that was, by far, the best dip I have ever seen," Mellon congratulated her.

Wyn blushed and suddenly could not meet their gazes, furious with herself for being so ridiculous. But a grin slid uncontrollably onto her lips and remained there as the lads chuckled and teased their way through a recounting of the events.

"Fergus chased me all the way to the Market," Desmond complained.

"A little exercise," Fergus explained. "Good for you."

"I about died."

"It was perfect," Mellon crowed. "By the time his lordship got disentangled from his soldiers you were vanished, and then he got entangled with our Whinny, here, and that was that. He was quite smitten."

"Shut up, you," Wyn grumbled, and gave Mellon a shove.

"Oh, my lord," Mellon continued in a squeaky falsetto. "Please help me, I feel faint at the sight of your very, very, tight, tight trousers."

"Ugh, he's ancient!" Wyn stuck out her tongue.

"I do have to say, and not to take anything away from what you just did, which, I may have mentioned, was the best dip I've ever seen, but you ladies have a huge advantage."

"Which one? The one where we're smarter? Or the one where we're better at everything?"

"Ha, ha... definitely not funnier. No, you cuddled right up next to him and he didn't peep. Can you imagine the baron letting me grab onto him like that?"

"It's your own fault, always thinking you lads are so big and strong and us girls are so frail and weak. 'Oh, I'd best comfort her!' Martyr's tears, what nonsense. Bloody men."

"What's wrong with that?" Desmond wondered. "Poor lass got knocked down, deserves a little pity."

"The only thing I deserve pity for is the fact I can't wear my woolies in this dress," Wyn muttered. "I'm freezing."

THE THIEF'S TALE

"One down, one to go," Mellon declared. "Come on, Tallywags… almost there."

Mellon had talked their way into possession of a disused night watchman's lodge beneath a brewery near Forge Hill, a towering stone building filled with copper vats and endless stacks of very tempting barrels of ale. The brewery was far from Scrivener's, far from Butcher's, and the brewer had never dealt with the Tallywags before. As near a perfect safehouse as could be asked for.

The lodge was buried in the cellar behind a wall of barrels and had been vacant ever since the old watchman had been caught selling barrels out of the back of the brewery and the brewmasters had decided to pay the local crew and the blackberries to keep their product safe, instead. The lodge included a front room with a fireplace and a stove, and a single bedroom against the back wall. They had hung a curtain across one corner for Wyn, right beneath the tiny window that peeked into the yard behind the brewery at ground level.

Wyn yanked the curtain closed behind her and beamed at the small cot and stool that were the minuscule nook's only furniture.

*I did it,* she repeated to herself for the umpteenth time. She could still feel the heavy weight of the key in her hand, even though she had only held it momentarily. *I pulled it. Best dip ever, says he, and that's no lie.*

Another smile spread joyfully across her lips. Her body sang with excited energy that demanded she leap and laugh uncontrollably. She wanted to climb Ruric's Tower again, just to stand on its summit and shout triumph into the thin air.

*What if it unlocks any lock? Maker, think of that…* Images of her approaching Nell Spicer's study door paraded through her imagination, but this time she gestured grandly with a key-shaped star ablaze in her hand, a Word thundered from her lips, and the doors swung wide as Desmond stared in awe.

THE THIEF'S TALE

Wyn laughed at the thought, then quickly stifled herself as she heard the door to the lodge's main room open. Footsteps crossed the bare floor and approached her curtain, Desmond's long stride.

"Wyn?" His voice carried tentatively through the curtain. "Are you changed? We're ready in the other room."

"No, I'm naked," Wyn lied.

"Oh… ah, I'll just let you… I'll go…" Desmond stammered. His footsteps hurried away and the door closed firmly behind him.

*Why did I say that?* she wondered. She glanced at the black dress she was still wearing, despite her declared intention to rid herself of it as quickly as possible. A strange reluctance had stayed her fingers from ripping the corset off, and Wyn realized that she did not want the other Tallywags to discover that her scorn for the dress had withered.

*They'd never stop teasing,* she reasoned, but that did not answer for the particular lie her mouth had chosen. Wyn did not understand why she was not curled up in mortified agony, but she was not. Instead, gleeful satisfaction at Desmond's hasty retreat curled her lips into a sly grin, and she chuckled quietly to herself at the image of his cheeks turning bright pink.

Wyn sighed and strolled in a circle around the stool, enjoying the sway of her hips and the swoosh of the dress against her legs. She pressed the heavy fabric of the corset against her stomach for one last moment, then reluctantly unhooked the buttons.

Her thick woolen leggings and long tunic were as soft and shapeless as they had been that morning, but Wyn felt smaller once she had pulled them on.

THE THIEF'S TALE

## CHAPTER THIRTEEN

# Always an Angle

Wyn joined the lads in the lodge's main room where they were seated around its table. It was not as large as their old table, and barely had room for Desmond's beautiful miniature rendition of the entrance to the Bathhouse, but it was much sturdier.

Murtagh's key gleamed in a place of honor next to Tillings's small Device. If the apostate's Device was actually a Veil, then they reasoned the closer it was to the key, the better.

"Someone should tell the Hawk we have the first of her keys," Wyn ventured. "I can do it if you want," she added quickly. "Just makes sense, since it were me she first thought to contact, and we stayed after in her carriage to chat and all," she finished in a rush.

"How sweet. But let's talk about that for a half a moment," Mellon said thoughtfully. "Have we decided we're trusting her? It weren't but a few days ago you thought she might be a Guild master."

"Well, she's not, is she," Wyn pointed out.

"True, very true, but that don't necessarily mean that we can trust her."

"Don't we want her to get rid of Quinn?" Wyn asked.

"Of course we do, but can you imagine what happens if we give her the keys and she crosses us? Or what happens if she doesn't pull whatever she has planned to deal with Quinn right away? We're proper fucked. I think we need a bit more assurances."

"Like what?"

"We tell her she has a deal if she gets rid of Quinn first."

Wyn frowned. "That's not what she said."

"She'll understand," Mellon assured her. "She'd want the same deal if she were in our place."

"But what if she says no?" Wyn slumped back, her arms crossed tightly to squeeze against the sudden swell of panic in her chest. *She has to get Quinn.*

"She won't. We still have a deal, we're just working the details. We don't even know what she's planning to do with Quinn. What if it's rubbish? What if it will take days and days?"

"I don't know," Wyn admitted.

"I'll tell you what," Mellon said grimly. "In that case we have to give the keys to Quinn, go back to your plan of watching him have fun with the Guild."

"He's right," Fergus said quietly. "We can't assume we're safe on her say-so."

"I… I know," Wyn muttered. "I understand. We're all dead unless the Hawk takes cares of Quinn, so we can't give up the keys until she does. It's just, this is our chance."

"I don't want to end up on a hook, either," Mellon assured her.

Wyn nodded glumly. The stink of Butcher's carving room and the brutal rip and tear of flesh that filled it lurked behind every thought, but Wyn realized that terror paled next to the anguish brought by the thought of placing the keys in Quinn's hand. *I won't die knowing I gave him what he wanted,* she vowed.

Mellon tapped a biscuit on his plate a few times, his gaze never leaving Wyn. "Perhaps I should talk to Lady Cailean," he ventured.

THE THIEF'S TALE

"I'll do it," Wyn said firmly.

"You certain?"

"I said so, didn't I?"

"You did," Mellon allowed. He slurped noisily at his tea as he considered Wyn over the lip of his cup. "Just wondering if you wanted any help explaining our position to her."

"I got it," Wyn muttered. "We don't trust you, m'lady, so you have to do your part before we do ours. Did I miss anything?" she asked sweetly.

Mellon sucked on his teeth for a moment, then raised his cup to his lips again. "No, that's it," he agreed.

Wyn ransacked her few belongings to find something to wear that might not shame her in front of the Hawk, but the results were pathetic. A single pair of worn leather trousers, cracked in every bend, scored by a thousand encounters with rough stone walls and quite a few encounters with rough stone streets. A ragged wool coat freshly stained with mud along the hem. Two frayed tunics, one grey, the other… *grey,* she decided after lengthy examination. Both featured hasty darns and split seams, and one smelled very suspicious.

And… that was it.

Wyn frowned at the meager pile and cursed the loss of the Wardrobe. *The Hawk wanted to talk to me because she heard I was a proper thief. I should look like a proper thief,* Wyn decided.

In the end, a quick raid on her comrades was required.

A small chest beside Fergus's cot donated a long, leather coat that almost reached her ankles, and a pair of low, black leather boots with steel buckles and thick soles that made her want to stomp things. Desmond had left unguarded a thick wool tunic, whose silver thread and bone clasps gave it a tough, rakish look that appealed to Wyn, and it was soft and warm and long enough to hide her all the way to her knees. She then acquired a pair of trousers baggy enough that she could wear every pair of wool stockings she possessed at the same time underneath, and added a big knife borrowed from Fergus's stash, jammed into one boot, which completed her version of the greatest thief in Kuray.

"What are you dressed as?" Mellon wondered when Wyn reappeared. "Are those my trousers?"

THE THIEF'S TALE

"Yes. Yours are the only ones short enough that I can wear without rolling them a thousand times," Wyn snapped back. "Thought it might be a good idea to look a bit respectable since it's the Hawk and all."

"You look proper flash," Desmond assured her.

"See?" Wyn told Mellon. She raised her nose and stared haughtily at the yellow and brown patchwork coat Mellon was brushing crumbs off. "Nothing wrong with a bit of smartening up."

"Absolutely," Mellon agreed vaguely, his attention already returned to his tea.

Wyn glared for another moment, but Mellon seemed blissfully unaware, and she frowned in disappointment as she turned to leave.

"Don't forget to get her ladyship some pretty flowers," Mellon called after her, but Wyn ignored him and stomped down the stairs, her hood pulled firmly over her head to hide the embarrassment blazing on her cheeks.

Fergus was waiting for her at the bottom of the stairs.

Wyn chewed her lip for a moment, then met the lean swordsman's gaze. "I'm going by myself," she informed him.

Fergus silently considered that declaration, then slowly shook his head. "I don't think that's wise."

"Look, last time we talked to the Hawk, you pointed a crossbow at her. We're meant to be partners now."

"You think she won't have her man, Cameron?"

"Of course. It's her house," Wyn said reasonably. "I'd wager coin that Grey Bastard is watching for us, as well."

"All the more reason for me to be there."

"She won't hurt me," Wyn assured him. "She came looking for me, remember? In any case, she needs us."

"That's no guarantee she won't change her mind."

"I know, but I need to talk to her alone. Show her that we trust her."

"We don't trust her," Fergus pointed out.

"Show her that she can trust us, then."

Fergus frowned at Wyn, his gaze never leaving hers, while Wyn willed her face into a stoic mask to match the swordsman's.

THE THIEF'S TALE

Everything she had said was true enough, but those reasons concealed a more shameful motivation that churned inside her.

*As long as we have a deal, she'll still want me to join her.*

Wyn had buried that promise, but it had somehow leeched into her thoughts along with the triumph of obtaining Murtagh's key and had settled contentedly there, tempting her to fantasize about that tantalizing future at every opportunity.

"All right," Fergus finally relented. "I'll go with you and wait outside."

Wyn shook her head. "You'll freeze! In any case, I want a ride in her shiny carriage."

"I don't think it's safe for any of us to go alone."

"You think Quinn's trolls will bother me after what he did at Butcher's?"

"No," Fergus admitted, "but there's worse after us than them."

"If Calixte knows where we are, there's nothing a sword can do to keep us safe."

Fergus raised an eyebrow. "He's a man, like any other. A blade will work fine."

"Go on with you." Wyn gave Fergus a shove on the shoulder that did more to push her away than move him. "A Guild master, just waiting for his chance to pounce on a wee girl, but too scared to have a go because there's a chap with a sword walking next to her. That's your thought?"

"That was my thought."

"Well, it's shite, isn't it?"

Fergus stared silently at her for a moment, then nodded slowly. "All right then."

"I'll be back in two shakes," Wyn assured him. "And if anyone gets uppity, I'll just show them this bloody great knife in my boot."

"If anyone gets uppity, run," Fergus corrected her.

"Aye, that sounds more like it," Wyn agreed.

The pale winter sun slowly drifted below the western rim of the valley during the long walk from the brewery to the upper east side, granting Wyn plenty of time for her thoughts to churn through countless variations of how she might ensure they had a

THE THIEF'S TALE

deal with the Hawk at the end of the night. *She'll understand,* began most of the versions. *Mellon's right, she must see we need her help before we dare to cross Quinn. She can keep the gold until we complete the job, that's fair.*

But even the umpteenth recitation of that golden outcome could not erase the other, disquieting paths the upcoming discussion might take. *If she sticks, what do I say? We can't give Quinn the keys, we can't get away from Quinn without help, and we can't deal with the Hawk trying to pull the job against us. We'll end up on the hooks, for sure.*

Wyn eventually banished all such scheming, for fear the repetition would somehow ensure that reality. But that left ample time for her mind to return to daydreaming as she ascended the eastern heights.

*She said I'd tell her what I deserved, but I still don't have a clue.* Wyn frowned at the cobbled surface of the avenue. *What do I want? Be nice to be rich, I suppose. Have a few bits to rub together. Could buy all those apprenticeships Brodie was talking about.*

Wyn twisted her lips as she gnawed at the thought. *She's right, coin is nice, but it don't signify, not really. There's always silver to be had. All right then, how about some bloody respect?* It took little effort to conjure the satisfying memories of deferential nods and admiring looks that she had enjoyed as word of conquering Ruric's Tower had spread. *Even caught the Hawk's ear,* she reminded herself. *Wouldn't mind a bit more of what's due, there.*

But Wyn soon realized that all such thoughts were too small. *I want what she has.* As she thought it, Wyn knew she was right. *She has it perfect. A legend, Mellon said, and that's right. Amazing jobs, everyone just shitting themselves over how amazing. I want to be a legend.* Wyn felt giddy exhilaration course through her at the thought. *I want to be her.*

Although the mountains still glowed orange and the sky was still bright enough to see by, lights already blazed from the entrances of the grand houses by the time Wyn reached the quiet lane which the Hawk called home.

*She's here, at least.* Every window of the manor glowed with warm light behind heavy drapes.

THE THIEF'S TALE

Wyn hurried to the end of the short carriageway that curled in front of the manor, paused to readjust her coat and tunic and sweep her hair out of her face, then squared her shoulders and strode to the door. A chain dangling from a raptor's beak produced a muted chime from within the house when pulled, and Wyn soon heard the heavy tread of someone approaching the door.

"Mistress Bronwyn," Cameron greeted her gravely.

"Master Cameron. It's just 'Wyn,' not that other." Wyn met his gaze for a moment, then decided the shining silver buttons on his waistcoat were a safer target. "Um, I need to talk with Lady Cailean."

"She said to expect you." Cameron stood aside and waved Wyn into the manor. "Come with me."

Wyn hurried to keep pace with the big man's long steps as he led her across the entry hall, resplendent in polished wood, and up a flight of wide, curving stairs.

The second-floor landing had only two doors on it, opposite one another. One led to a formal drawing room that ran the length of the house on one side, and the other to a library facing the garden. Cameron chose the library.

"She will be with you in a moment," he informed Wyn as he ushered her into the room.

Cailean's library was somehow cozy and elegant at the same time. Tall shelves filled with books lined the walls between pillars made of dark oak, and panels crafted from subtle patterns of mahogany, cherry, and maple graced the high ceiling. The center of the room was wide enough to hold several comfortable leather chairs and a settee, and a deep marble fireplace glowed with the lazy flames of a well-banked fire.

A thin pedestal stood in the center of the room, carved into the shape of intertwined branches that climbed a slender stalk, then spread elegantly to form a flat surface.

A box rested on top. It gleamed with intricate silver filigree, glowed with panels of black wood, and featured two prominent locks.

Wyn peered into the corners of the room, searching for Cailean, but no one was there. She frowned, then padded across

THE THIEF'S TALE

the floor to the box and peered at it. The more Wyn examined it, the more magical it seemed. The ornate flourishes she assumed were mere extravagance were actually layers of intertwined metal that bore minute channels etched in their surface. Wyn leaned so close that her breath fogged the polished surface, but still she could not follow the paths of the channels, nor unravel the web of tiny bands. She needed one of Desmond's lenses to have a chance.

The box itself was not very large, as long as her arm and merely a hand's-length wide. It would slip nicely beneath Wyn's coat, but she did not touch it.

"It is beautiful, isn't it?" Cailean's soft voice came from the shadows near the entrance, and Wyn whirled to face her.

The Hawk stepped away from the darkened doorway. She had traded the elegant gown she had worn in the carriage for a simple dress and soft leather coat, and she had unbound the sculpted magnificence of her hair and wore it spread across her shoulders.

"That's what this is all about, then? This box?"

"Yes," Cailean agreed. "You can look at it if you want to. I left it out for you."

"You knew I was coming?"

"I guessed it would be you. You do not seem to be a patient woman."

"You're not worried I'll just nick it? I also seem to be a bit of a thief, if I'm honest."

"Do you know, I am not concerned," Cailean admitted. "You cannot open it, and holding on to the box only puts you at risk, so why take it?"

"It's dangerous, is it?" Wyn asked. She placed her hands firmly behind her back.

"Not on its own. You could hit it with an axe or throw it in the fire, and no harm would befall it, or you. No, the danger comes from those who want what's inside it."

"Like Quinn?"

"Hardly," Cailean scoffed.

"What's inside that's worth two gold talens?"

"Ah, now that is a secret that I am not ready to share." Cailean joined Wyn beside the box and rested her fingers on the

THE THIEF'S TALE

lid. "Not yet. Have you thought about my offer? Not for the keys. For you."

"I did, yeah."

"Did you decide what you wanted?"

"I did. But it's not that simple, is it? I can't just leave the lads. They need me, and I need them. Couldn't I just work with you and them as well?"

"You can't serve two masters, Wyn, and if you tried, you would tear yourself apart." Cailean smiled sympathetically. "No, I need all of you, but that doesn't mean you won't see your friends. I won't chain you to an oar or banish you to a temple."

"I don't know what's right," Wyn groaned.

"You will," Cailean promised. "But there's time to sort it out. We're getting ahead of ourselves. First, there is another deal that needs to happen."

"Yeah." Wyn took a deep breath to steel herself. *Best to get it over with.* "Just to be clear, we provide the two keys, you'll give us two talens, and you'll deal with Quinn... that's the deal."

"Yes. It will give me great satisfaction, honestly. He's a dangerous animal, and I imagine I'll receive more thanks for dealing with him than for any job I've undertaken before."

"There's always an angle, with you." Wyn shook her head, her lips pressed into a thin line.

Cailean laughed. "Of course there is. It's difficult enough to make a name for yourself without giving up any advantage you can grab. I've worked hard to create 'The Hawk'... or do you think the citizens of Kuray naturally have enormous respect for presumptuous women from Dalby-fucking-Combe?"

Wyn snorted. "Not likely. Probably as much as they had for a wee squidge from the Temple orphanage."

"Exactly!" Cailean beamed in delight. "Maker, Wyn, that's why I like you. You prove yourself, over and over, not like all those bloody braggarts who think stealing from one another makes them hard men."

"Too right," Wyn muttered.

"Then, that is another reason we should help each other. Can you imagine? I would have the best thief in Kuray helping me, and you would have the mythical Hawk providing jobs that will be told as legends around all the right tables. But, most importantly, it would be us, not the murderers and sycophants and back-stabbers who have currently clawed their way to the top."

"Yeah, I mean, that sounds excellent, but it makes a difference how things go down, don't it." Wyn swallowed and tried to gather some sense into what she was saying. *Don't just blurt it out.* Wyn's jaw ached from clenching her teeth, but slowly the chaos of her thoughts stilled. *Don't fuck this up.* She took a deep breath and jumped. "What I mean is, the deal has to be that you take care of Quinn first, otherwise we have to give him the keys."

"That's not what we discussed. You get me the keys, I take care of Quinn for you."

"Yeah, but what are we supposed to do when he comes asking? Because he's going to come asking. 'Hang on a shake, don't kill us just yet, because we've got someone who's going to take care of you any day now.' I don't see that little chat working out in our favor."

"Then we had best take care of Quinn before that happens."

"We? Listen, your ladyship, there's no 'we.' That's on you. I mean, if we had a deal. Which we don't, unless."

"When I say we should be partners, that means working together, not just doing a job. I can't agree to a deal where my partner might back out just because it suits her. Wyn, I will do everything I can to help you, and you will do everything you can to help me, and there can't be any change of heart."

"That easy?"

"Why does it need to be more complicated than that?"

"It sounds pretty complicated to me. Sounds easier just to give Quinn what he wants and not get murdered."

"And you think you and Quinn will part as friends?"

"I'm not daft."

"Then what?"

"We do a good job for him, he has no reason to do us harm."

"Wyn... really?" Cailean's eyebrows rose incredulously. "I thought we were being honest."

"I am!"

"When has Quinn ever needed any more reason to do harm than it suits him? Perhaps you avoid the knife while you continue

THE THIEF'S TALE

to be more use than danger, but that means you're his dog. Up until the moment he puts you down."

Wyn glared defiantly at Cailean, but she managed to keep her lips pressed firmly together, a last bastion against the nearly overwhelming urge to blurt, *I told Mellon that!*

"Could be," Wyn finally managed to mutter. *How is this going so badly?* she wondered. *There was no arguing with Mellon. Now she's saying the same things I did, but when she says it, somehow it makes more sense!* Wyn tried to remember how Mellon had convinced her to agree with him. "But could be he's grateful, a bit, and if he's disappointed... well, that's the knife for certain, isn't it?"

Cailean tapped her lip with a finger while she studied Wyn, a slight crease deepening between her brows. Wyn squirmed under the attention, the urge to escape as quickly as possible warring with the churning shame that lurched around her stomach at the thought of abandoning Cailean to satisfy Quinn.

Cailean raised her chin slightly, and her eyes narrowed. "You don't even believe yourself."

"Look, your ladyship, I'd love to give you the keys. Trust me, I'd give anything not to help Quinn if there was a way. But there isn't. Unless he's gone, we have to give him the keys, and that's... well, that's just it. Because it's decided. I'm sorry."

"Decided? By whom... Mellon?" Cailean snorted her disdain. "And he knows what's best for you, does he?"

"I reckon he's done right by me, he has," Wyn said defiantly, her jaw clenched. "You don't know him, so how would you know? Mellon's as sharp as they come, and if he says something is right, then it likely is."

"Fair enough," Cailean mused, "but by the same coin, he does not know me, nor what I can give you. The Tallywags are a fine crew, but all it takes is for one bastard to twitch and you're gone." Cailean snapped her fingers and Wyn flinched at the sharp crack. "When that happens, all the scamming and conning in the world won't help you. Mellon has kept you safe by keeping the Tallywags small and useful, but that life was gone the moment you caught Quinn's attention. If Mellon thinks the best way to survive is by pleasing Quinn until you can slip back into obscurity, he's fooling himself. You are going to be Quinn's bitch, and you are going to spend the rest of your life hoping Quinn doesn't kick you."

"And partnering up with you is the only way out?"

"Not the only way." Cailean paused to let a smile creep onto the corner of her lips. "But it's the best way. Best for me, of course, but also best for Mellon. He'll be free of Quinn and can go back to finding the perfect scam to bring in a few more pennies until the next time you bump into a real bastard. And if you want to live like that as well, then maybe Mellon really does have your best interests at heart. But if you want your life to be about more than a few pennies and hiding from whoever takes Quinn's place, then this is the best path for you, as well. There's so much more than silver waiting for us."

"I like silver," Wyn muttered. "What's wrong with silver?"

"Silver is a tool, Wyn. A tool you use to get the real reward."

"What's that, then?"

"Control," Cailean said fiercely. "Owning every last bastard out there, one way or the other, until they're all begging to give us what we're owed."

"That sounds all right," Wyn said grudgingly.

"Well, that is your choice when the time comes."

"I don't always make the most cunning decisions, really."

"Whatever path you want your life to take, if you want more than to live in constant fear of the day Quinn decides you've outlived your usefulness, you need my help. Give me the keys, and it's done."

"How are you not worried? You'd be next on Quinn's list for murdering if you take his keys."

"Of course, I'm concerned. But if Quinn needs to be dealt with, there's no use pretending otherwise."

Wyn ground her teeth in frustration. *How can both decisions make sense at the same time?* she wondered desperately. She fought down the urge to simply give up and hide until someone else worked it all out, but she could not so easily deal with the terrifying excitement that made her breath catch and her fingers tingle every time she thought of wiping Quinn from her life. *Gone... what would that feel like? Better than silver between my fingers, I'll wager Cailean is right on that score, as well.* But that giddy dream could

THE THIEF'S TALE

not overwhelm the churning dread that surged into her throat at the same time. *I can't...* But she did not know what she could not do. *Can't fight Quinn? Can't give Quinn what he wants?*

Wyn was utterly bewildered, convinced she should run one moment, convinced she should hand over the keys the next, and her head ached with the strain of trying to unravel all the possibilities and match them with her instincts, which were to hide somewhere she would never be found.

"Ohhh," Wyn groaned. "I'm going to give you the keys... fuck!"

"Good. Then we're partners, Wyn."

"He is going to kill us..." Panic tightened around Wyn's chest like a noose, constricting her breath and forcing her heart to labor as terrible visions howled to escape their confinement behind her mind's locked door. Visions of blood and pain, yes, but worse than those was the aching memory of loss, of emptiness lurking behind a familiar door that should lead to comfort.

Wyn reeled as the memory overwhelmed her, as fresh as the day the priest had led her to the side of a bed in a shuttered room filled with the sickly scent of incense, her gaze desperately fastened on the cracked hairbrush lying in its place on the small table beside the bed, as if that shred of normalcy could drag the rest of her world back from the raw misery it had become.

The memory metastasized as her thoughts crafted further misery to accompany it, of new losses multiplying unbearably until Wyn thought she might drown in them. Anguish would come, despite her every effort to seal herself away from such vulnerability.

*It hasn't happened, it hasn't happened...* Wyn tried to reassure herself, but she knew it loomed like a thunderhead.

"Every person..." she tried, but the words emerged as a croak. She swallowed and tried to breathe deep, suddenly aware of Cailean's dark, unwavering gaze. "... he'll kill every person... I care about."

Cailean nodded as if satisfied, but there was nothing soft in her gaze. "Yes, he will. Unless he's stopped."

"I can't... there's nothing..." Wyn searched for words helplessly, and desperation bubbled into a hopeless laugh that

THE THIEF'S TALE

sounded like a sob. "Listen, if we're smart, we just disappear, hide until it's over."

"You know better than that," Cailean scolded her, disappointment creasing her brow.

"No, I bloody don't," Wyn snapped back, suddenly angry, although she was not sure at whom. "If you knew how many times I've had to run and hide to duck a beating, or worse."

"Wyn, a man like Quinn, you don't hurt and then walk away. Anyone you leave behind, anyone who tries to help you, is as good as dead."

"What then?"

"Sweetheart, there are times you have to fight."

"What good is fighting when a couple of big lads get their mitts on you? I'll tell you. When you're a twig of a girl, it doesn't mean shite. You get your fingers broken and your face smashed, that's what you get."

"When they left you bloody," Cailean asked softly, "did you give up and stay in the mud?"

"Not a chance," Wyn said defiantly.

"Why not?"

"Because… because fuck them," Wyn snarled. "I'll not give up to those bastards, I won't."

"That doesn't sound like hiding."

"But it never ends," Wyn said desperately. "It never ends. Everyone's looking for you to be weak, for a chance to take you down, doesn't even matter why except they can do it. I can't fight all that, no one can. Surviving's hard enough… trying to keep them that matters safe…" Wyn's voice caught, and she wiped uselessly at the tears brimming humiliatingly in her eyes. "Every fucking time… I've tried…"

Wyn took a shuddering breath, then another. Her body ached from holding back so much pain and misery for so long, from the loneliness of waiting long years for comfort that never came, a touch that she could barely remember. A third trembling breath fought its way past her throat, and with it came an icy calm that almost made Wyn gasp in shock. She shook her head as she suddenly realized the truth of what she could not do. *I can't live like this. I can't be scared my whole life.*

THE THIEF'S TALE

Wyn took another deep breath and raised her gaze to meet Cailean's. "All right."

"No more hiding," Cailean agreed.

Wyn nodded her head. "All right then. If we're not hiding, what are we doing?"

Cailean carefully smoothed the front of her dress into place, then met Wyn's gaze with a twisted smile. "For starters, we are going to a ball."

"We're going to... what?"

"Lady Huntley's Folly. A gala for the cream of society. She holds the ridiculous spectacle every year."

"We sneaking in to nick her jewels or something?" Wyn asked, bewildered.

"Not at all. We are invited to attend."

"We are?"

"Of course."

"You're the cream, then, are you? I thought all you had at home was sheep?"

"We also have fish," Cailean corrected her. "True, my family name would hardly get me an invitation. But I have given her ladyship reason to think it would be worth her while to befriend me, and we have several mutual friends who are most certainly on the list."

"All right, but never mind all that twaddle, why are we going? How does greasing up with a bunch of high-muckities help us take care of Quinn?"

"It doesn't," Cailean replied, as if that answered the question. "Now, we must hurry to get ready."

"I think I might have left my gown at home," Wyn snorted.

"I am certain you did," Cailean replied, undeterred. "You can borrow one of mine."

"They won't fit," Wyn predicted, desperation beginning to ooze into her stomach as Cailean brushed aside her objections. *She's not serious... oh please don't be serious.*

"Of course they will," Cailean insisted. "We are of a height and shape, near enough."

THE THIEF'S TALE

"We never are," Wyn protested incredulously, but Cailean ignored her and swept from the room before Wyn could muster another objection.

Wyn trailed behind, wary of whatever scheme Cailean had concocted to somehow sneak her into a dress, and her suspicions seemed to be confirmed when Cailean led her into the noblewoman's dressing room, filled with elegant gowns straight from Wyn's nightmares.

But Cailean ignored the parade of terror and searched through a chest of what looked like very sensible clothes. Trousers, leggings, coats, and vests, fancy, to be sure, but not so dissimilar to the clothes that Wyn liked to steal from Desmond.

"There you are." Cailean laid a selection of clothes on a padded couch. "Oh, and your mask, of course."

The mask was sable and silver and depicted a ferocious grin with an array of pointed teeth beneath wide, slanted eyes and two long, pointed ears. The metal was engraved with waves of thick fur and had whiskers made of silver so delicate they swayed with every movement.

"Oooo, isn't he lovely," Wyn gasped. "Look at those teeth... what is he? A dog?"

"A wolf." Cailean smiled to match the mask in Wyn's hands.

"I don't like wolves," Wyn complained, and she suppressed a shiver. "I remember they'd howl all winter and eat folks, and such."

"They do howl, but unless you're a sheep, you have little to worry about." Cailean's smile grew even fiercer. "Remember... you are the wolf."

"And why am I a wolf?"

"Because Lady Huntley's Folly is a costume gala," Cailean explained. "There will be an unending parade of birds and butterflies and suns and moons, and an equal number of idiots dressed as Queen Aoife and King Otho, all very dull and predictable."

"Are you going as a hawk, then?" Wyn asked innocently.

"Ha, ha!" Cailean chirped mockingly. "Not at all. You will see. Now, get dressed, and we will just have time for your hair."

THE THIEF'S TALE

Wyn peered intently at the strand of hair currently falling over her eye and gave it a surreptitious puff, but there was not any evidence that it needed any attention, as far as she was concerned.

The door closed behind Cailean with an oiled click of the latch. Wyn stared at it, suddenly stranded in the middle of the room without any apparent escape save for hurling herself out the window and never coming back. The low murmur of voices from somewhere on the floor above and the dry rustle of flames in the room's fireplace only reinforced the profound quiet, and Wyn suddenly felt very alone.

She crept to the door and pressed her ear against it. No creak of floorboard or sound of smothered breath gave away whomever Wyn was convinced was watching the door. Wyn gently pressed the latch and nearly gasped as it opened easily. She blinked at the freed bar in surprise, then carefully seated it back in its hook. Wyn considered the latch for another long moment, then wedged a high-back chair under the doorknob before returning to the stack of clothes Cailean had set aside for her.

But as she passed the chest that Cailean had opened, Wyn froze. Beneath a folded cloak there was a gleam of steel. Wyn set the cloak aside and drew out a coat of heavy, black leather, reinforced with hidden steel plates over the torso and shoulders. Under the coat was a padded shirt with steel rings and a belt with a long, thin blade sheathed on it.

Wyn gently drew the blade and held it to the light. Its steel was polished until it shone like silver, with one razor edge and a tapered point as narrow as a pin. Her fingers curled around the hilt and she tried a flourish. The blade produced a satisfying ripping sound as it sliced through the air, and Wyn tried another thrust.

"That's right," she hissed. "I'm the Hawk, you bastards."

Wyn whipped the supple blade back and forth, enjoying the lethal gleam of its steel. "Lady Wyn at your service, you bastards." She thrust savagely. "Oh, you're too slow." She twisted and swung wildly. "That's for sneaking up behind me, you scum." Another flourish and she struck a haughty pose as she stared down her nose at a frilly dress on a rack. "You think you can take the... the..." She caught sight of the black and silver mask lying next to the clothes. "…the Wolf? No, not wolf," she decided, her nose wrinkling in disgust. "The Cat? Gah, names are hard. The Silly Twit is more like it."

Wyn sheathed the blade and hefted the coat for inspection. It smelled of oil and polish and creaked luxuriously as she slung it around her shoulders. The steel plates pressed against her, but their weight made her feel strong, not burdened, and after tightening the bewildering array of buckles the coat settled into place on her shoulders and ribs and did not stop her from twisting or bending.

Wyn ran her hands admiringly down the front of the coat, marveling at its craftsmanship. *No one could tell it's not a regular coat, could they? Not until they try a jab and get a bit of a shock. I wager this is what the Hawk wears when she goes to meet some right bastards,* Wyn decided. She snuggled inside the leather until the coat settled perfectly in place. *Am I stupid to think I could be like her?*

Wyn picked up the blade and strode to the center of the room where she faced the frilly dress again. She gave the dress a savage grin, her chin thrust out defiantly, one fist on her hip, the blade tapping against her calf.

"You're fucked now," she told the dress. The blade's tip rose ominously until it pointed directly at the lace decorating the bodice. "You face the deadly blade of…" Wyn's thoughts raced furiously, then alighted on the memory of a scolding raven, soaring free from its concealed aerie in a high tower, and her mouth opened in surprise at her own brilliance. "… of the Raven!" she announced. She thrust the blade a bit more dramatically than she had intended and made a neat hole in the gown's collar, an embarrassing distance from the spot she had been addressing.

Wyn cursed and bent over the sliced fabric. The cut was small, but she could stick a fingertip through it. Wyn grimaced and quickly concealed the evidence of her crime beneath a hasty fold of cloth. The blade was returned to the chest with equal speed, but she hesitated a moment before taking off the coat. Truth be told, it was too heavy to be comfortable, and she could not really move as quickly as she would like, but she did not want to take it off.

THE THIEF'S TALE

Wyn sighed and worked her way through the buckles until she could shrug out of the coat and concealed it and the blade beneath the cloak. *Until the Raven flies again,* she told herself with a wry grin.

Wyn stepped to the stack of clothing on the couch with renewed confidence. *Now then, there's nothing wrong with this,* she decided as she held the jacket up for inspection. Soft and black and with a long tail.

The rest of the ensemble looked promising as well. The vest was made of creamy leather with black embroidery and buttons, the shirt fashioned from silk so smooth it shone with its own inner light. Wyn lost herself in the touch of the luxurious fabrics against her fingers and cheek until the sound of footsteps passing the barricaded door made her jump.

Wyn quickly stripped off her tunic and stamped off her trousers and began to dress, her skin prickling into goosebumps despite the warmth of the room. As Cailean had predicted, the clothes did fit, albeit far more snugly than any trousers or vest Wyn had worn before, although she had to admit that was likely because she had stolen most of her vests and trousers from Desmond. Wyn tugged and yanked in vain, trying to find a way that they might hang shapelessly around her, but the tight fabric was proof against her meddling. The coat was hardly better, with a pinched waist there was no chance of ever closing, even around Wyn's slender form. *Why even have buttons?* she wondered as she gave up trying to pull the front together.

*And, Maker, these trousers are tight,* Wyn groaned. She was forced to shed her warm woolen leggings just to get the trousers on, and still she feared they would split if she had to bend over. *At least the coattails hide my bum.*

"Ready?" Cailean's voice outside the door made Wyn flinch and hug her arms defensively against her chest.

"No," Wyn answered desperately. "I think they're too small, or something."

"Oh?" Cailean asked, but there was a trill of ill-concealed laughter in her reply that made Wyn's mouth twist in suspicion.

THE THIEF'S TALE

"Look!" Wyn yanked the door open and stood defiantly. "You can see all my… bits…" Wyn gestured vaguely, but her mouth ran out of words as she gaped at Cailean.

The noblewoman had donned a sweeping gown fashioned from shimmering fabric dyed a fiery red that made Wyn think of autumn leaves. The dress had no corset or petticoats and was bound around her ribs by a silver chain, allowing the fabric to glide like water over Cailean's waist and hips. Long sleeves draped elegantly from her wrists, and a wide, graceful neckline left her shoulders and collar bare.

A sparkling jewel set in shining silver hung around her slender throat, and a web of silver threads held her long hair in an intricate sculpture that artfully trailed strands against her neck.

"Let me see you in the light," Cailean instructed as she brushed past Wyn into the dressing room. The noblewoman's dress covered her from shoulder to heel, but as she crossed the room the way it flowed against her legs made heat rise uncontrollably up Wyn's neck.

"Come on, then," Cailean encouraged her, and Wyn swallowed and suddenly remembered the travails of her own wardrobe.

"This vest is squishing me as bad as a corset," she complained.

"You will certainly turn some heads, but that is the idea," Cailean assured her. "A lovely view to capture the gaze and divert the mind."

Wyn glared at the tips of Cailean's shoes. "Maybe if you were wearing it."

"Wyn, look at me," Cailean urged, but Wyn found she could not meet the noblewoman's gaze. *You're an idiot if you thought prancing around in her clothes made you like her,* Wyn sneered at herself scornfully. *You don't talk like her, you don't live in a fancy house like her, you're not scary like her, and you sure as shit don't look like her.*

"Wyn," Cailean repeated. Cailean gently pressed two fingertips against Wyn's chin. "Look at me."

Wyn chewed her lip, suddenly angry at herself. *Listen, you bitch, I may not look like her, but I'm the one who climbed Ruric's bloody Tower! I'm the one who stole the Queen's knickers! Maybe I'm not the Hawk, but*

THE THIEF'S TALE

*I'm not bloody useless. In any case, who gives a turd what you think?* Wyn lifted her chin defiantly and met Cailean's gaze.

"There she is… strong and fierce," Cailean said approvingly. Her gaze moved slowly across Wyn's face, her eyes dark save for streaks of amber. Wyn felt her stomach flutter as her blush spread to her cheeks with each pulse of her heart under the noblewoman's scrutiny. Cailean's gaze finished its tour and settled to meet Wyn's. "And so pretty," Cailean murmured.

Wyn snorted her derision.

"And so very annoyed!" Cailean laughed. "But I am not wrong."

"I look like a twig wearing a hanky," Wyn corrected her.

Silk rustled as Cailean slowly inhaled and then breathed out sharply. "Is that what they tell you?"

"What? No…"

"Ah," Cailean said softly. "That's what you tell yourself."

"I don't tell myself… that's just…" Wyn spread her arms helplessly. "That's just me."

Cailean laughed. "Well, you could use a few years of proper food instead of whatever you have been eating, or not eating more likely, and it will be years before you finish growing… but believe me, you are ready to break someone's heart with that smile."

"I wouldn't say no to some more proper food, and that's a fact."

"Lady Huntley sets a fine table."

"Well, why didn't you mention that in the first place?" Wyn demanded, her hands on her hips. "Let's go."

But first there was an eternity of fussing over her hair, until at last it was secured in its own web of silver threads to match Cailean's. Wyn could not stop touching the strange sculpture on her head, tracing the luscious curls with her fingertips until Cailean put an end to the exploration with an icy stare.

Cailean's carriage was waiting for them at the base of the steps, with Cameron holding the door. Wyn ducked under his gaze and settled onto the padded bench with her feet stretched as close to the glowing brazier as possible. Cailean settled on the opposite side and carefully smoothed her dress over her thighs, causing the fabric to shimmer from orange to red as it shifted.

THE THIEF'S TALE

"Are you going as a candle, then?" Wyn wondered.

"What? No." Cailean held her mask to her face for Wyn's perusal. Like Wyn's, the mask was crafted of polished metal painted in brilliant colors, but red and silver instead of black. The mask showed a sly smile under a pointed nose, and wide, cunning eyes that seemed to know far more than they should.

"Ohhh, a fox! It's lovely," Wyn cooed. "The masks are a bit useless, though, aren't they? They hardly hide who you are."

"No, they don't, but everyone will act as if they do so they can feel mysterious."

"High-muckities are quite stupid, aren't they?"

"People are quite stupid, for the most part," Cailean corrected. "Wealth neither improves nor worsens the odds."

Wyn smirked as she thought of Chuckles. "That sounds about right. But why do we have to hold the masks on a little stick instead of wearing them proper? They'll be in the way all night."

"Because we are delicate ladies. It won't matter. We won't be doing anything more energetic than a stroll, or perhaps a dance."

"Dance?" Wyn asked desperately, her stomach churning with dread.

"You never know when some twit will ask."

"You don't?" Wyn squeaked. *Oh, Maker, how could I possibly look more of an idiot than trying to dance? She'll wet her knickers laughing, and that's the end of it.*

The carriage rumbled slowly over cobbles and then gathered speed as Cameron turned it onto the broad, snow-smooth avenue that arced through the park.

"Now," Cailean began, tapping her lip with a fingertip as she gazed at Wyn. "I believe this is the perfect night to introduce to society a young woman who has come to visit her cousin in the city for the first time."

"It is? Is that me, then?"

"Yes, although I will tell everyone we're not really cousins, but dearest friends. Perhaps our fathers would hunt, or some such nonsense."

"I'm posh, am I?" Wyn asked.

"Absolutely. Well, a country girl trying to be posh. How is your accent?"

THE THIEF'S TALE

"Oh, m'lady Huntley, I am quite overwhelmed by how shiny your palace is. Pray, madam, where do you keep the filthy people?"

"Not terrible," Cailean decided. "Try 'my lady' as two words, and can you do it without sounding so timid? You are my friend, not my little mouse."

"Of course, dear Cailean," Wyn gushed. "I do miss our summers by the river. Do you recall the hedgepig who so startled us? It seems so silly, now."

"Better. Have you seen a hedgepig?"

"They're terrible spiky and such, aren't they? Do you hunt them?"

"No! They're dear little... oh, I see." Cailean rolled her eyes as she noticed Wyn's smile.

"So, if I'm your friend from Dalby Combe, what's my name?"

"Bronwyn, of course."

"My real name?"

"Yes."

"You see, we usually came up with fake names when we pull a job," Wyn explained hesitantly. *She must know that... why do I have to tell her this?* "You know... a fake name for a fake person, so when the job is over that person can disappear."

"Wyn, please don't ever change," Cailean replied. "Yes, I do know about taking on a role. But this is not a role. This is the new you, so no fake name, just a little massaging of your past."

"How do you mean, it's me?"

"You are going to be at my side... you, not a fake girl who might disappear one day when a job is over. Cailean and her friend Bronwyn... there they are, inseparable. We just need a little story to explain your sudden appearance."

"Oh..." Wyn sat quietly for a moment, then gazed from the window at the flare of passing lanterns while her thoughts churned. "Why do you care? I mean, about me?"

"Because you are like me, Wyn. Because everyone has tried to kick me aside, told me to hide myself away. But I won't do it. I will not give up until I've beaten them."

"Like Quinn?"

THE THIEF'S TALE

"Yes, like him. And worse."

"You sound as if you're looking forward to it."

Cailean sat silently for a moment as she rocked with the carriage's movement, her face disappearing and reappearing in and out of shadow as they passed the lanterns strung along the avenue. At last, she looked away. "Perhaps I am."

THE THIEF'S TALE

## CHAPTER FOURTEEN

# Lady Blackberry's Ball

The carriage creaked as it turned between high pillars and its wheels crunched on smooth gravel. Wyn wiped the fog and frost from a patch of glass and peered ahead. A long row of lanterns arced along the carriageway, soft, golden spheres of gentle light surrounded by the snow-lined branches of a well-manicured park. Ahead, the tall pillars of a grand mansion appeared through gaps in the trees, its façade draped with long banners illuminated by enormous, blazing braziers.

Gleaming carriages pulled majestically to the front of the mansion in a dignified queue, disgorging a flock of guests who preened and fluttered their way up a short flight of steps and through a pair of wide, bronze doors.

Wyn's fingertips squeaked against the glass as she hurriedly cleared away a fresh coat of breath. *There's so many of them,* she realized as she watched the latest gaggle of magnificently attired ladies and gentlemen alight from their carriage. Lady Cailean's carriage was drawing ever nearer the broad carpet and the army of footmen that marked the point of disembarkation. Most of the guests seemed content to stroll elegantly into the warm light of the mansion, but more than a few clustered together to fawn and exchange adoring compliments.

"What do I do if someone talks to me?" Wyn asked.

"Twist them. Tell them what they want to hear, so that they will want to give you whatever you ask of them."

"How do I know what they want?"

"Listen closely enough, they will tell you. I suspect that most of the time a wink from you will work wonders."

"How do you mean?"

Cailean glanced at Wyn. "Don't tell me you have never played the coquette to befuddle a mark."

"Played at what?"

"Twisted them with a winsome smile."

"I sort of blink at them and try to look helpless, and they get all stupid."

"Mmmm, helpless is good, but sometimes you need to give them a push. Give a hint that they have a chance to bed you and they will do most anything."

"Bed me..." Wyn blushed with such force that she was certain it was shining through her mask. She risked a quick glance at Cailean. The noblewoman was gazing intently at the cluster of guests currently blocking the entrance to the mansion, but her mask's sly smile seemed to be aimed directly at Wyn. "I wouldn't know what to say..."

"Nor do they," Cailean laughed. "Wyn, not everyone is as lucky as you. Some are favored to be strong, some to be wise, and some are blessed to be beautiful. Those are all tools. You have the great fortune to be gifted in many ways. Pretty is a tool, Wyn, a tool you can use, along with your courage, along with your skill. It would be a waste to ignore it, like trying to climb a tower with your hand tied behind your back."

"Always an angle," Wyn murmured, but there was no confusion, just a need to show the Hawk that she understood. Wyn held the wolf mask in front of her face and gave Cailean a sly smile. "Still think you're blind, though."

"Perfect," Cailean said with satisfaction. "And if anyone asks, we are Anariel and—"

THE THIEF'S TALE

"Indrithil," Wyn finished with as much nonchalance as she could muster. "Yeah, I figured that out when I saw your mask."

"Well, aren't you the elvhen scholar."

"Temple orphan, that's me."

"Of course."

"The Song of Valor is a good one, anyway. I liked it when Indrithil tricked the moon, the sly lad, and when Anariel nipped old Half-Tusk on his nose."

"He deserved it," Cailean agreed.

Then their carriage was next in line, and Wyn had only a moment to become a young lady from the country, giddy with the prospect of her first proper ball. Her eyes went wide as she gazed at the soaring portico of the mansion. She caught her breath in wonder as she stared at the beautiful dresses. She smiled in delight as she heard the first stirrings of music drifting into the night air.

Cameron handed them down between two ranks of footmen attired in long red coats and shining silver breastplates. Wyn skipped eagerly up the steps and urged Cailean to hurry and join her. "Oh, look," she breathed, enraptured, as she strolled between the doors and into the vast entrance hall of the mansion. She twirled slowly in a circle, her hands clutched together against her chest. "Oh, Cai, just look at them all."

Wyn met Cailean's gaze and gave her a quick grin, and the noblewoman smiled her appreciation for the performance in return.

"Perfect," Cailean whispered as she joined Wyn. "Ah, and here is Baroness Arglwyddes, first to the trough, as always."

Wyn followed Cailean's gaze and saw an ancient lady tottering toward them, attired in a golden dress with a splay of shimmering rays of metal in a curve around her head, so excessive that Wyn worried the woman's withered neck would snap at any moment.

"Oh, Indrithil and Anariel... Cailean, how perfect," the baroness gushed as she neared, her crimson lips making a puckered circle of delight.

"Thank you, my lady," Cailean replied, and she curtsied gracefully to the older woman. Wyn imitated her as well as she could, but it was a far more elegant move than the quick bob she had learned from Cara, and she was fairly certain she had made a mess of it.

"And who do we have here?" the baroness wondered, her gaze lingering on Wyn's face with such unabashed directness that Wyn was suddenly very grateful for the wolf mask that concealed her.

"My lady, may I present my very dearest friend, Bronwyn, who has joined me from Dalby Combe for the winter, or perhaps longer if her father will permit it."

"Very pleased to meet you, my lady." Wyn gave the baroness her brightest smile.

"And you, my dear. Bronwyn… such a joy to hear that beautiful name, and borne by such a darling creature. How do you find our city?"

"It is all that I had hoped," Wyn assured the noblewoman. She heaved a deep, wistful sigh and gazed at the sea of gaudy, self-satisfied shits strutting about the ballroom. "It is ever so much like a dream."

"How delightful that you think so," Baroness Arglwyddes agreed. "You must join us for tea, Cailean, and bring young Bronwyn so that we may help you brush the country off her. Never fear, my darling, you will soon feel that this is your home, and that we are your dearest friends."

"Thank you, my lady," Wyn replied gratefully.

"Adorable," the baroness insisted shrilly, and she laughed and tottered away, still crowing, "Adorable!"

"She is really strange," Wyn muttered.

"She's a tool."

Wyn snorted in agreement. "She certainly is."

Cailean's twisted half-smile appeared on her lips. "No, I mean she is useful. The baroness frequently dines with Duke Campbell and Reverend Bowen, as the duke is her cousin and the reverend her brother by marriage, and she does not miss a chance to spread a few rumors to ingratiate herself with her listeners."

"Oh." Wyn tried to figure out how any of that would translate into coin, but got no further than a vague notion of bags of silver being handed out to favorite arse-licks when she found herself being introduced to another ancient woman in an

THE THIEF'S TALE

overwrought gown, so similar to Baroness Arglwyddes that Wyn was highly suspicious that the women must be sisters.

Then they were waylaid by a group of willowy, drooping nobles who might have been cousins, but Wyn was not paying attention when they were introduced. Then a lord in an emerald green jacket with iridescent feathers jutting out of his mask. Then a ferociously sweating man squeezed into a suit of shiny armor. Then more. And more, until Wyn felt that her cheeks must soon crack from smiling and her mind whirled from the assault of banal invitations to tea, to visit, to meet, to dine, to drink, to introduce, to stroll, all delivered in an unending chorus of, "you must... you must... you must..."

*This is bloody useless*, Wyn thought ferociously. *What we need is a half-dozen dippers in here, and we would be set for life.*

A small gap in the stream of nobility allowed Wyn to lean close to Cailean and whisper, "What are we doing here? Tell me we're not just going to spend the night listening to a bunch of high-muckities prattle on about how amazingly important they are?"

Cailean did not answer, and instead simply offered her arm for Wyn to take. Wyn was not certain what to do with it. *Grab it?* But Cailean slipped her arm through Wyn's and guided her deftly through the mob of nobility surrounding the dance.

Cailean pressed close to Wyn, shoulder to shoulder, and breathed in her ear, "No, I have something much more interesting planned."

"Can we do it soon?" Wyn whispered back. "Before anyone asks for a dance?"

"What's that?" Cailean asked, a mischievous grin perfectly complementing her mask. "You would like to dance?"

"No, no, don't you dare," Wyn hissed desperately.

They strolled together through the whirl of bright fabrics and gleaming jewelry, and Wyn no longer felt buffeted by the overwhelming pageantry of the ball. The lights and sounds flowed around them and cocooned them together. Cailean's fingers were warm on Wyn's arm as she guided her, and her hip brushed against Wyn's on each slow step, and Wyn remembered the young

THE THIEF'S TALE

couple she had so envied in the park, just that morning and a lifetime ago.

The gentle pressure of Cailean's touch was more comforting that Wyn could have imagined. She did not dare consider the last time anyone had touched her with anything but contempt or violence. That memory was held hostage, locked away with the misery that coiled inextricably around it.

Wyn sniffed surreptitiously, and once again gave thanks for her mask. *Maker, I'm such a mess,* she lamented. *Can I not even be happy for a moment without boo-hooing everywhere like a useless scrub?*

She sniffed again, then dedicated herself to recapturing the assured confidence she had discovered in the park that morning. It was much easier than she had feared, as her body fell naturally into the rhythm of a long, graceful stride, her chin high to meet the gaze of the crowd with equal conviction as she matched the movement of the woman on her arm.

*You don't scare me,* she told the sea of glittering masks, and at that moment the thought became truth. *Whatever I want, you'll give it to me. Whatever you do to catch me, I'll slip away.*

She met Cailean's gaze for a moment, and the noblewoman smiled her twisted, feral grin and squeezed Wyn's arm, and Wyn smiled in return.

"Show me something interesting," Wyn told her. "I'm ready for anything."

"Right this way," the Hawk replied.

They reached the long gallery that led from the ballroom to the garden and perused the seemingly endless row of dour lords and ladies immortalized in glum oil on canvases that lined its walls. Half-way along, a small alcove housed a statue of a stern lady armed with an arrogant sneer and a haughty gaze. Cailean glanced to make certain no one had entered the gallery behind them, then stepped to confront the statue with disgust etched in every line of her face.

"Our host at her most pompous," she murmured, "the Honorable Lady Huntley." Cailean's gaze slid sideways and caught Wyn's, and she tapped a finger on the badge emblazoned on the shield at the statue's feet. "High Commander of the City Watch."

THE THIEF'S TALE

"The what?" Wyn asked, her voice the squeak of a mouse caught by an owl.

"Lady Blackberry, herself."

"What the shite are we doing in the chief blackberry's house?" Wyn hissed. "You never said we were going to Lady Blackberry's ball!"

"I thought it would be interesting to have a little look through her study," Cailean replied. She released Wyn's arm and stepped around the statue to the back of the alcove. "Which just happens to be on the other side of this cunning little fake door here."

"Martyr's tears, you're crazy," Wyn whispered. She glanced quickly down the gallery. Lords and ladies strolled past the open doors at both ends. The corner of her lips curled into a grin. She met Cailean's gaze. "Go on, then."

"Me?" Cailean asked, her eyebrows arching in mock surprise. "I thought I was in the presence of the best cracksman in Kuray?"

"Well, I could give it a go," Wyn replied, her smile spreading uncontrollably. She quickly retrieved the two picks she had stashed in the hem of her coat and carefully slid them into the small keyhole hidden amongst the carved flourishes of the paneling.

It was not until Wyn was delicately testing the notches on the lock's barrel that it occurred to her that Cailean might be examining her skill and not merely deferring to her out of friendliness. A sudden tremble made her pick lose its position, and Wyn forced a deep breath as a surge of pins and needles prickled her fingers.

*Maker...* she cursed. She heard a slight intake of breath from the woman beside her, and now Wyn was convinced that she was being judged. A drop of sweat trickled between her hunched shoulder blades as she re-set the picks and slowly drew one back to rake the pins. They dropped nicely, and the latch freed with a subtle click.

"There we are," Wyn said as unconcernedly as she could manage.

Cailean pushed the door open and slipped through the gap in a rustle of silk. Wyn followed and eased the door closed behind them.

THE THIEF'S TALE

Lady Huntley's study was lit only by a single long shaft of light knifing between the main doors, which illuminated a thin slice of a thick rug and the corner of a massive desk, but which made the shadows so dark that Wyn could not make out more than that the room was long and had a high ceiling. But Cailean quickly found a lantern on the desk, and with the dry rasp of the wheel flint and a quiet pop, the lamp blazed into life.

"There we are," Cailean said with satisfaction. She lifted the lantern and gazed around the room, her eyes gleaming. Heavy drapes shrouded one wall, while wide shelves packed with leather-bound tomes lined the others, frequently interrupted by shining marble busts set on tall pedestals.

"So, this is why we're here?" Wyn asked. "To pull a quick heist?"

Cailean smiled. "Of course."

"Always an angle," Wyn said admiringly.

"Always. What a waste of time to follow the straight path."

"We won't be able to carry much, not in these outfits, but I daresay I could fit a gem or two somewhere."

"What we're looking for, we won't have to carry," Cailean informed her, and she set the lantern on the desk and began to examine the dozens of scrolls bound in black ribbons spread across it. "Boring, boring, boring…" Cailean shuffled scrolls and parchment across the desk dismissively.

Wyn opened a drawer and crouched over it, her fingers delicately nudging and lifting the contents without disturbing them. "Oooo, that has a nice sound," she mused as her fingers encountered a small bag that clinked heavily.

"We don't need silver," Cailean told her.

"Ha, very funny." Wyn tried to find a pocket worthy of her haul, but the coat's were barely wide enough for a fingertip, and the trousers lacked even a single pocket.

"What's the matter with these stupid clothes?" Wyn griped. "There's no place to keep anything."

"Carrying things is so common," Cailean informed her. "Why have useful things when you need them, when you can just make someone else do it for you?"

THE THIEF'S TALE

Wyn stuffed a few coins into her coat pocket just on principle and returned her attention to the drawer. "Oh! Her seal!" Wyn gasped as a silver cylinder with an engraved head was revealed. "Des will love this!"

"Hmmm," Cailean mused. "Do you not think she might miss that?"

"Well, it is a burglary... sometimes things go missing in a burglary, I hear."

"Yes, but if she realizes her seal has been stolen, she will have a new one made."

"Good point, I'll just..." Wyn appropriated a piece of fresh vellum from the drawer and began to melt a small puddle of wax onto it from the black candle stored next to the seal. "What have you found?"

"A ledger that shows the City Watch's accounts, warrants of arrest awaiting her seal, reports from her captains... interesting, but not what... ah, speaking of warrants..."

Cailean held up a sheet of parchment with the seal of the Watch next to a second seal bearing a sigil that Wyn recognized instantly, the stag and cross of the Royal arms.

"Apparently the King's Chancellor has seen fit to offer a reward of ten thousand crowns for any information leading to the arrest of the persons responsible for a trespass of the Silver Keep."

"Ten thousand? Wait, is that me? For a handful of knickers!" Wyn whispered, aghast. She shook her head in dismay. "That's not right."

"King Arian probably thinks you defiled his precious Gabrielle by daring to touch her clothes," snarled Cailean. Wyn blinked in surprise at the venom that dripped from her voice. "He always preaches about honor, but in truth he's a feckless cunt."

"Do they know who did it?"

"It doesn't say," Cailean replied. "I doubt it if they are offering rewards to snitches."

"Ten thousand will turn a lot of right people into rats, I reckon," Wyn muttered.

"I expect so," Cailean agreed. "Now, what have we here..."

THE THIEF'S TALE

She plucked a smaller scroll from its place of concealment at the bottom of the pile, where its crimson seal stood out like a cardinal in a flock of ravens.

"What's that, then?" Wyn asked.

Cailean turned the scroll so that Wyn could see the seal. Two men dressed in flowing robes on either side of a rayed sun, their outstretched hands encircling the blazing orb.

Wyn felt her breath catch. "The Guild..."

"Now, what do you suppose the Guild of Artificers might be talking to the City Watch about?" Cailean began to unroll the parchment.

"Don't!" Wyn hissed. "There's likely a Ward or something!"

"You are absolutely full of surprises," Cailean said. "Did they teach you about Devices in your Temple orphanage as well?"

"No... I just know stuff..." Wyn muttered.

"I see. Well, it has already been opened," Cailean pointed out, "so I think we should be fine."

The parchment unrolled smoothly, revealing a few lines of cramped script above a scrawled signature.

"It appears that the Guild of Artificers has requested the City Watch's aid in tracking down an apostate seeking to sell stolen Devices in Kuray," Cailean read. "The Watch is instructed to investigate every lead and question every informant they have to find the apostate."

"Is that us?"

"How could it be?" Cailean mused. "The box is veiled against any Diviner, and there is no way the Guild could know the keys are even in Kuray."

"That's true, how would they know?" Wyn mumbled as her heart sank. *What will she do if she finds out it was likely Tillings that snitched to the Guild, and it was us who told him about the keys? That would be the end of 'my very dearest friend,' I'll wager, and too right. Maker, why did we ever go to Tillings?*

"All right then, let's put all this back the way it was."

"Is that all we're doing?"

"Yes," Cailean said firmly. "I wanted to determine what the City Watch knew, if anything, about your efforts. And although

THE THIEF'S TALE

the reward is not good news, and this interest of the Guild in stolen Devices is troubling, now we know."

They slipped out the concealed door and strolled into the mob, but this time Cailean avoided all entanglements with a sure step that brought them safely through the throng faster than Wyn had dared hope possible. A footman scurried to summon Cameron and the carriage, and they were soon ensconced in its padded comfort as it glided southward along the broad avenues of the New City.

"So… what do we do now?" Wyn asked.

"Now we confirm what we discovered tonight, and we use it," the Hawk replied. "First, we find out if they have unearthed anything about you with that reward. Then, we determine which blackberry captain is working with the Guild, and I send Dugan along to discover exactly what they are looking for."

"I sort of meant, tonight, but that all sounds good, too."

Cailean laughed. "Tonight, I take you home."

"Oh, yeah, I suppose it's a bit late. I just wasn't sure if we were done or not."

"For now," Cailean told her. "Get me those keys, Wyn, and next time we will be going home together."

"I'll get them," Wyn promised.

Cailean watched Wyn for a long moment, then leaned forward and grasped Wyn's hands in her own, her dark eyes gazing into Wyn's. "I know you will," Cailean replied softly.

Wyn nodded, suddenly content to never move again, to feel soft hands encircling hers, to bask in the gaze of beautiful eyes that trusted her, that promised her hope, forever. When, at last, Cailean released her and once more reclined against her cushions, Wyn was ablaze with a fierce urgency to make good on her promise, immediately. She perched on the edge of her bench, rocking gently with the motion of the carriage, as her mind raced.

*We'll figure it out, quick as you like, I know it.* Wyn began to plan out exactly how she would deliver the keys to Cailean, weighing the benefits of a nonchalant reveal in the Hawk's drawing room against a clandestine meeting in a dark courtyard.

A small worm of disquiet began to twist in the back of her mind. *What's the chance that Grey Bastard does find out what the Guild's*

THE THIEF'S TALE

*been up to? Pretty good, I'll wager. And how pleased will her ladyship be if she discovers I may have known a bit more about that than I let on? Disappointed won't half cover it, I'll wager that, as well.*

Wyn grimaced but could not think of a way to avoid that shame. Aside from coming clean.

"I think that message from the Guild might actually be about us," Wyn ventured into the silence.

"Why is that?"

"I think they might know the keys are in Kuray."

Cailean's eyes narrowed as she stared at Wyn, but she remained quiet as Wyn squirmed miserably.

"I mean... I know they do."

"You sound certain."

"Yeah. Master Calixte told me."

"What?" Cailean gasped, her eyes wide with shock.

"I was going to tell you, I promise, it just sort of slipped my mind, and then when I remembered I didn't know what I should say because it sounds so bad just to say it."

"That is an understatement. I think you should probably tell me the rest of the tale."

"I was visiting a jeweler Mellon knows, a funny old stick named Tillings, and I turned around and there was Calixte, just waiting for me, and he says, 'where's the key' and starts waving his staff around and the whole shop went to pieces. So I ran."

"I..." Cailean covered her mouth with her hand and turned to stare out the window, but Wyn swore she saw a smile twitch on her lips before she concealed it. "I imagine it was a bit more dramatic than the telling."

"Oh, yeah, it was proper scary. Poor old Tillings tried his best to help me, but I thought I was fucked, and that's a fact. Tables and benches and bottles wrecked, pieces everywhere. I didn't stop running until I was well gone."

"How do you know it was Master Calixte?"

"I overheard him in Spicer's study giving her adept the nuts."

"So, they know." Cailean frowned at the dim shapes passing beyond the carriage's windows. "Somehow, they know, and they know enough to lead them to you."

"Yeah," Wyn agreed quietly.

THE THIEF'S TALE

Cailean's lips pressed into a thin, pale line. "Someone must have told them."

"I suppose..." Wyn managed.

"There is no other explanation," Cailean insisted. "One of Quinn's is betraying him to the Guild. I'd wish the snitch good fortune if his scheme didn't put us in as much danger as Quinn."

"One of Quinn's, hey?" Wyn asked, grasping quickly at the rope. She snorted as much contempt as she could muster. "Yeah, I believe it. His crew is as shady as they come."

"All the more reason to deal with me, not Quinn," Cailean pointed out.

"I'm not changing my mind," Wyn insisted.

"Just reminding you what a wise decision you made."

"It's what I'm known for."

"I'm afraid this makes your task even more urgent," Cailean told her. "Now that the Guild knows the keys are in Kuray, I am certain they will quickly discover who holds them. I trust Nell Spicer to employ some sort of Veil to conceal her key, but Murtagh has no idea what he is carrying. The Guild will be visiting him soon."

"Actually..." Wyn began. "I may have also forgotten to mention that we snatched Murtagh's key this morning."

"You... what?"

"I didn't tell you?"

"No, I feel certain I would remember that."

"I meant to."

"I am sure you did. Where is the key now? You didn't bring it tonight, did you?"

"Oh, no," Wyn snorted. "It's back with the lads, safe and snug."

"Wyn, there's every chance Calixte has already paid them a visit. If he doesn't already have the key, we must move it somewhere he can't find it."

"No, no, no worries," Wyn assured the noblewoman. She grinned slyly. "We made sure to put it with a Veil, we're not idiots."

"You have a Veil?" Cailean shook her head in disbelief. "Of course you have a Veil, why am I surprised?"

THE THIEF'S TALE

"It's just a wee one," Wyn said modestly.

"Is it. And who amongst you is the adept who empowered it?" Cailean asked. "You?"

"Oh… uh…" Wyn stammered. "No. It was Tillings. The jeweler. He's an apostate. Was. I mean, probably was. Definitely was an apostate, probably is dead."

"So, you went to him for a Veil, and that's where Calixte found you," Cailean mused. "Was your association with Tillings known to those in Quinn's crew?"

"I dunno. Des apprenticed with Tillings for a year, so I suppose they could have sussed it out."

"It's unfortunate, but there was no way of knowing, and you did the right thing to seek out a Veil. How long will it remain empowered?"

"Uh… what does?"

"The Veil. If Tillings empowered it for you, someone who knows its Word will need to do it again once the effect of his Word expires."

"Oh. He didn't say."

"Then watch it closely. If it shows signs of weakening, you must bring me the key immediately so that I may conceal it."

They rode in silence as the gentle rocking of the carriage slowly gave way to heavy jouncing as they entered the Old City. Cameron's bellow was more than enough to clear a path, however, and they rolled to a stop outside Scrivener's far sooner than Wyn could have imagined. *I need a bloody carriage,* she decided. *Enough walking around forever every day.*

"Goodnight, Wyn," Cailean said as Cameron opened the door for her. "I look forward to seeing you again."

"It'll be soon," Wyn replied. She rose to leave, then suddenly stopped. "Oh… I'm still wearing your clothes."

"Keep them," Cailean told her. "You look stunning in them."

For an instant, Wyn readied herself to scoff. Instead, she blushed, a happy, awkward heat that was so different from the shame that typically reddened her cheeks that she could not help but smile.

"Goodnight, Wyn."

THE THIEF'S TALE

"G'night," Wyn murmured, and she stepped quickly from the carriage and watched it roll away before strolling happily into the tangled streets.

⎯⎯⎯⎯⎯⎯⎯⎯⎯⎯

*W*yn yanked the curtain closed behind her, skipped to her cot and leaped onto it, face-first. The walk from Scrivener's to the brewery had done nothing to suppress the exhilaration that coursed through her. Only after stifling an irrepressible burst of laughter with her pillow did she roll onto her back and kick off her boots, letting them thud to the floor.

Wyn stretched her legs above her, wiggled her toes, and sighed contentedly as she watched her small feet twist and point happily in the air over her face.

Visions of a golden key nestled in her hand, Baron Murtagh tipping helplessly from his saddle, spinning figures in lavish gowns, and a sly smile beneath a fox's cunning eyes whirled through her mind, a glittering cyclone of giddy joy and triumph that left her breathless.

There was still disquiet on the horizon, for certain. Awkward questions to be answered, terrifying enemies lurking, but Wyn buried those gloomy problems for another day. *Shit on all that,* she decided.

Wyn rummaged beneath her cot and collected her battered box, peered inside, and carefully extracted the Queen's knickers.

She hooked a thin strap of lace over her toe and let the bundle uncoil. The lantern made the red silk shine with a bright glow, as if the soft material was burnished metal. *I should give them to Lady Cailean,* Wyn decided as she gazed at the panties dangling over her face. *They'd suit a beautiful lady like her.*

But a frown creased her brow as she remembered the distant coldness Cailean had displayed when Wyn had mentioned the Queen's undergarments, and she reconsidered. *Must not be her style, I suppose. Maybe I'll just hang on to you, instead. I've done well by you so far, that's certain.*

THE THIEF'S TALE

Wyn stretched her toes until the panties dropped neatly into the waiting box, then removed the cracked brush. Her hair was starting to ache from its long imprisonment, so she painstakingly removed the dozens of pins holding it in its structured glory and dropped the silver thread into the box as well.

Then she began to brush out her hair with long, gentle strokes. As the bristles slid through her thick strands and dragged across her palm, the faint scent of lavender stirred. *I think I found a friend today,* she thought. *I hope you like her. She's fierce and strong, but maybe I am, too. She makes me feel safe, Mum, and I think she can show me the right things to do. I don't want to hurt the lads, but I want to be with her. Is it all right to want that?*

Wyn gave her hair a final stroke, set the brush in the box, and gently closed the lid. *I wish you were here to tell me what to do.*

Wyn secured the box beneath the cot, squirmed out of her coat, and curled into her pillow with a contented sigh. Her mind traced languidly over every moment spent with the Hawk. She dwelled on every glance, every smile, every fierce look, every laugh, every touch. She agonized over each word Cailean had uttered, repeated them endlessly to catch every nuance and inflection, and practiced them until they became her own. *I'll be her, someday,* Wyn promised herself. *I swear I will.*

Wyn yawned desperately, dragged a blanket over her shoulder, and yawned again, her eyes stinging with weariness, but her mind would not let her rest.

Wyn rolled over and tried to will herself to sleep, but as her thoughts finally began to quiet, the faint scraping of metal on metal from the main room crept to her ears through the silent lodge, and she could soon think of nothing else.

*This is stupid,* she decided. She rolled out of her bed, wrapped the blanket around her shoulders, and padded through the doorway to investigate.

Desmond was seated at the table, hunched over a cloth spread on the cracked wood. A lantern sat next to him, its light gleaming on a tidy array of metal picks and shafts. He held a key, chosen to match the overall size and shape of the star key, and in his other hand a slender pick. One of his wax molds stood open in

THE THIEF'S TALE

front of him, and he was slowly etching the blank surface of the new key with the same patterns that were pressed into the wax.

He glanced up as Wyn appeared in the lantern's circle of light and smiled, his eyes widening in astonishment.

"Look at you," he said softly.

Wyn spread her blanket to show off her fancy clothes. "I know, aren't they flash?" She presented one side to Desmond, then the other, before strolling gracefully to the table, where she struck a haughty pose. "What do you think?"

"You're... you look amazing," Desmond told her.

Wyn smiled, then huddled into the blanket again. Desmond's gaze lingered for a moment, then returned to the key.

Wyn settled onto a chair across from him and watched Desmond's hands work, mesmerized by the subtle movements of finger and pick, the delicate, certain, careful strokes across the metal.

"Maker, Des, how do you do it?"

"What's that?" Desmond asked, never taking his gaze away from the key. A thick flop of his hair had fallen over his forehead, but he made no effort to corral it, all his attention devoted to the wax imprint and the key under his reading glass. He frowned and chewed delicately on his lip, and his fingers moved slightly, drawing a tiny, intricate curve into the surface.

"How do you get all those little lines so perfect?" Wyn asked. "Every time, perfect."

"I don't know," Desmond replied from far away. He turned the key slightly and engraved another line with a precise stroke, turned it again, and connected the two shapes with an exact edge.

Wyn smiled happily and watched his fingers move confidently over the metal, then idly collected one of the small wooden figures from Desmond's completed model of the Bathhouse. He had captured most of the building with simple, confident carving that matched its proportions exactly, and had added flourishes to the areas that their plan had been most concerned with. A pair of windows leading to the changing rooms. A statue and a bench. The winding garden paths.

THE THIEF'S TALE

He had also finished a full set of figurines representing Murtagh and his guards, the Bathhouse attendants, the blackberries, and a dozen others, all the actors with a part to play.

Wyn turned the figure around in her hand and smiled at its pointed nose and prominent teeth. "We should probably hide this one before Ratter pays us another surprise visit."

Desmond glanced up for a moment, grinned, and returned to his work. "Probably."

Wyn experimentally pressed the figure's nose into the pad of her thumb a few times, then turned it back and forth to catch the light. "Do you remember what Pickle used to call him? 'Shatter.' "

"I remember."

"Then he'd always look over his shoulder to see if Ratter had snuck up on him."

"Yeah."

"Why do you think Pickle threw that stone?"

"Because he was an idiot."

"Des! Poor Pickle."

Desmond kept his gaze locked on the tip of his pick. "He was an idiot. You said so every day. 'Poor Pickle'… you hated him."

"I did not!" Wyn insisted.

"You called him a crying baby, and you said his name was Pickle because he had such a tiny dingle. Very friendly."

"Maker, I did, didn't I?" Wyn rested her chin in her palm. "Do you remember how he bawled when we made him come with us to Cowgate to dip? I reckoned he would cause such a fuss we could pick the crowd clean." Wyn screwed up her lips in a scowl. "I guess he was right to be scared, though, hey?"

Desmond finished the pattern and puffed on the gleaming metal, examining it at all angles, before he set the half-finished key on the table next to his tools and rubbed his fingers together.

"No, Pickle was an idiot. If he wasn't an idiot, Ratter would never have caught him, and if he wasn't an idiot, he would never have thrown that rock."

"I suppose."

"Wyn, how old were you when Ratter caught you in Cowgate?"

THE THIEF'S TALE

"Twelve." Wyn knew that for a fact, although her certainty about her age became very vague the further from that twelve she grew. *Seventeen, now,* she thought, but it might be more. *Or less.*

But twelve she knew. Twelve was the last year someone had cared enough about her to count for her, and the summer Ratter had caught her stealing in Cowgate had been her first summer alone.

"And how many times after that did he catch you?"

"None." Wyn knew that for a fact, too. As Ratter's leering smile had loomed over her, only varying slightly as he snapped her small fingers like twigs, one after the other, she had sworn never to be caught again.

And she had kept that promise.

"That's right, none," Desmond agreed. "That was the first thing you told me, do you remember? Don't get caught. How many times did he catch me?"

"Once."

"Once. That was enough for me, too. You and I learned. It wasn't good enough to fool your mark. It wasn't good enough to fool the blackberries. You had to be good enough to hide from Ratter, and if you couldn't, you stayed away from Cowgate. But not Pickle. How many times did Ratter catch him?"

"Three times."

"That's right. Fuck, how many times did Pickle's mark catch him? Even the blackberries caught him once. He never learned, always careless."

"I suppose so."

Desmond frowned at her.

"All right, I know so," Wyn admitted. "I still don't know why Pickle threw that rock, though."

"I don't know either, but he shouldn't have."

"No." Wyn probed the long gap Desmond had given the wooden Ratter's lip with her thumbnail. "No, Ratter got a gold tooth, and Pickle got beaten to death." She set the miniature Ratter back on the table, then carefully knocked it over with a jab of her finger.

"Yeah. Poor Pickle."

THE THIEF'S TALE

Wyn browsed the cluster of figures standing in front of the Bathhouse. A dozen featureless blackberries scattered in the park, a Murtagh with a ridiculously swollen chest, a slouching Mellon, and a scowling Fergus.

"What was I going to say?" she asked Desmond.

"Um... that you want another blanket?"

"No, no, no," Wyn muttered. "Where are we?"

"By the statue."

Wyn stood up and leaned over the table. There was miniature Desmond, his head poking from a shapeless ball of rags, waiting patiently beside the statue. Wyn frowned, momentarily unable to find a second figure, then saw it, standing triumphantly on the statue's shoulders.

The small carving was different from the others, less a caricature and more a sculpture. It twisted gracefully, its cloak and long hair a swirl of movement, its curves strong and supple and somewhat more prominent than Wyn knew she had a right to claim. It held a key slyly behind its back with one hand and raised two fingers defiantly with the other.

"That's me?" Wyn asked.

"Yeah," Desmond said softly.

"It doesn't look like me."

"Yes, it does."

Wyn snorted. "I wish. In any case, I was wearing that dress."

"I don't know why you made such a fuss. You looked right pretty in that dress, and all," Desmond smiled awkwardly, "and you look nice, now..." To her astonishment, he reached across the table toward her hand.

"What are you doing?" she snapped at him as she cringed suspiciously away.

"I just meant that you clean up well," Desmond said, baffled. "Martyr's tears, what's wrong with that?"

"Are you having a laugh?" Wyn crossed her arms angrily and glared at him.

"Shit, I take it back." Desmond held his hands out, palms facing her as if warding away a blow. "You look like a drowned rat. Better?"

THE THIEF'S TALE

"Thanks," Wyn said sweetly, putting as much scorn into her voice as possible.

"You're welcome," Desmond muttered. He snatched up his pick and the key and began another pattern, his lips pressed so tightly together they were white.

Wyn glared at him for a moment longer, then stomped angrily back to her cot to stare at the wall in the dark.

## CHAPTER FIFTEEN

# A Bottle and a Tale

"So," Mellon said, his fingers scratching idly in his beard. "That's not exactly the deal we wanted, is it?" He glanced around the small table, his questioning gaze meeting each of the Tallywags' in turn until he ended on Wyn. "What happened?"

"I tried," she told him. "I explained it all to Cailean, just like we agreed. She said no."

"I imagine you said, thank you very much, and walked out? Like we agreed?"

"No," Wyn admitted. "Look, I know you're angry, I know it's not what you wanted, but this is best, I promise."

"Tell me what changed your mind," Mellon asked, "so that I can understand, as well."

"Well, first of all, she's already helping us, just like you wanted, so there's that."

"That's good news, for a change. She let you in on her plan for dealing with Quinn? What, exactly, is she doing?"

"Not Quinn, no, but she took me to Lady Blackberry's mansion, and we found out there's a warrant out for me for the knickers, ten thousand if you can believe that, and that the Guild knows the keys are in Kuray. Well, we knew that part, but now she does, too, and she thinks it's a rat in Quinn's crew who told the Guild."

"And?"

"Well, and she said the same things I said, only better. Like it doesn't matter what we do, Quinn will do us over as soon as we're not useful to him, and we're just his dogs until he does. Cailean's going to help us, Mel, I know she will. You had to be there to see. She's wicked smart, just like you, and sees all the angles before I ever could, and she's that ready to fight. I know it's a terrible risk, but we can't give Quinn what he wants, we have to fight, too. Can't you see that?"

"I think I'm seeing pretty clear," Mellon told her. He sighed wearily and leaned back in his chair, which protested with a loud creak. "All right, what's done is done. You went to negotiate, and you thought this was best. You told her she had a deal, so that's what she has. For what it's worth, you were right at the start of all this, and I hope you're right now, I really do."

"Me, too."

"It does leave us with a bit of work to do," Mellon pointed out. "Our plan for Quinn was to leave him holding the keys for Master Calixte, but if we're to give them to the Hawk, that won't be possible."

"So we need to come up with a way to keep Quinn happy while not giving him the keys so Lady Hawk can keep her end of the deal before we're all killed. Of course, we first need to get our hands on Nellie's key." Mellon patted his stomach and peered at Wyn. "But none of that is as important as the last question."

"What?" Wyn asked, puzzled.

"Do we all get fancy new clothes out of the deal, too? Or was that just for you?"

Wyn grinned sheepishly. "Just me. I don't think you'd fit into one of her gowns, but I can ask if you'd like."

"Perhaps I'll pass. All right then, Tallywags, how do we get Nellie's key?"

Silence greeted the question as they glanced hopefully at each other.

THE THIEF'S TALE

"I could get into her study the same way as before and make the swap," Wyn suggested.

"A straight burglary, eh?" Mellon asked.

"Yeah?"

"I thought we hated that idea the first time," Desmond reminded her. "We don't know how she guards her study on a normal night. What if Pinhead is in there when you open the window?"

"We'd watch the place for a few nights, sneak in and see ahead of time."

"That's cutting it close," Fergus pointed out.

"What's your plan, then?"

"We go in while Spicer is at the Exchange with her guards, I deal with anyone who raises a fuss, and we take everything we can carry from the safe. Make it look like we didn't care about a key and left it behind."

"There's at least twenty servants in that place," Desmond said gloomily. "Plus those two blackberries at the gate. How're you going to keep all those quiet? They'll be running all over the place, screaming and shouting."

"I don't see mistress Callaghan agreeing, either," Wyn added, "and there's that weasel, Quany."

Fergus nodded, but Wyn was not at all certain whether the swordsman was agreeing or merely acknowledging the points.

"We could do the Wine Merchant!" Mellon beamed.

The announcement was met by a chorus of groans and eye rolling around the table.

"What?" Mellon asked, his grin fading as he looked around the table with a bewildered expression on his face.

"Anything but the Wine Merchant," Desmond begged.

"It's perfect," Mellon insisted, crossing his arms.

"It's not bloody perfect if I have to stand there and listen to him go on about the perfect bloody soil in bloody Criénne, again," Desmond muttered. "Wyn gets to be the assistant, this time."

"I do not!" Wyn protested.

"It's your turn."

"Isn't."

"Flip you for it."

THE THIEF'S TALE

"We've not agreed we're even doing the Wine Merchant," Wyn reminded him.

"It's perfect!" Mellon said defiantly.

"Mel, Spicer *is* a wine merchant," Wyn pointed out. "It'll never work."

"We will just have to use a bigger piece of bait." Mellon's smile had reappeared.

"Martyr's tears," Wyn sighed. "Des, get a penny. I feel lucky."

"Wyn, stop yanking on it," Mellon scolded her.

She pulled her finger out of her trim uniform's stiff collar and smacked her hand into her lap. "It's too tight," she complained.

"It's supposed to be tight," Mellon explained. "Nice and neat, proper smart."

Wyn scowled and twisted her head. The truth was she did not mind the uniform that much. For starters, it was black. A fitted black jacket, snug around her chest and waist, open down the front beneath her belt, curving in two long sweeps to her knees. The jacket buttoned up the side of the chest with a row of brass buttons, had brass cufflinks, and, annoyingly, a brass badge on either side of the high, stiff collar that was strangling her slender neck.

For seconds, its black trousers were roomy enough that she could wear her thick wool stockings underneath for warmth.

For thirds, the slim uniform, with its narrow waist and flared tails, gave her a hint of a figure, or, perhaps, if she dared to believe Cailean, revealed that she had a hint of a figure, a thought that, surprisingly, no longer made her want to huddle inside her tightly-wrapped cloak.

However, there was more amiss than just the collar. Mellon would not allow her to wear any kind of cap or hood, insisting that a uniformed attendant would never dare to sport such mufti, and had glared at her until she had pulled her hair up into a severe bun that felt like it was yanking her ears to meet one another across the back of her skull.

THE THIEF'S TALE

What she could feel of them, in any case. They were already numb at their tips, and so was her nose. Her cheeks were burning, and she suspected they were bright pink from the chill, as the inside of their carriage was achingly cold, despite the firmly shut and shuttered windows. Frozen air swirled into the carriage every time the wind howled past, along with bursts of snow that somehow found their way through the frames of the windows.

"Good thing we didn't bring any blankets."

Mellon waved away another blast of wind that rocked the carriage. "It's just a little blizzard. In any case, think of those two poor bastards up front." He grinned evilly, apparently unmoved by the plight of their comrades on the driver's bench.

The carriage jarred awkwardly and creaked in every joint, and Wyn grabbed for one of the leather grips that hung next to the wall.

"Oy!" Mellon bellowed, rapping on the front wall with the silver tip of his cane. "Careful, damn it. We just stole this bloody thing."

"I can't fucking see in this fucking storm," Desmond's miserable voice drifted back to them, and Mellon rolled his eyes.

"Avenues wide enough to allow four carriages, side by side, and he still hits the curb." He settled against the cushioned back and crossed one leg over the other, the picture of elegant nonchalance. Then his eyes narrowed, and he dove forward to peer into a small box mounted at the side of the bench that had sprung open when the carriage had bounced. "Oh, look what we have here."

He produced a long-stemmed pipe, crafted from golden, polished wood. "What a beauty," he announced. He began to fill the bowl from a small pouch in the box.

"What are you doing?" Wyn asked. "Maker, you're not going to smoke that?"

"Of course I am," Mellon replied. He found a wheel flint in the box and ground sparks into the bowl as he sucked on the pipe.

"That's been in someone's mouth," Wyn objected, her nose wrinkled in disgust.

"That it has," Mellon agreed as he sat back on the bench, contentedly blowing clouds of smoke into the air. "One day, when

THE THIEF'S TALE

you're a bit older, you'll realize that sometimes it's very nice to have parts of other people in your mouth."

"Ewww." Wyn certainly would not mind trying, if someone ever volunteered, but it was quite disgusting to think of things like kissing when Mellon was grinning at her with his foul smoke making her ill.

The carriage creaked as it turned sharply, then it trundled to a stop. Two thumps on the roof let them know they had arrived at Nell Spicer's palatial home.

Mellon gave the blue jacket and cream vest he had acquired a careful tug into place, then thumped back.

The door was yanked open a moment later. Snow whipped into the interior, stinging Wyn's cheeks and snapping Mellon's coattails. He jumped down, and Wyn followed, clutching a long, polished wooden box in both hands. Fergus gave her a nod as she passed, his hood and coat completely covered in snow, then he slammed the door closed and leapt back onto the driver's bench as Desmond cracked the reins to drive the carriage around to the carriage house in the back.

Wyn and Mellon stumbled through the tall front doors and into the grand circular entrance hall. The massive doors closed behind them, muffling the shriek of the wind so completely that Wyn could hear the squeak of Master Parker's shoes as he approached.

"I am very sorry not to meet you at the door," Parker said stiffly, "but what with the weather, we were not expecting visitors."

"I suppose not," Mellon replied, clearly unconvinced of the merits of Parker's argument. He had added a slight accent to his normal high-muckity voice, a trace of a vibrant, exotic tone that teased around his vowels and altered his cadence.

He produced a silver case from an inside pocket and extracted a card boasting Desmond's best calligraphy and gold leaf.

"If you would care to wait in the parlor while I announce you, ah… my lord," Parker concluded with a glance at the card.

"Of course," Mellon agreed and strolled across the entrance hall in Parker's wake, barely acknowledging the majestic pillars and

THE THIEF'S TALE

sweeping stairs. Wyn hurried behind, the box held precisely flat in her hands, the perfect servant.

Wyn stifled a grin as they were left in the Garden Parlor, and Mellon posed nobly in the window overlooking the horse statue. A servant appeared to provide refreshments, and Pinhead appeared to provide glowering silence.

Wyn arched one eyebrow at the burly guard and stared back, as seemed proper for an attendant who clearly boasted the neatest, blackest uniform with the shiniest buttons in the room.

Mellon had finished a glass of sweet, golden wine and was beginning to repeat his repertoire of noble poses when the doors to the parlor opened, and Parker returned.

"Madam Spicer will see you now," he announced, and led them along the hall to the wide doors of Spicer's study.

The Honorable Nell Spicer sat at her desk, its broad surface bare save for a thick, leather-bound book and a silver candlestick. The drapes had been pulled back from the tall windows, exposing a sweeping view of streaking, swirling snow, and a fire roared in the wide fireplace to battle the freezing air that emanated from the window's glass panes.

"Lord Jenner," Parker announced, and withdrew. The doors swung shut behind him with no apparent impetus from Parker or Spicer.

"Now then, my lord," Spicer began. Her voice carried effortlessly across the vast room, her accent dripping with the cultured resonance of the New City. "I do not believe we have been introduced."

"No, madam, yet your name is known to my associates and me as far more than a profiteer of trade, but as a connoisseur of true masterpieces."

"That would depend on what goods your associates represent. If you have a trade proposal, it would be more proper to leave your credentials with Master Parker, and we might arrange a meeting at the Exchange at a future date."

"I have been sent to offer you a singular purchase, Madam, and I assure you, it would be most improper to discuss it at the Exchange."

THE THIEF'S TALE

"I see." Spicer leaned forward and interlocked her fingers. "And what type of purchase do you refer to, my lord?"

"My associates and I have the good fortune to represent a legendary vintage. Peerless in every way."

"I already have partners in Venaissin with whom I am very satisfied."

"Madam," Mellon said graciously, "I believe you misunderstand. I am not a representative of a vineyard. I am a representative... of this." Mellon beckoned grandly, and Wyn carefully placed the wooden box on Spicer's desk. Mellon produced two steel keys and snapped the locks open, then swiveled the case to face Spicer and opened it with a flourish.

Inside the case a single bottle was nestled in a bed of black silk, held in place by silk cords. Thick, white wax with the imprint of a proud, rearing horse sealed the bottle's top. The glass was sparkling clean, but there were other signs of age. The wax was discolored around the edges, and there was a slight nick in the otherwise smooth bottom edge of the bottle.

Spicer leaned forward, and Wyn saw her eyes go dark and wide as her gaze fastened on the seal.

"What is..."

"A treasure beyond compare," Mellon sighed with pleasure.

Spicer frowned, and her hands retreated to her lap. "I have seen wines from the White Horse vineyards, before. I have two in this very house. They are exquisite, but hardly incomparable."

"Of course, Madam, if this were simply another bottle of wine." Mellon tilted his head to concede her point.

"Then, what, exactly, am I looking at?"

"If Madam would permit me to become nostalgic?" Mellon asked, and continued as Spicer gave him a brief nod. "You are acquainted with the beautiful hills above Criénne, I take it. A glorious landscape, bathed in sun such as you can only dream of here in your beloved, rainy realm. In the valleys, of course, there is such abundance that your farmers would weep to see it, but on the hillsides they grow a much more delicate crop. And if you were to travel two days north of Criénne, you would reach a valley where soil, sun, and rain combine to create a perfect... no... mystical... place. For centuries they grew grapes there until no one could tell you how old the vines were, and the wines they made were the finest in the world."

"The White Horse river," Spicer agreed. "I know all of this."

"Ah. Then Madam surely knows of the tragedy that befell the world twenty years ago..."

"Of course. The White Horse vineyards were wiped out. Some kind of pest that ate the roots."

"Pestilence, indeed," Mellon agreed sadly.

"Which is why the bottles are so rare. And so expensive," Spicer mused. "Are you saying you wish to sell me a bottle of White Horse wine? It would be rash, indeed, to take your claim at face value. Whom do you represent? Where is the note of authenticity?"

Mellon chuckled as if sharing a particularly witty joke. "There is no note, and I am not trying to sell you one bottle. I am trying to sell you an entire case."

"You have a dozen bottles?" Spicer's mouth opened slightly, closed again, then opened as she sought for words. "That is... ludicrous. If someone were selling a case of White Horse, the world would know."

"Absolutely... but this is no bottle of White Horse wine... as I said, this is something without compare... a wine made from a process so closely guarded, many believe it is mere fantasy."

Spicer laughed a single hiccup of sound. "The tawny red?"

"The tawny red," Mellon agreed.

"Pissed out of a dragon, no doubt." Spicer dismissed them with a wave of her hand.

"Not at all. The winemakers would crush the grapes in granite troughs, then introduce a special blend of sweet liquor to the juice to fortify it. Then it was placed in a wooden cask, not to be touched, while it aged."

Spicer's eyes had grown wide. "Maker... you do know... you have the technique?"

Mellon sighed. "Sadly, no. That knowledge is guarded too well. No one knows the liquor they used, no one knows when to introduce it, and, most sadly of all, no one can replace the grapes. What I do have is a case of the very last tawny red ever bottled in the White Horse vineyard, stored away before the vines were

THE THIEF'S TALE

destroyed, a single case, hidden beneath the stone floor of the manor by an enterprising worker when the fires were set to contain the spread of the pests."

Wyn watched Spicer's face. Mellon had set the hook deep, with the right amount of unthinkable glory tarnished with just a touch of disappointment to make it real. Nell Spicer was one of the shrewdest merchants in Kuray, perhaps in Albyn, but she had no tools to judge such a tale. Still, she was no stranger to negotiations, whatever the stakes.

"The tawny red is a legend… I've heard tales of it before."

"Of course," Mellon allowed.

"All I see is a bottle."

"Of course."

"I am not paying you for a bottle, no matter the story."

"Ah!" Mellon gasped and raised his finger as if he only now realized her reluctance. "Of course not, Madam, I would not think of it."

"Then…?"

"I have brought a single bottle to show my bonafides, and, if you are inclined, I will establish introductions between yourself and those who can provide proof, all before a single bit has exchanged hands."

"I will want to meet the principals."

"Of course. Criénne is lovely in the spring."

Spicer examined Mellon in silence, her eyes narrowed, her fingers tapping on the polished wood. Wyn saw her glance at the bottle, a flicker of the eyes in their slits, no more, but she knew the fish was landed.

"I shall need the details of the proposed partnership, and an intermediary of my choosing in Criénne to make the first contact before I proceed."

"Entirely expected," Mellon bowed.

"How many competitors do I have?"

Mellon swallowed, apparently caught for an answer.

"Don't be foolish." Spicer waved her hand grandly. "You would hardly propose a sale of such magnitude to only one partner."

THE THIEF'S TALE

"I regret that you are correct," Mellon apologized. "However, you are *my* only potential client. Others have been contacted, but I do not know who they are." It was Mellon's turn to wave his hand. "We do not imagine that all such meetings would be as… sanguine… as this. It seemed prudent to restrict the information any single courier might possess."

Spicer nodded. "Very well. What shall we do with this bottle?"

Mellon smiled. "Shall we open it? We should toast our… opportunities."

"Open it?" Spicer gasped, astounded.

"Of course. How else to prove its worth?"

Spicer licked her lips, suddenly as nervous as a child holding a broken precious. "I… absolutely… I insist."

Mellon snapped his fingers, and Wyn carefully folded back a small, hidden insert in the wine case, revealing two crystal glasses. She arranged them on the table, released the bottle with a twist, and stepped deferentially away. Mellon rose majestically to his feet, his face set in dignified reverence. He raised the bottle from its nest as if it were an infant, so tender was his touch, cut the seal with a flourish, and carefully poured a finger of velvety-red wine into each glass.

A rich scent of plums, cherries, and chocolate filled the study, making Wyn's mouth water. Mellon raised his glass and waited for Spicer to join him. She hesitated, a final breath before the plunge, then grasped the second glass forcefully enough that the wine sloshed.

"To opportunities," Spicer muttered.

Mellon beamed in return. "Opportunities," he repeated, and raised his glass, letting the smallest sip pass between his lips. He savored it and swallowed appreciatively. Spicer joined him, and Wyn saw her eyes widen.

"Wonderful," she crooned after swallowing. "Sweet, yet such a backbone."

"Yes," Mellon agreed. He drank again, and Spicer followed suit. Soon the small measure in each glass was gone, and Spicer set her glass down with a sigh.

THE THIEF'S TALE

"It was not what I was expecting," she admitted. "Smooth… it is like nothing I have ever tasted."

"Heavenly…" Mellon rhapsodized.

"I…" Spicer managed before her eyes rolled up and she pitched forward. Wyn caught her before she could strike the table and eased her into her chair.

"Maker, finally," Mellon sighed. "Never met someone so set against being given a bag of gold."

"You loved it," Wyn accused him, already opening the concealed door of the vault.

"I did," he admitted with a grin. "Master merchant, my arse, I hooked her with nothing but a bottle and a tale."

Wyn carefully felt for the pins of the outer door with her pick. "A bottle of bloody expensive wine. I've never bought anything that dear. And it didn't even taste that nice."

"Your rearing is showing," Mellon humphed.

"My what is showing?" Wyn asked, craning to peer over her shoulder.

"Never you worry, your bum is well safe. Unless you fiddle a bit longer with that door, then both our arses are in trouble. I thought you said you could pick it quick?"

"This is quick," Wyn snarled as the last pin in the inverted row dropped. She swung the door open to reveal the massive inner door, and Mellon whistled softly.

"You weren't having a laugh, were you?" he whispered.

"No, it's right easy, this one," Wyn replied bitterly, delicately turning the four wheels into place. "The laugh's on us if she's changed the numbers."

The last wheel slipped into place, and the four handles turned with satisfying clunks. Wyn darted inside, fumbled in the hem of her coat for Desmond's forgery, and swapped it for the real key before taking a breath. The key vanished into the same concealed pocket in a flash, and the door thudded closed. Wyn returned the dials to their places, locked the outer door, had the false panel closed in another instant, and faced Mellon with a wide smile as she smoothed the fabric of her coat.

"Done."

THE THIEF'S TALE

"Right you are," Mellon congratulated her. "Back into place, then."

Mellon returned to the desk and stood with glass in hand while Wyn settled behind him, hands folded neatly over each other in front of her.

" 'Didn't even taste that nice,' " Mellon muttered.

"It didn't," Wyn insisted. "Made my tummy burn."

"Well, it cost us almost everything left in the stash, so I hope you enjoyed that burn."

"Tasted better once we poured that blackberry plonk into it."

Whatever Mellon had been about to say was cut off as Nell Spicer suddenly snorted, muttered, and frowned at him. Mellon smiled brilliantly and returned his glass to the table.

"Most kind," he said. "The remainder I leave with your Honor, as a token of our commitment to this endeavor."

"Very gracious," Spicer muttered, still somewhat dazed. But she forced herself to her feet to offer best wishes and hopes for a quick and satisfying conclusion to their dealings, rang a silver bell, and Wyn and Mellon were ushered from the mansion with far more dignity than they had been allowed in.

Wyn settled into the deep cushions of the carriage and wrapped her arms around herself against the cold, but Mellon merely beamed through the window as they trundled along the broad avenues of the New City.

"You don't think she'll eventually wonder where we've gone?"

"She'll reckon we made the deal with someone else. She'll never think we were there to rob her bloody great vault while we sipped wine, and even if she does for some reason suspect, what will she find? Nothing taken. Nah, we're set, we are."

"With her bottle of nasty wine."

"I'd wager gold she never drinks it again. Too valuable. She'll top it off and have the wax sealed tight, no doubt." Mellon grinned happily at Wyn. "I would."

THE THIEF'S TALE

## CHAPTER SIXTEEN

# Murderous Bastard

The Penny Angel pulsed with wealth. It gleamed from the walls, striped with brown marble of every hue from chocolate to gold. It shone from the polished tabletops, crafted from single slabs of burnished mahogany. It shimmered from thousands of crystals in ornate chandeliers. It clung to the intricately carved panels of the ceiling, their wood painted a deep cream trimmed with shining gold. And it throbbed in the murmur of voices from the elegantly attired clientele seated at the tables, unhurried as they discussed vast sums and society with equal concern.

Wyn sat stiffly, still dressed in the crisp, black uniform she had worn for her role as Mellon's assistant, her hands itching to investigate the heavy, gold-plated cutlery and porcelain cups arranged on the table in front of her.

Mellon lounged in his padded, high-backed chair, entirely at ease, breathing in the refined air as if it fueled his contentment.

Ratter did not seem as relaxed.

"Mellon," he hissed through a rigid smile. "What if Spicer shows up?"

"She's at the Exchange, dear boy," Mellon said grandly. He crossed his legs casually and waved his new long-stemmed pipe at Ratter. "I thought a proper cup of tea was in order, to celebrate the successful conclusion to our business."

"You have both of them, then?" Ratter's eyes gleamed eagerly.

"Both, indeed." Mellon puffed contentedly on his pipe. "Surely an impossible job, yet accomplished, nonetheless, and with time to spare."

"You want some of that smoke up your arse?" Ratter snorted. "You'll have to do it yourself. Let's see the keys."

"Absolutely, as soon as there is some sign of the promised payment."

"I've got it."

"Of course." Mellon made no move except to savor another long drag on his pipe. "Wyn, dear, are the custodians still watching our friend, here?"

"They've not glanced away," Wyn smirked. The tall, fit young men in perfectly tailored black jackets who maintained the decorum of the Angel had fastened on to Ratter the moment he walked through the doors, despite him having Mellon's invitation in his hand. "Looks like they don't trust you, Ratter. Shame."

"Oh, my." Mellon grinned. "It seems we do not have time to say ridiculous things such as, 'I've got it.' Perhaps we should move on to the actual production of the coins?"

Ratter's smile failed and was replaced by a furious scowl. But he reached into his coat and brought out a small, leather purse with an iron ring around its neck. He placed it on the table and released the latch, then sat back.

Wyn scooped it up and peered inside. Silver gleamed back at her, dozens of coins, a heavy weight in her hand. But not enough. She dug into the mass, making a quick count.

"You have another of these to hand over?" Wyn asked Ratter. "Otherwise, we have a problem."

"Half now, half when the client pays us."

"It seems like the time to mention that particular wrinkle would have been at the beginning of the enterprise," Mellon said stiffly.

THE THIEF'S TALE

"That's the deal," Ratter replied, his smile returning, cold and amused.

"Perhaps we just give you half the keys, then?" Mellon suggested.

Ratter leaned onto the table. "Here's the way this works, Mellon," he said with a sneer. "If I get up from this table without both those keys, the first thing that happens is my lads beat your boys hiding across the street until they wish they were dead. Maybe a bit more, things like that can get out of hand. Then, when you find the balls to walk out of here, we do the same to you and Whinny. Your prats in their pretty coats won't give two shits what happens to you once you're out those doors. So, you just give a thought on how much of a prick you want to be right now."

Mellon glanced involuntarily through the window next to their table, seeking a sign of Fergus and Desmond across the street. But Wyn understood that if Ratter had mentioned them, he knew they were there.

Wyn scowled uselessly at Ratter, but Mellon's shoulders slumped in resignation, and he nodded reluctantly to Wyn. "Give them to him."

"What?" Wyn hissed. "Mellon, you must be fucking jo—"

"Give them over, Wyn," he replied, his voice hard.

Wyn glared at him, then produced a small wooden box and shoved it across the table.

Ratter grinned cruelly at her, then collected the box.

"Don't be mad, Whinny," he chuckled. He flipped the latch and carefully opened the lid, and his eyes widened as he saw the beautiful shapes within.

"Fuck you," Wyn said sullenly.

Ratter ignored her and took his time examining the keys. Finally satisfied, he stood, tucked the box into his coat, and beamed at the two Tallywags. "It was a real pleasure. I'll bring you the other half of the payment when it's ready."

"We'll see you then," Mellon said gruffly.

Ratter sauntered out of the Angel and quickly disappeared in the swirling snow.

THE THIEF'S TALE

"That went all right," Mellon decided. "He actually paid us half the money."

"You looked as if you were going to cry," Wyn said appreciatively. "I swear I saw a tear. How did you do that?"

"I thought about our dear friends, shivering in the cold," Mellon claimed. "Are you going to finish that tea?"

"Yes," Wyn told him firmly, and she grabbed her cup protectively in both hands.

"I suppose now we find out how much Quinn knows about Devices," Mellon mused.

"I'll wager doing Fergus's dishes that Quinn wouldn't know a proper Device if it were presented to him in a box."

"No bet." Mellon grinned. "You're stuck with those dishes, my lass."

They stared contentedly out the window until Brodie appeared on the street to give them a wave, and then they joined Desmond and Fergus and strolled the fifty paces to where they had left their borrowed carriage.

"How did it go?" Mellon asked.

"They had four or five big lads staking us out," Fergus replied. "Other than that, boring."

"And you?" Mellon asked Brodie.

"Keeva and Vail have Ratter. We'll know where he goes with those keys, and they'll send Two-Bits when there's word."

"Then we need to lose whatever idiots Ratter left to tail us, and you need to get ready for a bit of lurking," he told Wyn.

Wyn nodded happily. "Let's go."

Wyn went slowly insane as she paced the small rooms behind the wall of kegs, occasionally standing on her cot and peering through the tiny, dirty window to watch the snow steadily pile up in the yard.

Two-Bits arrived in a flurry of snow shaken off his boots and hair to announce that Ratter had returned directly to Butcher's, but no further news came as the afternoon passed, until Mellon

THE THIEF'S TALE

wondered if Quinn's client was to meet with Quinn at the slaughterhouse to receive the keys.

By evening bells the snow had finally stopped, but little else had changed. Not long after, however, Two-Bits returned with news that Quinn and Ratter had left Butcher's, accompanied by a half-dozen brutes, headed through the Cow Gate and into the Old City.

"All right, then, Wyn?" Mellon asked in that kindly way he had that made Wyn forget how annoying he was most of the time.

"Yeah, I'm all right," she assured him. "Feel like I'm going to puke. Just want to get going." She always felt the same before a job. Nervous as a cat before, then giddy with the thrill of it once the job had started.

Mellon nodded. "You take care of her," he told Fergus.

The tall swordsman pulled his coat tight and settled the split in its side so that the hilt of his sword poked through. "I will," he answered.

Fergus and Wyn left the brewery and hurried south toward Cowgate, pausing at pre-arranged landmarks to meet with the steady procession of Wee Ones sent to update them on Quinn's heading.

Deeper and deeper into the Old City they followed Quinn's crew, past the lively streets and past the brooding slums, all the way to Goldenfields.

"He's just gone into one of those old mansions," Brodie told Wyn when they came to the final rendezvous.

Brodie led them to a street that had been ancient when the Cataclysm struck, centuries ago. Old manor houses lined the road, the relics of the first enclave of the wealthy of Kuray before the New City had risen to lord over the valley. Most of the houses had rotted to the marrow, long-since scraped clean of anything of value, and were now refuge only to squatters.

At the low end of Goldenfields a rambling ruin capped the street, its vacant windows glowering with sullen contempt for the filth that had invaded its domain.

Wyn gazed at the decrepit edifice and shivered. The bare branches of gnarled trees and the dried husks of nettles bursting from a crust of snow framed the short driveway and the steps

THE THIEF'S TALE

leading to the manor. Yellow plaster peeled from the weathered bricks in swathes, leaving leprous wounds. Boards greyed by exposure shrouded the long row of arched windows.

"That's the one," Brodie whispered as they crouched in the shadows of a nearby ruin.

Wyn stuck out her tongue. "Lovely. All right, Brodie, well done. Off you go, now, and see if you can't follow whoever shows up to meet Quinn when they leave."

"Will do, boss," Brodie whispered with a grin, and he vanished into the ruins.

"Come on, let's see the back," Wyn said to Fergus. "I don't fancy knocking on the door."

They crept through the remains of the neighboring building, a dilapidated wreck that was more rubble than ruin. Wyn sniffed and bit her lip as she examined the manor that Quinn had entered. Her gaze was drawn to the gaping holes in the roof nearest them, lined with ragged beams that jutted from the wounds like broken bones.

"I'll go straight up the side, right there, then through that hole next to the busted tower on top," she whispered to Fergus. "Easy as wishing."

"Where do you want me?"

"Right here, I reckon," Wyn told him. "Stay quiet and watch the windows. I'll come and wave or flash a lantern if I need you."

Fergus nodded silently, his brow furrowed. "I'll be here."

Wyn stripped off Desmond's thick coat and Fergus's heavy boots, leaving her with only her threadbare tunic and torn leather trousers, but she had never found kit that suited her better for lurking, and lurking was needed, tonight, not warmth. She added her fingerless, woolen gloves and a pair of slim boots, soft enough to let her feel for footholds in an old broken wall, and she tucked her hair in a woolen cap that covered her ears.

"Ready?" Fergus asked as he bundled her discarded clothing.

"Yeah, I'm going, before I freeze," Wyn told him. She slipped through a ragged hole in the collapsed brick wall they had used for concealment, gave the windows of the manor house across the alleyway a lengthy, silent examination, and scampered across the stone's-throw of empty space between the buildings.

THE THIEF'S TALE

The wall was as easy to climb as Wyn had predicted, only offering the occasional crumbling handhold to make the ascent challenging, and she reached the roof without effort.

The attic was a ruin of fallen beams and rotten flooring covered in snow, dirt, and bird droppings. Wide gaps had melted into the lower floors, and the beams that remained were so soft that Wyn's boot left a deep gouge in the wood when she slipped.

She carefully maneuvered around the most suspect stretches and reached a hole that opened onto a small hallway in the floor below. She slowly uncurled from the lip and dropped soundlessly into the grimy passageway.

The hall ran above a courtyard in the back of the manor, and Wyn paused as she passed a window. A black carriage, gleaming with polish, rested in the yard. Two matching black horses stood patiently in front of it, their breath steaming in the chill air.

*I suppose that means the client is here,* Wyn guessed. *I need to hurry.*

She followed the hallway toward the front of the house, creeping next to the wall to avoid creaking floorboards, and her anxiety grew with every tiny step. *Come on... you can't be late...*

The dim glow of a distant lantern leaking through an empty doorway soon rewarded her. Wyn crawled to the frame and peered around it.

She found herself on a small balcony with an ornate iron rail that overlooked a vast room. The chamber seemed likely to have been a ballroom during the manor's heyday. An immense wheel of carved wood depicting flowers and suns and ivy, all withered behind cracked, faded paint and blotched with filthy smoke stains, crowned the ceiling. The walls were featureless save for water-stained plaster and mold, although Wyn could see where wood paneling had once covered them.

The original floor could have been made of wood, or gold, or dragon scales, for all that Wyn could tell now. It had vanished, likely into fireplaces across the Old City, and Wyn could see through the remaining massive beams into an impenetrable darkness that might have been the cellar, or an endless well. Crude planks crossed the gaping beams haphazardly, but in the center of the room the planks had been arranged more carefully, creating a

THE THIEF'S TALE

small island on which a lantern had been placed next to two ancient, straight-backed chairs.

Quinn was alone in the room, standing rigidly next to one of the chairs, but he did not have the room to himself for long. A door across the chamber from Wyn ground open and two figures stepped through.

Wyn gripped the iron railing as her legs suddenly lost their strength and the room seemed to sway. *No,* she begged. *Oh please, no...*

As Cameron stood to the side, his gaze never leaving Quinn, Lady Cailean entered the room, and Quinn turned to greet her.

Cailean nodded to Quinn and sat gracefully in the chair nearest her. She had donned her leather coat with the concealed metal plates for her meeting with Quinn, along with slim leather riding leggings, and looked every bit the legendary Hawk. Quinn remained beside his chair and tried to stand haughtily, but he held an awkward stiffness in his pose that Wyn had never seen before.

Wyn stared desperately at the noblewoman, pleading with her to say something that would explain away how she was here.

"I hope there is good news," the Hawk told Quinn, and Wyn sagged helplessly to her knees, her breath reduced to ragged gasps that she could hardly contain.

"Aye, there is," Quinn replied in his thick drawl. "I have the keys."

"Your thieves were entirely successful, then?"

"They were," Quinn admitted grudgingly. "In the end."

"Good." The Hawk perched on the edge of her chair and indicated the empty one with a tilt of her hand. "Only three days left. I was growing concerned that you would not deliver."

"We got them," Quinn scowled. He sat heavily in the chair, then slumped back, his eyes thin slits. "We've done our part. You ready to do yours?"

"Of course," the Hawk agreed with an easy, wide smile. "I have your final payment. As agreed, it is yours once the keys are tested. Cameron, will you ask Kieran to join us?"

The tall swordsman returned to the doorway and called softly, and another figure entered the room, a thin man with lank hair swept back on either side of a long face, sporting a thick mustache

THE THIEF'S TALE

and a tiny patch of beard under his lip. He was dressed in a long robe, but Wyn could see from her perch that it was patched with cast-off fabrics and loose stitching, and its hem was stained with mud.

*Her apostate,* Wyn realized through her haze of misery. *He must be…*

He approached the two chairs, his hands clasped in front of him, and stood awkwardly, his gaze darting between the two seated figures.

"Go on, Kieran," the Hawk told him. "Quinn will not bite, I promise."

Wyn was not sure she was correct, but Kieran managed to stumble forward and hold out a hand. Quinn stared at him for a moment, then dug inside his coat and produced the small wooden box Mellon had given to Ratter at Penny Angel's. The Hawk's gaze sharpened as the box appeared, keen and bright as a blade.

Kieran took the box and opened it, and his awkwardness disappeared. He raised first one key then the next, turning them to catch the light, gently probing the intricate patterns with his fingertips.

Then he returned them to the box and shook his head silently.

"That is disappointing," the Hawk said quietly.

"What do you mean?" Quinn asked, his voice a dangerous growl.

"These are not the real keys," she explained. "They are fakes."

"I'm supposed to accept that on his say-so?" Quinn demanded, jabbing his finger at the robed man, who took a prudent step backward.

"You may accept what you want," the Hawk said smoothly, "but I am not paying you for these." She gestured to the box in Kieran's hands. "You may take them, or leave them, whatever you prefer, but you now have only three days to bring me the real keys."

"Ratter!" Quinn's voice echoed from the decrepit ceiling. A moment later the warped door opened again, scraping across the sill, and Ratter appeared, his usual sneer replaced by a tight-lipped grimace.

"She says these are fakes," Quinn announced.

Ratter's face darkened, and he took a hesitant step toward the box in the apostate's hands. "Fake? But…"

"You fucking idiot!" Quinn screamed, and Ratter stepped warily away from his boss. "Mellon tricked you."

"He must have," Ratter agreed in a low voice.

"Maybe you should have a word," Quinn suggested, suddenly calm as ice. "Make sure he understands how disappointed I am."

"Yes, boss," Ratter snarled, and he turned to go.

"Let us remember that we do not have the keys yet," the Hawk mentioned casually. She glanced at Ratter, then Quinn. "It would certainly be a shame if we lost them now, just because we could not keep our tempers. That would disappoint *me*. Very much."

Quinn stared at the noblewoman for a long moment, then called to Ratter. "Have a word with Mellon… politely. Find out what he wants with all this foolishness."

Ratter nodded and strode from the room. The door closed behind him with a scraping thud.

"I should have known I couldn't trust Mellon," Quinn grunted. "But I'll have those keys."

"The Tallywags certainly made a fool of you." The Hawk smiled her twisted smile, but her eyes were hard as stone. "Let us hope they were as successful in obtaining the real keys."

She stood and settled her cloak around her shoulders. "When you find them… if you find them… don't make another fool of yourself. I am not sure our partnership could survive that."

"Is that a fact?" Quinn asked, as if bored by the conversation. But Wyn could see his eyes were fastened on the Hawk with a predatory look, and so could Cameron, as he stepped forward and placed his right hand on his sword's hilt.

But Quinn was not one to be intimidated by a sheathed sword. "Seems you might not want it known that the Hawk twists deals when it suits her. You may have a hard name, m'lady, but I'll make sure you choke on it if you try to stiff me."

THE THIEF'S TALE

"Two keys," the Hawk said, holding up two fingers as if to make certain Quinn understood such a large amount. "By the day after next, or they are no good to me, which means they are no good to you." She shook her head sadly. "There is no sense in bickering, Quinn. I want to make you rich, and you want to give me those keys. That can still happen, but we are short on time."

"Then why make a fuss about how I ask those fucking Tallywags where they are?"

"If your way does not work, there is no other way," she said reasonably. "This Mellon has played you, yes, but I am certain you have made the consequences of that clear to him, and he did it anyway. That means he has planned for your response."

"There's planning and then there's being asked the question."

"Let's not take that risk," she said sweetly, but the conversation was clearly at an end. "All business, until I have the proper keys in my hand. What is the harm in that? There's all the time in the world, after, for any other satisfaction that might be required."

Quinn rose from the chair and towered over the Hawk, his glare cold. But he nodded acceptance when she held his gaze. "Aye... all business, until."

"I knew I made the right choice." She pulled on her soft leather gloves and accompanied Kieran from the room without another word, Cameron following cautiously behind, never taking his eyes off Quinn.

Wyn held her breath, desperate to crawl away, but Quinn still stood silently in the room below, and she did not dare move.

But at length Quinn departed as well, his thick lips fixed in a sneer of hatred, and Wyn eased blood into her cramped legs as she listened to his boots thump across the entryway and out the shuddering front door.

Then, at last, Wyn allowed herself to slump to the floor and release the shuddering sobs that threatened to choke her, her hands pressed miserably over her face. *How could she? She let me believe she was my friend, that she cared about me, that she was going to protect me... she promised me...*

She groaned and rolled slowly onto her knees, her eyes stinging. *Was everything she said a lie? That I was strong, that I could fight? That I could be like her… that's all gone, isn't it?* Wyn ground her teeth savagely together. *Mellon's going to fucking laugh, why didn't I listen to him?*

A fresh wave of despair overwhelmed her and bent her over until her forehead pressed against the floorboards. But within her anguish she felt fury stir, as hot and sharp as a sword glowing beneath the smith's hammer. Her mouth twisted as the fire burned away her distress. *Fight for justice, eh? I'll make you wish you'd never taught me that, you bitch.*

Wyn clambered to her feet, wiped her eyes, and stepped through the dark archway at the rear of the balcony.

She flinched away as she caught a sigh of movement in the shadows the instant before something crashed into her stomach like a battering ram, folding her double, driving the breath from her lungs.

Wyn staggered, her knees buckled, and she stumbled to the floor, her body curled around the agony seething through her abdomen. She struggled to rise, but her legs would not obey.

A leering smile glinted gold in the darkness.

Wyn moaned and dragged one foot under her as a figure emerged from the shadowed hallway and crossed the faint patch of light from the ballroom.

"Hello, Whinny," Ratter crooned.

Wyn snarled and rose to her feet, but her legs shook and she could not straighten.

"I'm not best pleased with you, luv," Ratter tutted. He stepped forward and lashed out with his fist. Wyn saw it blur from the shadows and lurched back, her legs too slow, too weak, and her head exploded with light as he caught her above her ear.

The blow spun her into the wall, and she collapsed to her hands and knees amidst a shower of cracked plaster. The side of her head throbbed dully as if muffled by thick wool, and Wyn blinked stupidly at the splintered floor between her hands, wondering what was happening. Then the dull ache peeled her skull apart and thrust a white poker of pain into her head, and Wyn choked on a scream of agony.

"Not pleased at all," Ratter whispered in her ear, and Wyn tried to shove herself away from his voice. A boot caught her hip

THE THIEF'S TALE

savagely, and the world reeled around her as she tumbled through the archway. She sprawled against the railing of the balcony, her feet clanging into the iron curlicues, her arms flailing uselessly in the air.

Wyn groaned and rolled onto her knees as splinters of red agony ground deep in her hip. The tiny blade she used for slipping latches dropped into her hand with a shake of her wrist. She grabbed the iron railing, threading her fingers through it, and hauled herself upright. Ratter's boots crunched on broken plaster behind her, and Wyn whirled, her knife a shining line through the shadows.

She felt its edge catch on cloth, scrape uselessly over leather, and then slice across skin, and Ratter's breath hissed between his teeth. Wyn slashed again, but Ratter stepped close and her wrist struck him awkwardly on his shoulder, jarring the small knife from her hand. His hand closed around her slender neck with a grip like steel, forcing her head back.

Wyn smashed her fist into his cheek, grabbed a handful of his coarse hair with her other hand, and smashed her fist into his face again. She screamed in fury and swung again, but Ratter jerked back and to the side, leaving a fistful of hair in Wyn's hand, and she missed. Ratter snarled in anger and slammed his shoulder into Wyn, crushing her against the railing. Her back ground against the marble bar and she tipped backward. She clawed at his arms as her legs kicked out for purchase, finding none.

Then his hand clamped over hers and twisted it. Wyn screamed as pain lanced through her wrist to her elbow. She grabbed his hand and tried to bend it back, but Ratter was too strong, and his weight kept her pinned against the rail.

"I thought you remembered the punishment for being where you shouldn't," Ratter whispered through his bared teeth.

Wyn thrashed desperately, trying to pry his fingers free from her trapped hand, and she scratched long strips of bloody skin from his wrist.

Ratter jerked and there was a sharp crack like a dry twig splitting, and Wyn shrieked as agony sizzled up her arm.

"There's one," Ratter sneered. He twisted again, and Wyn choked as another finger snapped.

THE THIEF'S TALE

"You bastard!" she screamed. She sank her teeth into his hand, and hot blood spat into her mouth. He yelled in pain and tore himself free. Wyn lurched after him, reaching for his face with her good hand, but he slapped it away and lashed out at her head. Wyn ducked low and felt the wind of his punch on the back of her neck, straightened, and drove her knee between his legs.

He staggered back and Wyn leapt for the rail. Her boot landed firmly on top and she lunged into the air, but even as she extended, she felt the railing give way with a shriek of metal and a dry crack of shattered stone.

Wyn arched her back and twisted toward the floor. A beam rushed at her and she crashed into it chest-first. The impact drove the breath from her body and snapped her teeth closed on her tongue. Her legs swung wildly, she clawed at the beam's rotten wood, and then her weight dragged her free and she spiraled into the darkness beneath the ballroom.

She hit far sooner than she had feared, awkwardly on her back and shoulder. She curled onto her side and let a shower of wrought iron and stone shards from the balcony pelt her back. Daggers stabbed her sternum when she gasped, her head throbbed with dizzying pain, her stomach felt as if it had split open like a burst water skin, fresh pain dug fingers into her shoulder, and she retched as blood poured into her throat from her tongue, but all paled next to the shards of glass being ground deep inside the crooked fingers of her left hand with every pulse of her heart.

She moaned, too overwhelmed to scream, and slowly drew her legs underneath her. They still worked, somehow spared the vicious assault of fist and boot and fall.

"Maker's breath, Whinny, are you dead?" Ratter called from above. He spat heavily, and Wyn heard a splat in the darkness near her. "You better hope you are."

"Oh... Martyr..." Wyn sobbed. She lurched to her feet and staggered forward, stumbling over unseen debris, uncaring what lay ahead in the shadows.

A glimmer of light drew her like a moth, zigzag shadows promising stairs out of the pit. She clambered up the steps and was disgorged into a narrow hallway lined with black doorways. At

THE THIEF'S TALE

the end was a square of pale space and the foot of a grand staircase. But Wyn had only taken one step in that direction before she shrank into the gap of one of the doorways as a dark figure filled the opening.

"Wyn?" Ratter called. "I'll trade you a finger for a key, how's that?" He laughed, the sound echoing as it curled around her as if it were alive. Wyn risked a peek around the doorframe, but he was gone, the end of the hall as empty as the foyer beyond.

Wyn sank into the gloom, slowly pressing herself against the wall, feeling its crumbling plaster run rough over the tips of her fingers. Her heel found the lip of a step, and she backed up the stairs, feeling for each step, not daring to take her gaze from the thick shadow in front of her.

Another slow step, and another. Enough light seeped from the floor above to see she was in a square stairwell. Wyn peered into the open space and lurched against the railing as she swayed, dizzy and nauseous. She snarled and spat, and forced herself to climb, clinging to the rail.

A turn, another, and another. The increasing moonlight showed her water-stained plaster, scarred from the removal of elegant paneling, and stairs so choked with rubble and dirt that some of the steps were vague impressions only. At the top, a vaulted ceiling and a pair of warped doors wedged open by the piled chunks of plaster.

"Whiiiiiinny!" Ratter's voice sang from the depths of the ruined mansion. "Just like old times, eh? You running, me catching you."

Wyn shoved herself through the gap, leaned on the wall on the other side, and reluctantly raised her left hand to examine it. Her first and second fingers stuck out rigidly, trembling in agony. When Ratter had caught them as children, Desmond had set her fingers, and she had set Desmond's, but now there was little choice but to do it herself.

She gripped her first finger, breathed deeply, and pulled it up and out. A thin, high noise came from her as she doubled over her injured hand. Then, before the pulse of agony had faded, she did it to her middle finger.

The Thief's Tale

Red pain overwhelmed her so that the world dimmed and she sank to her knees, her head pressed against the cold floor, her good hand jammed into her mouth to stop her sobs.

The red faded to black and began to press on her like a great weight, pushing her eyes closed, driving her body to curl on the floor and give in.

Leather scraped across stone as she pushed one leg under her, then again as she forced herself up. The wall was cold and damp against her cheek as she caught her breath. She raised her hand again. Her fingers no longer bent the wrong way, a vast improvement, but she still could not move them.

Slowly the frozen air pushed back the nauseating dizziness, and Wyn steadied her breathing as she listened for telltale sounds amidst the trembling creak and groan of the ancient house.

*You murderous bastard,* she snarled. *I'm not done, yet.*

She licked her suddenly dry lips and peeked around the corner of the landing. A hallway stretched silently into the manor, and bands of moonlight created stripes of silver and black that slashed across rubble and crumbling, stained plaster.

She darted across the hall and crouched in the shadows between two windows, then crept silently down the passageway, ears straining to detect any sound through the pounding of her heart.

The creak of an ancient floorboard from the stairwell behind her dissuaded her from slowing. She padded faster, the light touch of her boots on the warped boards no louder than a brush of wind, yet it seemed to echo in the still air.

Wyn risked another look behind her. The end of the hall near the landing was impenetrable darkness. *How long for him to reach the top?* she thought desperately. *Not long enough...*

Wyn slid through the gaping mouth of an empty doorway and felt her way across the dark expanse within. Her fingers brushed against the rotten upholstery of a chair, then the upended legs of a table. A soft rustle of crumbling plaster made her flinch as she passed too close to the wall, and she clenched her teeth, desperately willing the small crumbs to cling to each other for a moment longer.

THE THIEF'S TALE

A second door provided an exit, and Wyn eased through it into a large room lit by moonlight flooding through wide balcony doors. The carcass of a twisted chandelier and the rotten remains of a settee rested, abandoned, amidst a sea of debris, chunks of plaster fallen from the walls and ceiling, snow and dirt piled in mounds.

The balcony doors called Wyn to them, their twisted, warped iron sighing softly as icy fingers of wind curled around them. Broken glass covered the floor in glittering shards, and Wyn's boots crunched as she stepped to the doors despite her caution.

Wyn pushed carefully on the balcony door, but the iron frames would not move. The lock was bulbous with rust, and long, orange stains coated the stone around the hinges. Wyn tugged at the latch, then pushed firmly on the door, again, but it would not shift.

The sound of plaster crunching underfoot trickled into the room through the door, and Wyn froze. The wind moaned against the ruined iron, and the trees beneath the balcony scraped their bare limbs together, but her ears caught a second, slow crunch, and the scuff of leather against stone.

Wyn scurried across the room and curled into the shadow behind the settee, crouched on the balls of her feet and the fingertips of her good hand, and poised herself to bolt.

Wood ground over rubble as the door to the room opened wider. Boots scuffed softly on thick dirt, then pressed carefully on warped wood as their owner trod slowly toward the settee. Wyn forced her breathing to slow, her body to still, as she became as dark and silent as the mildewed, soggy frame against her shoulder.

Another slow step brought Ratter to the opposite side of the settee. Leather creaked softly. Another step, this one muffled on dirt as he started around the end of the settee behind her.

Wyn exploded out of her crouch and raced for the doorway. Three steps brought her to the chandelier and she leapt high, brushed its tip with her hip, and regained her feet at full sprint on the far side.

She threw herself to the side as metal hissed through the air and obliterated a broken vase against the far wall in a shower of shards and a chiming rain of porcelain debris. Wyn sprawled onto

THE THIEF'S TALE

the filthy floor, slid on her stomach, and rolled to her feet in one smooth movement.

Ratter charged toward her, nimble despite his size, a long knife gleaming in his hand.

She dove to the side as the blade sighed past her and scrambled on hands and feet toward the door, desperate to flee. A hand grabbed her ankle, and she twisted and hurled a chunk of plaster. Ratter jerked away and raised an arm, but the missile hit him over his eye with a dull thunk and a shower of grime, and Ratter cursed.

Wyn rolled over her shoulder and came to her feet, darted to her left, then back to her right as Ratter lunged at her feint. But he recovered as fast as a snake and the toe of his boot caught her ankle, sweeping her leg into the air. She twisted desperately and managed to land on her shoulder and roll instead of sprawling uselessly into the wall, but her momentum took her crashing into the small table.

Wood shattered and tore at her as she tumbled. Her feet found the floor and slipped as her slim legs churned into motion before she could come to a rest. A heavy boot thudded into the floor next to her, and she lashed out as she rose. Her fist smashed Ratter's lip and snapped his head back. Wyn screamed and struck again, but it was clumsy and wild, and Ratter knocked her arm aside with his own.

Wyn spun away and darted toward the door, but Ratter was there before her, cutting her off with a few quick steps as she circled around him, out of reach of his knife. Wyn tried the other way, but he cut her off again, slowly herding her back to the wall.

"Oh no," Ratter whispered, licking at his split lip, his teeth stained black in the moonlight. "No, Wyn, you aren't getting out of this."

The balcony doors exploded into the room. Shards of glass tinkled and shattered, twisted iron shrieked, and splinters of stone clattered against the floor as a figure landed in the room. Wyn caught a glimpse of a gaunt face and long, lanky hair as Fergus gathered his legs under him and hurled himself toward Ratter.

Ratter whirled and his knife flashed across the room, but his aim was rushed, and the blade careened off the wall behind Fergus with an explosion of plaster chunks. Ratter's long blade hissed into his hand an instant later, but Fergus had reached him. He seized Ratter's wrist in both hands and twisted so that the sword clattered into the corner of the room.

Ratter slammed his fist into Fergus's cheek, snapping his head back as bone cracked against bone. Fergus ducked beneath the next blow, yanked Ratter forward, and slammed his forehead into Ratter's face.

Wyn heard a snap of bone as blood spurted across the floorboards, but Ratter was unfazed. He spun and slammed his hip into Fergus, lifted him, and hurled him into the wall, upside down, his legs splayed uselessly.

Ratter was on him in an instant. His boot crashed into Fergus's arm and chest as the pale-haired warrior rose to one knee. Ratter kicked again, but Fergus caught the extended leg under his arm and drove his shoulder into Ratter's stomach, lifting him off his feet and slamming him onto the settee. The ancient chair split with a tearing crack, but as Fergus fell on Ratter amidst the splinters, he was met with an out-flung boot that caught him in his chest and threw him back with a grunt.

Wyn snatched Ratter's sword from the floor and hacked at him as he struggled from the ruins of the settee. He jerked away once, twice, her attacks deadly fast but wielded awkwardly, and on her third he knocked her arm aside.

She ducked beneath his fist as it streaked over her ear and whipped the sword at his face. He dodged away, again, but then cursed as Fergus's strong hands grabbed him by his shoulders and hurled him headfirst into the wall.

Fergus followed with short, quick strikes, his fists thudding into Ratter's face and arms as Ratter twisted to defend himself against the assault. Blood sprayed across the wall as Fergus caught Ratter above the eye, but Ratter recovered too quickly. He threw his elbow, then a sharp jab, forcing Fergus back to avoid the blows, then struck savagely, putting his weight and shoulder into an attack intended to take off Fergus's head.

Fergus stepped under the punch and slammed his hand into Ratter's throat. They staggered together, crashed into the wall and

THE THIEF'S TALE

then to the floor. Fergus pinned Ratter with his knee and pressed his grip around his throat.

Ratter strained against Fergus's wrist, then clawed his face. Fergus grimaced and caught Ratter's thumb with his free hand, twisting the arm down and across his chest, trapping it against the floor.

Then Fergus put his weight behind the arm pressed into Ratter's neck, pushing down relentlessly as Ratter gasped and strained, his boots slipping on the grimy floor. His free hand clutched uselessly at Fergus's tunic as his head was pressed into the floor, his eyes staring desperately at Wyn as she watched, unable to turn away.

There was a wet, tearing sound and Ratter's mouth gaped soundlessly. His fingers convulsed against Fergus, then slid along his arm, strengthless, until at last his arm fell across his face, mercifully hiding it from Wyn.

Fergus released Ratter's body and strode to Wyn's side.

"Are you hurt?"

"YES!" Wyn croaked, then spat blood and coughed. "I'll live... Maker, you killed him."

"Turns out I am like him," Fergus said calmly. Blood trickled from a gash on his brow and another over his boney cheek, and there were bright red streaks along his forearms, but his breathing was no harder than if he had just run up some stairs.

"Guh," Wyn muttered. "My head." She blinked and slumped to her knees. Whatever strength she had somehow borrowed while fighting for her life was quickly fading, and her body was demanding restitution immediately. She tried to spit blood as her mouth filled again, but she lacked the strength, and it drooled from her lips in long strands.

"Looks like you took a fair beating," Fergus said, as if examining an unfortunate nick in his sword.

"You should see the other guy," Wyn said thickly, tried to grin, and drooled more blood. Her gaze drifted to Ratter's twisted body, then flinched away.

"Do you think you can walk?"

"Absolutely," Wyn mumbled. "Give us a hand up."

THE THIEF'S TALE

She draped her injured hand over Fergus's shoulders, and he curled his arm around her back and hoisted her to her feet. Pain arced across her chest and ribs, and she groaned and sagged against Fergus's iron grip.

"Mother... fucker..." she gasped. The room teetered as if she were drunk and started to recede behind a red haze.

Fergus ignored her mumbled protests and slipped his other arm under her knees and lifted her as effortlessly as a child.

"I've got you, lass," he assured her, and Wyn curled into the iron cords of his arms and rested her head against his chest, feeling the hard creak of leather on her cheek as he strode through the manor, and she knew she was safe.

THE THIEF'S TALE

## CHAPTER SEVENTEEN

# Agony and Fear

W yn was not certain which part of her hurt the most. Each time she focused on a wound it blazed to new heights of pain, but, unfairly, the agony did not recede when she forced her attention elsewhere.

Fergus tilted her head to the light, his fingers relentlessly probing her blood-matted hair despite her squeaks of protest. "What happened to your head?"

"He hit me. And I whacked my chin on a beam. And I bashed it on the ground. Ow! You're making it worse!"

Fergus ignored her. "Your skull isn't cracked, and clearly your jaw isn't broken. May need stitches for your chin."

"Good thing her head is so hard," Mellon muttered, but his face was pale beneath his scruff, and he could not muster a grin.

Desmond pushed a dripping cloth at Fergus. "For her cheek," he murmured.

"Whas the madder wid my cheek?" Wyn asked. Her tongue felt twice its proper size, and it was a chore to speak normally.

"Nothing," Fergus assured her, wiping her cheek with the cloth. It came away dark with blood, and Wyn's eyes went wide.

"You call that nothing?"

"You're a bit of a mess, that's all."

Desmond rinsed out the cloth in a basin and pushed it at Fergus. "Here, her hair."

"Maker, stop it." Wyn shoved the cloth away. She could not endure Desmond's hovering concern, nor Mellon's stricken worry. They made her feel helpless. "You two, fuck off so that Fergus can fix my fingers."

Desmond opened his mouth to object, hurt, but he caught her glare and stomped from her nook instead. Mellon chewed on his lip for a moment, then followed Desmond out and hooked the curtain closed behind him.

"Finally." Wyn sighed wearily and let her head rest on the wall, wincing as it bumped gently.

"They are concerned for you."

"Yeah, well, I don't need a bunch of old hens clucking at me."

Fergus frowned at her until Wyn looked away guiltily, but she did not relent. She could not bear for them to see her in pain. It made her feel weak and helpless, so they had to go.

"Fingers?" she suggested to Fergus. The thought of the coming pain nauseated her, so she wanted it over with.

Fergus splinted her fingers and bound them tightly in place, and Wyn only groaned a little, proud that she had made it through without boo-hooing.

But Fergus was a long way from finished.

When at last he released his patient, Wyn had been prodded and cleaned and stitched and wrapped every which way, as efficiently as a sheep on shearing day, and she considered it fair odds that she hurt worse now than when he had started.

"Watch for blood when you make water," Fergus told her, "but I don't think you are bleeding inside."

"You sure know how to sweep a girl off her feet, with that charming talk of yours." Wyn slowly pushed herself upright, her hand pressed against her waist, where Fergus had discovered a mottled, purple and red bruise spreading across her hip and abdomen. "Bloody pee, bad, got it."

"Also, you can get the spins from a cracked head, sometimes to puking."

"Yeah, I noticed," Wyn sighed, then winced as thorns of pain dug into her ribs despite the bandages wrapped tightly around her chest. The world was slowly stopping its spin, she thought, although everything remained strangely slow and blurred, as if each movement stretched and then rebounded an instant after it should have.

Wyn found a wadded tunic lodged behind her cot, not so much clean as without bloodstains, and struggled into it one-handed. "Done this before, have you?"

"A few times," Fergus admitted. "When the fighting's over you get the hurt back on their feet, a sword in their hand, quick as you can, because there's more fighting to be done." He watched her silently for a moment, then held out his hand to her. "You ready to fight?"

Wyn gazed at his hand, suddenly aware of the steel strength in Fergus's fingers. She could see the lattice of dozens of pale scars across his weathered skin, and even the iron rings on his fingers showed nicks and scratches, enough pain and blood to make any man cringe and huddle away, their tail between their legs. Yet there was no hesitation in Fergus's strength, just the comfort of his unwavering resolve to persist despite the pain, despite the fear, because there was more fighting to be done.

Wyn tried to find the same steel within herself, but the weary agony of her body threatened to overwhelm her.

"I don't know..." she replied.

Fergus's hand did not move. "Yes, you do."

Wyn met his gaze, and at that moment she knew that the pain, the fear, the wounds that had cut deeper than just flesh, all were merely scars that would someday be no more than tiny pale lines. None had scored the steel of her resolve. She was not certain where that strength had been forged, but she could feel the heat of its tempering still burning within her, and it was inviolable.

She took his hand and pulled herself to her feet.

"There you are," Fergus said approvingly.

Wyn smiled, suddenly bashful and proud at the same moment, and she quickly busied herself in a halfhearted attempt

THE THIEF'S TALE

to tie her tunic with her one good hand. "What about... the other?" she asked.

Fergus took the threads from her hand and knotted them securely. "The killing, you mean?"

"Yeah, that."

Fergus inhaled deeply, then let it out in a long sigh. "You know I have."

"I figured you had... I guess I didn't... know it."

Fergus nodded and held her gaze. "I can't remember them all. Some I never saw their face. Just saw someone with an axe, or came up behind them... pretty certain I've killed some of my own, it's that easy to do when the shield wall breaks and you don't know which way you're turned or who's behind you and it's hard to find room to swing your blade. I've killed in battles, I've killed crawling through a pitch-dark tunnel, can't even see their blades coming at you, just hear their breathing. One more piece of shit doesn't make a difference in all of that."

"It's so easy to talk about killing and revenge, but when it happened, it didn't feel real," Wyn said softly.

"But it is," Fergus said flatly. "One moment he's a man, the next he's meat. Nothing is more real than that."

Wyn nodded. "I've seen... people... die." She swallowed against her suddenly constricted throat and forced herself to speak. "I can't..."

"There was no other way—"

"I know," she interrupted. Her bruised lips stung as they tightened. "I'm... I'm glad he's dead."

She had hated Ratter for so long, and been terrified of him for so much longer, it was hard to comprehend the relief she felt knowing she would never have to be afraid of him again. But as she spoke, she realized there was a darker satisfaction lurking beneath the relief, beyond survival. *I... I wanted him killed. He deserved it, and I wanted him punished. Maker... I wanted to kill him.* But his desperate gaze stared at her every time she closed her eyes.

"I'm glad, too." Fergus took a deep breath. "Here." He held a long, curved knife by its sheath, its simple, steel hilt facing her. "I think this one is a good weight for you."

THE THIEF'S TALE

Wyn slipped the fingers of her uninjured hand around the hilt and drew it free. The blade shone in the candlelight, its single edge a perfect arc that rose to a needle point, the steel of its pommel a cold weight against her wrist. Wyn turned it slowly. It felt heavy, but its weight made her hand feel stronger, as if the weapon were a part of her fist.

She made a half-hearted pass with the blade. As far as Wyn was concerned, the knife looked like it had killed a thousand people, easy. It knew its business, but her hand did not. The blade wavered as she turned it.

"I don't know, Fergus," she said softly. "I'll likely just kill myself with it."

"Well," he replied, gently moving the point to the side with his finger. "That's wrong. First lesson."

"I couldn't hit Ratter with a sword, what chance do I have with a knife?"

"Swords are heavy, they'll make someone your size slow," Fergus replied. "You're as quick as a cat, and you need a weapon that suits you. This one won't slow you down, and a blade this sharp can cut cloth, leather, skin, muscle. It's long enough to reach the vitals, no problem."

Wyn grasped the thin hilt more firmly.

Fergus reached to her hand and gently rotated the knife so that the blade aligned with her forward knuckles. "Like that."

She liked the way it sank into her hand, that was certain. "I suppose…"

"Wyn, I want you to have it. It will make me feel better, knowing you have that if you need it. I hope you never do. I hope I can be there every time. But…"

"Do I stab with it, or slash, or what?"

"Both. Quick, controlled. No big movements. Speed, not strength."

"What do I aim for?"

"Here." He took her hand again and placed the tip of the blade against his neck. "Here. Here. Here." He moved the point under his sternum, the inside of his arm, the inside of his thigh. "You get your blade in any of those places, he's killed. Here." He

THE THIEF'S TALE

pressed the blade against his own knuckles as his fingers curled into a fist. "He'll flinch away, maybe drop his knife."

"Show me how." Wyn tried to look her fiercest, ready and determined, not aching and exhausted and dizzy.

"Wyn, you are not ready for a proper lesson. We'll get to that, I promise, when you're healed."

Wyn agreed reluctantly, and Fergus helped her re-thread her belt around her hips so that the dagger was held snugly against the small of her back where it would not poke out and snag on everything.

They rejoined Desmond and Mellon in the small area behind the barrels, and Wyn eased herself onto one of the rickety highbacked chairs around the table with as little movement as possible. Parts of her she did not dare move, as there was little chance any movement would not hurt. Parts of her she was not sure she could move, given how tightly Fergus had wrapped her bandages.

She shifted uncomfortably and plucked at the wrappings, but they were proof against her meddling.

"Are you all right?" Desmond asked. He held out a small threadbare cushion that smelled of cat as if it could somehow heal swelling and knit bone.

"I can't breathe," Wyn informed him archly. She grimaced and shifted again. "Not sure I want to breathe, to be honest. Feels like a dagger sticking me when I do. Might just give it up."

"Here." Desmond tried to give her the pillow again.

"Maker, Des… leave off!" Wyn snapped.

"Seems that your tongue is just as sharp as ever," Mellon observed. "Whatever you did to it, you didn't bite it off."

"I'm sorry, did my getting beat hurt your feelings?"

"Never in life," Mellon assured her. "Just wondering when you might turn that temper onto those who deserve it."

"I'm ready now." Wyn glared at him.

"I'm ready, too." Mellon glared back.

"All right, then."

"All right, then," Mellon agreed. A grin crept onto the corner of his lips. "That means not me, right?"

THE THIEF'S TALE

"No, not you," Wyn relented. "Just stop fussing. I hurt enough without having to tell you to fuck off every two shakes."

"Right. We'll give no shits about you, starting… now." Mellon's grin faded. "It hurts us to see you hurt, Whinny, that's all, and it sticks in my craw not to have been there. It doesn't mean nothing more than that, and I'll say no more. Except, I want to hurt those bastards."

"Well, I'll tell you, it was not as fun as it sounds."

"No, perhaps not," Mellon allowed.

"What do we do now?"

Desmond placed the two real keys next to Tillings's Veil on the table, nudging them until they were perfectly aligned with each other. Wyn eyed the little grey Device dubiously. The small circle of markings, which had once glowed such a soothing blue, now showed barely a flicker of light.

"They know we have the keys," Fergus said gravely. "They're going to come after us."

"And what?" Mellon asked. "We hide until… when?"

"Until they're dead."

"And we tell everyone we care about to hide," Wyn added.

"Aye, them as well," Fergus agreed.

"What else?" Mellon asked. "We agree we can no longer give the keys to the Hawk?"

"How is that any different than just handing them to Quinn?" Desmond asked. "We'd be murdered the next day."

"I don't know." Mellon glanced at Wyn. "What do you say about our Lady Hawk? You know her best."

Wyn snorted, then regretted it instantly as pain laced through her skull. She blinked back tears and swallowed carefully. "She made a complete fool of me."

"So twist it back on her," Mellon urged. "She didn't do it for free, and I'll wager there's more to be read if we take another look, now that we know her true color."

Wyn closed her eyes as she tried to stir her thoughts from the thick morass they were mired in. It was difficult to think back on the time she had spent with Lady Cailean without flinching away in shame, but Wyn forced herself to examine each cunning lie,

THE THIEF'S TALE

each twisted smile, and let the humiliation fuel the hot fire of rage that crackled and spat in her chest.

"She really wants the keys," Wyn said softly. "More than anything. She doesn't give two shits about Quinn, nor us, nor anything else."

"She might get rid of him if that's what is required to get the keys?"

"She might."

"Do you trust she'll actually hold to her end of the deal if we deliver?"

"Trust her?" Wyn shook her head slowly. "Never again," she swore.

Mellon sighed. "All right. We're a bit short on options, then."

"There's only one option," Wyn whispered. "There was only ever one option."

"If we're back to saying no to Quinn, it's a bit late."

"No, you were right. There was no saying no to Quinn. We were going to be here the moment I grabbed those knickers, no matter what. Whether it was Quinn or the next bastard who came along, there was no more hiding for the Tallywags. That's what Cailean told me, that night I went and told her she had a deal."

"Wyn, she told you that to make us agree to her deal."

"I've not forgotten that, but she's not wrong. And I'm not saying we shouldn't have done the panty heist. We're nothing without a name, it's just we hadn't thought it all the way through. Now we have."

"And did her ladyship have any advice for what to do about that?"

"Yeah." Wyn shook her head in astonishment. *I'm actually saying this,* she thought, bewildered. "She said that if Quinn needs to be dealt with, there's no use pretending otherwise."

Fergus nodded his approval silently, while Mellon grunted and huffed like a pig for a moment before meeting Wyn's gaze and giving his own, resigned nod.

Desmond glanced around the table miserably, his face pale save for two bright spots of pink on his cheekbones. "What do we do, then?" he asked.

Wyn could hear the Hawk's voice clear as a bell, despite the thick fog of pain that clouded her thoughts. She smiled, her mouth twisted around her swollen lips.

"Sweetheart, there are times you have to fight."

**W**yn stopped to retch behind the wreckage of an old cart before staggering up the narrow alley to the small, black door beneath the sign of a candle. The sickening dizziness that accompanied the pounding ache in her head had grown steadily worse as she trudged through the dark streets until the few lanterns still shining bobbed and weaved and lurched as if they floated on an insane sea.

The snow had returned, falling in silent, muffling curtains that caused the stone buildings to shift and dance as if they were made of paper, and the narrow alleys soon filled with thick piles that concealed treacherous, slippery, uneven cobbles.

Mellon had done his best to keep her ensconced at the brewery, but Wyn refused to listen.

"The first thing we do is warn everyone we know that Quinn's going to be looking for us," Wyn had insisted.

"Too right," Mellon agreed. "But that doesn't mean you have to do it."

"Why is that?"

"You've had a hell of a night."

"I can walk and talk."

"What's that?" Mellon had leaned toward her and cupped his ear. "I'm sorry, I couldn't hear you with all the blood drooling out of your mouth."

"Don't be stupid," Wyn chided Mellon. "I'm not staying here when I can help."

Mellon had grumbled but Wyn refused to listen, and in the end, he gave in with bad grace.

Wyn paused when she reached the black-painted door and leaned her forehead on the brick frame, pressing her sweat-soaked skin against its chill surface. To add to her misery, her hip was stabbing her on every step, and somehow her broken fingers still throbbed painfully, even though they were now numb with cold.

She inhaled the frigid air and tried to still the reeling world. Wyn pulled her hood as low as possible to conceal the scraped and swollen flesh on her face and her bruised neck, stretched for the iron knob, and let herself in as the bell tinkled in the gloomy recesses of the shop. Another breath steeled her resolve, and she managed to walk steadily across the floor and down the stairs without mishap.

"Maker, lass… what happened?" the Candlemaker gasped, leaning his bulk against the table as Wyn stepped into the light. For a moment, the iron-hearted fence sounded almost concerned.

"Ice…" Wyn muttered vaguely.

"I see," he said thoughtfully. His eyes narrowed as his gaze lingered on the splinted fingers poking from her cut-off gloves. "Down in Cowgate, was this ice? You should be more careful. Who else will bring me such fascinating treasures?" The Candlemaker licked his lips in anticipation, greed overwhelming momentary compassion like a spring flood washing away a child's twig dam.

"I don't have anything tonight," Wyn told him as she eased into the chair across the table from the Candlemaker. "Wanted to let you know there may be others come asking about us, besides Faithless Todd."

"Might there, indeed?"

"Yeah. Wanted to remind you we had a deal. You give us fair warning before you give us up."

"We do have a deal, I've not forgotten. Did you find the, ah, person you were asking about, last time you were here?"

"Yeah, I did, and you were right. I wish I hadn't."

"The Candlemaker is always right," he replied smugly. He stared at Wyn for a moment, cleared his throat, squirmed uncomfortably in his chair, and cleared his throat, again.

"I guess I'll be going, then," Wyn said.

"It occurs to me…" the Candlemaker said suddenly. His fingers drummed frantically on the table for a moment. "It occurs to me that our deal may not be entirely square."

THE THIEF'S TALE

"I can't pay you any more," Wyn said, fighting the tears that burned her eyes, helpless rage and fear blurring her vision with stinging shame. "I've got nothing left."

"No, I don't think you understand. I feel that you may have overpaid."

"I... what?"

The Candlemaker slumped back in his seat, his bright eyes darting everywhere except meeting her puzzled gaze.

"After all," he continued, "we're just talking about a quiet word, aren't we? A professional courtesy? No need for silver, really."

"But..." Wyn managed, but her voice caught before she could continue, and she could not stop the tears from sliding down her cheeks. She wiped helplessly at her eyes with her sleeve, but it made no difference to the torrent.

The Candlemaker busied himself searching his robes and set two small stacks of silver on his table.

"Here," he said roughly.

"I knew you were an old softy," Wyn told him between sniffles.

"Don't tell anyone," he grumbled. "In any case, Faithless Todd's promised mountain of silver has, predictably, not appeared, so there's nothing for me to warn you about."

"There'll be more than Faithless asking, now," Wyn warned him.

"I know who it will be," the Candlemaker assured her. "Here, take your silver."

"Keep it," Wyn decided. "The next time I bring you something lovely, you can just figure it into the deal."

"As you like," he agreed. "Good luck to you, lass."

Wyn levered herself painfully out of the chair and hobbled for the stairs, her hip grating. But before she had taken three strides the bell chimed brightly somewhere above, and the Candlemaker hissed in annoyance.

"Most inconvenient," he sniffed. "More inconvenient if anyone should see you with me. Here, into the hole..."

Wyn followed his bloated finger to an innocuous stretch of shelving against the cellar's wall which clicked open to reveal a

THE THIEF'S TALE

spacious hidey-hole. Wyn gazed at the space in horror. All she could think of was the door locking behind her, caging her in, helpless.

"Hurry," he hissed. Heavy boots clomped across the floorboards above their heads, shifting dirt in a hazy curtain.

Wyn stopped at the brink of entering the concealed room, her every instinct screaming to flee, to hide. She shook her head. "Not there."

Wyn scuttled to the back of the cellar and clambered painfully into the shadows above one of the thick beams that supported the ceiling. She wedged herself into the narrow gap, sliding deep into the shadow until she became a part of the ancient, blackened beam, a patch of welcome darkness as silent as the depths of a well.

The Candlemaker scowled but had no time to argue. The boots were on the stairs, and he barely regained his seat before the footsteps left the wood for the stone floor of the cellar.

Wyn lifted a corner of her hood, enough to see the pool of light surrounding the Candlemaker's table. His massive bulk sagged over the arms of his chair and around the back, his red robes the color of blood in the shadows. Vague figures moved toward him from the stairs, and Wyn caught her breath as they stepped into the glow of the lantern.

"Quinn," the Candlemaker mumbled. "Always a pleasure."

Quinn gazed down at the Candlemaker, slowly pulling his heavy gauntlets free one finger at a time. The dim light made his face seem bloodless, his thick lips and close-cropped hair as bleached as his smooth cheeks. Only his eyes had life, dark slits that glinted as he examined his host.

Two men stepped out of Quinn's shadow and stood on either side of the table. One had grey whiskers that drooped to his chest, a granite face lined with deep cracks beside his nose and around his eyes, and arms as thick as Wyn's thighs crossed over the barrel of his chest. The second was tall enough he had to stoop beneath the beams, his tangled black hair hanging limply around his face. A deep scar ran through his lip and nose, lending him a permanent sneer

THE THIEF'S TALE

"Candlemaker," Quinn said softly. At last his gauntlets were free, and he laid them carefully on the table next to Wyn's coins.

"Have a seat, please." The Candlemaker gestured to the empty chair. Quinn examined it with a brief, sneering smile, then seated himself with his elbows on the table, his fingers interlocked.

"I hear you do business with the Tallywags," Quinn stated.

The Candlemaker shrugged. "People come down those stairs, I do business with them."

Quinn tilted his head slowly to the side, examining his host as if he were a cut of meat hanging from a hook. "That's not a yes, nor a no."

"Quinn, you know I love you, but questions cost coin," the Candlemaker wheezed.

The thick leather of Quinn's sword belt creaked as he slowly withdrew a hand to his waist. Wyn held her breath, willing the Candlemaker to reach for the trigger of his crossbow. But Quinn's hand returned above the table without drawing steel, then produced a silver penny, holding it between thumb and forefinger.

Quinn eased back in the chair, the coin slowly working its way across his knuckles, glinting in the lantern light. Then he tossed it casually onto the table. It bounced and rolled and clattered on the pitted wood, taking every gaze in the room with it.

Wyn stifled a gasp as Quinn suddenly erupted from his chair. His fist flashed in a brutal arc over the table and smashed onto the Candlemaker's hand. The huge man shrieked and tried to rise, but he lurched awkwardly and sank onto his knees, his chair tumbling backward with a crash. Quinn's knife was buried in the Candlemaker's hand, the long, curved blade sunk deep into the hard wood of the table beneath it.

The Candlemaker screamed again, the fingers of his pierced hand splayed uselessly as he stared at the knife. He grabbed his wrist with his free hand, then lunged beneath the table, groping for his crossbow.

Quinn stepped calmly to the side as a hollow thrum vibrated through the room. The chair's back shattered into a shower of splinters, and the chair twisted away as if yanked by an invisible rope.

Wyn's fingers dug into the wooden beam in desperation as she watched the Candlemaker sag against the table, his quivering hand clutching the knife's hilt.

"There's my coin," Quinn said quietly. "Now, my questions."

The Candlemaker pulled on the knife and screamed piteously as the steel shifted between the bones of his pinned hand. He abandoned the knife and slumped, a mass of shining skin in a filthy, stained robe as his blood pooled on his table amongst the scattered silver coins. "Take it out!" he begged. "Take it out!"

Quinn frowned. "How is he going to hear my questions with all that squealing?"

"Stop your mouth, you fat fuck!" Whiskers bellowed at the Candlemaker. He stepped forward, his massive arms reaching for the sobbing man's head.

The Candlemaker shrieked and whipped his free hand at Whiskers. In his pudgy grip was a heavy cleaver, its broad blade shining silver in the flickering light. Whiskers cursed and stumbled back, tripped, and crashed into a rickety shelf of candles.

The Candlemaker screamed again, spit spraying from his lips as he reversed his cut and slashed at Quinn.

Quinn stepped quickly forward and the Candlemaker's arm whacked uselessly into Quinn's hip, the cleaver waving in the air behind his back. Steel flashed in Quinn's hand, and he drove it into the Candlemaker's gut once, twice, three times in the space of a heartbeat, then Quinn stepped away.

The long knife in his hand, a twin to the one impaled in the table, dripped blood from its narrow point, and Quinn flipped it around twice before slipping it back into its sheath beneath his cloak as he watched his victim.

The Candlemaker struggled once more to rise, but his scream was a hacking moan of pain, and his robes glistened wetly in a fast-spreading stain across his gut. He waved the cleaver, but his movements were slow and clumsy, and Stoop snatched the weapon from his hand without trouble.

"It's good to see there are some bones beneath all that fat," Quinn growled. "But you've got a fucking problem now." Stoop handed the cleaver to Quinn silently, and Quinn hefted it, judging its weight.

"Where are the fucking Tallywags?" Quinn spat. "They been here? They tell you about the keys?"

"You bastard..." the Candlemaker gasped.

Wyn bit her lip as a scream built in her throat. Her legs gripped the beam as if it were coated in ice. *Stop!* she screamed, but her throat would not move, would not utter a sound. *No no no no... oh, Maker, tell them,* she begged the Candlemaker, but still her jaw would not unlock, her lips would not form the words, and she cowered silently in the shadows.

Quinn shook his head slightly, his eyes dangerous and sharp. When he moved, it was the sudden explosion of the hawk's strike on the rabbit. He twisted violently and there was the sound of wood being hewed. Small objects flew into the air and landed with a faint patter. Wyn felt the world lurch and bile rush into her mouth.

The Candlemaker stared at his pinned hand in horror. The cleaver's blade quivered in the wood where his knuckles had been, streaked with blood.

He choked and tried to scream, but all that emerged was a wet gurgle.

Quinn leaned over him. "Where are they!" he screamed. Spit splattered across the Candlemaker's waxy face. "What did they tell you!"

"You bastard!" the Candlemaker choked out in a gurgling shriek. He lurched upward and grabbed the hilt of the knife pinning his hand and wrenched it free of the wood with a horrifying squeal.

Quinn grabbed the Candlemaker's wrist before he could swing, twisted it savagely to the side, and smashed his other fist into the Candlemaker's face. The huge man crashed to the floor like a felled ox and Quinn followed him down, pinning the arm holding the knife beneath his knee as Quinn gripped the Candlemaker's head in his powerful hands.

"What did they tell you!" Quinn bellowed. He smashed the Candlemaker's head into the floor, again and again, until he was

THE THIEF'S TALE

pounding a shapeless mass of dead meat against the blood-drenched stone.

Quinn rose to his full height over the sprawled mass of the Candlemaker. His face twisted and he spat, then he retrieved his knife from the Candlemaker's lifeless fingers.

Stoop yanked the cleaver from the table and tucked it in his belt as Whiskers climbed from the wreckage of the shelf, rubbing at his arm.

"Fucker got me," he said disbelievingly. A long, ragged cut crossed his flesh just above his elbow.

"Search the place," Quinn said quietly, his rage vanished, his face emotionless again. "If those keys are here, find them."

Stoop and Whiskers nodded silently and hurried to tear apart the shop while Quinn methodically wiped the blood from his hands and face. They soon found the hidey-hole, along with a concealed chest in the floor and a hidden latch that opened the heavily reinforced door guarding the Candlemaker's stash. Gem-encrusted silver and gold treasures were tucked into pockets as fast as they were found, but all the crashing and splintering could not reveal keys that were not there, and the two lackeys soon had to skulk back to Quinn to report their failure.

Quinn nodded silently, then fixed them with a glare. "Find Ratter, wherever that bastard has gotten to. He'll know where they are."

"Yes, boss, sorry, boss," Whiskers said.

Quinn shook his head. "They weren't here." He shrugged. "Just a waste of time." Quinn stomped up the stairs and his thugs followed, and the cellar was silent save for the spatter of blood dripping from the table onto the worn floorboards.

She ran. The freezing air burned her lungs, the soft snow clung to her boots, and the pain from her hip made her gasp, but she flew across Tinkers Square, leaving a trail of indignant cries and shocked stares behind her.

The Thief's Tale

The cobbler's shop appeared through the white veil of snow, and Wyn sped across the lane and tore the small, weathered door open, calling out as she leapt down the narrow stairs.

The dim hallway was empty, and there was no answering call. Wyn desperately raced into the main room and stumbled to a halt. Two dozen faces stared back at her in astonishment, their owners frozen in place around the rickety table, some with food poised half-way to their mouths. Brodie was on his feet, a steaming pot in his hand, a smile faltering on his lips.

"Wyn, what...?"

"You have to go," Wyn panted. "Get out, right now, it's not safe!"

Several of the smaller children cried out in fright and started from their places on the bench while the rest stared, bewildered, at Wyn.

"Wyn, what's going on?" Brodie asked as he placed the pot on the table.

"You have to go!" Wyn pleaded.

"Wyn! Stop it!" Brodie snapped. He glanced nervously around the table, then strode to Wyn, took her arm, and marched her to the far end of the room. "You're terrifying them," he accused her.

"I'm sorry..." Wyn tried to swallow her panic. "Brodie, get them out of here. It's Quinn. He's murdering everyone we know. No telling how long before he comes here."

Brodie's eyes widened as he peered at her face. "Martyr's tears... Wyn, what happened to you?"

"Brodie, please, listen," Wyn pleaded. "Quinn killed the Candlemaker, he's going to come here looking for us, and when you don't tell him what he wants to know, he's going to kill you all."

Brodie's face turned pale as ash, and he glanced nervously at the silent table. "Oh, shit... what do I do?"

"Get out of here, hide for a few days, that's all you'll need."

Boots clattered down the stairs and Wyn whirled to face the door, her heart in her throat, then thought she was going to pass out with relief when Desmond shouldered his way into the room, his face flushed, his breath ragged.

THE THIEF'S TALE

"All right… all right…" Brodie muttered. He inhaled sharply and set his shoulders. "All right, Wee Ones, everyone run to your cots and dress in your warmest clothes and come back as quick as you can. Vail, Elise, load all the food and the stash into the cart as soon as you are dressed. Keeva, run down to Littlemarket, find Jester and Thorn, and get them back here."

The pack swirled into motion, children hurrying in every direction as Wyn paced frantically back and forth between the stairs and the main room. The bairns stared wide-eyed at her as they slowly congregated in the main room, wrapped in old coats and mittens. Some were crying, not sure what was happening, but the older children comforted them and held their hands, waiting on the stragglers. Finally, everyone was ready and the precious food and silver gathered, and the minute crew tromped upstairs and into the back alley.

"I'm going to take them to—"

"Don't!" Wyn stopped him. "Just in case…"

Brodie nodded, his eyes wide with fear, but he steeled himself, nodded to Wyn, and ran after his charges.

Wyn listened to his boots clump up the stairs and the door slam shut behind him. She turned to follow and caught sight of the table, the mismatched bowls of broth abandoned, the pot still steaming, and misery sucked the strength out of her. She tried to breathe but gagged on a sob, and a thin wail squeezed out of her aching throat as her eyes burned and the room blurred.

Then Desmond was there, his face twisted by anguish, and she collapsed into his arms, sobbing. He held her tight, and she felt as if she were a girl of twelve, again, torn from her mother, her body broken, her heart shattered by loneliness and fear, finding comfort in the soothing strength of the quiet boy who stayed by her side, no matter what.

"I've got you," he whispered to her, his breath warm on the back of her neck, and she pressed against him as another sob shuddered through her, burrowing as deep into his arms as she could. "I'll take care of you, you'll take care of me, remember?"

"Uh-huh," she managed, nodding against his chest.

A distant thought urged her to hide her pathetic weakness, to stand and glare fiercely, but she could not find the will to be strong, anymore. She sagged to her knees and Desmond knelt with her, and a torrent of misery wailed from her. There was too much fear, too much pain, and too much sorrow to contain. Sorrow for an avaricious man who had died because she had sold him some jewels. Sorrow for a friend who had killed for her, choking out a life on a dirty floor. And sorrow for the realization that she wanted to see death, again. Wanted to watch Quinn's eyes bulge with fear, wanted to see his life extinguished. Wanted to feel it happen under her own hand.

She was not certain how long they stayed that way, but when, at last, she realized she was breathing normally, her throat was raw and the cloth of Desmond's coat was soaked against her face. She let herself rest for another moment, enjoying the warmth of his arms around her shoulders, then gently pushed herself away.

Desmond's cheeks were bright pink, the way they became when he was embarrassed or happy or excited or drunk, and he held her gaze, his green eyes wide with concern. She managed a weak, apologetic smile and turned away, embarrassed by what she was certain she must look like, with puffy eyes and red, running nose, her face covered in scrapes and bruises.

"I'm all right," she said softly. "Sorry about your coat."

"It needed some snot, I always thought so."

Wyn snorted a little laugh, then sighed, exhausted.

"Maker, Des, I'm a mess."

"Yeah, but I still love you."

"That's because you're an idiot," she replied easily, but her thoughts froze on his words for a heartbeat. *What if that were true?* she wondered, before she shredded that hope. *Don't be stupid, who could possibly love me, anyway?*

She clambered to her feet and wiped her face on her sleeve, then tried uselessly to tame her hair with only one hand, but gave up and let it hang around her face and fall in a tangled mass down her back.

"What are you doing here?" she asked.

"I was coming to warn them when I saw you running," Desmond said simply. "I thought Quinn was here... Did he really kill the Candlemaker?"

Wyn nodded mutely.

THE THIEF'S TALE

"Maker…" Desmond frowned and shook his head, then suddenly stared at Wyn in concern. "Wyn, who else have you warned, tonight?"

"Just the Candlemaker and here."

"You haven't been to the Padraigs?"

"No, not… have you?"

"No, that's where I was headed, next."

"Oh, Des," Wyn whispered, her voice tight with fear. "Oh, no… we have to go now… he knows they were working with us, he could be going there now!"

"Not without Fergus," Desmond said firmly. "No, Wyn, you're not. If he had caught you at the Candlemaker's, you'd be dead. If he were here, you'd be dead. If he's at the Padraigs', you'll be dead. It'll take me two shakes to get Fergus, then you can go."

$\mathcal{W}$yn inhaled deeply, digging for the strength to keep going. She could not remember the last time she had slept, but it was before pain and death, and before an endless night slogging between places to puke across the Old City.

There was no talk as they stamped their way through the snow to the Padraigs' quiet street. Fergus stared straight ahead as if sheer determination would set things right, but Wyn had no time to worry about anything except the grating pain in her hip. It awoke with a vengeance as they hurried up the stairs from the Wee One's cellar and hobbled her as they trudged through the snow-muffled streets. To her relief, the pain finally relented as they neared the Padraigs' house, becoming an uneasy ache that promised to betray her on every step.

Most of the houses on the Padraigs' street had the snow shoveled off their steps, although the evening's fresh fall was steadily undoing that work. A snowman stared at them from amidst a swath of trampled snow, its coal eyes somehow forlorn under the bonnet that had been smushed onto its head.

The Padraigs' steps had not been cleared. Snow piled against the door, and no smoke curled from its chimney.

THE THIEF'S TALE

"No one home…" Wyn murmured as she stared at the house from the street.

"Why would they not come home?" Fergus wondered, and Wyn felt her heart lurch as cold fire prickled her spine.

"It's not right," Wyn decided. She strode to the door and hammered on it, then twisted the knob. To their surprise, it turned and the door swung open. Wyn clutched at the hilt of Fergus's knife as she peered into the dark hallway beyond.

"Padraigs!" Fergus hollered into the house. "Hello!"

They waited anxiously for a reply, but there was none, and eventually, Fergus stepped cautiously into the house. Wyn followed, her heart thundering in her throat.

Fergus stopped at the drawing-room door, and Wyn heard him curse.

She looked. She did not want to, but she could not stop herself, desperate to discover, somehow, that the dread she felt leaking from the house was not real. But it was.

The room was foul with blood. Long arcs were sprayed on the walls, thick stains covered the threadbare rugs, long rivulets meandered from body to body across the soiled floor.

Wyn pressed her fingers to her mouth, unable to look away. She could not tell who she was looking at. The corpses were strange, butchered meat… how could they be people she knew? But her terrified gaze found the proof she did not want to see. Faces familiar despite their empty eyes, despite the agony and fear twisted into them.

She heard Fergus calling out, and she wondered why. They were all gone, that was as certain as death, their bodies lying somewhere in their small home. *Killed just for knowing me…*

Wyn flinched as she bumped into the wall at her back, unaware that she had retreated from the horror spread across the drawing room. She slid to the floor, her legs too weak to support her.

"There's four more in the kitchen," Fergus said grimly as he returned to the front hall.

"He was learning to write," Wyn said softly. Skinny looked so surprised, his eyes wide with shock as he stared at the floor beneath his head.

THE THIEF'S TALE

Fergus crouched next to her with a slow creak of leather. "Come on," he said softly. "There's nothing we can do for them."

Wyn clambered slowly to her feet and followed Fergus along the hallway without a word, but she balked at the kitchen door.

"Is… is Bloody…?"

"No, she's not in there," Fergus replied. "Some must have gotten away."

"She would have fought," Wyn insisted.

"She might not have been here." Fergus gripped Wyn by her shoulders and bent to bring his face level with hers, his gaze gentle but unrelenting. "Wyn, we have to go. This didn't happen long ago."

Wyn nodded silently and followed Fergus out the back door without a word. They hopped the wall into the small lane behind the row of houses, followed its concealing shadows to the wagon house at its base, and cut across the yard toward the twisting maze of streets beyond.

A figure stepped into the archway leading from the street and Wyn froze, dragging on Fergus's arm. A second figure joined the first, and a third, their shapes muffled by long cloaks.

She spun as a scrape of metal on stone carried from the shadows inside the wagon house, and two more figures eased into the yard.

"Wyn, run," Fergus whispered. "Get out of here."

"Back to the lane," Wyn urged, "quick!"

But figures were materializing from the shadows all around the yard, now, pairs stepping confidently from the wagon house door and the nearby alleys, surrounding them. Wyn darted toward the back gate, then jerked to a halt as two figures pushed through it into the yard. She spun in place, a groan of frustration leaking through her clenched teeth.

The group under the archway stepped into the moonlight. Wyn recognized the broad shoulders and drooping mustache of Whiskers at their center.

"Quinn would like a word," Whiskers growled across the rapidly shrinking stretch of paving stones that separated them. "He's not well-pleased."

THE THIEF'S TALE

Fergus glanced carefully left and right. "Takes ten of you to deliver a message, does it?"

"Depends on the message," Stoop's quiet rasp sounded from the figures in the wagon house doorway. The tall brute slouched from the shadow behind the faded wooden door. "This message takes ten."

Steel whispered as Fergus drew his blade, and Wyn flinched at the sound.

"Careful lads, he's right quick with that sword," Whiskers growled. The crew began to spread out, and the moonlight glinted on knives, axes, and short blades being readied.

"Wyn, go," Fergus whispered. His arm swept out and tried to herd her behind him. "As soon as they come for us, run."

"Not a chance," Wyn hissed back. Her hand groped for the hilt of Fergus's knife behind her back, and she slipped it free from its leather loop and forced herself to stand like Fergus. Her stomach convulsed at the thought of staying, and she tasted sour bile. Her legs trembled with the need to flee, and her hand shook and she could not stop it as she desperately tried to remember even one piece of his instructions. "Not a chance…"

"Not quick enough against all of us," Stoop sneered. He produced a pair of small, wickedly hooked hatchets from beneath his coat and tested their weight.

"Quick enough to do you and your bitty axes," Wyn spat at Stoop, but her voice sounded like the squeak of a mouse, even to her, and the tall brute barely glanced at her.

The circle closed to within a few steps and halted. Eyes glared hungrily at Wyn, narrowed suspiciously, stared eagerly, darted nervously between her and Fergus. There was a soft sigh of cloth as Fergus's cloak curled to the cobblestones and a creak of leather as he shifted into his stance.

"Oh, fuck," Wyn whispered.

Stoop hurled his hatchet and Fergus bent like a reed as it flew past his nose to bury its blade in the wood of the courtyard gate. Whiskers bellowed and charged, and with him the rest of his crew leapt forward.

Whiskers' axe flashed in a wicked arc, but Fergus danced aside, and his blade flicked across Whiskers' ribs as its razor edge tore through his leather vest and slashed a long, red stripe into his skin.

A short man with oily black hair and a forest of bristles on his cheeks stabbed at Fergus, but the swordsman knocked the thrust aside and whipped his blade through a tight spiral, severing the man's hand, and he fell to his knees, gaping at the stump.

Fergus stepped forward in a long lunge and his point slammed home beneath the jaw of a tall, gangly man with drooping mustaches and a fat-bladed dagger, then he grabbed the tunic of a leathery-faced man hacking at him with two hatchets, drove his knee between the man's legs, then stabbed upward into his stomach three times before Wyn could blink, his shining blade jutting from the man's back and disappearing like magic.

A bald man with a pointed nose and a tiny, snarling mouth leapt toward Fergus with his axe raised high, and Wyn dove into his legs without hesitation. His knee drove her breath from her in a whoosh and they sprawled into a mass of thrashing limbs. A boot thudded into her hip as she tried to roll away, and she cursed and kicked at a glimpse of a sneering smile. It disappeared with a crunch and a spray of blood, and Wyn lashed out a second time, just to be sure, before scrambling to her feet.

A body stumbled against her, sending her staggering as its weight sagged into her legs, then someone collided with her from the opposite direction, knocking her off her feet. She tripped and frantically caught her balance just in time to plow into Stoop as he raised a hatchet to throw.

Wyn sliced wildly at Stoop's face, but he jerked away and swung viciously at her with his hatchet. She ducked beneath the first swing, then leapt away from the next. *Quick and controlled,* she chastised herself, but everyone was moving too fast to think ahead, and only her reflexes were fast enough to keep her safe.

A huge man with a shining, pink, fat head staggered past her, clutching a dripping stain across his enormous belly, screaming in terror as he pushed past.

Wyn followed his trail back to Fergus. The lanky swordsman had scampered free of the scrum in the middle of the courtyard and was carefully circling behind a row of sturdy wooden pillars beneath the wagon house portico. A thin man with gaunt eyes and a wiry beard lunged at him with an iron hook, but Fergus stepped nimbly away, his blade leaving a long spray of blood across the brick wall as its tip sliced the man's face from lip to ear.

A powerfully built man with a bristling beard and coal-black hair pounced on Fergus and wrapped his thick arms around the swordsman's chest. Fergus snapped his head back and smashed the man's lips, but the brute just grinned redly and heaved Fergus to face Whiskers, his boots slapping against the pillars as they swung through the air.

"Hold him," Whiskers spat, and he struck heavily with his long axe. But Fergus curled and twisted to the side, yanking the bearded man with him, and Whisker's axe thudded deep into the man's shoulder. The man cried out and staggered backward, clutching at the dangling limb, and Fergus skewered him through his arm and deep into his broad chest.

Whiskers cursed and swung wildly at Fergus's head, but Fergus swatted the axe aside with his sword. Whiskers whipped his axe back, but Fergus struck faster, stabbing the thick man deep between hip and ribs. Fergus pulled back to thrust again, but before he could, a young man with a square jaw and narrow, squinting eyes lunged from behind him and jabbed his dagger into Fergus's back.

Fergus spun and kicked the youth's legs out, sending him staggering into Whiskers. A hatchet whirled from behind Wyn, so close to her head that she felt the swirl of air puff against her neck. Fergus slashed at the spinning weapon with his sword and metal clanged sharply against metal. Fergus staggered as the hatchet clattered to the ground, and Wyn saw a gaping red wound open along Fergus's thigh where the blade had gouged him as it ricocheted past.

Whiskers wrenched the young man away from him and leapt at Fergus, his axe high. Fergus twisted and parried the curved blade away, but the force of Whiskers' rush slammed him backward, and Fergus bounced off the brick wall with a grunt. Whiskers barely paused. He bellowed and swung again, and the axe hissed as it tore down Fergus's back. Sparks flew as the axe bit into the cobbled pavement as Fergus staggered out of reach, but

Whiskers was after him in a heartbeat, his teeth bared, spit flying from his curled lips.

Wyn stepped toward Whiskers, Fergus's knife raised, when a blow caught her on the side of her head and sent her sprawling to the stones. The knife skittered away from her fingers as she smacked her cheek on the ground and tasted blood. She crawled toward the blade, but Stoop's heavy boot slammed onto her wrist and ground it into the stone.

She screamed in pain and tried to jerk away, but the boot pinned her.

"Now we'll see," he muttered, and there was a long scrape of metal as he drew the Candlemaker's cleaver from his belt.

"No!" Wyn shrieked at him. She clutched at his boot, but her splinted fingers could not gain a purchase.

Stoop raised the cleaver, his stare fixed on her fingers, splayed on the cobblestones beside his boot. Wyn slammed her shoulder into the side of his knee and shoved with her legs, her boots slipping on the wet stones. Pain lanced into her neck and back, but Stoop cursed and wrenched away from the impact, clutching at his knee.

"Gah! You bitch!" he shouted.

Wyn scrambled forward and grabbed Fergus's knife. Her arm screamed with pain, but her fingers worked just fine, and she twisted to face Stoop, the knife held warily in front of her as she crouched low.

Stoop grimaced as he put weight on his leg, then snarled as he stepped forward, the cleaver sighing through the air. Wyn tumbled to the side and felt the heavy blade tug the cloth of her hood. She lashed out with the knife and Stoop pulled back, then hacked at her again.

Wyn dodged away and collided with the brick wall. Stoop raised the cleaver and stepped into his swing.

Fergus's blade slid into Stoop's body under his raised arm, and the steel rasped home. Stoop's legs buckled and he crashed to his knees, blood spattering to the ground in a great gout that burst from his side. Stoop grabbed the blade as he collapsed, desperately pulling at the slim length of steel.

Fergus yanked it back and twisted as Whiskers' axe caught him above his hip. The blade bit deep and drove Fergus to his knee, and he gasped in pain.

"Die, you bastard!" Whiskers screamed. He wrenched the axe free, spraying blood in a narrow arc across the wall and Wyn's face. She flinched away as the warm drops stung her cheek.

Fergus spun, his blade a shining arc as it scythed through the air. It traced a narrow path across Whiskers' stomach and sang sweetly as its tip came free from his tunic. Whiskers stumbled back, his eyes bulging with panic as he clutched at his abdomen. Blood rushed between his fingers in a torrent as a great wound opened, and the heavy axe dropped to the ground with a ringing clang as Whiskers collapsed to his knees.

"No, you die," Fergus told him softly. The swordsman slumped heavily on his heels, his sword clattering to the cobbles beside him.

Whiskers choked out an animal moan and tried to rise, but his thick legs had no strength and he pitched onto his back. Coils of grey meat oozed from the wound across his belly, and he coughed thick blood as his legs trembled and scraped on the ground.

Wyn rushed to Fergus and knelt beside him. She slipped her arm around his ribs and tried to haul him to his feet. He groaned and slumped against her.

"Come on!" she shouted at him.

"I'm not going anywhere," he whispered, his hand clutched against the deep wound in his side. Bright red blood coursed from it and was already pooling around his knees.

"Come on! Somewhere safe, then we'll stitch you up," Wyn insisted.

The scrape of leather on stone made her gasp and look frantically over her shoulder.

The young man with the square jaw stood a few paces away, staring dumbly at the sprawled bodies and the thick slick of blood. His skin had turned grey, and his narrow eyes were wide with terror and fear.

THE THIEF'S TALE

His gaze snapped to Wyn's, and he flinched away and stumbled toward the entrance of the alley. She rose and gripped her knife, ready to give chase.

"Wyn…" Fergus's voice was a dry rasp. "Don't…"

"He stabbed you in the back—"

"It doesn't matter… let him go." Fergus groaned and began to clamber to his feet, and Wyn had no choice but to sheath the knife and help him. "I'm the killer, not you…"

"Maker, you're a mess," Wyn told him as she slipped under his arm and tried to support him. The lanky swordsman was as thin as a branch, but his legs had no strength, and Wyn's legs trembled as she struggled under his weight.

They stumbled together across the courtyard and reached a small staircase of cut stone leading behind the wagon house. Fergus managed three steps before his legs gave way, and he pulled Wyn to the ground with him.

"Damn it," Wyn sobbed. Her tunic was plastered to her side with Fergus's blood, warm and sticky, and more blood squelched against her fingers as she tried to grip him around his chest. "Please, Fergus, get up…"

"Wyn, where's my sword?"

"Who cares?" Wyn struggled to drape his arm over her shoulder. "We'll get you another one… one from Dorcha, remember? Maker, hold on to me, Fergus, come on…"

"Get my sword… I'll need it… if they catch up to us…"

"Here's your knife."

"You hold on to that," Fergus groaned. "Ahhh… Maker…"

"I'll get it, I'll get your sword," Wyn told him desperately.

"Never mind… Wyn, I'm sorry…"

"Don't be sorry!" She pulled him into a sitting position, trying to find some leverage, but he slumped against the wall and weakly waved away her hands.

"I am sorry…" Fergus sighed. He closed his eyes wearily.

"No, no, no…" she sobbed.

"It's done, Wyn," he gasped. "It's done…" His eyes opened, and he held her gaze.

THE THIEF'S TALE

"Don't leave me…" Wyn whispered, but it was too late. Fergus's gaze was fixed, his eyes suddenly cold and unseeing, and he was gone.

Wyn tried to sob, to scream, but no sound emerged. Pain and sorrow boiled into her throat, clogging it, forcing upward so that she could not breathe, could not make a sound. She rocked on her knees, mouth stretched, as agony flooded through her. At last, a wail of anguish leaked out, desperate and thin, and it seemed to have no end.

THE THIEF'S TALE

## CHAPTER EIGHTEEN

# What They Deserved

"I**t doesn't seem real," Desmond whispered.

"Feels real," Mellon muttered.

Wyn's gaze drifted between the two, unable to find purchase, as if she watched from some remote, detached place. She could barely remember how she had returned to the brewery, just a vague jumble of dark streets and cold stone brushing against her fingertips that had no sequence.

Even the bright gleam of Desmond's silver buckles was muted, compared to the sharp, black splash of pain that cut through her memory, black as blood against churned snow in the moonlight. The bright candle flame in the center of the table shuddered slightly and drew Wyn's eye, and a thin stream of smoke curled upward like the last breath between thin, grey lips.

*That's what's real,* Wyn realized. She swallowed against the choking despair that swelled in her throat. *One moment he's a man, the next he's meat. Nothing is more real than that,* Fergus's voice whispered to her.

"One got away?" Mellon asked.

Wyn blinked at him, confused, then slowly nodded her head. "One got away."

"Then we don't have much time," Mellon sighed.

"Time for what?" Desmond asked.

"To run, that's what."

"Why are we running?" Wyn asked, her brows wrinkled in confusion.

"Because right now Quinn's crew is heading out to catch us. He'll have silver in the pockets of the blackberries at the gates, silver for whatever snitch spots us first, and a blade for anyone that helps us. We have to get out before all that silver hits the streets. With any luck we can clear the city and be long gone before Quinn hears about it."

"We're going to let him get away with it?" Wyn asked.

Mellon looked away. "No." He tapped his finger on the two golden keys on the table. "We'll drop these bitches in the river. They'll never find them."

"I didn't mean the keys. I meant—"

"I know what you meant. We can't go after Quinn now."

"You mean now that Fergus is dead?" Wyn asked. "You think Fergus would stop fighting if one of us were dead?"

"No, I don't, but fighting is what he was, lass. That's not us."

Wyn picked up the keys and gently tapped them on Tillings's grey Device. "We toss these, we run, we let Quinn go, what was it all for?"

"Des," Mellon said quietly, "go get your coat for a moment."

Desmond retreated to the small bedroom, his gaze probing Wyn's face until the door closed.

"You going to make it, lass?" Mellon asked.

Wyn nodded once.

"It was a hard night. None harder, I'd say," he continued. "None would say otherwise, no matter who they were."

Wyn nodded again, her gaze fixed on the keys in her hand.

"Fergus didn't die for those keys, Wyn. He wasn't fighting for them, nor to get revenge. None of that. He was fighting for us, for you, so that you could live. Don't throw that away."

"Throw it away? You think Fergus died so we could live like this? Running and hiding until we're all dead? No, Mel, he died

THE THIEF'S TALE

fighting for our family. How can we not do the same? If we don't, then we're not what he thought we were, and I won't let that happen. I can't."

Mellon rubbed his eyes wearily. "We can't fight Quinn."

"We have to."

"Wyn, I'm not going to let you run out there and kill yourself. I couldn't..." He breathed in deeply, then placed a gentle hand on her shoulder. "Don't lose hope, lass. You can stay here for now, we'll take care of everything, no worries. But if you're coming, you need to put last night behind you, find your strength, Wyn. We need you, not... this."

"I'm not sad," Wyn said softly. That was somewhat true. She could feel a red ball of misery churning in her chest, aching to burst out of her clenched throat, and she was terrified of the depths that swirled in its heart. But she had locked its twin behind sturdy doors for years, and she knew she could imprison this fresh sorrow, as well. No, she was not certain what she was feeling, only that it was washing through her like a cold wave, numbing her, drowning her, leaving her as still as the ice on the surface of a well.

"Fine, you're not sad, but whatever you are, grab what you can carry and get on with it."

"I need to change," she said quietly. "I'm covered in blood."

She walked purposefully into the cramped bedroom and hooked the curtain across her corner. Her hands shook as she peeled off the blood-soaked tunic, and she cursed at them, but they would not stop. The only clothing she had left was the black uniform she had worn to Spicer's, so she donned the slim jacket and fumbled the buttons into place as quickly as possible. She wrapped Fergus's belt around her hips and pulled it tight, and adjusted the sheathed knife until it rested perfectly against her spine.

She glanced around the cubicle, pulled her hair back, and tied it in a knot.

*There's no use pretending otherwise,* she told herself, then she stood on the cot and squirmed through the small window into the yard.

THE THIEF'S TALE

The Old City was so still under the pale blue, pre-dawn sky that Wyn was mostly convinced she was dreaming. A few wisps of high cloud glowed yellow and purple as they caught the sun's first rays, and the very tips of the Ironbacks flared gold above their purple flanks.

The city appeared soft and clean under its cover of fresh snow, with only a few tracks from nocturnal prowlers blotting the surface. The comforting smell of wood smoke drifted in the still air, and the only sound aside from the soft creaking of the snow under her boots was the faint tinkling of a dairy wagon trundling toward the market with its load of still-steaming milk.

*A dream.* Wyn frowned. *Must be.* How else could she explain that she was on her way to kill someone?

The Cow Gate was open, and one of the blackberries gathered around their snapping fire in the gatehouse gave her a cheery wave as she passed through. The market was empty, and only the lowing of a cow in one of the stockades and the caw of a raven perched on Butcher's iron gate could be heard.

Butcher's appeared dark and empty, its narrow windows shuttered, its stained bricks bleached of color in the grey light. Wyn stopped at the entrance to the wide marketplace, a slender, stark figure in her long, black coat. The cold air stirred against her, brushing her cheek with wisps of her golden hair, and Wyn let it play.

Butcher's looked empty, but it was not. *He's in there.* She was certain of it, waiting for her. Was he even now imagining her on a hook, blood draining from her and swirling into the troughs with the remains of cows and pigs? Or was he anticipating the first cut?

Wyn licked her lips against the dryness of the frigid air.

"All right, then," she whispered. "Here I come."

She strode across the market, her small boots leaving a line of black prints in the snow as straight as an arrow. She tried to watch all the windows in Butcher's at once, seeking the first hint of movement in their dark recesses that would signal that she had been seen. But there was no cry, no startled face peering at her, no stir of motion.

The raven cawed raucously and launched from its perch. Its wings beat heavily in the cold air as it fluttered to the peak of

THE THIEF'S TALE

Butcher's eaves, where it settled on an exposed beam, its head cocked to the side as it tracked her progress across the open space.

Wyn reached the gate and hopped over it with an effortless swing of her legs. Her boots hit the ground inside the fence, and she hurried to the side of the building, certain that now, at last, she would be seen. But still there was no sound of alert.

She pressed against the wall, sliding along it until she reached the wide doors that led into the slaughterhouse. The latch swiveled open with a faint squeak, and she shoved the door open enough to squeeze through.

The vast, dank room smelled of flesh and death despite the chill. The scent seeped from the stone like smoke from an ashen coal. Wyn stepped into the shadows against the wall and gazed silently around, searching for any sign of life. Iron chains swayed slightly, clinking forlornly, and wingbeats echoed amongst the beams of the high ceiling. Wyn stilled her breath and closed her eyes, her head tilted to one side, as if made of ice.

She was not alone, of that she was certain. She could hear them, like rats in the walls. The faint reverberation of a snore. The creak of a floorboard. The grumbling murmur of hushed conversation. The sounds drifted to her from every direction through the floors and walls of the slaughterhouse.

Wyn glanced about the abattoir, her gaze darting between the rows of hanging carcasses, their flesh hard as stone in the frozen air. She was not certain how much time she had, but Wyn knew she could not simply wait for Quinn's crew to rouse themselves.

The slowly shifting form of a cow's carcass caught her attention, and her gaze followed its pale shape up to the iron hook from which it dangled. Wyn suppressed a shiver at the sight of the brutal curve of iron, but the chain had given her an idea. She hurried to the simple cleat that secured the chain to a nearby pillar, peered at it for a moment, then knocked the pin free.

The chain released with a clanking rush and dropped the carcass on the floor with a thud that echoed hollowly through the cavernous room. Wyn quickly retreated behind the ranks of butchered meat and waited.

THE THIEF'S TALE

Footsteps approached from a side passage, slow and hesitant, and the yellow light of a lantern gleamed on the stones. Wyn watched a figure linger in the doorway and peer about without entering, and a frown creased her brow as she recognized his lank orange hair and thick jowls. *Chuckles, you bastard. Come on, then, what are you waiting for?*

She could hear him giggling nervously to himself as he moved cautiously into the space, his lantern jerking left and right as he crept between the rows of carcasses.

Wyn slowly slipped her fingers into her coat pocket and withdrew one of the heavy metal shapes that pressed against her ribs. It glimmered as it caught the lantern's light and channeled it across its intricate engravings, beautiful and mysterious. It had been simple enough to palm the keys without Mellon noticing, and Wyn felt a twinge of guilt at the thought of his face when he realized they were gone, but she needed them far more than he did.

Wyn's lips pressed together in a thin, determined line, and she carefully tossed the key toward Chuckles.

It bounced harshly against the stones and slid to a stop. Chuckles whirled to the sound, hesitated a long moment, then slowly shuffled toward the golden Device.

"What the fuck?" he muttered. He swung the lantern in a circle and laughed nervously.

"Here, puss-puss," Wyn called to him, and Chuckles stumbled away from her in fear as she stepped into the light. "You tell Quinn I'll show him where the other one is if he comes and has a little chat with me," she instructed Chuckles. "Go on, you bastard. Run."

Chuckles scooped up the key and hurried away, his footsteps slapping echoes from the high ceiling as he went.

Wyn inhaled deeply and walked slowly to the center of the room, away from the hideous hooks and swaying meat. Her stomach was clenched with fear, but far stronger was the cold fire that burned in her chest, her hands, her legs. Her eyes narrowed to fierce slits as she glared in the direction Chuckles had vanished. *I don't want to run,* she realized. *I don't want to hide.*

THE THIEF'S TALE

Figures began to enter the room in ones and twos, encircling her in the shadows. A dozen pairs of eyes glared at her, but none of the figures approached.

Heavy footsteps sounded from the depths of the slaughterhouse, and then he was there.

Quinn stared at Wyn, his pale eyes cold and reptilian. He held the gold key and tapped it against his palm as he examined her, his thick lips twisted in contempt.

"Search her," he murmured to Chuckles, and the thug giggled shrilly and hurried forward to obey.

Wyn glared defiantly at Quinn as Chuckles groped her. His fumbling fingers soon found the second key, and he held it up triumphantly for his boss. "Look!" he crowed.

"Oh, no, you found it," Wyn congratulated Quinn, her voice as thick with mockery as she could manage.

Quinn ignored her. "Anything else?" he asked.

"Just this." Chuckles laughed, and he pulled Fergus's knife free from its sheath and held it up.

"All right," Quinn said softly. He stepped forward and took the key from Chuckles, who immediately grabbed Wyn's arms and pulled them savagely behind her back. Quinn scrutinized the keys, running his thick fingers across their intricate designs. He glanced at her, and his fist closed around the keys.

"Where's Ratter?" he asked quietly. His gaze slowly dropped to her hand. "I see he found you."

"Yeah." Wyn raised her stitched chin defiantly. "He said it was just like old times. But do you know what? Turns out it wasn't. Turns out, Shatter isn't so hard when he's not beating on little children."

Quinn nodded slowly. "Where is he?"

Wyn shrugged as nonchalantly as she could in Chuckles's grasp. "Left him for the rats."

"You think you can kill Ratter and just walk out of here?" Quinn spat in sudden fury, and his lip curled back over bared teeth.

Wyn snorted her contempt. "I didn't kill him." She gazed around the circle of Quinn's crew. "Cor, there's not many of you left, are there? Do you think that's enough?" she asked Quinn.

THE THIEF'S TALE

"Enough to stop Fergus?" Quinn sneered. "I heard there's not much of Fergus left."

"No, not Fergus," Wyn said coldly. "I'm the one who's going to kill you, Quinn."

"You think so?" Quinn's eyes widened and his nostrils flared in fury. He whirled and stalked to the rack of carving implements against the wall and yanked a long knife free. "We'll see," he growled as he eyed the blade's long, razor-thin edge. He faced Wyn, his thick lips puckered in writhing contempt. "We'll fucking see."

"We will," Wyn promised him. "But you're not going to do shit, not until the Hawk says those keys are real. Or are you going to fuck that up, again?"

Quinn stared at her for a long, silent moment, suddenly calm as ice once more. "Someone's been peeking where she shouldn't," he said softly. "You think the Hawk cares if I kill you now or later?"

"I'll wager two gold talens you don't have the balls to risk it."

"You have been a sneaky little bitch, haven't you?" Quinn murmured. "I'm glad. I was going to let you live, use you on a few more jobs, but now…" He tapped the long blade against his thigh and nodded his head. "Now, I don't have to wait."

Quinn stepped close to Wyn and stared coldly at her. He smelled of death, of blood, thick and foul. Wyn felt Chuckles pull back, thrusting her forward like a shield.

Quinn exhaled in a long, satisfied sigh. "Your friends died screaming," he told her softly. "At first, they cursed me, but do you know who they cursed at the end?"

Wyn felt her breath turn ragged and her mouth twisted as she glared at Quinn, but she could not speak, and her eyes burned with tears that she could not wipe away.

Quinn nodded slowly. "That's right. They cursed you." He leaned near, his mouth so close to her ear that she could feel his breath slide across her skin as he spoke. "So will your brats, and so will your precious Tallywags. I'll make sure of it."

A faint tremor carried through the thick slabs of the floor and up Wyn's leg, and a moment later a dull echo drifted into the slaughterhouse. The iron chains swayed and clanked, and the

THE THIEF'S TALE

circle of thugs gazed around in confusion. Quinn looked away from Wyn, frowning thunderously.

"Uh oh," Wyn said softly.

Quinn glanced at her, and Wyn could not stop a triumphant grin from curling across her lips. "Do you not have a Veil?" she asked innocently.

"Go," he ordered, and two of his men hurried toward the upper levels of the slaughterhouse. "The rest of you, ready for blood."

Blades hissed as knives were drawn and axes appeared in white-knuckled hands as Quinn's crew prepared themselves.

Wyn glanced over her shoulder and met Chuckles' gaze. "You're going to die, too," she whispered to him with a grin. He started to laugh, but all that emerged from the puckered hole of his mouth was a wet choke of fear.

A heavy, measured tread sounded on the wooden steps that led upstairs, and a tall figure slowly descended to the slaughterhouse floor. He paused at the base of the stairs, his dark, disdainful gaze sweeping the crowd of thugs awaiting him.

"Where are the keys?" Master Calixte demanded, his voice smooth thunder that rolled across the stone floor and reverberated in the shadows.

More boots sounded on the stairs, and Calixte's two soldiers joined him, their armor gleaming in the faint light that pierced the abattoir's gloom. One of the soldiers was massive, with a chest like a tree trunk and arms that looked as if they were carved from whorls of weathered oak, his skin a burnished copper beneath his gilded helm. His companion appeared to have been sculpted from deep umber iron, his skin stretched tight over ridges of muscles, with a powerful jaw and high cheekbones.

Oak and Iron flanked the Guild master, broad-bladed, wickedly curved swords in their hands, their red cloaks the color of blood.

Quinn gestured quickly with a flick of his hand, and his crew spread out, drifting in and out of shadow as they encircled the intruders.

"I don't know who you are," Quinn growled, "but you just fucked up."

THE THIEF'S TALE

Calixte extended one arm toward Quinn, his fist closed. His fingers opened and released a small, shining star that soared to the vaulted ceiling, paused for an instant, pulsing softly against the grime-crusted brick, and then swooped toward Quinn. He held up an arm to shield himself, but the bright light settled gently against his skin and dispersed into a mist.

Quinn frowned in confusion as he examined the spot where the light had touched him, then his mouth twisted in contempt. "Kill them," he growled.

His men pressed forward, wary of the soldiers' swords, but confident in their overwhelming numbers.

Calixte did not wait. He strode toward Quinn, his staff ringing against the stone floor with every step.

Quinn's thugs rushed to meet him. A thin man with staring eyes and gaunt cheeks leapt forward, and a long axe scythed through the air toward Calixte. The Guild master did not pause. There was a flash as if the axe had struck steel in the air above Calixte, and a crack of thunder as the curved blade shattered into splinters that pelted stone and flesh like hail. The thin man screamed in agony and staggered back, staring at the bloody claws of his ruined hands.

Calixte's Word shook the slaughterhouse, sending the heavy chains dancing as the pillars creaked and groaned. The tip of his staff caught the thin man in the chest, tearing him apart and spraying chunks of flesh in a great arc across his stunned companions.

In the shocked silence that followed, Wyn heard blood pattering across the floor like rain. Then chaos erupted.

Quinn's crew hurled themselves in all directions. Some rushed for the doorways, others flung themselves toward the Guild master, howling in rage, but Calixte's gaze never left Quinn. He raised his staff and brought it savagely down, and violence tore through the heavy slabs of the floor in a dreadful wave. Iron gratings twisted into the air and stone cracked and shattered into splinters as Quinn was engulfed by a choking cloud of dust.

A flash of gold caught Wyn's gaze, and she watched with wide eyes as a key bounced and tumbled through the air. It struck the base of a wooden pillar, skittered across the floor, and was

THE THIEF'S TALE

kicked by a heavy boot as it slid beneath the stampede of men racing toward Calixte. It clanged musically as it bounced and spun to a stop only two paces from Wyn.

Wyn twisted away from Chuckles in an instant and spun low. Her boot smashed into the side of Chuckles' injured knee, and he shrieked in pain and staggered away, his fleshy cheeks grey with shock and fear. Behind him, Calixte swung his staff in a wide arc.

Wyn dove sideways and curled tightly behind a pillar as the staff's path of destruction intersected with Chuckles. His thick body wavered like porridge and his mouth gaped like a dying fish, then he was gone, leaving behind a gale of red mist and sodden rags that cascaded to the ground.

Wyn twisted into a crouch, balanced on her fingers and toes, and peered around the pillar. Men shrieked and bellowed in rage and agony. Thunder cracked as a huge man with iron-grey hair and a face hideous with scars lost his knife against Calixte's unperturbed neck. A man with a head as pink and hairless as a baby's whipped an axe savagely at Oak, who turned it contemptuously aside and took the man's arm, leg, and head with three smooth swings of his massive sword.

Wyn darted from her hiding place, weaved through the running figures, threw herself onto her knees, and reached for the key, but she was knocked aside as a man stumbled into her. She cursed and pushed herself clear of his flailing legs, only to see another boot strike the key a glancing blow, sending it spinning crazily across the floor.

Wyn dashed after it. She whirled past staggering figures as she danced through the chaos. An axe lashed out wildly at her and she slid beneath it, then scrambled forward and snagged the key the instant before a body landed heavily on the same spot.

Wyn grinned in triumph. *Now then, where's your friend?* she asked it. But she had taken only a single step when a figure blocked her path and she found herself staring into Calixte's eyes. As their gaze met his eyes widened in recognition, then glanced quickly at the key still clutched in her fist.

His staff whirled toward Wyn as she burst into motion, launching herself into the air, her back arched, twisting as she curved over the scything arc of the staff's tip. Stone erupted

THE THIEF'S TALE

beneath her with a thunderous crack that swatted her aside. She tumbled, her feet hit the ground awkwardly, and she pitched headlong across the floor, finally coming to rest upside down with her legs sprawled helplessly against a pillar.

Wyn groaned and struggled to her feet as Calixte strode toward her, his face twisted into an arrogant sneer. She staggered away, pushing desperately between rows of ice-heavy carcasses, and dove beneath a thick, scarred slab of a table as she felt Calixte's Word thunder toward her.

Massive pillars of wood shattered. Frozen carcasses tore apart and were flung aside, jerking frantically on the ends of their chains. The great beams that formed the lattice of supports crossing the abattoir twisted and ripped away from the remaining pillars. Chunks of wood as thick as tree trunks cascaded to the ground, smashed the supports of one of the vast rending vats, and spilled the boiling liquid across the floor in a seething rush.

Wyn huddled beneath the carving table and buried her head under her arms until the floor stopped shaking. The butchered carcass of a cow landed next to her with a wet thud, and debris thundered against the thick table over her head.

Wyn crawled cautiously from her makeshift shelter. One end of an enormous beam had fallen across the table and wedged against the floor. An iron hook had carved a furrow through the tabletop before being yanked to a stop, deeply embedded in the scarred oak.

As the echoes of the collapse faded, Wyn was shocked to discover that the clangor of battle had also died. Her stunned ears could pick out faint sobbing and a wet, coughing choke, but gone was the clash of metal on metal and the screams of pain and fury. She could also hear the crunch of boots slowly approaching, and she scurried behind the jagged end of a fallen beam and crouched in its shadow before risking a peek.

Master Calixte surveyed his work, his thick beard jutting proudly. Iron joined him, wiping his blade clean on a piece of ragged cloth. Wyn could not see Oak, but nor could she see any of Quinn's crew. Alive, in any case. Corpses littered the slaughterhouse, and their blood slowly filled the deep sluices that crisscrossed the floor.

THE THIEF'S TALE

Wyn glanced about, but she could not spy an easy path of escape. The sheer wall of the chamber was at her back, and the piles of debris offered her concealment only if she remained still.

Calixte said something to Iron and gestured vaguely in Wyn's direction. She could not understand the words, but the meaning was clear. *That's right, I'm in here,* she thought fiercely. *But I might not be as dead as you hope.*

Wyn shifted carefully onto her toes, then froze as another set of footsteps crunched nearby, this time from along the wall. She turned her head slowly and let a small groan of frustration slide between her lips as Oak stepped around a pillar and into view.

Their gaze met, and the soldier opened his mouth to call out. Wyn smiled brightly at him, and Oak smiled back, suddenly uncertain. Wyn climbed wearily to her feet, stretched her back, and took a languid step toward the soldier. At the last moment, Oak realized what she was about to do. His befuddled grin transformed into a frown in an instant, and he lunged for her, but Wyn was already in motion.

She hurled herself away from the soldier and sprinted for a jumble of wrecked beams and torn carcasses. Two quick strides and she gathered herself to leap.

Steel-hard fingers grasped her collar and yanked her brutally off her feet as she clutched vainly at the wrist behind her head. She was wrenched one way, then hurled the other, her legs swinging wildly in the air as she crashed onto the carving table with a bone-shaking thud that drove the breath from her chest in a choking gasp. Oak's grasp tore free and Wyn bounced and tumbled off the far side of the table, the slaughterhouse spiraling around her as she slammed into the floor.

The two soldiers did not give her a moment to recover. Steel-shod boots rang against stone as they closed on her, faster than Wyn could believe a man in armor could move. She sprang to her feet and leapt onto the long beam that had plunged from the rafters, landed in a crouch, and sprinted toward the ceiling, the shaft twisting and rocking under her with every step.

A quick glance behind her showed that one of the soldiers was not hesitant to pursue her into the air. Iron was already halfway up the angled beam, moving effortlessly despite his heavy

THE THIEF'S TALE

armor, a fierce grin baring his teeth as he met Wyn's gaze. Oak had apparently decided climbing was more suitable for his smaller comrade, and stood glaring at Wyn from below with his massive fists planted firmly on his hips.

*Well, one is better than two,* she tried to convince herself, but she was not at all certain she had received the easier half of that bargain. Iron did not have Oak's size, but he had the lean, coiled strength of a predator, and it seemed limitless. She hurried to the nearest pillar, tucked the key into her belt to free her good hand, and scrambled up as her boots slid and scraped against the grime-slippery wood.

She could hear Calixte calling out to Iron from the floor, urging him on, and a quick look back revealed that the soldier had grabbed ahold of a thick chain and was ascending it, the powerful muscles in his arms rippling as they hauled his weight smoothly upward.

*That's not fair!* she thought bitterly, and she gritted her teeth and climbed grimly onward.

The highest level of rafters was a chaotic web of shattered beams and twisted chains woven from the destruction caused by Calixte's staff. Iron joists were bent and torn or simply sheared through, and wooden beams swayed heavily against each other as the structure shook and groaned under its unbalanced weight. Wyn reached the nearest joist only a moment before Iron, frowned at the single intact bolt keeping the beam attached to the pillar, and then started to edge across the beam toward the wall.

The thick beam rocked and swayed alarmingly, a dozen carcasses and another massive beam that hung beneath it, tangled in the chains, bumping and wobbling and clanking with each movement.

Wyn set her jaw and kept going. The loose end of the beam was tantalizingly close, and it was only a small jump from there to the wall, and only a short climb to the small windows that lined the top of the wall.

A deep groan reverberated through the beam as it slowly twisted. Wyn crouched and rode the long, pendulous swing, waiting for it to return. But as it shifted, she heard a rending shriek as one of the chains pulled from its anchor and swung free,

THE THIEF'S TALE

dragging the end of the beam after it. The beam shuddered as it was wrenched downward, and there was a sharp crack as the last of the iron bolts holding it to the pillar sheared through.

Wyn leapt from the beam as it dropped away from her. She slammed chest-first against another beam, her arms wrapped around it and her feet swinging madly below. For an instant, the beam shuddered and bucked under her weight, then the end ripped free with the long, slow tear of a tree falling.

Wyn gasped as she felt the beam give way. She shoved it away and strained to reach one of the flailing chains. Her fingers closed around the iron, and her fall was yanked to a stop. She swung wildly across the chamber, then the chain pulled free and she fell again. The heavy links roared across a beam, snagged, and yanked her to another stop, bouncing and twisting high above the stone floor.

Her fingers slipped, caught, and held firm, and she quickly wrapped her legs around the chain and clung to it as it swayed perilously amongst the web of loose debris. *Knew I could make it,* she gasped.

Wyn craned her neck to look upward. Her chain was wrapped around a beam that had pulled entirely free of its joist and now hung suspended from a dozen other chains, creaking and groaning from their unaccustomed load.

A quick glance down made her grip tighten even further. Beneath her stood one of the vast, bubbling rendering vats, spraying boiling fat across the floor as chunks of wood and iron splatted into it. Even if she missed that she would land on solid stone at the feet of Master Calixte, who gazed at her with a grimace of disappointment etching his thin lips. Wyn scowled and started to climb, but she froze as a gleam of gold caught her gaze.

A key balanced on a chunk of wood a short distance beneath her. Her hand went to her belt and found it empty, and she groaned in dismay. Wrapping her legs more securely around the chain she hung upside down, her fingers stretching toward the golden prize. Her fingertips brushed it and it slid toward the edge of its perch, snagging at the last moment on a ragged splinter.

THE THIEF'S TALE

Wyn felt her chain shudder as it pulled against its anchor. A voice called to her, and she saw Iron clinging one-handed to a nearby pillar, his other hand stretched out to her.

"Come," he urged her, his accent awkward and thick, his brow creased in concern. "Come... I catch you."

*I can get it,* she decided. She slid slowly down the chain, her fingers straining for the key. The vibrations grew savage, jerking her chain back and forth and sending the piece of wood with the key dancing and spinning. Her fingers brushed against metal, but it was gone too quickly to grab, and she cursed.

*Come on!* she groaned. She lunged, and for an instant her fingertip touched the key.

Then, with a terrible rush, her chain gave way. Wyn wrenched herself desperately toward Iron. Their hands slapped together and his fingers closed firmly around her slender wrist. He swung her away from the cascade of steel and wood and deposited her gently on a splintered nub of a beam just below him.

Wyn twisted to watch the key, her gaze riveted to the tiny gold speck as it tumbled free from its perch and spiraled toward the rending vat.

"No!" she screamed.

A hand shot out and grabbed the key before it hit the bubbling surface. Calixte smiled in satisfaction, stepped away from the oozing heat of the vat, and held the key up to the light to examine it.

Wyn groaned as relief and dismay fought each other for ascendency. She puffed savagely at the long strands of hair that had fallen across her face, then glanced up to meet Iron's gaze.

"Thanks," she said quietly.

He smiled and nodded, then consoled her in his rich, southern language, his deep voice rolling through its elegant rhythms.

"Whatever you're saying, you can keep on saying it," Wyn decided. She grinned at Iron to show her appreciation, then began searching for the best escape route, pausing to glare resentfully at the sight of Calixte fondling his new key.

Wyn gasped as a figure suddenly emerged from the shadows behind Master Calixte. Quinn's face was streaked with blood and

THE THIEF'S TALE

dust, and he snarled as he lunged forward, his powerful hands empty of weapons. Oak barked a warning, but Quinn was on Calixte before the Guild master could react. One hand wrapped around Calixte's wrist and yanked him forward, the other curled into a fist and exploded into Calixte's chin with a sharp crack that rocked the taller man's head back.

Calixte staggered and Quinn followed with another blow to the Guild master's head that split Calixte's cheek open and dropped him to his knees.

Wyn heard Iron curse and begin to scramble down, but he was a long way from his master. Oak was much closer, and he leapt toward Quinn, his sword a vicious blur of steel. Quinn was forced back, bellowing in rage. He feinted and lunged, but Oak was far too quick, his blade far too deadly, and Quinn could not close with him.

*Get him!* Wyn urged the soldier as he backed Quinn away from Calixte, and the powerful warrior seemed to hear, as he pressed forward, forcing Quinn to dodge away a finger's-breadth from death again and again.

Quinn lurched to the side and Oak struck in a blur. But his sword plowed heavily into thick iron chains, and Quinn howled in triumph as he leapt forward and smashed his forehead into the soldier's face.

Oak staggered, but he was far from beaten. His fist rocked Quinn's head back with a savage blow, then he forced Quinn against the rendering vat, the soldier's massive arm wedged under Quinn's jaw as he strained to hold Quinn against the searing metal. Quinn roared, twisted savagely, and wrenched Oak from his feet. The two men crashed to the floor, tearing at one another for leverage.

Oak lashed out with his elbow and caught Quinn across the brow, but Quinn merely grunted and drove his shoulder savagely against the soldier's arm, wrenching it back. Oak strained against him, every tendon in his arm standing rigid as a cable, but Quinn threw his weight against the pinned limb, driving it back, twisting it with his huge hands, until there was a wet crack and Oak screamed.

*No, no, no!* Wyn cursed. She urged Iron on, willing him to climb faster.

But Quinn had plenty of time to deal with a crippled opponent. Oak tried to twist out of Quinn's grasp, but Quinn slammed his head onto the stones, then rose up over the dazed soldier and smashed his fist into Oak's head, again and again, until blood coated the floor beneath him.

Satisfied, Quinn turned to Calixte.

Iron leapt the remaining distance to the floor and landed heavily, but his sword hissed free from its scabbard without hesitation as he closed on Quinn, his face dark with fury.

For an instant, Wyn thought Quinn would throw himself on the soldier, but he suddenly scooped the golden key from the floor, whirled, and sprinted toward the stairs.

Iron gave chase, but Wyn could see that his formerly smooth gait was now awkward, favoring one leg. Quinn was gone long before the soldier reached the stairs, but Iron did not give up and disappeared through the doorway after Quinn. Wyn could hear the soldier's footsteps fading as she slipped down a chain to the floor and stood, surveying the slaughter.

A groan caught her attention. Calixte had clambered to a knee, his beautiful robes in disarray, his face twisted by bitter wrath. Wyn frowned in annoyance, found a chunk of wood, and smacked the Guild master in the side of his head with it, a triumphant smile lighting up her face as he sprawled back to the floor in a heap.

Wyn shoved Calixte's staff into the fire beneath the rendering vat, scooped up Fergus's knife from where it had fallen amidst Chuckles' remains, and raced through a door into the empty courtyard behind Butcher's.

She slowed to a halt, shocked by the sudden, gentle quiet of the snow-muffled morning, the sharp bite of the crisp air. Then she trotted to the gate, where a single drover waited outside, two shaggy cows peering disinterestedly at the iron bars and the yard beyond.

"Good morning!" the drover called hopefully.

THE THIEF'S TALE

346 | WHAT THEY DESERVED

"Morning," Wyn answered. She leapt onto the gate, grasped the top bar, and swung over in one fluid movement, dropping to the snowy cobbles next to the surprised man.

"Do... um... are they open?" he asked.

"Not open," Wyn told him as she strode away. "I'd go somewhere else today."

Wyn hurried to the corner of the slaughterhouse and peeked around. A body sprawled face-down in the snow a dozen paces from Butcher's side door, a dark mound surrounded by a sea of pristine white broken only by the trail of churned red snow connecting it to the building. *Not Quinn,* she realized immediately. *Good.*

Iron was trudging grimly back to Butcher's, his sword unbloodied. She stayed carefully hidden as he gave a last, bitter glare around the market square before he disappeared inside.

A flicker of movement drew Wyn's gaze beyond the corpse, and she caught a brief glimpse of a figure ducking into an alley on the far side of the slaughterhouse.

Wyn's mouth curled into a fierce smile. She sprinted across the market, snow flying from her boots, leapt onto a wagon and then the roof of the cooper's shop next to the alley. She scrambled across the pitched shingles and slid into place against the squat, soot-stained chimney at the far end.

She watched from her perch as the figure strode along the alley. Quinn's determined pace devoured the distance, but he did not seem hurried or frantic. He turned at the end of the lane without looking back, and Wyn chased after him, hopping from the roof onto the wall of the cooper's yard and from there up the side of the next building, scrambling nimbly up the thick iron drains that led to its roof.

Wyn loped across the slate tiles, following Quinn as he turned and then turned again, heading along the great curve of the city wall away from the Cow Gate. A leap across a narrow gap kept him in sight as he entered a short passageway between two buildings built against the massive stones of the city wall itself, and Wyn watched with a satisfied smile on her lips as he shoved his way through the door of one of the buildings.

THE THIEF'S TALE

The windows of the building were boarded up, but Wyn soon found a loose plank that could be pried free, and she curled through the breach and lowered herself to the bare, dusty floor in silence. She crept across the warped floorboards and peeked through a crack in the door. The interior of the building appeared abandoned, with shafts of grey light probing tentatively through gaps in the window coverings to find only swirling dust and shifting shadows.

Wyn slipped through the half-open door, crossed a narrow balcony that overlooked the entryway, and peered between the cracked balustrades into the murky shadows of the floor below.

A faint odor tugged at her, sweet and smoky. *A pipe.*

She followed the scent downstairs and across the entryway to the rear of the house, where she found a rough-cut staircase that led beneath the stone foundation of the building.

Wyn paused at the top, crouched on toes and fingertips for balance, as she probed the silence below her. A faint murmur of voices. A clink of metal. A scrape of wood on stone. She lowered herself onto the steps and crept into the darkness.

A deep cellar stretched from the bottom of the stairs, running the length of the building. Thick pillars crowded the space, and heavy beams crossed it to support the brick-lined vaults above.

Wyn crept from pillar to pillar, her boots a whisper against the stone floor. At the far end, an open door led to a long passageway, and she leaned against the wall next to the doorway and listened.

Three voices… perhaps four, speaking in low tones, gruff and harsh. A quick peek showed her that two doorways pierced the hallway's walls, and warm light washed from them along with the voices. At the end of the corridor was a third door, painted black, almost invisible in the shadows save for a small glow through the keyhole.

Wyn shrank into the shadows as the black door opened. A tall figure appeared and entered the hallway, shutting the door firmly behind him. He strode toward Wyn, then turned through one of the open doors.

"What did he say?" a voice asked.

THE THIEF'S TALE

"Just not to let anyone in, and be ready to go at two bells… I think something bad happened."

"Why's that?"

"He had that fucking look," the second voice answered, much softer than before.

"All right…" the first voice trailed off, then found new vigor. "Well, get some more wood in the stove, then. Sounds like we're going to be here a little longer."

Wyn heard a squeak of a hinge and the thud and crackle of wood being fed into a fire.

"Pile it in," the first voice exclaimed. "Yes, lovely… ahhh, I can feel my fingers again."

"Think of those fuckers searching out in the cold all night, hey? I'm glad I'm not with them."

"Too right," the first voice agreed. "I heard there was quite the bloodbath last night… oy, you're blocking the fire, you fat fuck."

Wyn chewed her lip as she glanced around, searching for a way past the two doors. She could risk a quick dash past, but if any of the guards should be looking anywhere near the doorway, they would see her illuminated in the fire's glow as easy as if it were bright summer's noon.

She scowled at the thought. She had not come here to be grabbed by a bunch of brutes. Then her glance found the dim shape of the heavy beams bowed under the weight of the house above. The beams ran the length of the underground chamber and clearly passed over the thin walls that divided the back rooms from the empty cellar.

Wyn took two quick steps, leapt, and caught the beam with her fingertips. She swung back and forth and then curled upward and wrapped her legs over the beam.

There was room to crouch between the beam and the vaulted ceiling, and Wyn began to move carefully toward the far end of the room, stepping quietly around the joists as she went. Warm light played on the underside of the beam and against the thick, brick ceiling. Wyn paused at the edge of the light and peered down. Four men were playing cards at a table near an iron stove. Several cots were shoved against the walls, and coats and cloaks were strewn across them and on the floor. One of the men took a contented drag on a long-stemmed pipe and blew a stream of smoke across the table.

Wyn moved slowly along the beam and over the room. She could read the card faces, she was so near. She froze as one of the men stretched and yawned, but he never looked up. Instead, he rose to check the hallway, then stood near the stove and held his hands to warm them while the game played on without him.

"Wall of Spears to the Black, you fuckers," one of the men crowed.

His comrades moaned good-naturedly and tossed their cards on the table, and Wyn crept silently away.

A partition had been fashioned to form the end room, but the carpentry was shoddy and had left a ragged gap next to the beam. Wyn slowly squeezed through, careful not to snag the rough wood.

A dull glow from the embers of a fire lit the room on the other side. There was enough light for her to see a man slouched in a chair before the fire, his heavy boots crossed on the stone hearth. He held a metal cup loosely in one hand, sloshing its dark contents so that drops pattered onto the rug beneath him.

Wyn slowly lowered herself onto the beam, then slipped over the side, clinging with one hand while she uncurled and stretched for the floor. She dropped the short distance without a sound. Her hand found the hilt of Fergus's knife and slipped the leather loop, and she took a cautious step toward the chair.

The man in the chair drank deeply from his mug, then set it on the floor next to him. Wyn froze, uncertain whether she had made some sound to disturb him, or, worse, if he had chosen that moment to rise. But he simply uncrossed his boots and slumped deeper in the chair's battered upholstery.

Wyn took another step, then another, as silent as the spread of ice across a pond. A final step and she stood directly behind the chair. She could hear the heavy sound of his breath, smell the sour stench of his skin.

A bead of sweat left a frozen trail down the skin of her back, and she shivered as she understood the certainty that she was going to kill someone.

THE THIEF'S TALE

Fergus's knife sighed as it slid from its sheath, and the man shifted slightly. Wyn's gaze found the pale skin across his throat. 'Here...' Fergus whispered in her thoughts, and she clutched the hilt of Fergus's knife in her sweat-soaked hand. A flicker of shadow beneath his jaw drew her gaze as she tensed to strike, his pulse throbbing beneath his skin, rapid and strong, and her breath caught as she saw the rigid strain of the corded muscles on his arms and realized that he waited, a killer coiled and ready for his prey to come close enough to strike.

Wyn lunged, Fergus's knife a pale blur in the dim light.

Quinn twisted and rose from his chair at the same instant, faster than Wyn could believe. Fergus's knife sliced through the skin along Quinn's jaw, opening a deep gash so narrow it seemed bloodless. Quinn savagely swept his arm around, his forearm smashing into hers, knocking Fergus's knife from her stinging fingers.

Quinn's thick lips curled slightly as his left hand closed around her slender neck and drove her into the wall with two quick steps, his pale gaze alive with murder. Blood coursed from the long cut across his jaw, coating his neck in a wet sheen.

"Wyn," he spat. "I should have guessed you would be stupid enough to come after me. You should have run."

"No," Wyn hissed fiercely, her lips parted in a snarl of resolve, her gaze narrowed as she challenged the scarred man who loomed over her. "If I ran, when would I get to kill you?"

"You think that's what is going to happen?" Quinn said in his strange, soft voice.

"I know it."

"I can feel you shaking." His grip tightened relentlessly around her throat. She tore uselessly at his arm, hard and thick with muscle, and her splinted fingers ached as she strained for purchase.

Quinn's mouth twisted in disgust. He wrenched her forward and slammed her into the wall again. Wyn felt her breath cough past his fingers as her head sang with pain.

Quinn leaned close, his breath thick against her face. "I'll cut your fucking fingers off for this," Quinn said quietly, as if he were

THE THIEF'S TALE

discussing a disappointing meal. "But I'll let you watch me do the same to your fucking friends before I kill you."

Cold fire washed through her, prickling her skin, surging in her veins. She gasped, eyes wide, nostrils flared, and her trembling fingers became as still as ice as one hand dropped away from Quinn's arm.

Wyn glared into his eyes, never blinking, binding his gaze with unwavering hate. She deliberately parted her lips, curled her tongue, and spat.

Quinn sneered as the spittle hit his cheek with a quiet splat. He slowly wiped the moisture away with the back of his hand, his cold gaze never faltering. "I'll have that fucking tongue of yours, too," he promised as his hand dropped to his belt for his knife.

"It's so easy for you," Wyn choked out, forcing the words through a throat suddenly too tight to breathe. "Maybe it's that easy for me."

Wyn slammed her fist into the pale flesh just beneath his ribs and held it there. *'Here...'*

Quinn's grip on her throat loosened. He snarled, tendons rigid in his neck. Wyn drew in a gasp of air, then another as his fingers twitched beneath her jaw.

Her boots found the floor as she slowly slid down the wall. Quinn was panting now, his thick lips open as he sought his vanishing strength.

He wrenched his gaze from her eyes and searched for his knife, then frowned, confused, as he saw the empty sheath on his belt.

"Looking for this?" she hissed through bared teeth. Her fingers were curled around the slippery hilt of Quinn's knife, its blade buried deep beneath his ribs.

He tried to shove himself away, but Wyn stayed with him. His legs buckled and he sagged to his knees, gazing down at the bright blood streaming from his stomach, a flood that spread around him in a glistening pool. Wyn knelt at Quinn's side and carefully pressed his knife deeper. Quinn made a soft, animal noise as she slid it home, then she sat back on her heels and watched his eyes.

THE THIEF'S TALE

"You…" he gasped, his breath bubbling in his throat. He reached toward his knife as it swayed with each breath, but Wyn brushed his fumbling hand away. "Look what you've done…"

"I'm looking," Wyn told him. She leaned forward so that her face was over his, close enough that she could feel his breath on her lips. "Goodbye, Quinn."

"No…" he hissed.

"Shhh," she whispered to him. She pressed against the knife's pommel and watched his eyes widen even further with the pain. "All my life, so scared of you… all that fear…."

Quinn gasped frantically, his breath caught, and a last sigh wheezed from his open mouth.

Wyn felt it brush against her lips and depart, slowly pushed herself back, and drew in a deep, satisfied breath. "… gone," she sighed.

She waited for herself to change, for some terrifying realization that would turn her eyes haunted and her heart cold and black. But all she felt was utter relief, a solace that unwound the dread that had knotted her stomach and squeezed her heart. Every breath came easier, and she crawled to the wall and sagged against it. Her head tilted back and her eyes closed, reveling in the solid soothing comfort of the silent stone.

Then she waited for someone to kill her. She was certain that one of the guards would have heard the thump of her body hitting the wall or the wet slap of the knife being buried in Quinn's heart. But as her breathing calmed and her pulse slowed to a tranquil throb in her throat, she realized no one was coming.

She opened her eyes and glanced around the room, puzzled. Then she hauled herself to her feet and peeked out the door. The hallway was unchanged from when she had peered down it from the other end, a lifetime ago.

"Celestial Tower, you fuckers," one of the guards cried triumphantly, his voice as clear as if he was in the room with her.

THE THIEF'S TALE

Wyn frowned. She had not really considered leaving, but now that the chance presented itself, she discovered that she was eager not to get caught.

She searched through Quinn's pockets until she found the heavy shapes of the two keys, reclaimed Fergus's knife, and scrambled back onto the beam. None of the guards considered looking up this time, either, and the house was as empty and silent as it had been on her arrival.

Wyn stepped into the street and breathed in the chill air. The sun was still not above the eastern ridge, but the mountains to the west were fully illuminated, their sheer sides sharp and clear and crisp.

The same blackberry waved her back through the Cow Gate. The streets started to come alive with carts and wagons forging trails through the snow, crowds congregating around the first open stalls, shopkeepers clearing drifts from their stoops with brooms, shovels, or whatever came to hand, and dogs sniffing hopefully at every doorway before dashing madly across the street with whatever prize they had claimed.

The keys pressed against her ribs with every step, and for a moment Wyn was tempted to veer to the nearest well, hurl them into its dark depths, and be done with them. But that was no guarantee Calixte would not eventually find them, and she was not about to allow the Guild master to get his grasp on her prize. The thought of Calixte made Wyn hurry her steps. *He's had a hard morning, and I reckon that gives me a bit of time, but best not waste it.*

After all, she still had one more visit to make certain everyone got what they deserved.

THE THIEF'S TALE

### CHAPTER NINETEEN

# An End to Hiding

The sun's rays were just kissing the eastern ridge of the valley as Wyn returned to the Hawk's manor. Their light traced the valley rim in blazing gold and set the tall spire of the Silver Keep shining against the endless blue of the newborn sky.

The awakening bustle of the city could not penetrate the secluded eyrie of Kuray's nobles, and only distant birdsong ruffled the hushed quiet of snow-smothered avenues and gardens.

Wyn crouched beneath the eaves of a neighbor's stable house and watched the rear façade of the manor with her knees drawn up to her chin and her fingers shoved under her arms. A steady stream of white smoke rose from the kitchen's chimney, but the other fireplaces showed no such activity and the heavy drapes over the tall windows on the second and third floors were still firmly shut against the slow progress of the sun's golden rays.

*M'lady is still abed,* Wyn decided, but she stayed concealed, for she knew without doubt that the manor was not as unguarded as it seemed. A twitch of the drapes on the second floor caught her eye. The heavy fabric drew apart for a moment and Wyn was granted a glimpse of Cameron's silver whiskers as he inspected the garden.

Wyn glanced over her shoulder to check the golden glow spreading over the eastern valley crest, then turned her attention back to the Hawk's manor. *Any moment now…*

She was rewarded as the tallest chimneys transformed from grey to glorious honey as the sun's rays touched them. Wyn urged the light downward and it obliged, creeping lower until the manor's slate roof sparkled as if it was encrusted in diamonds, then lower still until the windows blazed like molten metal.

Only then did Wyn slip to the ground, hugging the shadow beneath the stable house's roof. A garden wall separated the manor from a narrow lane that ran behind the tall houses, and she slid over it without a sound and dropped into the shadows behind a row of ornamental trees.

Wyn crept to the back wall of the manor, where the kitchen door opened next to a coal bin with a hutch over it. A bewildering array of iron drainpipes gave easy access to the kitchen roof, then the upper floors, and Wyn used the lattice of pipes and the dozens of wide window ledges to reach the roof quickly.

A window led into the attic, a small crescent of dirty glass and wood, and she lowered herself into the gloomy space, peering into the cluttered shadows as she learned the hushed sounds of the elegant building.

A low door led to a cramped landing that gave access to the small bedrooms at the front of the house. Wyn peered cautiously down the stairwell. Each landing was broader and grander as it descended. Simple wooden railings gave way to ornate iron balustrades and polished stone, narrow steps to sweeping flights, bare wood to plush carpets.

As she watched, a door sighed open on the second floor, and Cameron appeared on the landing, resplendent in a burgundy coat and creamy white vest despite the early hour. He sipped from a porcelain cup as he descended the stairs to the ground floor, peered through the front windows, and then crossed the entryway to disappear into the back of the house.

Wyn crept down, finding the sturdy steps so that her boots did not produce a tell-tale creak as the wood took her weight.

THE THIEF'S TALE

Once on the third floor she paused to listen carefully for any sound of Cameron's return or of a distant bustle of a housemaid embarking on a trip upstairs, but the house was perfectly still. Satisfied, Wyn stole across the landing and along the short passageway that led to the Hawk's bedroom.

Wyn pressed her cheek against the polished oak door. She could hear the faint shift and pop of an old fire, but nothing else. *Well, if she's in there, she's not giving it away.* Wyn gently opened the door and slipped inside.

The bedroom was protected from the invading sun by thick drapes pulled across its wide windows, but the fierce glow spilled around the edges of the heavy fabric and spread across the outer wall, etching the engraved panels in orange and red. A single brilliant shaft of gold bifurcated the floor, blazing across polished wood, luxurious carpets, and the corner of a great canopied bed, its curtains swept back. A few motes were captured in the beam's path and danced there wreathed in fiery halos.

But the bright light only served to make the shadows deeper, and Wyn paused with her back against the door as she peered beyond the beam, trying to discern what lurked on the far side of the room. She could make out a dark shadow upon the soft pile of pillows against the headboard. Wyn held her breath and tilted her head toward the bed. A soft breath sighed from the shadows, and Wyn slowly exhaled. *She's here.*

Wyn padded softly across the room, her boots soundless on the thick carpets. At the foot of the bed she stopped and rested her hand on the pillar of wood that rose from the footboard.

Cailean was deeply asleep, a small mound curled beneath the layers of thick duvets. Her hair spread across the snowy white pillows in total disarray so unlike its usual elegance that Wyn peered intently for a moment to establish the occupant's identity, suddenly certain that Cailean had given her bed to one of the housemaids as bait for any intruder.

Wyn gazed at her face. The twisted smile and the knowing frown were smoothed away by a peaceful vulnerability that Wyn had never seen while Cailean was awake. Wyn was suddenly overwhelmed by the urge to stay motionless, to preserve that state for as long as possible, but there was no knowing how much time she had to complete her business before a housemaid arrived with a steaming cup of tea to awaken her ladyship.

Wyn's lips hardened into a thin line, and she took one last, deep breath to steady the tingling burn in her fingers.

Then she sat gently on the end of the bed.

The polished wood creaked softly under her light weight, but it might have been a hammer tempering steel for its effect. Cailean twisted upright and pressed against the headboard in one violent motion, and the ray of sunlight caught the razor edge of a thin blade in her clenched fist and traced it in gold. Her teeth were bared in a snarl, and her eyes wide with fierce anger.

"Wyn?" Cailean asked. She blinked once and shook her head to clear away the last befuddling mists of sleep. "Martyr's tears…" She pushed a tumble of chestnut hair from her face and glanced from Wyn's stitched chin to her splinted fingers. "You seem to be a bit worse for wear. What's happened?"

"Fergus is dead," Wyn said flatly.

"Oh, Wyn, I'm sorry," Cailean said softly.

Wyn nodded quietly. She had not really thought that Cailean had anything to do with setting up the ambush behind the Padraigs' house, and she did not believe the noblewoman's surprise and sympathy were faked. *Not even the Hawk could pull that off, not just woken up and sitting in her nightclothes,* Wyn decided.

"Me, too," Wyn whispered.

"How?"

"Quinn's crew jumped us. We went to warn some friends, and there they were, waiting for us to show up." Wyn's fingers traced the hilt of Fergus's knife behind her back. "A bunch of them."

"You were with him? Martyr's tears… how awful. Is that how…?" Her fingers traced the tip of her chin.

Wyn held up her broken fingers. "This? No, Ratter had a go at me, but Fergus stopped him. Killed that bastard. Saved my life, did Fergus. Twice. Fergus killed them all, every one of those bastards, except one lad he let get away because he weren't much older than me, and looked to be pissing himself to boot." Wyn forced herself to let go of the knife and pressed her hands into her lap. "He died to protect me."

THE THIEF'S TALE

Cailean placed her knife on top of the thick duvet and crawled across the bed to sit next to Wyn. Cailean took Wyn's uninjured hand and slipped her fingers between Wyn's. "I know it must be awful, I can't imagine. But we will pay Quinn back for Fergus, I swear it. You'll get your revenge."

"Revenge, eh?" Wyn asked. "Yeah, that's what you said, wasn't it? Fight back and all, do them before they do you."

"That's right. Put an end to them, put an end to hiding and fear and sorrow."

"Does it make you feel better?"

"Sometimes."

Wyn nodded. "Well, no need to worry about getting revenge on Quinn, no more. I killed that fucker this morning."

Wyn heard Cailean's breath catch, and her fingers abruptly stilled against Wyn's grasp.

"You..."

Wyn sighed, suddenly weary. "Stabbed him in the heart and watched his eyes until he was gone." Wyn jerked as a laugh snorted through her nose. "Thought I would feel cold and dead, but I don't. I'm glad he's dead."

"I am, too," Cailean assured her. She squeezed Wyn's hand again. "I'm proud of you."

"But I still hurt," Wyn said softly. "Here..." She pressed her fingertips against her chest. "Why don't I feel better?"

Cailean stayed quiet, then retrieved a hanky from her nightstand and offered it to Wyn.

"No, I don't need it," Wyn told her. "You'd think I'd be boo-hooing all over after last night, but not a tear right now."

Cailean sat on the bed facing Wyn, her fingers linked over her knee. Wyn could see the noblewoman's dark gaze fixed on her as she waited, her eyes narrowed and a faint crease between her brows.

"Perhaps the hurt will fade, in time," Cailean said. "Perhaps it won't. Perhaps it shouldn't. Justice is not about feeling better, or evening the score, or gaining some small vindication. Justice is not for your convenience or satisfaction. Justice is ensuring those that deserve the hurt are the ones who reap it."

THE THIEF'S TALE

"I don't know about justice," Wyn decided. "I just wanted Quinn dead."

"Did he deserve it?"

"You know he did."

"Then that's justice," Cailean declared. She hesitated for a moment, her lips slightly open as she re-considered whatever had been on the tip of her tongue. She rose from the bed and walked quickly to an armoire against the wall.

"It's freezing in here," Cailean muttered as she produced a housecoat from the depths of the armoire. She donned the housecoat and huddled inside it as she hurried to the fireplace, her bare feet padding softly on the thick rugs scattered across the floor. "The bloody fire has gone out," Cailean grumbled, and she crouched and began prodding the ashes with an iron.

Wyn watched her quietly. Cailean was as elegant and beautiful as ever, despite being disheveled and engaged in a menial chore, but Wyn was struck by how small the noblewoman suddenly seemed, as if she were somehow diminished. Wyn glanced to where the slim knife had rested on the bed covers, but the blade had vanished. Wyn nodded to herself, then rose from the bed and joined Cailean by the fireplace.

Cailean gave the pile of ash-coated wood a last, savage poke with the iron and stood, stretching her back as she surveyed the results of her assault. Grey tendrils of smoke slowly uncurled from the heart of one charred lump, and a pale flame tentatively probed the surface before vanishing.

"Hopeless," Cailean decided. She replaced the iron in its rack and pulled her housecoat tightly closed, her fingers clenched deep in the thick fabric.

"Here," Wyn offered. She knelt and began to poke the remains of wood into a proper stack, surrounding the deep embers with unburnt shells. The wood was soon smoking, and an orange glow began to build, and Wyn held her palms to its warmth.

"Magic," Cailean sighed.

"You learn when there's no coin left for more wood."

THE THIEF'S TALE

"I…" Cailean started, but she clamped her lips closed before she could say more and took several steps away from the fire, her back turned against Wyn.

Wyn stood and brushed her hands against her trousers. *Time to get on with it,* she decided. She did not want to. She wanted to find a way to return to a time when Fergus was waiting for her outside, when she could imagine a golden future at the side of the Hawk, when she did not know what death felt like against her lips. But that time was irretrievably lost, Wyn knew. All she had, now, was what she could forge for herself.

That prospect should have terrified her. It would have terrified the girl who was Wyn just a few days ago. But that girl was gone as surely as the past she craved, and Wyn realized that she was not frightened of whatever came next.

"I brought the keys," she said quietly.

Cailean tensed, her shoulders rigid, her breath stilled. Just for a moment, but before she could force a calming breath, Wyn saw the Hawk's excitement and relief as plain as if it were gilded in gold leaf.

"I'm glad to hear it." Cailean glanced at Wyn over her shoulder. "I did wonder, of course…"

"Yeah," Wyn acknowledged. She drew the two keys from her pocket. Their heavy weight shifted slightly in her grasp, and Wyn clutched at them as if they were the crumbling lip of an endless precipice. Slowly, Wyn forced her fingers to open, releasing her last grip on that tenuous safety, and extended her hand to the Hawk. "Here they are."

Cailean nodded and slowly drew in a deep breath while Wyn listened to the quiet pop of the fire and the thunder of her heartbeat surging in her ears. Then Cailean crossed the room to meet Wyn, slowly, as if content to savor the graceful brush of her nightdress against the thick rugs, her expression serene save for the slightly twisted curl of a smile that dimpled the corner of her lips.

But Wyn saw the rigid strain of the muscles in Cailean's slender neck and felt the noblewoman's fingers tremble against her hand as she reached for the keys, and Cailean's breath escaped her in a gasp of relief as she lifted the Devices.

THE THIEF'S TALE

"You should be proud, Wyn," Cailean whispered. The tranquil mask she had worn melted away in an instant. Her eyes were wide and dark, her mouth a fierce line, her chin raised defiantly. "That's justice you have delivered."

Wyn flinched from the predatory hunger in Cailean's gaze, and her hand curled instinctively away as if her fingertips had touched a searing coal. But as her limbs tingled with the need to flee, she hesitated, her gaze suddenly riveted to the gleam of a single teardrop perched on Cailean's cheek. Wyn felt her breath catch as she discovered an echo of the misery that lurked beneath her own fierce anger, mirrored in the tremble in the noblewoman's lip, the shining gleam of more tears held rigidly at bay in her eyes, the pale sheen of sweat on her brow.

Wyn hugged her hands to her chest as the last vestiges of fear were banished by a nearly overwhelming urge to reach out to Cailean.

"Who hurt you?" Wyn asked softly.

Cailean's mouth twisted as she glared at Wyn, but a moment later her gaze slid away from Wyn's, and her shoulders slumped. Cailean drew breath to speak, hesitated, then her lips closed into a sad smile.

"It doesn't matter who he is," Cailean whispered. She gently wiped the escaped tear from her cheek, and when she raised her head all traces of fear and pain and fury had also been wiped away by a cold certainty that frightened Wyn far more than the wounded rage it replaced. Cailean's hand closed into a fist around the keys. "What matters is that I will finally get justice."

"And he gets what he deserves, right?"

"That's right."

Wyn nodded. "Speaking of deserves…"

"Of course," Cailean agreed. She walked briskly to a small writing desk near the windows and drew a purse made of black leather from its drawer. She unhooked the iron ring that closed it, laid two squares of metal on the desk with precise clicks against its polished wood, and dropped the empty pouch next to them. The metal's deep, burnished yellow seemed to throb gently in the light spilling around the drapes.

"Two talens, as promised."

THE THIEF'S TALE

"Don't you want to check the keys?" Wyn asked flatly.

"Check them?"

"Don't you want Kieran to check they aren't forgeries?" Wyn continued coldly.

"I…" Cailean's lips tightened into a pale line and she slowly inhaled. She closed her eyes and nodded, then exhaled in a rush and met Wyn's gaze. "You were there."

"Yeah. You were, too."

"Is that where Ratter caught you? I am sorry." Cailean sighed sadly. "I told Quinn I wanted no violence."

"That's right. Your man, Ratter, as it turns out."

"Never," Cailean snapped, stung. "He was a tool, that is all, just like Quinn."

"Just like me."

Cailean shook her head. "No, Wyn. Perhaps at first, yes, but not once I knew you. You must believe that."

"Is that right?" Wyn asked. "Well, I don't believe a fucking word. You've not played straight with us since the start."

"Imagine if I had," the Hawk said. "Imagine if I had simply hired Quinn and never approached you. Now Quinn is dead, no keys for me, no gold for you. No one wins."

"Yeah? Well, I can imagine, too. I can imagine what if you had come straight at the start and just trusted me. Then Fergus isn't dead, Skinny isn't dead, the Candlemaker isn't dead, and you get your keys. How is that for winning?"

"Quinn would still be alive, as well."

"I'd make that deal in a heartbeat."

"Wyn, I wish it could have happened that way, I truly do. But I couldn't trust someone I didn't know. Not with something as important as this. I hoped that we could make a straight deal, but if we couldn't, I still needed those keys. That's why I hired Quinn and his crew."

"I'll wager it wasn't chance that had him come to us, neither."

"Of course not. It was always you I wanted for this job, so I told him to hire you. He took some persuading."

"Why'd you go through Quinn, then?" Wyn asked, astonished. "Brutal bastard like him."

THE THIEF'S TALE

"A mistake," Cailean admitted. "One I am sorry for, especially as it has caused so much hurt. You don't know me, would not trust me, so I thought an intermediary, one I'd used before."

Wyn's eyes narrowed. "No, you chose him *because* he was a brutal bastard, didn't you? You knew we'd be fucked without your help. You sat in your carriage and told us exactly that, and all the while it was you that had put us in the shit."

"He was just leverage to help you make the right decision. Once you saw that, eliminating Quinn was a perfect bonus. He needed to be removed, but that didn't mean he couldn't be used, one last time."

"Always an angle, right?"

"Yes, exactly."

"Your angle is what caused all the problems!" Wyn snapped.

"You're an idiot if you don't plan for when things go sour."

"I've been called worse."

"Wyn, you must see that I did everything I could to help you."

"Everything except actually dealing with Quinn before he killed my friends. But you couldn't, could you? Not while you had to have your backup plan. In case things went sour, right?"

"That's right. In case they did."

"Fuck you."

Cailean frowned. "You're angry and I understand why. You feel betrayed—"

"And what do we do with them that stab us in the back?" Wyn gasped in mock surprise. "Oh, that's right. We give them what they deserve, don't we? We give them justice."

Cailean's eyes narrowed dangerously and her nostrils flared. But when she spoke, her voice was calm as ice. "I may have lied to you about Quinn, but everything else I told you was the truth. If you can see your way past your rage and your grief, you can still have that life. Everything you've done has proven to me that you are the woman I hoped you were. More than I'd hoped. We would make such a team. Now that I have the keys, you just have to take my hand and we can do anything we set our minds to."

THE THIEF'S TALE

Wyn shook her head. "I'm such an idiot. Tell them what they want to hear, you said, so that they will want to give you whatever you ask of them. You told me what you were doing, and it never once occurred to me that you were doing it to me."

"Just because you wanted to hear it doesn't mean it's not true. Don't you see, Wyn? We need each other. That is why you can trust me, not because of anything I say to you."

"I would have given anything to be like you."

"Then why not take my hand?"

Wyn was not certain she could answer Cailean. It was so easy to remember the Hawk that she had dreamed of becoming, and the aching desire and desperate hope she had felt when it seemed that dream could be real. As easy as it was to see that the rage that drove the woman in front of her now had burned her hollow with its cold, consuming flame.

*Am I any different?* Wyn wondered. She could feel that same fire within herself, fierce and bright and eager to blaze anew. It had burned away the fear that had crushed her in its inky darkness, but what had it revealed? *Am I as empty as Cailean… nothing left but old pain and anger?*

Wyn could not answer that, either. She did not dare examine the torn cloak of who she had been, nor the fresh wounds of who she was. She was overwhelmed by conflicting emotions, worn too thin to endure the broken shards of grief and hope that swirled within her.

But she knew her heart ached from the pain Cailean had caused, and she understood that, no matter who she had become, she could never be the Hawk.

Cailean's hand still reached for hers, open, welcoming. Wyn desperately wanted to feel the warm comfort of her fingers entwined with her own. But she gently shook her head.

"No."

"Wyn, why?" Cailean asked.

"Because you're not the person I thought you were," Wyn told her sadly. "So I'll just have to try to be me, instead."

Cailean's lips tightened. Her hand dropped to her side as she gazed silently at Wyn.

"Where does that leave us?" Cailean asked. She turned to the writing desk and rested her finger next to the golden talens. "Do we still have a deal? Or do you believe I owe more than gold?"

Wyn's eyes narrowed as she gazed at Cailean's back. *No, not Cailean,* Wyn realized. The woman in front of her was poised, a predator ready to strike. Wyn's fingers twitched as they sought the safety of Fergus's knife, but she forced her hands to remain at her sides. *Why don't I hate her?* Wyn wondered. *All the pain she caused...* But beneath her anger, Wyn only felt pity.

"Hawk," Wyn called out to her. Wyn's stomach was curling in on itself, but she knew what she needed to do. "The Tallywags always deliver."

The noblewoman glanced at Wyn, her brows creased in suspicion. "That easy?"

"No, not easy at all," Wyn snapped. "What you did... maybe you deserve the worst, but I won't hurt you. I know what it's like to be hurt so bad you can't... I just feel sorry for you."

"I don't need your pity."

"Well, maybe that's how we're different, then," Wyn decided. "Lucky for you I give a shit about people besides myself."

The noblewoman closed her eyes and let out a long breath, and as she did, her shoulders sagged wearily. "It makes you weak."

"Yeah, well..." Wyn stepped next to the Hawk. "I'm the girl that stole the Queen's knickers. I'm the girl who cracked the unbreakable safe. I'm the girl who nicked two Devices and got away clean from the Guild." She held the talens to catch the ray of sun between the drapes and admired their rich blaze of color. "And the last fucker who came after me is lying cold with his own knife shoved in his heart, and he was the hardest bastard you'll meet."

Wyn caught the Hawk's gaze. "So if you think I'm an easy mark, you're welcome to have a go." She raised one faint eyebrow in query.

The Hawk's lips curled into her twisted smile. "No," Cailean said softly. "I don't think I shall." She held Wyn's gaze for a moment more, then relented and strode to the door. "Thank you for the keys, Wyn. I am certain we shall see each other again soon." The diminutive woman stepped through the doorway

THE THIEF'S TALE

without looking back, and left with a parting, "You can let yourself out."

Wyn exhaled with a rush, pushed her hair out of her face with both hands, and let her shoulders sag. Then she carefully tucked the gold talens into the pouch before something could happen to them. The small squares of metal were much heavier than she had expected, and were warm to the touch, as if their glow was more than reflected light. Wyn hooked the iron ring around the pouch's neck, opened it again, checked the talens were really there, stashed the pouch in a pocket, then repeated the process again.

*Martyr's tears, get on with it, you stupid girl,* she chastised herself.

The main stairwell was just as deserted as it had been on the way in, but Wyn no longer had the comfort of believing that she was unobserved. The dark hallways leading from the landings were no longer sanctuary, but seemed to harbor watching eyes, and the closed doors sheltered lurking presences ready to leap out if she came too close.

Wyn hurried up the stairs to the top floor and squirmed through the low door into the attic, then down the iron drainpipe, retracing her steps to the shed at the base of the garden.

"Two keys for two talens… nothing to it," Wyn whispered softly to herself.

THE THIEF'S TALE

## CHAPTER TWENTY

# Long Live the Queen

T he sun was well above the rooftops when Wyn returned to the brewery. Someone had barred her window behind her, and the cellar door was locked, so Mellon and Desmond had apparently been smart enough not to wait for her. Wyn was not concerned about finding them. She would manage it, somehow.

She retrieved her box from beneath her cot and returned to the streets, following a meandering path that gradually led to the high western wall of the valley, where the cobblestones slowly gave way to rutted tracks that twisted up the slope.

As the sun reached its zenith she arrived at a ridge where an abandoned watchtower teetered on a narrow shelf. Its paving stones lay half-buried under tangled nettles and the roots of a gnarled pine. A curling flight of worn, stone steps led to the tower's base, where tumbled blocks of stone languished amongst the weeds.

She stood on the edge of the shelf, carefully resting one boot on a weathered lump of parapet. Beyond the lip, Kuray tumbled into its valley, a web of sparkling, frosted chaos that spilled like a stream into a stony bed until it merged into a sea of haze.

The city seemed impossibly remote. Its screaming, shrieking, bellowing, clattering life inaudible behind the faint rasp of a breeze through the thin needles of the pine tree, and its wretched stench submerged below the cold scents of ice and stone.

"Best thing ever," Wyn said softly. She smiled to herself and gently corralled the hair wafting around her face, then perched on a stone and wrapped her arms around her knees, hugging them to her chest as she watched the distant city.

A faraway bell sounded faintly on the breeze. Then another, not the cascading tones that tracked time for the denizens of Kuray, but harsh and strident. Another bell took up the clangor, and another. The deep voice of the Whitetemple tower, the bright resonance of the Lord's Bell, the flat timbre of the Watchtowers, and the booming note of the Silver Keep, all discordant, all frantic.

*What is happening?*

Wyn picked her way down the slope, more puzzled than anxious, but as the bells continued to sound unabated, her pace quickened.

The bells were deafening in the narrow streets as Wyn pushed through the people crowding the way. She saw her own bewilderment echoed on many of the faces, but as she reached Forge Hill, she began to see grim anger, shock, and even open tears.

A pack of young boys scampered past and Wyn grabbed one by the arm before he could escape.

"What is happening?" she asked, shouting to be heard above the din.

"The King's dead!" he said excitedly, and tore free from her grasp to pursue his fellows.

Wyn remembered a young woman, her smile white against tawny skin as she heard news of a letter from her love. *Oh, no,* Wyn thought, and that brief memory became intimately painful as she knew the grief that now must engulf the Queen. *Poor thing. She must be so sad.*

THE THIEF'S TALE

A mutter of conversation between two blackberries caught her ear, and she tapped one vigorously on his arm until she had his attention.

"What did you say?"

"King Arian was murdered," he repeated, his cheeks flushed with the importance of his news. "Assassinated, right in the Keep."

"He never was," Wyn objected.

"He was," the blackberry insisted. "Watch commander told us. We're sealing the gates."

"How?"

"They're not saying, but it happened just after sunrise, this morning."

Wyn stared at the blackberry, stunned. *He died just after I left the Hawk's manor, near enough...*

"Is the Queen...?" Wyn stammered.

"She's alive," the blackberry assured her. "Long live the Queen, I suppose."

"Yeah..." Wyn agreed distractedly. She stared at the growing crowds, many of the people now openly sobbing as they heard the news of the death of their young king. But Wyn knew what to do with the sharp twinge of pain she felt when she thought of the Queen's grief. She pushed it behind doors deep in her heart and slammed them shut on the memories.

Then she began to collect all the purses and jewelry she could, before the stunned and grieving crowds could recover.

THE THIEF'S TALE

## CHAPTER TWENTY-ONE

# Epilogue

Wind ruffled the great raven's feathers as he soared above the city. His dark gaze swept the distant streets and rooftops as he circled, and his wingtips flared to tickle the wind spirits that played around him. The city squatted in a haze of its own smoke, but the murk could not conceal the stark white blanket that frosted its buildings, plazas, and gardens, nor the stark black banners that streamed mournfully from windows, towers, and flagpoles across the city, so that it looked to the raven as if he flew above a weed-choked river, dark fronds waving in the current.

The raven dipped his wings as a gust tried to tumble him, and he slipped away from the wind's grasp and arced toward the rooftops, cawing loudly in delight as he taunted the breeze.

The pungent air of the city was thick with interesting smells, and the raven's beak gaped as he skimmed over the rooftops, his tongue tasting every scent. The smell of ice and river-mud called to him, and the raven settled on an iron signpost amidst the thunder of his wings and the clatter of his talons against metal. Below him, wicker baskets set in piled snow displayed juicy fishes in their shining grey armor, a feast that had attracted many of the raven's lesser cousins as well as a pack of dogs. The raven carefully arranged his feathers with long strokes of his beak as he eyed the red-faced person who guarded the fish, waiting to see if his attention might waver.

The red-faced person spoke to other people who came to take his fish, his voice quiet and sad. They replied in their own quiet, sad voices, or simply nodded mutely, too downcast to speak. Many of the people wore black cloth to match the banners and streamers slowly twisting in the cold breeze. Black cloaks. Black armbands. Black coats. Black bonnets. Black dresses. So much black that the occasional brown or green cloth seemed like a burst of color instead of the drab tones they really were.

But not all the people were sad. The raven abandoned his preening and watched as a sun-haired person strode beneath his perch, joyous and incandescent as a spark leaping from a fire.

Her body bore stories of pain and fear and struggle, and the raven listened to the tales of torn skin and broken bones and bright blood. But the sun-haired person herself no longer listened to those stories, or, at least, she rarely heard their muttering.

How could she, when so many more exciting stories burst from her like the song of flashing sunlight on the surface of a tumbling stream?

The raven croaked contentedly as he recounted the tale of the sun-haired person for his cousins and the dogs and the red-faced person. How the wind spirits could not pull her from the silver people's tower. How she danced in the shadows so that the cow-killers could not see her. How she laughed when she leapt across the sky. How she smiled as she gazed over the treasure she had gathered in a small, buried room that smelled of boiled cabbage.

And he preened with pride as he related how handsome she thought him, and how he had shared the secret of his nest with her.

The raven cocked his head as he watched her a moment longer. She chattered like a lark and weaved a dance of skipping, whirling steps amongst the plodding, morose people who clogged the street.

THE THIEF'S TALE

The flicker of her fire burned some of the people it brushed against, reminding them of a time when they, too, had a spark of joy that was now quenched. But some people her fire warmed, and they smiled as their own ember pulsed for a moment, shedding the grey clouds that obscured it.

# THE END

BOOK ONE OF
THE CHRONICLES OF THE MARTYR

# *THE MARTYR'S BLADE*

FINALIST FOR THE 2018 INDIE BOOK AWARDS
PRIZE FOR FANTASY

When a series of gruesome rituals are discovered in the icy hinterlands of Albyn, three of the realm's most storied guardians are sent to track down and bring those responsible to justice.

Lord Bradon, veteran commander and warrior, driven by his unabating love for a woman forever beyond his reach. Sir Killock, a Templar knight more at home in the endless wilderness than in any castle or court. The paragon Danielle d'Lavandou, heir to the Martyr's Blade, a legendary weapon guarded by her ancestors for generations.

What they uncover is far more than simple murder: a terrifying threat to all the realms of mankind, thought sealed away so long ago that it now exists only as legend.

AVAILABLE NOW

# About the Author

Joel Manners has created rich worlds and memorable characters in video games for more than 30 years. He brings his talent for storytelling to the epic fantasy genre in his critically acclaimed series, *The Chronicles of the Martyr*. He lives in Austin, TX with his wife and two boys. And this dog his wife made them get, but honestly, she's pretty sweet. The dog. His wife too. Although he suspects that might change if she sees this.

Made in the USA
Middletown, DE
23 December 2021

56947379R00229